BATTLEMAGES

Margaret,

Hope you enjoy!

Contents

Chapter One 3

Chapter Two 17

Chapter Three 35

Chapter Four 57

Chapter Five 81

Chapter Six 101

Chapter Seven 110

Chapter Eight 143

Chapter Nine 181

Chapter Ten 207

Chapter Eleven 246

Epilogue 263

Chapter One - The Boy Amongst Men

The quill hammered hard against the parchment as James crowned his work with a final full stop. Three months, eighteen thousand words, finally done. At least, that is what he told himself. Of course, the reality was that about sixteen thousand of those words were the product of the last two weeks... but nobody had to know that.

He scraped his essay from his desk and into his backpack, springing up from his seat and glancing out of the window. By the position of the sun, it wasn't quite noon yet - his cramming was an astounding success. A smug grin on his face, he adjusted his scruffy brown hair in the mirror and looked his reflection up and down. His weak, little body was no less unimpressive than usual and his tangled mess of brown hair was a total disaster, yet he wore a confident look in his scarlet eyes nonetheless.

Slinging his backpack over his back, James took one last look around his dorm before slipping out into the hallway. As he barrelled across the hallway and down the winding flights of stairs, he lamented as he often did the agony of living on the fifth floor. Although, he did have to feel sorry for the poor souls on the eighth floor.

As he swept through the reception, the vibrant red carpets transitioned to marble tiles and again into red brick pavement. He skidded out into the street and onto the campus of the College of Arcana.

The streets that ran through the campus were a sight to behold - spiralling, gravity defying water features, flawlessly cultivated foliage of a hundred different colours and shimmering magical streetlights. All of this was surrounded on every side by beautiful grey spires tipped with slender black roofs accented with gold. Like much of the city of Abenfurt, it was perfect, but the College in particular was something truly incredible.

"There you are!" Nearchos snapped. "By Ivarrion, I'd nearly given up waiting!"

James smirked as his impatient friend peeled himself from a nearby lamppost and came marching towards him. Nearchos had always been strict with himself when it came to his education and hated the very idea of poor punctuality.

He was a fairly average looking young man, yet he stuck out like an abhuman in a church with his tan skin so typical of Thyresians. His jet black hair was slicked back and groomed to perfection as usual, making way for his rugged yet chiselled face.

"Calm down!" James laughed as they crossed the street and headed into the central tower. "We've got plenty of time."

"I tell you this every day, James - you should always arrive early to your lessons!"

"Says nobody else…" James smirked.

"When you're late, I'll be the one laughing," Nearchos chuckled. "Mark my words."

"Words marked."

"Good. So, did you successfully cram your entire essay?" Nearchos asked.

"Pft, what do you take me for?" James scoffed.

"Someone with incredibly poor time management," Nearchos sighed. "And barely a clue what he's doing."

"Ouch… yeah, I crammed it. Very successfully, I'll have you know."

"Which explains why you have bags under your eyes."

"Don't be ridiculous," James laughed. "I've never been more awake!"

A smirk on his lips, Nearchos raised his finger and spat a jet of water from its end, splashing James' face as he stumbled off to the side. "I'd say it took you a whole second to react to that," he chuckled. "Hopefully, it woke you up."

"Can you do something to send me to sleep?" James groaned, wiping down his eyes.

"You might want to ask *her*," Nearchos said, nodding down the hallway.

James followed his gaze to the end of the corridor, where Zahra hurried to meet them. If Nearchos stuck out amongst his fellow students, Zahra shined like a star. She was novekhiri, the first of her people to grace Verdenheld's soil, and she had the brown skin and thick accent to make it known. Many had feared her upon her arrival, but the gifted mage had been nothing but a pleasure to all those around her.

Physically, she was fairly weak, with a tall and slender frame supporting a head heavy with knowledge. For as pretty as she was with her dimpled cheeks and sensible, black bun, it was her smarts that were beyond compare. One had to wonder just how talented the mages of Novekhir had to be to produce a prodigy like her at such a young age - the girl had potential far beyond that of her classmates, showing an aptitude for the school of illusion like few ever had.

"James!" she yelled, running at him with her arms spread wide.

His face was blank as she approached, prancing like a deer towards him. As she drew close, her fist clenched and suddenly, the incoming hug was something far more terrible. James threw up his hands in terror, only to peer through his hands and see nothing but an empty corridor.

"You really are gullible," Zahra laughed, scaring her friends out of their skin as she appeared behind them. "You fall for that one every time!"

James groaned as Zahra slid to his side and they continued onwards. "Maybe if you didn't change the illusion every damn time, it wouldn't scare me as much."

"That would defeat the point, would it not?" Zahra smirked. "Anyway... how is James?"

"James is good..." James said. "Hey, guess who's finished his essay! Eighteen thousand words and a few minutes to spare!"

"Wait... what essay?" Zahra mumbled.

"Wha- you haven't done your theory essay?!"

"Oh, the theory essay!" Zahra laughed. "Sorry, I turned that in something like two months ago, I totally forgot about it! I think I did... thirty thousand words?"

James' face dropped and his body sagged. That girl was far too adept in magical theory. He often wondered if she was this good with her illusions - he had never seen her in action beyond a few party tricks.

"I know that look," Zahra smirked. "Don't worry, I'm sure your essay is great! Mine is just astronomically better."

"Yeah, thanks..." James muttered.

They came to a stop before the door to Class B, where Nearchos wasted no time in barging in and storming for his seat. Zahra wandered after him and James followed glumly in their shadows. The classroom was alive with chatter and the cracks and fizzles of magical spells. Bruno roared as usual with laughter, Isadora drew on one of the six desks with her knife and Brooke was tossing discs of scarlet energy into the air for Ava to blast with violet ice.

James trudged past Professor Elisa Moreau, who sat at her desk marking essays. She had her typical disinterested frown on her aged face, fiddling with her greying, blonde locks as she glared down upon an essay. James always felt sorry for her - teaching twenty powered students with no essence of your own must have been a nightmare.

As James passed down the aisle, his eyes widened at the sight of an incoming, scarlet hand. The tips of Lucia's fingers glided through his hair, leaving behind them a trail of dancing yellow flame. James was quick to pat it out, having dealt with that plenty of times before - it was almost ritualistic at this point.

He glared at Lucia out of the corner of his eye, receiving back a smug grin. Her raw, red skin creased as she stretched her cheeks, the blotched remnant of terrible burns that cloaked much of her body. Tendrils of scarlet snaked up her pale face and grasped for her fiery, yellow eyes, those which always burned with intensity akin to the fire she wielded. A mass of coarse, blonde hair sat atop her head, tied in a short, crude ponytail and scorched with blacks and browns.

James turned away with a sigh and continued towards his seat, while the warning hand of Hasso reached out for Lucia's shoulder. Poor Hasso - that was the only way people referred to the boy nowadays. Red headed and soft faced, he was well renowned as being sweet and kind - nobody could guess how such a nice person could end up with somebody like Lucia.

"Oh, grow a pair!" Lucia hissed with her usual intensity, shoving his hand aside.

"Lucia, you need to accept that-"

"I'll accept your death warrant!" Lucia snapped. She crossed her arms childishly and glared over her shoulder at James as he took a seat at his desk.

James collapsed into his seat beside Zahra, who smirked at his tired, empty face.

"If it's any consolation, the bald spot looks great," Zahra smiled. She broke into laughter as his eyes shot wide. "I'm kidding, I'm kidding!"

"You're the worst," James groaned, burying his face in the table.

"Alright, before we begin, have I got everybody's essays?" the professor asked. Moreau sighed as a skinny arm rose slowly from the back. "Yes, Florence, you've told me of your deadline extension six times already. Anyone else?"

Zahra glanced to James with a smirk and leaned into his ear. "Your essay, James," she whispered.

With wide eyes, James shot up out of his seat. "Wait!" he gasped, stumbling into the isle and barrelling to the front.

"Early as ever, James," Moreau sighed as the boy skidded to a halt before her, panting for breath. She took the paper with a roll of her eyes and cast it onto her desk. "And I suppose that makes everyone."

James trudged back to his seat under several demeaning gazes. The elite of Abenfurt had always treated him with such pity and many at the College were little different. He didn't care though - the only opinions he valued were those of his friends. They saw him for more than just his worth in coin.

"Thanks…" he sighed as he slumped back into his seat beside Zahra.

"What would you do without me?" Zahra chuckled, her brow suddenly rising as she glanced towards the front of the room.

The chatter of the class began to die low as Moreau drew a large scroll from behind her desk and began to slowly unravel it.

"Now, with that out of the way, you've officially completed your second term - feel free to pat yourselves on the back."

The class simply glanced to one another in silence. Hasso drew back his hand to pat Lucia's back and froze as the girl's fist ignited explosively with

6

violent flame. Moreau glared at Lucia as Hasso shrivelled away, receiving back a sweet, innocent smile.

"Anyway... with summer on its way, it's time we started thinking about what comes next," Moreau explained.

Nearchos and Zahra chuckled as James leaned forward in his seat, excitement burning in his eyes. It had completely slipped his mind, the thing he had been waiting for all year. No, all his life!

"As you probably already know, the College hosts an annual competition in which all first year students must compete, the Triarcanum," Moreau muttered. "For those of you who have been living under a rock, the tournament consists of a number of challenges to test your magical expertise, versatility, yada yada yada..."

The class was beginning to shuffle and whisper with excitement. Everybody's eyes were already falling upon Lucia, desperate to call her ally rather than enemy.

"I'll leave the rules at the front for anyone interested," Moreau said. "But for now, you'll want to organise yourselves into teams of five. I'm meant to give you some team building advice... but I don't have any. Class dismissed - have at it."

As the professor slumped back in her chair and gazed with a smirk at James' essay, the class erupted into chaos. The screech of chairs against floorboards pierced the air as half of the students jumped up and stormed towards Lucia in a desperate frenzy. The girl sat with a smug smile as she was consumed by a tide of bodies, all shouting and chattering, pleading and begging their cases.

"Well, I guess we know whose team we're *not* on..." Zahra muttered.

"I want nothing to do with that no-good snob anyway," Nearchos scoffed, folding his arms in defiance. "She has a disgusting lack of respect and an abhorrent attitude to learning."

"Nearchos, you're a hydromancer, not a playwright," James laughed. "But you're right - I wouldn't want to team with her, even if she did think I was worth her time."

"Alright!" Lucia boomed, plunging the swarm around her into silence. From amidst the crowd, she rose atop her chair with her arms planted commandingly at her sides.

"Lucia, get down from there," Moreau sighed.

"*Shut up!*" Lucia growled. The professor raised an eyebrow before returning to James' work with a careless shrug. "Okay, listen up! I already got my team in mind." Her eyes scanned the mass of students before her. "Hasso, Matheas, Josef, Isadora. Rest of you, scram!"

"*Two* abjurers?" Nearchos scoffed as the crowd glumly dispersed. "Her team totally lacks versatility!"

"Yes, but it suits Lucia perfectly," Zahra said. "High offensive capabilities, abjurers to shield their artillery and an enchanter to provide support. You must remember Nearchos - nobody here is a fool. Lucia has thought this through."

"Well, looks like we know the team to beat," James grinned. "Let's get to work on our own."

Zahra smiled warmly at James' determined grin. All he had ever wanted was to be a battlemage and the three of them knew well this tournament's grand prize - a month's internship with the city guard as trainee battlemages. It was an excellent opportunity for any aspiring mage, but it was a prize that James sought beyond all else.

"Indeed!" Zahra declared. "Between us, we already have pretty good offensive and support capabilities - we need a defender."

"Agreed…" Nearchos muttered, scanning the room and homing in on the green eyed brunette across the room. "What about the Tarantis girl? She's an abjurer."

James glanced over at Caesia Tarantis, who despite the chaos, sat reading in the far corner of the classroom. She wasn't much to look at - ghostly pale skin, her hair a sensible brown bob and her body practically skeletal. To most people however, she appeared an alien with her abnormal green essence.

"I don't know…" James muttered. "I've never seen her in action, is she any good?"

"No idea," Nearchos sighed. "But hey - in the combat round, everyone will be too scared to attack her!"

"I doubt that," Zahra smirked. "Surely Verdenheld's aristocracy isn't *that* intimidating…"

The gormless looks on her friends' faces said it all.

"Oh… well in that case, maybe we should-"

"Zahraaaaa!" cried the banshee voice of a girl from across the classroom. "Can I be on your team?!"

From amidst the crowds of students slipped a tiny runt of a girl. So small was she that her ashen grey pigtails barely reached the shoulders of those around her. Her crazed, hot pink eyes gazed through a pair of round, crooked glasses that magnified them to a massive size. Strangest in her appearance were her clothes, a sensible Vilandil Academy uniform - there was no guessing why she still wore her elegant black skirt, grey leggings and her tidy maroon overcoat, but she looked utterly adorable in it all. Cute as she appeared however, there was insanity in her burning gaze.

"Goddess…" Zahra sighed in defeat as the girl thundered across the classroom.

"Who in Elarios is she?" Nearchos scoffed. "I've never noticed her before."

"Emilia Arrenni," Zahra muttered. "I got too cosy with her on the first day and now she's attached to me like a dunestalker."

"A what?"

"It's not relevant," Zahra smirked. "A word of warning - she's crazy. When she tells you she has pink essence, don't deny it... for your own safety."

James and Nearchos glanced at each other with a mix of concern and terror. Neither one of them knew what hell was about to rain down upon them, but they were both equally afraid. They watched anxiously as the girl battered Brooke aside and leapt before their desks.

"Hi! I'm Emilia, you've probably heard of me!" Emilia smiled, her voice rapid and crazed and her eyes flaring with energy. "No doubt you know about my gift!"

"Yeah, sounds... amazing," James muttered.

"Wonderful! Of course, you'll be happy to know I can bring more than just fame and notoriety to your team!" Emilia declared. "I'm also an *awesome* biomancer!"

"And she has the modesty of Thedonius to boot!" Nearchos chuckled.

Of course, nobody around him knew who Thedonius was, but that did not stop Emilia from glaring at him as if she was going to rip the essence from his body.

"Come on, none of you know Thedonius?" Nearchos scoffed to an audience of blank faces. "The man given incredible acting talent by Artimenner, yet he remained a humble man and lived a modest life? No?"

"I'm pretty sure that's a no," Zahra smirked.

"Ah, you people are so uncultured..." Nearchos muttered.

"Thedonius aside, I'm not sure you're what we're looking for," James mumbled, shrinking into his seat as Emilia's eyes exploded into a burning glare. "We're kind of looking for a defender..."

The girl's bloodthirsty stare quickly subsided and formed into a smug grin. "Defence is it?" she sneered. "Well, you're in luck - I can do *anything*!"

A doubtful silence hung over the trio as Emilia's face darkened. Nobody believed her, but they all feared to dispute her.

"Hmph, must everybody hold the school of biomancy in such low esteem?" Emilia scoffed, a sudden snobbery in her once erratic voice. "As a biomancer, I can absorb enemy attacks like they are nothing. If you need someone to keep enemy attackers at bay, I'm your girl!"

Glances were exchanged between the group as they mulled over Emilia's words. They were afraid to be around this lunatic for too long, but she did make a good point. A biomancer was an excellent alternative to an abjurer and could act as a potent buffer between their team and the enemy.

"Come to think of it, Nearchos could be as effective a defender as any abjurer," Zahra mused. "And combined with Emilia, could keep James and I defended just fine."

"Wouldn't using Nearchos for defence kinda neuter our offence?" James asked.

"Well, we've still room for one more," Zahra smiled. "I say we let Emilia join, any objections?"

A wide grin crept across Emilia's face as she monitored the blank faces of her teammates. With a gleeful squeal, she slid behind Zahra's chair and threw her arms around the girl's neck.

"Thank you, Zahra!" she cried, burying her face in Zahra's shoulder. "When I'm super famous, you can be a main character in my biography!"

"I'm not sure that's how biographies-" James thought it best to stop as Emilia's eyes rose from Zahra's shoulder, her throbbing pink pupils swamped in darkness by her ashen fringe.

"Well, that makes four," Nearchos sighed, still unsure if he was happy with this. "Now… we just need one more."

"Any ideas?" James asked, searching the room carefully. Everybody had been quick to assemble their teams - there was nobody left! Even Caesia had been reluctantly dragged from her seat by Bruno and his band of rejects. "Hm… I guess we'll have to find someone from a different-"

"Not so fast!"

Zahra shook off Emilia's grip and the four of them stared across the room. Laurent Bouchard stumbled out from the bulging mass of students still drifting around Lucia and her team, hoping that she would kick somebody out in a blind rage - a fairly likely circumstance.

"Freedom!" Laurent cried as he patted himself down. "I thought that mass of skin and sweat would be my tomb!"

From his ragged state, Laurent quickly returned to form. He flicked back his flowing, blonde hair and returned a smug smile to his flawless, round face. Known above all else for his style, he straightened his crimson doublet and glided smoothly to their side, his vibrant, purple eyes fixed upon James.

"If you seek a fifth, my friend, Sir Laurent of Gerasberg is happy to oblige!" sang his silken, effeminate voice.

"*Sir* Laurent?" Emilia laughed at the sight of the man. "My cat was more knightly than you!"

"Looks can be deceiving, I assure you!" Laurent declared heroically. Everybody's eyes fluttered in surprise at the fact that he actually had a knighthood at such a young age. "You will find my skills as a warrior *and* enchanter much to your liking!"

"Do we need an enchanter?" James asked Zahra.

"Well, I-"

"Of course you do!" Laurent boomed. "Enchantment gives me access to a host of offensive and defensive abilities alike! You will find no teammate more versatile!"

"That's a pitch I can't argue with," Nearchos grinned. "Anyone object?"

"My powers don't need a boost!" Emilia snapped, looking away in petty defiance.

"Three against one," James chirped. "You're in, Sir Knight."

"Happy days!" Laurent gushed, spreading his arms wide in praise of the lord. "I shan't disappoint!"

"Well, I guess that's that..." Zahra muttered, looking back and forth at her teammates. It was quite the dysfunctional band, but it had promise. "What now?"

"First things first," Emilia grinned sinisterly. "I would like to put myself forward as team leader! No objections? Good."

The original trio simultaneously sighed, already fatigued by the girl, while Laurent stood listening with chivalrous respect for the lady.

"No offence, Emilia," Zahra mumbled, stiffening as the girl's smiling face turned slowly to meet her. "But I don't think we should be letting the sixteen year old lead the team..."

"Wait, you're sixteen?!" Nearchos scoffed. "How in Ivarrion's name did you get in?!"

"Isn't it obvious?" Emilia sneered. "The faculty were so excited to behold my gift that they allowed father to admit me early!"

While her eyes were closed in a prideful smile, the rest of the group looked to each other with doubtful smirks. They knew full well that it was the wealth of House Arrenni that had gotten the girl her place.

"You've a gift?" Laurent mused, drawing groans from the rest of his team. "Do tell, my lady!"

One could perfectly pinpoint the moment in which Emilia processed his request, her eyes lighting up like hot pink fireworks. "Well, hasn't someone been living under a rock!" she giggled. "My name is Emilia, the miraculous girl born with pink essence!"

"Pink?" Laurent scoffed. "First the Tarantis girl with her green essence, now you? What is the world coming to?"

"Don't invoke that pretender's name!" Emilia snapped, before suddenly returning to normal. "The powers that be have blessed me with great power, the likes of which the world has never seen!"

Zahra stared blankly into the distance, her shoulders sagging further and further down as she succumbed to her terrible reality. What had she gotten herself into?

"Blessed by God..." Laurent gasped. The group's eyes widened as he fell to one knee and bowed his head low. "My lady! Allow me to be your sworn blade, to defend you from the nefarious powers that might seek your God-given gift!"

There were no words to describe the sheer emptiness of mind that James, Nearchos and Zahra were experiencing. Of all the talented mages in their company, they had managed to end up with, by far, the two densest of the lot.

"Hm... I can't imagine I'd need protection," Emilia mused, her head rushing with ideas. "But yes, Sir Laurent of Gerasberg! I will have you be my sworn servant!"

"I am humbled, my lady," Laurent mumbled, bowing his head further. "The Lord as my witness, I pledge to you service undying, that I might stand at your side until world's end."

"Okay!" Zahra boomed, jumping up and yanking Laurent to his feet. "As I was saying, I don't think *her majesty* here is quite appropriate for the role."

"*I'll make you eat those words, you b-*"

"Calm yourself, mistress," Laurent said calmly, resting his hand gently on her shoulder. "Zahra of... Novekhir, I demand that you retract your words!"

"Ala'mir..." Zahra sighed.

"Zahra is right," James said, avoiding eye contact with Emilia at all cost. "No offence, but I think we need someone a little more level headed."

Emilia's eyes violently twitched as her anger boiled, yet a deep breath calmed her temper. "What do you suggest?" she hissed, her body stiffening as she buried her fury.

"I suggest Zahra," James smiled. Zahra's eyes shot wide open and snapped to stare at James in panic. "She knows her way around magical theory better than any of us, which should make her a pretty good strategist."

"I- what?!" Zahra gasped, her mouth falling ajar and her throat constricting. "No, no, I can't lead! Get Nearchos to do it, he's sensible!"

"I agree with James," Nearchos muttered, only sinking Zahra further into distress. "You're an illusionist. Your backfield support role will allow you to study our situation without distraction, make us more adaptable."

Laurent bent down to Emilia's shoulder. "They raise a good point, my lady," he whispered. "Were you to lead, I fear you would struggle to grasp the battlefield in its entirety."

Emilia was momentarily infuriated, seconds away from punching her unfaithful servant before she plastered on a smile. This was fine, she thought - less time spent leading meant more time spent displaying her awesome power!

"Very well," Emilia muttered. "But I'm taking second in command."

Zahra's head was in a spin. The concept of leadership terrified her - Like James, she had always been quiet and studious, never really interacted with many people until she came to the College. What use was she in such a role?

"Now hold on!" she snapped. "You can't just thrust this role on me without my consent!"

"Oh, it's happening," Emilia grinned.

"We're not forcing anything on you," James said gently, pushing Emilia away. "We just think you'd be a pretty awesome leader."

"I... what can I do?" Zahra sighed. "I've not a speck of charisma in my body."

"We don't expect you to give us any rousing speeches," Nearchos smirked. "We just need a strategist and there is no candidate even close to your smarts."

"That's not true..." Zahra groaned. Alas, they were right. As poor as she would be in all other departments of leadership, she was sure to shine in strategy. She knew what this meant to James and thus, she found herself willing to take one for the team. "But fine, I'll do it."

"Wonderful!" Laurent sang, casting his arms into the air. "And should you find yourself under pressure, I'm sure Lady Emilia would be happy to bear your burdens!"

"Do not speak for me, knight!" Emilia hissed. "But yes, what he said."

"Then I guess it's settled," James smiled, sliding out of his seat. "I'm sure you'll do great, Zahra."

"Undoubtedly!" Nearchos grinned as he sprang up after his friend.

With all that out of the way, James scanned the other teams assembled throughout the room. He could only guess at most of their abilities, for his evocation classes were shared only with Brooke, Harmodius and Bruno.

First, of course, was Lucia's team. The girl made no secret of her abilities - fire, and lots of it. Hasso was naturally by her side, watching with an attentive smile as she talked strategy. Across from him stood Matheas, a quite handsome and well-mannered young man who like Hasso, had no business associating with Lucia. Also like Hasso, he was an abjurer, no doubt there to protect his fearless leader while she set the foe alight. That left Josef and Isadora, electromancer and enchanter respectively. James knew nothing of their abilities, but they had to be good to be acquired by Lady Severin. Isadora in particular was unusual amongst the class - the fair-haired Thyresian was an athlete and had the slender build to suit it. One had to wonder what enchantments someone like her might make use of.

Next was Ava's team, no doubt led in equal parts by Brooke - the two of them were the best of friends and did practically everything as a duo. Ava was a cryomancer, paired cleverly with Leopold for the versatility of ice and fire. Meanwhile, Nicolas' abjuration would combine with Brooke's evocation for a strong defence. James knew well that Brooke's evocation power scarcely mirrored her plain appearance, far more potent than the rest of their class. Finally, there was Galen - the team's wildcard. As an illusionist, only Zahra and Class D's Vivienne had ever seen what he could bring to the table. To the rest, he was an unknown.

Last of all was Bruno's team, one scraped together largely from the rejects of the class. Bruno was rather large, not in muscle yet physically imposing all the same. He was renowned amongst their evocation class from steering away from the usual focus on weaponry and instead pursuing magical armour to further amplify the perks of his size. At the behemoth's side stood Harmodius, his friend and fellow evoker, specialising in defensive evocation. Together, they were a wall of magical might to stand ahead of their team. Then came Emeric and Florence - Emeric was quiet and reserved, more of an 'I'm only here to learn' type, while Florence was equally quiet yet also a bubbly bundle of joy. They were electromancer and biomancer respectively, each capable of offence and support. Last of all was Caesia, who was slumped against the wall reading her book. It was scary to think what she might have been capable of, what nasty surprises that green essence of hers could have in store.

"We should take a look at the rules," Zahra sighed, sliding reluctantly from her seat.

The rest of the team followed suit and they marched to the front, where most of the class was gathered around the end of Moreau's desk. Emilia pushed apart Florence and Harmodius, revealing the scroll and all its dictations.

"No lethal spells?!" Emilia scoffed, throwing her arms high in disgust. "Well, this is going to be far more boring than I'd hoped."

James breathed a sigh of relief at the fact, staring across the room at Lucia. He looked the rules up and down - the structure was quite simple. Three stages, the first two being a mystery and the last pitting students against one another in a combat stage. Though lethal spells were not permitted, anything else was fair game. All manners of physical and mental harm were on the table.

"Well, this is simple enough…" Zahra muttered. "And really, *really* dangerous."

"Don't be silly, it's going to be fun!" Emilia chirped. "There's nothing quite like obliterating the dreams of helpless children."

"You're the youngest one here," Nearchos said.

"Did I ask for your input, you blithering fungus?"

She and Laurent stalked off to the door and, as Lucia came storming to the front, the rest of the group thought it best to do the same.

"Out of the way, pimples," Lucia growled, shoving Brooke out of her path and straight into James.

Her shoulder slammed straight into his chin, bouncing the two of them away from each other. "Sorry, sorry!" Brooke gasped as he stumbled back from him. "A-Are you okay? I... I'm really sorry."

"Um, yeah, I'm fine..." James muttered, holding his jaw in his hand. "It's not your fault."

"Heh, you're right... silly me!" Brooke smiled. Pale faced and stiff as a broom, she edged slowly back to Ava's side. "Good, uh, good luck with your training!"

"Oh yeah, training," James mumbled as he re-joined his team.

Zahra's eyes floated slowly to her friend. "James... you have been training, right?"

"I... have been busy," James mumbled shamefully.

"Busy procrastinating, I expect," Nearchos sighed. "Looks like you've got your work cut out for you."

"Don't worry, Jake!" Emilia chirped. "I haven't started either!"

"That's not a good thing!" Zahra hissed. "If we want to win this, you two need to get your acts together. We need to train like we've never trained before!"

"You can count on it," James smiled. With his essay finally out of the way, he had only one thing on his mind.

They stepped out into the hallway after the rest of the class, which mostly dispersed towards the libraries and training yards.

"Bye, everyone!" Brooke chirped, skipping off down the hall. "Have fun!"

"What a lovely girl," Laurent smiled. "So! What is the plan, team leader?"

"Um... just train, I guess," Zahra muttered. "I'm probably going to spend some time in the library today."

"As will I," Nearchos said. "But I think it best we meet up regularly. Train as a team, you know?"

"Ugh, do I have to?" Emilia groaned.

"Yes, Nearchos is right," Zahra insisted. "How is everybody for ten tomorrow morning?"

The group glanced back and forth in silence, along with a few shrugs and subtle gestures.

"I… guess that's a yes," Zahra sighed. "Alright, we'll meet up tomorrow and discuss tactics and training and all that."

"Great!" Emilia smiled, turning to Laurent. "Sir Knight! I require a chariot!"

The others watched as Laurent shuffled to one knee and lifted Emilia's tiny frame onto his shoulders. The two of them rose, Emilia kicking her feet childishly as Laurent stood up straight.

"Where to, my lady?" Laurent asked, heroism in his voice despite his embarrassing situation.

"To the red dorms!" Emilia yelled, thrusting her finger ahead. "Mush, Sir Knight!"

James watched blankly as Laurent thundered off down the corridor with Emilia giggling like a maniac on his shoulders - they truly had acquired some characters. The team dispersed across the campus, more eager than ever to put in all the work they could. The Triarcanum was but a week away and there was no time to lose.

Chapter Two - Dysfunctional Dynamics

Procrastination… one of life's greatest foes. The day was through in an instant and James had not a moment of training under his belt. It was only when he tucked himself into bed that his eyes snapped open at the realisation of it. Alas, as much as he cursed himself for such practices, it never stopped him from repeating them. I'll start tomorrow, he told himself.

Feeling fresh and raring for the day ahead, he stepped once again out of the red dorms and onto the campus, where Nearchos awaited him yet again.

"Nine-forty…" Nearchos smirked, glancing at the distant, archaic clock tower. "You're actually punctual."

"What can I say?" James grinned. "I'm gonna win this."

"I suppose you've been training hard then?" Nearchos asked.

"Yeah… absolutely," James mumbled. Nearchos didn't have to know about his failures - today, he was getting his act together. "Where's Zahra?"

"Oh, she said last night that she'd be in the Gardens. Don't know why…"

"Gardens it is then," James smiled. "Let's go."

They headed into the centre of the campus, a short walk from each of the equidistant dorm towers. It was another beautiful, cloudless day, as was often the case in Abenfurt. Like much of the Kingdom of Verdenheld, the city was blessed with warm summers and snowy winters, the best climate in the known world. Unless you asked Zahra, that is, for she insisted that Novekhir was far greater. How is a desert a good climate?

The campus was rather easy to navigate now that the term had come to a close, the roads and pathways no longer choked with bodies. A few minutes later, they found themselves stepping into the College Gardens. The expansive grove nestled at the campus' centre was a vibrant paradise of all kinds of life. Plants of every colour from all across the world graced its grounds, whether gifted by nations or torn from their lands by force. A glistening, artificial river flowed through its centre, pulled all the way from the canal by means of hydromancy. It was a beautiful place, yet quite the maze to navigate.

James scanned the gardens carefully, yet he could barely see beyond the treeline ahead. As usual, many alchemists roamed the area, stalking from plant to plant and analysing their alchemical properties. Aside from them, a few biomancers were wandering the grounds and honing their skills. James' eyes fell upon Florence, who was standing at the gardens' edge manipulating the ragged vines hanging from one of the Strausian jungle trees. Hopefully, she would know where Zahra was lurking.

"Florence, hey!" he called. "How's it going?"

Florence's head snapped upright, the vines around her arm drooping as she stared blankly at him, short of breath. It was nothing unusual for her to freeze under the threat of social interaction, but she was always quick to recover. She cleared her throat and loosened up, a sweet smile spreading across her face as she shook off her vines.

She was easily the cutest of the girl's in James' class, in the same sense that one would call a baby so. Her crimson eyes were large and exaggerated, her pasty cheeks swamped with a hundred freckles. Her fiery, orange hair was clustered in a simple bob that wrapped around her face, curling as it reached her feeble jaw.

"Oh, uh… Hi, guys!" she stammered. "Yeah, I'm good and… stuff. Just practicing my eco-manipulation and-" Her face dropped and she stared off blankly into the air, uncertainty in her eyes. "Am I allowed to tell people that?"

"I think it's pretty obvious either way," Nearchos smirked. "And it looks like it's coming along nicely."

Florence locked up at the impact of his compliment, her eyes shrinking into her head as she fumbled for words. "Oh, I- you… you think so?"

"You could barely move grass at the start of the year, right?" Nearchos chuckled. "We've all come a long way - James couldn't even cast a spell before he came here!"

James sighed with embarrassment - he did not need reminding how inferior he was to his fellow students.

"I guess we have," Florence smiled. "And I'm not even at my best today! It's too dry, not really good for the plants, you know?"

Nearchos' face lit up with purpose, drawing a smirk out of James. Every mage relished an opportunity to apply his trade, hydromancers especially.

"Maybe I can help with that," Nearchos smiled. "Stand back, if you would."

Florence nearly tripped over herself as she stepped away, staring blankly at the ground and glowing red with pent up breath.

Nearchos drew forth his finger and spewed a slender jet of blue water into the dirt around the plants nearby. A smile grew on her face as she lifted her hand high and met a vine that reached down for her. As Nearchos stepped away, she gently maneuvered her hand and drew several vines to her waist, joining them like a thick rope draped from the tree.

"Thanks," Florence mumbled as she nestled between the vines and lifted her feet, rocking gently back and forth on her organic swing. "So…

18

what are you guys doing here anyway? N-not that you can't be here! I'm just wondering, that's all... you don't have to tell me."

"We were just looking for Zahra," James explained. "You seen her around here?"

"Zahra... I think I might have," Florence muttered. "Last I remember, she was by the memorial fountain."

"Right next to all the novekhiri flora," Nearchos sighed. "We should have known."

"Ah, we're in no rush," James smiled. "Thanks, Florence. Good luck with your training."

"Yeah, um... you too, guys," Florence said, before slumping back on her swing with a sigh of relief. She watched James and Nearchos march off into the Gardens, humming a rhythmless tune as they went and internally kicking herself for being awkward in front of boys again.

"You chivalrous bastard," James chuckled. "Allow me to water your plants, my lady!"

"Oh, come now," Nearchos muttered. "There was no chivalry about it, I was simply being polite!"

"That's what chivalry is!" James laughed.

"Chivalry is a complex system of morality common in knights. Politeness is simply not being an ass."

James rolled his eyes - Nearchos was never one to take a joke when it came to matters of education or manners. He was far too strict when it came to rules and conduct, always striving for perfection. It would have been admirable were it not so annoying.

They wandered through the Gardens and towards the eastern edge, where the foliage opened up into a lush clearing. Only the distant twitter of birds disturbed the peaceful grove, rows of vibrant plants encircling a flawless, sandstone fountain that trickled crystalline water into small canals, slowly feeding the plants around it. It was the Sianna Everic Memorial Fountain, a subtle monument commemorating the headteacher turned battlemage whose battalion saved Abenfurt from the Oppressor's armies during the Elarian War.

Perched on the fountain's edge was Zahra, her eyes shut tight and her hands drifting gently about in front of her. Now that term was over, her hair was loose at her shoulders - she had always insisted upon tying it back during term time in order to look presentable, but much preferred it this way. She turned to James and Nearchos with a smile as they approached, yet her eyes remained shut.

"Morning, gentlemen," she smiled, tilting her head as if looking around the clearing. "I see you've found my lair."

"Yeah, nice place," James muttered, never much for the beauty of nature. "We're not, er…"

"Disturbing me?" Zahra smirked, lifting herself gently to her feet. "Of course you are, but it's no fuss. After all, we've got work to do!"

As she sprang upright, Zahra looked up into the sky with her eyes still closed and let slip a gentle whistle that seemed to last an age. James and Nearchos followed Zahra's imaginary gaze and jumped out of their skin as a yellow blur bolted towards them.

Zahra chuckled as the two of them staggered aside, Nearchos letting slip a pathetic gasp as the blur swept overhead with a chilling screech. She extended her arm high and grinned with delight as the sand drake came to rest on her wrist. Her eyes peeled open, fluttering as they adjusted to the sun, and fell smugly upon her friends.

"What the- is that a drake?!" James stammered, wheezing for air as his heart thundered.

The creature's beady, orange eyes stared blankly at James, setting him incredibly on edge. The smallest of the draconid family at only half Zahra's height, it was still as intimidating as it was beautiful. Its yellow skin was painted almost golden by brown ridges, wrought across its rough, scaled skin and giving way at its shoulders for battered wings that folded as it squatted on Zahra's arm. At the end of its long, winding neck lay a maw of innumerable razor teeth that dripped oily mucus onto its master's shoes.

"*Sand* drake," Zahra smiled. "Her name is Amani."

"And… why have we only just met her?" Nearchos asked.

"Because I've been keeping her a secret since I arrived," Zahra grinned deviously. "She's going to be my trump card in the tournament."

"Is that allowed?" Nearchos asked with an eyebrow raised in doubt.

"I'm told I can bring any animal I wish, so long as I can fully control it. Me and Amani have been a team since I started at Al-Acazar Academy, so it's a bit of a no-brainer."

"So, you can control that thing?" James scoffed.

"*Her*," Zahra hissed. "And yes, I've trained for years to do so."

James could scarcely believe what he was seeing. He knew that Zahra was good, but suddenly she pulls out a fire-breathing lizard that she had all along? James could barely evoke a stick, what use was he compared to her?

"Qess jabal, Amani," Zahra smiled, her hand glowing with yellow light as she brushed it past the drake's head.

Nearchos sprang out of the way as Amani leapt from Zahra's wrist, spreading her wings and sailing off into the sky. Zahra sighed as her pet disappeared over the rooftops and turned back to her friends.

"Anyway, we'd better fetch the others," she said.

"And where are-"

James was cut short as he caught a yellow blur out the corner of his eye. The trio watched as Amani swept onto the roof above and skidded to a stop beside a bird nest.

"Ti, Amani!" Zahra snapped.

A jet of flame exploded from Amani's mouth and utterly consumed a helpless pigeon, the sustained stream of fire cooking it on the spot. Nearchos' mouth fell ajar as the creature snapped up the scorched carcass of the bird and threw back its head, guzzling the entire thing down its slender throat. After a few moments of gargled gulping, Amani chirped innocently and swept off into the sky once again.

"Zahra…" Nearchos sighed. "That thing is *not* safe to have on campus."

"She won't hurt anyone, she was just hungry!" Zahra urged. "Drake's have quite the appetite, you know."

"Which is exactly why she's dangerous," Nearchos insisted. "What if she gets peckish and the only thing around to eat is… I don't know, Emilia?"

"I think in that scenario, *Amani* might be the one being eaten," James smirked.

"That won't happen, Nearchos, I promise," Zahra smiled. "Amani is trained to be around people, she won't be a problem."

With a begrudging groan, Nearchos relented. Having a carnivorous, fire-breathing creature on campus was unnerving to say the least. He trusted Zahra's word, yet he intended to keep a close eye on the beast.

"I'll hold you to that," he muttered. "Now, let's go find the other two."

"Oh, no need!" Zahra chirped. "I spotted them while I was flying Amani around, they're just through the treeline. I was going to go over there, but… I was afraid to disturb Emilia. I think she's trying to concentrate."

"Speaking of which, I was meaning to ask - what is her problem?" James asked as they set off along the path.

"I don't know," Zahra sighed. "I generally tried to avoid her, so I never quite figured it out. All I can say for certain is that she thinks she has pink essence and that gives her a seriously massive ego."

"So, she's not actually special."

"No. Either it's a mutation in her essence or her eyes - one way or another, it's definitely not real. Of course, she won't listen to a word anyone has to say against it. I suppose there's no harm in letting her have her wild fantasies."

"Wild fantasies?" James laughed. "What, does she think she's some kind of god?"

"She thinks she's gifted," Zahra smirked. "You should have seen the look on her face when the Tarantis girl walked in on the first day."

"Damn, that must have hurt…"

"Actually, I'm pretty sure it just made her angry. Like, *really* angry," Zahra said. "I'm pretty sure she intends to destroy the poor girl in the tournament."

"Poor girl?" James said. "What's Emilia going to do to her? She's tiny!"

"That's the question," Zahra mumbled. "And I'm scared to learn the answer."

James furrowed his brow, baffled by the notion. Caesia might have been terribly skinny, but Emilia was perhaps the shortest person he had ever met. Surely, she could do no harm.

"She really is crazy, huh?" James laughed.

"Absolutely out of her mind," Zahra said. "It's kind of cute. In a way…"

They stepped through the treeline, where Emilia sat cross-legged in the grass by a small pond. Laurent stood at her side, toying with his hair and leaning on a silvered mace. The weapon's grip was wrapped with crimson cloth and its blunt head hummed with subtle, purple light. He glanced up from his master and waved to his teammates as they approached.

Zahra stared for a moment at him, waiting for him to break his silence before turning to the girl. "Hey, Emilia…" she whispered, approaching with caution. "What are you-"

"Shhh!" Emilia hissed. "I'm listening to the grass."

She glanced up at Laurent, who simply smiled and shrugged. Nearchos and James looked to her with doubtful smirks, sharing silently in their amusement.

"What does it say?" Nearchos asked.

"They're saying *shut the hell up I'm trying to concentrate!*" Her eyes shot open and she plunged her fist into his gut, watching with an emotionless glare as he staggered away.

"Emilia!" Zahra hissed.

"I tend not to tolerate disobedience," Emilia muttered as she clambered to her feet. "You lowlifes have a lot of nerve interrupting me like this."

"Well excuse us, my lady," James said. "You weren't actually listening to the grass, were you?"

"Of course bloody not!" Emilia snapped. "Do you even know what biomancy is?"

"Making plants do things?" James suggested. "And healing. Maybe *with* plants."

The look on Emilia face was one of utter disgust. "I've met statues less thick that you," she hissed. "Biomancy is about more than telling plants what to do! It's the power over life and death itself! The means to harness the very stuff of creation!"

"Isn't that just necromancy?" Nearchos smirked as he edged hesitantly back to her side.

"Why don't you tell me, Water Boy?" Emilia growled, smacking her hand down upon his arm.

Nearchos' eyes widened in terror as his skin began to harden. In a panic, he shook his arm back and forth, detaching her feeble hand and staring down in horror at Emilia's handiwork. His skin had warped and bent beneath her grip, leaving behind a crude, phallic shape etched into his flesh. James descended into hysterics at the sight of it, while Zahra tried desperately to bottle her laughter as she watched her friend's horrified stare.

"W-what did you do to me?!" Nearchos cried, shaking his hand violently in a fruitless attempt to remove the brand. "Get it off!"

Emilia cackled maniacally, revelling in his anguish. "What do we say, Water Boy?"

"I'm sorry, I'm sorry! Just… just get rid of it!"

His face dropped as the girl folded her arms in defiance, raising her chin high. "Insincere!" she snapped. "Admit your mistake calmly and coherently."

Nearchos glanced up longingly at his friends, who watched intently as they awaited his embarrassment. "I'm sorry that I insulted you. Biomancy is an excellent school for which I have a lot of respect… and you are a truly amazing biomancer."

With a smug grin, Emilia wiped her hand across Nearchos' arm and returned the flesh to normal. "Let that be a lesson, you watered down shit stain," Emilia sneered. "Now, for what dull purpose have you intruded upon me?"

"They are your team, my lady," Laurent whispered. "For the tournament?"

"For the- yes! Yes, of course," Emilia gasped. "What does my favourite trio of fodder need?"

"We need to talk tactics," Zahra said. "I was thinking we could go to the library today and put a plan together."

"That sounds… really boring," Emilia groaned, glancing to Laurent. "Oh, don't look at me like that."

"You must be cooperative, mistress," Laurent insisted. "Even with your astounding gift, you cannot win this tournament alone!"

"Don't tempt me," Emilia warned. "Fine. We'll talk about your silly 'tactics'. On one condition."

Zahra sighed into her hand. "What is it?"

"I need someone to complement my hair," Emilia said. "I'm still not sold on the pigtails, I feel like they detract from my natural beauty."

"Yeah, yeah, they're great," Zahra muttered. "Can we go now?"

"Could you explain your reasoning?" Emilia asked.

"They… they bring out your eyes… you know, because, uh, because they cover up your ears."

Emilia narrowed her eyes, yet a smile slowly began to crease her cheeks. "You're so right!" she gushed, patting down the sides of her head. "Less exposed skin means more focus on my *gorgeous* eyes!"

"Mm, yeah. Let's go."

Zahra waved the team along and Emilia skipped along with them, shadowed by Laurent.

"So, where are we going?" Emilia chirped as she leapt and bound down the path.

"I told you, we're going to the library," Zahra groaned.

"Well, I wasn't listening," Emilia said. "Why exactly are we going there?"

James sniggered as Zahra buried her face in her hands. "You're messing with me, aren't you?" she asked.

"Maybe."

"My lady, I believe that Zahra of Novekhir is feeling rather stressed right now," Laurent warned. "You may want to stop antagonising her."

"Antagonising?!" Emilia scoffed, her hand over her heart. "What kind of half-witted degenerate do you take me for? I thought you were on my side, but it is clear to see that your loyalty-"

The thud of a distant explosion quaked the ground beneath their feet. Lampposts shook, trees rustled and stone crumbled from ledges.

"What was that?" Laurent gasped.

"Sounded like it came from the training yard…" Nearchos said.

"Oh, I want to see!" Emilia cried, charging off down the pathway.

The others hurried after her, down the winding trail and towards the thick walls that bordered the training yard. They piled into cover at the entrance and Emilia clambered onto Laurent's shoulders as they peered around the corner. A large swathe of the dusty ground was painted black and flickered with yellow flame. One of the walls had crumbled into a pile of smouldering rubble, before this remained the ashen stump of a vaporised training dummy.

"You fucking idiot," Lucia growled, standing over Brooke as the girl scrambled to pick up a number of burnt books. "The hell were you thinking?"

"I-I'm sorry!" Brooke cried as she stumbled to her feet, grasping her auburn bob as she cowered. "I didn't know, I thought... I just..."

"You walked right into the blast zone is what you did!" Lucia snapped. She drew back her fist and punched Brooke hard in the shoulder, sending her reeling. "You're lucky to be alive, you wart-faced, little freak!"

Lucia shook her head as Brooke squeezed her books tight and fled from the yard, tears streaming down her acne spattered cheeks.

"Maybe we shouldn't be firing off the big stuff around here," Hasso mumbled. "Someone could get hurt or-"

"If someone gets hurt, it because they're stupid," Lucia muttered. "And no, I'm not worried about the property damage. What are they gonna do, expel me?"

"There's only so many times you can push the limits," Hasso urged.

Chuckling to herself, Lucia flung out her hand. "Watch me."

Yellow flames erupted from her hand and exploded across the yard, obliterating the rest of the wall and incinerating another dummy. The colossal bang left ears ringing and walls trembling. Lucia withdrew her arm with a smug smile and surveyed the startled faces of the students around them.

"We're so dead," James sighed.

"That was *amazing*!" Emilia gushed, vibrating on the spot. "The rush of heat, the glorious boom! Tell her to do it again!"

"Nearchos, you specialise in an elementa sub-school," Laurent said. "Can you do something like that?"

"I could do either the size or the power, not both," Nearchos said. "I knew she was good, but that kind of spell is beyond what any first year should wield."

"I heard her essence awakened early," James whispered, taking cover as Lucia marched out of the yard. "That means she's had more time to get to grips with it than the rest of us."

"Never mind the whys, we should be talking about the *hows*," Emilia hissed. "Like how we're going to crush that uppity blonde and her team of nobodies!"

"Uppity, huh?"

James, Zahra and Nearchos simultaneously froze as Lucia stepped around the corner.

"Please, that's hardly original," she smirked, folding her arms and tilting her head. "I could say the same about you, but I'd rather go with something like... I don't know - a diminutive wretch with a toxic ego the

25

size of her family's own wealth. A spoilt, little daddy's girl, told all her life she's special when she's nothing more than a mutant freak of nature. How's that?"

Emilia stared blankly at her, slowly narrowing her eyes. A smile creased her face as she descended into subtle yet manic laughter.

"Excuse my insolence Lady Severin, but as Lady Emilia's sworn protector, I demand that you relinquish your words!" Laurent growled, stepping forward and raising his finger to her. "Apologise for your rudeness or by my own hand, I shall-"

Lucia grabbed his wrist and clenched it tightly in her heavy grip. "Touch me and you won't have a hand," she smiled.

Laurent maintained his glare as flames crept from Lucia's sleeve. She chuckled as his face twitched and trembled in an attempt to keep his cool.

"Oh, give it a break," Emilia sighed, shoving Laurent aside. "I like her style. She gets a pass."

Lucia's glare shifted to a look of confusion as Laurent shuffled glumly away. "Quite the pair of weirdoes you got here, Zahra," she sneered. "I didn't think it possible, but you've redefined 'scraping the bottom of the barrel'."

She swivelled on the spot and marched off, twitching her hand and chuckling as Nearchos jumped in fright. Hasso looked back over his shoulder as he turned to follow, his usual apologetic look on his face. There was scarcely a time when he didn't appear sad and exhausted.

"I'd wish you all luck, but I doubt you need it," Lucia called. "I'm sure Tiny can just *bribe* you into the finals."

Emilia chuckled, but her eyes told a very different and far darker story. The rest of the team waited for Lucia to turn the corner before expelling their pent up breath.

"Vekh alaghar," Zahra groaned. "What is that word that everyone whispers behind her back?"

"Bitch?" James suggested.

"That's the one…" Zahra sighed. "Ugh, she really is the worst."

Laurent hung back as the rest of the group continued on. With an impatient groan and a roll of her eyes, Emilia dropped back to his side.

"I'm sorry, my lady…" Laurent sighed, hanging his head in shame. "I have failed you."

"Shut your trap, I can take care of myself," Emilia muttered. "You don't need to go threatening people every time they insult me."

"I'm your knight… it is my duty to defend your honour."

"Look, I think need to have a little talk about the whole… dynamic here," Emilia said. "I don't need your protection, so stop trying to stand up for me."

"But... what is my purpose, if not to protect you?" Laurent mumbled.

"Think of yourself more as a vessel of my will," Emilia smiled. "Just do what I say, ferry me around and..." Her voice became hushed as she shuffled close. "Be my friend."

Laurent looked down at her with an eyebrow raised. She smiled up at him and eventually, he smiled back. "I can do that."

"Good man," Emilia grinned, slapping his back with unnatural force. "If anyone asks, this conversation never happened."

"As you will it, my lady."

Emilia grinned with utmost delight, swelling with giddiness as they caught up with their team.

The group headed across the campus to the library, a six-story monolith of grey stone, filled with thousands upon thousands of spells, lore and theories. Ancient tomes had survived for nine hundred years on the towering shelves that stacked every floor, looming like titans over the surrounding tables and desks. Zahra found her team an empty table on the second floor, in the shadow of several hundred abjuration tomes, where they gathered to discuss a plan of action.

"Right. Strategy," Zahra said, tapping her quill against the desk. "Strategy, strategy, strategy..."

"Wow, you're terrible at this," Emilia laughed. She rolled her eyes as Zahra shrank away in shame. "The only thing we can prepare for right now is the combat stage. We don't know what team we'll be against yet, so we can figure out team composition later. Right now, we ought to figure out our roles and talk about what abilities we need to work on in our training."

She narrowed her eyes as James and Nearchos stared at her blankly.

"What?" she hissed.

"Nothing..." James mumbled. "Just kinda surprised how much that made sense."

"Well, I'm full of surprises," Emilia smiled, venom in her voice. "I'll start!"

She sprang from her seat, sending her chair skidding across the hall as she stood tall and planted her hands on her hips.

"Here we go," Nearchos sighed.

"*I can hear you!*" Emilia growled, smacking Nearchos over the head and filling the library with an echoing crack. "Oh, you've got a really slappable head! Anyhow, my biomantic powers specialise in manipulating my physical properties. By changing my strength and density, I can fill just about any role - offence, defence, anything in between!"

James groaned and stuck up his hand. "Hey, can you just stop with the ego for-"

"However! You want me on offence," Emilia grinned. "Believe me, you won't regret it."

"Should we really be entrusting our offence to a sixteen year old?" Nearchos asked.

"You'd rather entrust her to defence?" Zahra sighed.

"I'm right here!" Emilia snapped. "You people need to start taking me seriously. You think they'd let me into this damn place if I didn't know what I was doing?"

Nearchos buried his head in his hand. "They let you in because your father paid them t-"

Another visceral crack echoed throughout the library, turning the heads of many disgruntled students and scholars.

"What I'm trying to say is that I'm on offence, no ifs, no buts," Emilia hissed, falling back into her seat. Even Laurent had to hold back laughter as she collapsed to the ground, staring up at the seat that lay a whole metre across the room. "You people are mean, you know that?"

She scrambled to her feet and dragged her chair back to the table. Slumping grumpily onto her seat, she folded her arms and huffed a heavy breath.

"You'll see... I'll win this stupid tournament single handedly. You losers will be falling at my feet and singing my praise!"

"Okay..." Zahra sighed. "Laurent, what can you do?"

"Well, as it would happen, I too am rather versatile," Laurent smiled. "My enchantments give me durability and quite a bit of hitting power. Depending on which I decide to use, I can fill either role."

"Do you have a preference?" Zahra asked.

"Hm... If I had to choose, I'd probably go with defence. With my equipment on hand, I can take a great deal of punishment and keep the enemy at a safe distance from yourself."

"And what about our loveable water boy?" Emilia sneered. "Are you spells as wet as your personality?"

"What is that supposed to mean?" Nearchos scoffed, receiving only a smug smile in return. "My spells are pretty straight forward - I can create water and manipulate liquids."

"Speaking of which, I'm parched," Emilia sighed. "Can I-"

"No," Nearchos snapped. "I can do defence, but I'm probably better on offence. From the backfield, I can use jets of water as artillery, blast people while someone else keeps them off me."

"Sounds like you'd combine well with Laurent or Emilia," Zahra said. "Focus on your offensive stuff. James, you can make a good shield, right?"

"Uh, yeah..." James mumbled. "It's not very big, more of a personal thing. I can do a weapon to... kind of."

"Kind of?" Nearchos asked.

"It's fine. Don't worry about it," James smiled. "You probably want me up front. I'll at least be decent at getting in the way."

"Someone sounds a tad ashamed..." Emilia said, leaning forward intently. "Have you something to share, Justin?"

"I... I can kind of only make a baton," James mumbled, sinking into his seat as Emilia erupted into hysterical laughter. "It's still a good weapon! I can knock people out with it!"

"A baton!" Emilia cackled, slamming the table with her fist. "That's hilarious! You're *so* bad!"

"Emilia!" Nearchos hissed.

"She's not exactly wrong though..." Zahra said. "You don't really stack up to the other competitors."

"I know," James sighed. "But I'm good with my shield, I promise. I'll just stand in the way while you all... be useful."

"I'm sure you'll do great," Laurent smiled. "And what about you, Zahra?"

"Oh, do tell!" Emilia chirped. "You funny-coloured people are meant to be really good at illusions, right?"

Everybody sank into silence as Zahra stared vacantly at Emilia. "Excuse me?"

"What, am I just colourblind?" Emilia asked. "I'm not the only seeing brown here, am I?"

"Getting back on topic..." Zahra hissed. "I can manipulate a person's perception of reality - make them hallucinate, black out their vision, put them to sleep... Only thing is, it requires a lot of concentration."

"Which means you'll need someone out in front," Nearchos said. "What about the drake?"

"Amani can open people up for attack and distract them when need be. I can control her directly, but basic commands should do us just fine."

"You know, we've not got that bad a team," Emilia mused, kicking up her feet on the table. "So long as the frontline holds up, which it will, we could dole out some serious damage."

"Emilia, get your feet off the table," Nearchos commanded.

"That'll be a no, my soggy friend," Emilia smiled. "Actually, what am I saying? We're done here!"

She swivelled on her chair and leapt to her feet, grabbing Laurent's wrist and pulling him up after her.

"Where are you going?" Nearchos asked. "We should be training *together*!"

Emilia looked him up and down, a mix of disgust and pity on her face. "I'll be honest. You two - wet willy and the baton boy... you're not exactly

29

my favourite people. Don't get me wrong, in comedic value you're the best, but really… I-I just don't like you, okay?"

The rest of the group, Laurent included, stared at her in shock as she span around and dragged her knight to the front door.

"If it's all the same to you losers, I'd rather spend as little time around you as possible," Emilia called as she marched off. "See you in a week!"

"Don't worry, gents," Laurent whispered as he was dragged by. "*I* like you very much!"

"Uh, thanks," James mumbled, turning to Zahra and Nearchos. "Well… that was blunt."

"She didn't mean that," Zahra sighed. "She just thinks you're idiots."

James looked glumly to Nearchos as Zahra chuckled to herself. "Ah, that's fine then," he muttered. "So, what are we getting up to?"

"Training, I guess," Zahra said. "You're both okay with me practicing my illusions on you, right?"

"Is there any risk?" Nearchos asked.

"Not aside from a headache or two. Though, there was this time I locked someone in mental stasis on accident. Took me three hours to get her out… but that was years ago!"

"You didn't have to include that last part," James groaned. "Fine, training it is. Just don't make my nightmares reality or something."

"Of course not," Zahra smiled. She watched intently as James slipped from his seat, only to jump in fright and collapse against his chair.

"I am *not* afraid of Emilia!" James growled.

"You should be," Emilia smiled. "Sorry, I was eavesdropping. I'll go now."

James watched as she scurried back to Laurent and into the stairwell. "Was that…"

"Real? Yes," Zahra chuckled. "I expected you'd go the other way."

His instincts got the better of him and he peered over his shoulder. Zahra giggled as he quaked and grasped his chest, his head sinking to the table.

"That's not funny," he mumbled into the wood. "That was a private memory and you should feel bad."

"Aw, I'm sorry," Zahra smirked. "But seagulls? Really?"

"It was scary!" James snapped. "You've clearly never been attacked by birds."

Zahra shook her head and rolled back her left sleeve. "Try being attacked by a drake, then get back to me."

James shivered at the sight of the deep teeth marks indented in her skin. "There were a lot of them…"

"You should give up now. Before I tamed Amani, I tried my powers on a terak'ra."

He stuck out his hand as she reached for her trouser leg. "Okay, I get it!" he laughed. "No need to make my childhood trauma a competition."

"Why, because you'll lose?" Zahra sneered, hopping to her feet. "Right, no more slacking. Let's get to work."

James and Nearchos followed hesitantly as Zahra led them out of the library and off campus. A short walk through the streets of Abenfurt brought them to the edge of the city, where they passed through the towering, wooden gates and over the canal.

"Remind me again why we're out here," James groaned as they trudged through the flawless plain of grass that severed the city from the Abenwood.

"Well, the training yard was on fire last we checked and I didn't want to disturb the gardens," Zahra explained. "The guards should have no problem with us firing off some spells out here."

"I really don't like the grass here," Nearchos muttered as his boot phased through several blades. "How much of this stuff is an illusion?"

"All of it," James smirked. "Pretty sure half the Abenwood is fake as well, got cut down ages ago. I wonder what it would look like if you dropped some sladium around here."

"Just like home," Zahra laughed. "I can't imagine it being anything but-"

She yelped as an arrow struck the ground in front of them and spat dirt from beneath the illusory grass. Its shaft lit up with blue light and whined as it released a pulse of magical energy, ripping away the illusion in a rippling wave. The ground surrounding the arrow was reduced to a lifeless husk of cracked dirt, a festering blotch in the vibrant field.

"Well, that answers that," James sighed, watching Zahra gasp for air. "Should we be worried about that?"

"I don't think so," Nearchos said. He pointed towards the edge of the Abenwood, where a pair of tan legs dangled from amidst a tree. "Isadora?"

"Hey, hey!" Isadora chirped. Her leg whipped up into the tree and her head poked upside-down from the canopy. "Sorry, did I scare you?"

"Just a little," Zahra gasped. "What are you doing up there?"

"Parkour. What brings you lot out here?"

They stepped beneath the tree and stared up at her. She was hanging by her bulky legs from a branch, her battered, old quiver between her feet. No passer-by would ever guess that Isadora went to the College - her dull, blonde mane was filthy and unkempt and her worn face was almost always spattered with grime. Everywhere she went, no matter the occasion, she

31

dressed in the same sweaty shirt and ragged shorts. Nobody questioned it - the Thyresians were well known in Verdenheld to be an unusual people.

She swung herself up and planted herself gracefully atop the branch. "Shouldn't you be training?"

"We are," James called. "Shouldn't you be with Lucia?"

Isadora chuckled quietly as she shuffled to her feet. "Well... to quote our fearless leader - 'If you're going to rely on me, you're not worth my time. Piss off and train yourselves'. So, here I am!"

"Hm, I can't tell if that's good leadership or bad," Zahra said. "Must be terrible having her boss you around."

"I like her, she's fun," Isadora smiled. "Too many people around here are all prissy and proper. Lucy's not the nicest person, but she's a breath of fresh air."

"I wouldn't say her that to her face, if you know what's good for you," James laughed.

"Maybe, but I like to live on the edge," Isadora said. "Why else would I join Lucy's team?"

"I'm not sure you had a choice," Zahra smirked.

"And *I'm* not afraid of a little fire. Believe me, I had a choice," Isadora smiled. "Not even Vera herself could scare me."

"Hm, so humble," Nearchos smirked.

"A person is humble because they don't value what they have," Isadora said diligently. "A god said that... I assume. Probably Isoripes. Maybe."

"That doesn't make any sense," Nearchos said. "A person can't be humble if they don't know what they have."

"That... is what Isoripes was trying to teach us!" Isadora declared. "You passed the test. Well done!"

"I'm pretty sure the god of judgement wouldn't-"

"Well! I'd best not keep you all. We have training to do, after all."

"Yes, we do," Zahra smiled as she dragged Nearchos away. "Good luck with your... tree climbing."

Isadora furrowed her brow as they disappeared back into the field. "It's parkour!"

"She is weird," James sighed.

"Everyone here is weird," Zahra laughed. "At least she's not quite hit Emilia levels of strangeness... Is something wrong, Nearchos?"

He looked totally vacant - lost in thought and utterly baffled. "I just can't get my head around what she was talking about," he said. "I just don't remember Isoripes saying that."

"Nearchos..." James sighed. "I don't know much about this Isoripes guy, but he probably didn't say that. I'm pretty sure she was making that up."

"Then why would she lie?" Nearchos scoffed.

Zahra leaned into James. "It's not worth it," she whispered. "Let's just get to training. Who wants to be my test subject?"

James looked longingly to Nearchos, who was still mumbling to himself in a world of his own. They came to a stop amidst the field, where Zahra turned to him with a smile.

"I guess it's you then!" Zahra chirped. "Don't worry, my spells are completely harmless. Unless I decide to make you brain dead…"

"Come again?"

"Don't worry about it!" Zahra smiled "You just stand there and I'll… I'll make you see some butterflies."

James took a deep breath as Zahra raised her hand. With a sudden flick of the wrist, she disappeared. Everything disappeared. The grass, the trees, the city - all reduced to nothing but blackness.

"Zahra?" James mumbled, breathing heavily as he scoured the empty void. "Zahra, what did you do to me?!"

"Calm down!" called Zahra's voice from amidst the abyss. It echoed a hundred times in his mind. "It's just an illusory void."

"Illusory- that's not butterflies!"

"The unsuspecting mind is a mind most vulnerable," Zahra said. "Image-based illusions don't work if you know they're coming! Hold on, I'll pull you out."

He tensed as the sound of her voice disappeared and left him in total silence. As anxiety began to creep into his mind, he began to hop up and down on the spot, trying to take his mind off the endless abyss.

"This is fine. This is fine!" he whispered to himself squeezing his eyes shut. "This is not fine! Zahra, I'm freaking out!"

"Oh, don't be such a baby!" Zahra moaned. "Look, I… I may have messed this up a little, just let me get the spellbook."

"What do you mean, a little?!" James cried. "Zahra? This isn't funny!"

"Will you quit your whining?" Zahra snapped. "I need to concentrate, now hold still!"

The rush of colour that surged back into reality set James' head in a spin. The light of the sun exploded across his vision like a fireball and his mind rang with a terrible ache. Gasping his every breath, he swayed groggily on the spot as his eyes adjusted and narrowed into a glare.

"You're the worst…" he groaned.

"I admit, that spell still needs some work," Zahra muttered, stepping slowly closer. "Why don't we try a sensory spell?"

"No way!" James snapped. She threw up her hands in resistance as he tried to shove her away. "Practice on Nearchos, he's-"

Zahra's hand slipped between his arms and planted against his head. "Sleep!"

She giggled as he collapsed into her arms and deposited his limp body in the grass. It was an adorable sight, so peaceful and innocent, drooling into the dirt as he slept.

"Better let him calm down," Zahra sighed, spinning around to Nearchos. "How's it going?"

"I've run into a problem," Nearchos said, staring blankly at the ground. "It's nothing but dry dirt under this grass - not exactly the best spot for hydromancy."

"Ah… I don't suppose you want to be my-"

"Not really, no."

With a nod of her head, Zahra turned back to James. She sighed as she stared down upon him, so precious and cute. She almost felt bad, taking advantage of his weakness as a mage, but it was all in good fun.

"Are you going to wake him up?" Nearchos asked.

"Not yet," Zahra smiled as she shuffled to the ground beside him. "He needs the sleep."

She lay back in the grass, arms spread wide, and took in a deep breath of the fresh morning air. The hard dirt beneath her was of no comfort, but the caress of the illusions against her skin created a strange, almost euphoric sensation. What better place to work on her telepathy with Amani?

Only a few minutes later, Nearchos turned his head and groaned at the sight of his friends, both sound asleep.

Chapter Three - Gladewatch

The week rolled by at a startling speed and before the students knew it, summer had arrived and the Triarcanum was ready to commence. The campus, once desolate, swarmed with nobles and merchants, chattering in anticipation of the most incredible of Verdenheld's annual celebrations. The turquoise banners of House Tarantis flew from every building, their six pointed star reminding the innumerable patrons of who made it all possible.

Nearchos watched the campus gates from afar, perched with his feet hanging into the canal. With the whole city crammed into the College's towering walls, it was an unusually peaceful spot - an excellent place to take a break. He glanced down into the gentle water, staring anxiously at his distorted reflection. It was beyond intimidating to think that all those people would be watching, to know that the eyes of the world's most powerful men and women would be fixed upon him. He supposed it was something to get used to if he was to be an admiral like his family before him, but he could not help but fear the bustling crowds.

With a deep sigh, he planted his hands on the canal's edge and pushed himself over, landing with a meagre splash atop the water's surface. He started down the river, bypassing the crowds and strolling undisturbed into the campus. Nearchos could not help but wear a smug smirk on his face as he stepped out of the canal and into the gardens, for he was particularly proud of his intuition.

"*Come on!*" Emilia growled. "I can take i-"

Nearchos had not even time to pinpoint the girl's position before a deafening clang broke the tranquillity of the gardens. A pink blur whipped past his sight and crashing into the treeline ahead of him. His jaw dropped as two beds of flowers, a rare shrub and several tree branches were obliterated by the meteoric impact of Emilia's body.

"Are you harmed, my lady?" Laurent called as he dropped his mace and hurried after her.

The foliage shifted as Emilia burrowed from the brambles and burst from the pummelled plantlife unscathed, fists raised triumphantly in the air.

"That was awesome!" she cried, wading back onto the grass and crushing several more flowers on her way. Her skin was rigid like the bark of a tree, hardened to the strength of steel by biomantic power. Her clothes on the other hand, were shredded and scarred, reduced to tattered husks.

"Emilia!" Nearchos snapped, winning a cheeky grin from the girl. "What in Elarios are you doing?!"

"Uh… practicing?" she answered smugly, shrugging her shoulders without care.

"You just destroyed several items of College property!" Nearchos hissed. "An act of vandalism like this could see you disqualified from the tournament!"

"Ugh, you really are a killjoy, aren't you, Water Boy?" Emilia sighed. "Sir Knight, would you please fetch the ginger girl with the freckles."

"Of course, ma'am," Laurent said, jogging off with utmost haste.

His face deep in his palm, Nearchos groaned with total agony. "You'd do well to be more respectful of the rules…" he muttered, despite knowing full well that Emilia did not care for his advice. "Anyway, I guess Zahra isn't here?"

"Maybe her drake saw you coming," Emilia smirked. "Oh no! It's that water guy, here to *rain* on all the fun! Best go get my umbrella!"

"Must you be so difficult?" Nearchos sighed.

"Yes," Emilia grinned. "But if you must know, she went to find Joshua in the training yard. I might have gone with her… but I dislike his kind, so unhygienic."

Nearchos sighed and folded his arms. "I just can't figure you out," he muttered. "What's your problem?"

"Pft, my problem?" Emilia laughed. "Well, I keep running into this guy, he's a total loser, most boring person I've met in my life."

"Very funny," Nearchos groaned. "Come on, tell me. Is it all ego or are you just looking for attention?"

Emilia stepped closer, narrowing her eyes. "Oh, you think you know it all, don't you?" she hissed. "You think you've got me all figured out. Well, let me tell you something, *detective* - the fact is-"

"I return with the girl!" Laurent boomed, charging back into the clearing. "Florence Belveau, I present to you Lady Emilia Arrenni."

"Ah, you're here!" Emilia chirped, skipping merrily to Florence's side. "I've discovered a scene of terrible vandalism wrought by an unknown criminal and you are just the girl to fix it!"

Emilia had spoken so fast that she had sent Florence's head into a spin. It took a fair few seconds before the girl recovered from her dazed state with a flutter of her eyes.

"Oh, er… okay…" she mumbled, staring timidly into the grass. "I mean… I can try, but I'm not that-"

"Great!" Emilia smiled. She slapped Florence heavily in the back, smirking as the girl let slip a pathetic whimper. "Come, gentlemen! To the training yard!"

She rushed off with not another word, Laurent scraping up his mace and following in her wake. Nearchos glanced with a sigh to Florence, who was still fumbling for words and looking the scene of destruction up and down.

"Sorry…" he muttered as he turned to follow.

"Th-that's okay," Florence smiled, distress in her trembling eyes. "It'll be good practice! I think. I hope…"

With a hesitant nod of the head, Nearchos trailed out of the gardens and left Florence in her lonesome. The journey to the western side of campus would be a gruelling one with the enormous crowds in their path. He just hoped that they could escape the city before the nobles finished their celebrations, else the road to Gladewatch would be swarming with bodies.

The sweltering heat of the sun had all but drained James of energy. He withdrew his cylindrical, scarlet baton from the training dummy and slumped to the ground. Sweat dripped from every inch of his skin and sagged his hair down the length of his forehead. He felt like death after barely five minutes of practice.

Across the training yard, Catelyn and Meridian from Class A were making no attempt to hide their amusement as they laughed and pointed his way. A laughing stock once again - nothing new there.

"Bloody sun…" James moaned as he shuffled to his feet.

He took up stance before the dummy, raising his baton to its wooden figure. As he understood it, the laws of essence meant that the weapon in his hands could achieve any properties he might choose - it could slice through steel, shatter rocks, vaporise matter! Alas, his meagre understanding left it good for little more than hitting people over the head. The impact buckled him more than it did the wood as he slammed it down upon the dummy's shoulder.

"Quite the mighty weapon you got there, Serith!"

James' body stiffened at the sound of Lucia's voice. It was as if she actively sought him out, as if she had nothing better to do than make his life miserable. He heaved a heavy sigh and took another swing at the training dummy, his back to the waiting girl.

"Ignoring me, huh?" Lucia smirked. "No… you're listening to my every word. It's sad how petty you look, trying to be the better person."

It wasn't that at all - James simply wished to preserve his life. He had seen from afar the terrible results of angering Lucia, like when she accidentally set a Master Menard on fire after being threatened with expulsion. Her volatile temper made her dangerous and James feared to end up on its receiving end.

"Look, there's no way I can say this without sounding like an asshole…" Lucia sighed. "But you should quit this tournament while you can. You won't get *anywhere* with that crappy little thing, let alone the finals."

He knew that she was right; it was a reality he was all too aware of. He stood no chance against the other students.

"And if you get in my way... hell, anyone's way - you're going to get obliterated," Lucia warned. "The Triarcanum is no place for a peasant boy with a stick."

Peasant boy - is that what he was to her? He was no street urchin, he was from Abenfurt! It was clear she was being cruel for the sake of cruelty, for she seemed to rather enjoy it.

Lucia's brow furrowed and she began to pace around the dummy. "Maybe you aren't listening after all..." she hissed, her voice becoming abrasive as her patience wore thin. "People like you sicken me. You think you're so much better than me 'cause you're all silent and reserved, think you're *so* perfect!"

He glanced up from the dummy and into her eyes. There was not a time when they didn't burn with hate, though they now twitched with impatience.

"Is that it, Serith?" she growled, planting her hands upon the dummy's shoulders. "Answer me."

She growled as his eyes fell back to the dummy and he readied his baton for another swing. Smoke seeped from beneath her fingers as they burned deep into the wood. Her pupils flared with a fiery glow and her teeth clenched tight like those of a snarling wolf.

"*Answer me!*" she roared, slamming her hands against the dummy's back.

James leapt back as it exploded into flames, the wood blackening as it withered and crumbled away. The sweat on Lucia's brow began to simmer as she marched back around the blazing figure, confronting James with fury in her fiery eyes.

"You're pissing me off, James..." Lucia warned, her tone escalating into a manic growl as her right arm flickered with dancing flames. Steam began to drift from her scarred skin as her temper reached boiling point. "I don't think either of us want that."

His throat dried out as her heat washed over him like a burning wave. Yet, even as he was overcome with dread, he was calmed by the sight of a golden drake perched atop the wall above. His heart might have been thundering, but Amani's presence gave him a flicker of confidence in the face of terror.

"How could I ever think I'm better than you?" he sighed. "You're better than me in every way... but that doesn't mean I'm hopeless."

The flames on Lucia's arm died slowly out and her dark expression gave way suddenly to an amused grin. "You think you have a chance?" she laughed, her anger an absolute thing of the past. "That's adorable, Serith, but you really ought to be realistic."

"I am," James growled, dispelling his weapon and screwing up his fists. "I might not be all that good, but I've got the best team I could ever hope for."

"Do you now?" Lucia smirked as she turned her back. "You might have the smartest girl in class on your team, but you also have a sixteen year old girl, a wannabe knight, a stick-up-the-ass Thyresian and... well, you."

At that, she sprang down the steps and waved carelessly over her shoulder, leaving James alone with the scorched remains of his dummy.

"But, I digress - Best of luck, Serith," she sneered. "Who knows... maybe I'll see you in the combat stage."

Gritting his teeth with contempt at her words, James watched as Lucia strolled off into the lower yard, flicking her hand aside and vaporizing a passing wasp for no particular reason. It was hard to refute the disadvantage James was at, nor the sheer power that Lucia and many of his other classmates held over him. That only meant that he had to try harder, that he had to prove her wrong. Whether he was capable of such a feat... he would prefer to find out first hand.

A smile returned to his face as Zahra slipped out from beneath the yard's surrounding balconies, swaying with hands behind her back as she wandered to meet him. Amani launched from atop the wall above and swept into the sky, circling the yard at a distance.

"What was that about?" Zahra called as she ascended the steps to the upper yard.

"Ah, she just wanted me to know I'm going to lose," James smirked. "I'll enjoy the look on her face when I'm strapped up in Tarantis blue."

The uncertainty in his voice was more obvious than he liked to believe.

"If she doesn't kill you first," Zahra chuckled, nodding towards the crumbling dummy at his side. "I suppose that's her doing?"

"Yeah, I... tried to ignore her."

"Big mistake," Zahra grinned. "That sort of tactic only works when the nuisance in question can't burn you to death in seconds flat. Anyway...you ready?"

"As I'll ever be," James sighed, that meaning not at all. He had spent so much of the year struggling with magical theory that he had scarcely had time to work on his evocation.

Zahra took a deep breath as she watched him squirm. "You're still worked up about your powers, aren't you?"

"Of course, I am - How can I not be? I'm terrible."

"Don't be so hard on yourself."

"It's called being realistic, Zahra," James said. "Lucia is right, I'm hopeless against the other students. I'll never be on their level."

"You will," Zahra urged, grasping his wrists. "These things just take time. You started at such a disadvantage and... and if you ask me, you've done incredibly to get this far!"

James managed a dwindling smile. "That still doesn't change how awful I am."

"And I'm an awful leader," Zahra smiled. "We have to make do, even with this scuffed, dysfunctional band of idiots we've put together."

James laughed hesitantly. Zahra always knew how to perk him up, but she was terrible in the field of optimism. He felt no more confident about his odds, though he would certainly give it his all.

Zahra's eyes darted across the yard as an unmistakable head of ashen hair came hurtling around the corner. A satisfied grin graced James' lips as Emilia shoved Catelyn aside and sent her vial of perfume spiralling from her hands. Catelyn shrieked as it shattered against the ground, while Emilia skipped by merrily, ranging ahead of Laurent and Nearchos.

"Zahraaaaa!" she cried, breaking the collective concentration of every mage in the vicinity with her piercing squeal. "I wanna go to the festival!"

"The festival?" Zahra scoffed. "Emilia, the festival isn't for us, we need to be training!"

"Everyone else is going!" Emilia insisted. "Well, not everyone... but most of them are!"

"All of whom will be at a disadvantage for doing so," Zahra said proudly. "If we put in the extra work now, we'll be a step ahead of the rest."

Emilia stared for a moment through sinking eyelids. "Ugh, you're such a nerd!" she groaned. "Train all you want, *I'm* going to the festival."

"Emilia-"

"I... kind of agree," Nearchos muttered, clearly displeased to utter such words. "A break would do us good. If everyone else is down there, it couldn't exactly hurt."

"Nearchos, are you feeling alright?" James smirked.

"Yes, and I understand the importance of recreation in regards to one's health," Nearchos declared.

Zahra fumbled for words as her opinion was washed away by the people she was meant to lead. "But I-"

"Going!" Emilia snapped, spinning around and charging across the yard.

"If you still want to train, I don't mind sticking around," James said to Zahra as they watched their teammates march off.

"Thanks, but... well, I don't want to ruin everyone's fun," Zahra sighed, shooing him off with a flick of her hand. "You go have fun. I'll spend a bit more time with Amani before I come down."

"You sure?"

She glanced up at her circling drake with a gentle smile. "Yeah. She's all the company I've ever needed."

"Right," James smiled as he hurried after his team. "Guess I'll see you down there!"

"I should hope so!" Zahra called as Amani swooped onto her wrist. It was a shame to miss out, but she was perfectly happy alone with her best friend.

One teammate down, the group started out of Abenfurt and into the Abenwood, following the Stefismeyr River into the darkness of the forest. The woods that dominated House Tarantis' lands were cloaked by a sprawling canopy that buried the ground beneath it in a veil of shadow. Luckily, the pathways carved through the forest split the canopy above and shone beating sunlight down upon their route.

Much of the journey was spent tolerating Emilia's feverous rambling as she proclaimed her dominance over all other students and explained the impossibility of her failure. It certainly dragged, but they soon found themselves emerging from a treeline in the very centre of the Abenwood.

Dominating the enormous clearing ahead was the fortress of Gladewatch. The Interregnum era castle had been refurbished to accommodate events after its fall to House Barethia - its stone walls were pristine, the surrounding grass flawless. Many tents, mostly turquoise in colour, swarmed in the shadow of the castle's walls, bustling with noble guests. A racetrack encircled the site, stretching around a marble amphitheatre and disappearing behind the fort.

"I spy... something beginning with T," Emilia said from atop Laurent's shoulders. "And I promise it's not a tree this time."

"It's a tree, isn't it?" Nearchos groaned.

"I can neither confirm nor deny that statement," Emilia muttered.

"There is an entire castle in front of us and you still pick the damn trees!" James snapped. "If you're going to play this stupid game, put in some effort!"

Emilia stared down upon him, an eyebrow raised. "Wow. I'll be honest - didn't expect that reaction. For a lowborn wretch like yourself, you've certainly got some fangs."

"Yeah, listening to your crap for an hour will do that."

"Hmph... perhaps you've got some fight in you after all," Emilia smirked. "Very well, I will be quiet."

Her elbows dug into Laurent's head and she buried her face in her hands. As they wandered into the festival village, Emilia began to hum, then to tap her fingers and then to whistle incredibly poorly. They had barely passed the first tent before she groaned with agony.

"Ah, forget it, I'm booored!" Emilia moaned, beating Laurent's chest with her feet. "What even is there to do here? I mean, it's just a bunch of tents in a muddy-" She paused, staring wide eyed at a distant tent as her face lit up with excitement. "Games!"

She leapt from Laurent's shoulders and shattered the dirt beneath her upon impact. Amplifying the density of her hands, she slammed Nearchos aside and toppled him to his knees before prancing off into the field. Laurent jogged with her to the tent, while James helped Nearchos up.

"Remind me to keep a metre's distance from her at all times," Nearchos muttered as he brushed off his mud-caked knees.

They followed Emilia loosely through the shifting tide of visitors as she darted into the shadow of the large, turquoise tent. It was about as simple as a game could get - people stood upon a designated mat and threw balls at a stack of cups only a few metres away. Surely, Emilia could do no harm here.

As the gamemaster extended a ball to an approaching child, Emilia leapt onto the mat and shoved the small boy aside, swiping the ball from the man's grip in a swift motion.

"Step aside, filthy peasant!" she sneered, narrowing her eyes upon the gamesmaster, who stumbled back in fear. "Prepare to witness a feat of raw physical prowess!"

Her gaze fell across the tent to the stack of cups at its far end. Clenching the ball in her hand, she reeled it back, manipulating the density of her arm for maximum power. As she readied to strike, her face dropped suddenly into a scowl.

"I said step aside, you half-eaten cabbage!" Emilia barked, hurling the ball at the gamesmaster and smashing his shoulder with a subtle crunch. "I can't concentrate with you just... standing there! Looking at me with that ugly face, trying to make me feel sorry for you - go on, get!"

Everybody around her shrank away in terror as the gamesmaster trudged to the very edge of the tent, whimpering quietly and grasping his shoulder in his hand. He could see the glow of essence in her eyes - no regular person dared defy an angry mage.

"Boy, fetch me another two," Emilia demanded, smiling as the terrified child retrieved more ammunition. She snatched them from him and returned her attention to the game. "As I was saying, behold my power!"

A cleaving, overhead swing sent the ball hurtling like a comet into the stack, obliterating it in a shower of shattered cups. The gamesmaster sheltered his face as ceramic shards sprayed the vicinity like a hail of blades.

"Another flawless victory," Emilia chirped, thrusting her hand towards the stack of prizes in the tent's corner. "The sword."

The gamesmaster edged hesitantly to the pile and plucked out a children's wooden sword, one that would be far to small for anybody but Emilia. She took the blade in her hands and held it up to her face, inhaling the fresh scent of the wood in a euphoric high.

"I'll call you... *Deathblade*," she whispered, before sliding the remaining ball into her hand and staring down upon it, breathing manically. "Hm, one to spare..."

Emilia gripped the ball tight in her hands as darkness came over her. Her thirsting eyes searched the area and a devious smile grew on her face. Without a word, she whipped around and hurled the projectile into a nearby crowd of people, cackling quietly as it glanced off Caesia's forehead.

"Aw, I missed," she sighed, a villainous grin on her lips. "How unfortunate..."

She swivelled around and skipped off, waving her sword back and forth, completely careless of the dirty looks she was receiving from the entire Tarantis household. Laurent hurried after her, leaving James and Nearchos frozen in shock.

"Uh... maybe we should let Emilia have her own fun," James mumbled. "I don't wanna be executed."

"I couldn't agree more," Nearchos muttered. "But what do *we* do?"

"Dunno... all of these games are for kids, so maybe a good place to start would be lunch."

"Lunch?" Nearchos scoffed. "It's ten o'clock."

"And I had breakfast at five. Come on, we're going on a food hunt."

At that, the two of them began to sweep the festival grounds for some good food. Most tents were simply shelter for gaggles of nobles to converse beneath, while others doled out noble delicacies or hosted intriguing, magical performances. The jolly melodies of a band were amplified throughout the site, filling the village with a wondrous atmosphere that drowned the feverous chatter of its patrons.

After much deliberation, James decided that he would choose a meal more filling than the fancy morsels on show. He would find his prize at a tent that bellowed steam and oozed the intoxicating scent of sizzling meat.

As it turned out, this was not just any tent - it was home to one of the College's foremost pyromancers, Master Gerin. Draped in his crimson robe, the scruffy old man oversaw a large pit of lashing, purple flame and the swarm of pork and chicken suspended above.

"This is extravagant…" Nearchos muttered as Gerin levitated a leg of pork into Harmodius' hands.

"Who cares?" James laughed. "It's food!"

He marched beneath the tent, where a wave of magical heat washed over him and the compelling scent of pork overwhelmed his senses. In his hungering trance, he was oblivious as he wandered right into Bruno's back.

Bruno was a goliath of a man, a mass of muscle that towered over the rest of his class by a fair margin. His jet-black hair and rigid face leant him a rather intimidating appearance, but that was far from accurate. Like most from the city of Schardenhelm, he was an unusual mix of jolly and gruff, often found laughing and gloating, yet sometimes brooding in a calculative silence. Harmodius at his side was rather plain in comparison. His sponsorship by an Apilistian general had seen him grow chiselled and muscular, with groomed, blonde hair and a jaw so rigid it could parry a blade. Nonetheless, he was dwarfed by his monolithic friend.

"Oh, um, sorry…" James mumbled as he recovered, staring up at the titan's slobbering maw.

"Ah, James!" Bruno boomed through a mouthful of chicken. "You *must* try this chicken! It is perfection in poultry form."

James stumbled back as Bruno thrust a second chicken leg into his face. "You sure? A few more pounds might do your tiny self some good."

Bruno erupted with hearty laughter, spewing a hail of chewed poultry over a disgruntled Harmodius. Wiping his slimy lips, Bruno tore another chunk from his meal and discarded it into a nearby bin.

"Not as much as it'd help your weedy arms," he chuckled, shaking the remaining leg back and forth. "Eat up, little man."

"Alright…" James sighed, plucking the leg from Bruno's meaty hand.

Bruno moved for another leg and glanced to Nearchos, who raised his hands in denial.

"I had a big breakfast," he said.

"Smart man!" Bruno laughed. "Care to join us for a stroll, gentlemen?"

"Why not?" James said, shrugging as they stepped out from beneath the tent.

"That's the spirit," Bruno smiled. "So, chaps! How are we feeling about our teams? Confident?"

James glanced to Nearchos with a deep sigh. "Well… I don't suppose you've met Emilia Arrenni?"

"The grey haired one, right? Seen her around, but we've never talked," Bruno said as he obliterated a mouthful of chicken. "I find it's good practice to avoid people that spend all of dinner talking to themselves."

"Yeah, that's a pretty accurate assessment," James muttered. "She's mad, absolutely crazy. Worst of all is she doesn't think we're worth her time."

"You think she'll struggle to work as a team."

"I know she will," James said. "And then there's Laurent... he'll just follow Emilia. Idiot swore an oath to protect her."

"You could always just go with them," Harmodius suggested. "She might not be the leader, but it's probably better you stick together."

"Maybe, but I'd rather stand by Zahra as our leader," Nearchos said. "I trust her intuition far more than that sociopath."

"And Zahra *really* needs a boost in confidence," James said. "What about your team?"

"Honestly, I'm not sure," Bruno mused. "I've no doubt about their talents, but it's their commitment that worries me. Florence is a sweet girl, but the whole thing terrifies her. Emeric doesn't care in the slightest and Caesia seems more intent upon studying other students and testing weird hypotheses than actually trying to win."

"That's what we get for picking the quiet ones," Harmodius muttered.

Bruno chuckled and shook his head. "Harmodius thinks I made a mistake, but he'll see."

"Whatever you say..." Harmodius sighed.

"Why *did* you pick them?" Nearchos asked.

"Because he felt sorry for them," Harmodius said. "This big idiot has too much heart."

"You can never have too much heart!" Bruno triumphantly declared. "And as I've tried to explain to my pessimistic friend - the quiet ones are always set to surprise. I still don't know much about Emeric, but Florence and Caesia might have a bit more fight than people expect."

As they stepped around the corner and into the centre of the village, they paused before a sizable crowd that swelled around a nearby tent. Several curious visitors joined agitated students to spectate whatever transpired in their midst, their hushed chatter breeding a contagious tension.

"What is this?" James whispered.

"Maybe a really good performer..." Bruno said. "Or a fight. You want to find out?"

James shrugged, which was enough for Bruno to march into the crowd. It parted without resistance before his towering form and he waded swiftly to the front. His companions peered around his side, where the scorched, blonde hair of Lucia was easily picked out - the look on her face was a strange mix of amusement and contempt.

"Oh, this doesn't look good," James mumbled.

At Lucia's side was the rest of her team. Josef and Matheas lurked a metre back, trying their best not to associate themselves with her. Hasso stood by to suppress her, yet he could barely get close as she waved her hands in violent gestures. Then, there was Isadora who cheered at her leader's side and pumped her arms in excitement.

Opposite them stood a group of students from Class D. Waiting off to the side were a tall, shaggy Nord, a makeup-caked girl with a thick, blonde bob and a chubby, redheaded girl slathered with freckles. The fourth of their number James knew, a girl mentioned by Zahra on many an occasion - Vivienne. According to Zahra, the Abenfurt born illusionist was about as stuck up as it got. With pristine makeup and perfect, braided brown hair, the lanky girl certainly looked the part.

Last of all was their leader, he who had the guts to oppose Lucia. His blonde hair was slicked aside and perfectly groomed, topping a pasty face that wore a smug grin. His icy blue eyes burned with disgust behind a visage of supreme confidence, that which matched Lucia's like no other could.

"You must be bloody delusional!" Lucia laughed. "You can't seriously think your gang of snobs is better than me."

"Is that right?" the boy sneered, folding his arms and raising his chin. "From where I'm standing, it's terribly obvious that you're team is doomed. I mean, how is your team going to function when their leader is too busy blowing things up to think strategy?"

One could see the veins bulging from Hasso's skin as he tensed ever more, fearing that one word too many from the boy could send Lucia into a violent rage.

"Sure… I'll let you think that," Lucia smirked. "I'll just look forward to burning your uppity ass in the combat stage."

"Straight to burning, is it?" the boy chuckled. "I shouldn't be surprised, but don't you think it's a little… poetic, given your past grievances? Though I suppose boiling isn't quite the same thing."

Lucia's eyes darkened and her hand drifted to scratch at the raw, red flesh of her neck. "You'd better watch your mouth, you cocky, little freak," she hissed. "You'll be wishing I'd fried your sorry ass once you're in hot water with House Severin."

"Hot water… interesting choice of words," he grinned, narrowing his eyes deviously. "And why should I be scared of House Severin - a house with no allies, dwindling power and nothing but a man-child and his sister left to hold it together?"

"And eight hundred thousand soldiers," Lucia smiled with a plastic sweetness.

"Cowering behind your men as always," Reiner sneered. "Where were they, I wonder, when your army rebelled? Surely they weren't *all* having their way with your mother."

Her face slowly dropped as his words sank in. Flickering embers drifted from her skin as it began to hiss with escalating heat. Even Vivienne looked to her leader with distress as everybody froze in anticipation of an impending blaze. Even so, the boy maintained his smug gaze, unmoved by the rapid brightening of Lucia's pupils.

"Alright, that's enough!" Bruno growled, barging in between them and thrusting his hands out. "We're all here to have a good time, let's just keep it friendly."

He shivered as Lucia glared up at him, a darkness like no other festering in her eyes. With a reluctant groan, she span around and marched back to her team. Their audience breathed many sighs of relief and slowly began to disperse. As Bruno stepped from between them, a smug grin grew across the boy's face and with a flick of his hand, the gentle breeze shifted into motion. Sensing the change, many swivelled around, only to watch with wide eyes as the back of Lucia's skirt was swept high by rushing wind.

A silence fell over the crowd, some looking away in horror while others stared in total disbelief. Lucia stopped dead in her tracks, the cleaving force of her feet carving trenches from the soil. As she turned slowly back around, many witnesses ducked for cover or prepared defensive spells, knowing full well what would surely come next. Rage flared in the girl's eyes as she stared back at her opponent, grabbing her skirt and thrusting it down over her legs. Suddenly, her expression shifted to a devious grin and she glanced over her shoulder.

"Brother!" she called, straining not to smile too wide as she tried to remain serious.

Her audience followed her gaze to a group of men loitering near the wine tent, to the back of a man's head - that of Lord Alvus Severin. Uttering an apology to his peers, Lord Severin turned to his sister and marched to her side. A shaggy brown beard decorated the young lord's face alongside a slender scar down the side of his head. He met her with a hearty slap on the back and a welcoming smile to those around him.

"Lucia!" he boomed. "What's all this commotion about?"

"This belligerent twit thought it wise to insult me," Lucia smugly explained. "Not only has he been tremendously rude, but the bastard used his magic to up-skirt me!"

Lord Severin glanced up at the boy, who had totally locked up before him. The colour had drained completely from his face, his eyes trembling despite his attempt to keep a straight face. Alvus grinned mischievously, knowing well his sister's intent.

"Up-skirting a lady?" he scoffed, clearly trying not to laugh. "Why, such an ill display of manners is cause enough for public execution!"

Despite his upbeat and outgoing attitude, everybody around him were frozen in silence. The lords of Verdenheld were terrifying, their power absolute. As the man who controlled over two thirds of the kingdom's military, he was feared above even King Friedrich himself.

"Tell me, sister - beheading, hanging or burning?"

"You certainly lack creativity, don't you?" Lucia smirked. "How about we take him to Windspire and see if his aeromancy can help him survive the drop from the Grand Cathedral?"

Vivienne rolled her eyes and stepped forward, grabbing her leader by the arm and dragging him back. "She's bluffing, Reiner," she spat, glaring at Lucia with malice. "We'd best not waste anymore time."

Lucia chuckled darkly as Reiner and his team retreated and the crowd began to silently disperse. She turned to her brother with a wide grin and received back a pat on the shoulder.

"If he does that again, you have my permission to flame him," Alvus grinned as he wandered back to the wine tent.

"Figuratively or literally?" Lucia called after him.

"I'm being vague for a reason!"

Swaying merrily back and forth, Lucia glanced smugly to an exhausted Hasso before scanning those who still remained around her. "Ah, look who still came!" she chirped to James as she wandered off with her team in tow. "Don't say I didn't warn you, Serith…"

"Was that a threat?" Bruno whispered.

"No… more of a pre-emptive 'I told you so'," James muttered. "Lucia thinks I should opt out of the tournament because I'm not that good."

"Seriously?" Nearchos scoffed. "The nerve…"

"Honestly, she's probably right," Harmodius sighed, shrinking away at the dirty looks received from his peers. "What? Bruno, you've seen James in action too - he's barely got a hang of the novice spells. Everyone else is at least at an apprentice level, how can he stand against that?"

Bruno shook his head, smirking as James hung his in shame. "Being successful in this tournament will be more than a matter of magical prowess," he smiled, folding his arms in a display of confidence. "Above all else, good teamwork is the key to victory. If there was ever a weakness in a team like Lucia's, that is surely it."

"You think I stand a chance?" James mumbled.

"Enough poetry, Bruno," Harmodius groaned. "We need to find the others."

"Indeed we do!" Bruno laughed. "Best of luck, James. Maybe I'll see you in the combat stage."

"I guess we'd better find our own team," Nearchos sighed as Bruno marched off. "Wouldn't want to miss the opening speech."

"Are we that bothered?" James muttered, immediately recognising the foolishness of his words as Nearchos took a deep breath and raised his finger.

"Of course! It is important that we respect the traditions of the tournament and immerse ourselves in the experience. It would be an injustice not to-"

"Alright, I'm going!" James groaned, trudging off towards the village's edge. The tension was killing him, but Bruno's words had given him much to distract his mind with. Perhaps there was more hope than he imagined - all they had to do was work as a team. Easier said than done, but doable all the same.

Zahra gazed down from one of the myriad balconies that peppered the slanted face of the Gladewatch's eastern wall. Tapping her fingers anxiously against the marble guardrail, she surveyed the venue of the upcoming round from above. It was fairly unsuspecting - a massive, circular area cloaked in plantlife and peppered with the occasional building. There was no guessing what manner of trial could take place in this portioned off wilderness, but she had a bad feeling in her gut.

"Zahra… I'm hungry!" Emilia moaned from her perch atop Laurent's shoulders. "Can I eat your drake?"

"No, and it's far too late now," Zahra sighed. "You should have grabbed something while you had the chance."

"Fine. Sir Knight, to the food!"

With a pained groan, Zahra reached out and grabbed Laurent by the wrist as he leapt into action. "*Lady Emilia* is perfectly capable of finding food herself," she growled, glancing up at a disgruntled Emilia. "You two are hardly ever here, I'm not having you dragging him off all the damn time!"

Emilia glared at her with a sinister contempt, but quickly returned a smile to her face - she couldn't be mad at her best friend in the whole world.

"Very well," she sighed, swinging her legs back and shuffling off Laurent's shoulders. "Hey, you think I can make it to the bottom if I jump?"

"I don't- what?!"

Before Zahra could fully process Emilia's question, the girl had planted her feet on her knight's shoulders and leapt over the guardrail. Laurent gasped as she plummeted past in a pink blur and struck the ground two balconies down with a thunderous crack, punctuated by the shriek of terrified nobles.

"Ala'mir, se cafala…" Zahra muttered into her hands as she recovered from the fright, watching as Emilia strolled casually onto the staircase and softened her skin. "I don't suppose you're beginning to rethink that oath of yours?"

"Well, Lady Emilia is certainly a handful, but I will not waver," Laurent smiled proudly, his hands on his hips. "Tis the noblest of charges, to defend a damsel. Not that my lady is as much for suffering distress as causing it."

"You're really going through with this?" Zahra scoffed. "You do know her essence isn't special, right? It's just a mutated red."

"Oh, I'm well aware," Laurent chuckled, much to her surprise. "I simply play along so that I might continue my servitude. Finding a ward is no easy task for a young knight such as myself."

Zahra raised an eyebrow, shocked to find even a slither of intelligence in her teammate. This chivalry nonsense made no sense to an outsider like herself, but she could see that he was no fool at all - he was simply being a proper knight.

"I have been wondering," Zahra mused. "How did you come to be a knight at such a young age?"

"Ah, it runs in the family. My father was a knight and his father before him!" Laurent declared. "The Bouchard family is so acclaimed in the Heartland that father managed to talk the king into knighting me. King Friedrich is assured that I will be nothing but stellar, just as my predecessors were!"

"Wow, that's a lot to live up to…" Zahra sighed. "You think you'll meet their expectations?"

"I've not a doubt!" Laurent laughed. "Lady Emilia may seem cold around others, but she has assured me that my performance is second to none!"

"I suppose even the most legendary knights would struggle to keep up with her," Zahra smirked. "Considering I didn't expect you to last a day, I'd say you're going above and beyond."

"Thank you, Zahra of Novekhir," Laurent smiled.

"Is it too much to ask that you stop calling me that?" Zahra groaned.

"What would rather I call you?"

"Uh… Zahra? Just anything but that, please."

"I see," Laurent mumbled, hanging his head in shame. "I apologise, Zahra. I preferred to address you formally until I could gain a better understanding of your culture. I did not want to risk offending you with informalities."

Zahra giggled quietly into her hand. "You really are a gentleman, aren't you?" she sighed. "Trust me, I'm not as different as people think I am."

"Right you are," Laurent chirped. "You know, when I first arrived at the College, I was rather terrified to hear that there was a Novekhiri girl in my class. I'd heard nothing but bad things about you people... yet here we stand!"

"Well, relations got off to a pretty shaky start, I guess. That's why *I'm* here - to prove that the Caliphate has something to give."

"Is that so?" Laurent mused. "A rather noble mission, coming all this way for the sake of bettering your nation's reputation."

"It wasn't my choice..." Zahra muttered. "My mother sent me here expecting me to blow some minds. Novekhir knows a great deal more about illusion magic than Verdenheld does and she was hoping that I'd prove it."

"And never has there been a more perfect opportunity! What better an occasion to show off your skills?"

"I wish it was that easy. Illusion isn't an easy magic to get in the spotlight, seeing as it works mostly in the head. It's possibly the most potent arcane school, but it's difficult to display in non-academic means."

"So, what will you do?"

"I don't know... I guess Amani might be my only hope, though I'll have to keep her under wraps until the combat round. I'm just... I guess I'm a little scared. If I don't excel, I'll have failed my country, my parents, myself... and if I do something stupid, there's every chance they'll pull me off the course and drag me back to Novekhir."

"I fail to see the issue," Laurent smiled. "You're one of the most-"

"I'm baaaaaack!" Emilia sang, prancing onto the balcony and flailing a colossal chunk of pork in her tiny hand.

"That was fast," Zahra muttered.

"Yeah, I legally acquired this from a very generous, fully grown individual," Emilia smiled. "Does anyone have any salt?"

"No..." Zahra groaned.

Emilia waited for a moment in silence before falling upon her meal. Her jaws crashed down upon the pork and shredded its hide with ravenous efficiency. Tearing off a chunk half the size of her head in one fell swoop, she threw back her head and guzzled it into her mouth like a starving beast.

"Ah, our teammates arrive!" Laurent boomed, his words jolting Zahra in fright as her focus was ripped from Emilia's violent dining.

She watched with a growing smile as James and Nearchos wandered up the stairs to meet them. As they approached, it became quickly apparent that Nearchos was caked in sweat and panting for breath, jogging with all his might several metres ahead of James.

"Don't just stand there!" he cried as he passed. "Lady Amelie is soon to give her opening speech!"

The trio made not a single move as Nearchos continued up the staircase, all watching with smirks as he staggered unathletically to the top.

"Does he know we've still got a few minutes?" Zahra called to James.

"Ah, you know how he is," James sighed. "Everyone ready?"

"Oh, you have no idea, Jacques," Emilia growled, spewing fragments of meat into Zahra's hair with her every word. *The grass will run red with the blood of the weak.*"

"Okay…" James mumbled. "You know the combat round is the last-"

"One wrong word and you'll go the way of this pig," Emilia said darkly, taking another chunk out of her meal and gnashing it loudly. "Come, Sir Knight. Let us partake in this 'opening speech'."

Laurent followed as Emilia skipped ahead, who deflected a chewed pig bone off James' forehead as she went. With a deep sigh, Zahra waved James along and tailed her teammates at a distance.

"Hey, you've got a bit of… pig in your hair," James said, raising his hand to her head hesitantly.

"I know," Zahra sighed. "I was going to tell her how offensive that was, but she wouldn't care."

"I'm not sure I'd go as far as offensive…"

"We don't eat meat in Novekhir," Zahra muttered. "I don't really mind other people eating it, but spitting dead pig in my hair… that's a little much."

"Huh, I guess that *is* offensive," James said. "Isn't meat really important though? Like, for nutrients?"

"Not at all - we eat this fruit called hakhmat, it's got all the essential stuff you get from meat," "My father does a lot of mercenary work in Athaea nowadays, so he keeps me stocked up."

"Your dad's a mercenary?" James scoffed. "How does a merc pay for college tuition?"

"Well… more like mercenary *general*," Zahra said with an innocent smile, embarrassed to flaunt her privileged upbringing. "And if your parents could afford it, why not mine?"

James knew Zahra meant well, but that one hurt. His father had worked overtime almost every day for a decade to get him into the College, a fact that often had them eating morsels for many a week. Even so, it seemed miraculous that they ever could have afforded it.

They stepped onto the vast terrace that sprawled across the renovated eastern wing. Dominated by a lush garden and a sprinkling of tables, chairs and parasols, it was set up as a seating area for those less concerned with the games and more so with drinking and discussing the political landscape. A crowd of students and nobles gathered in the gardens before a large, wooden platform. The podium was backed by a pair of large, turquoise banners marked with House Tarantis' six pointed star, flanking on either side a flawless, white fountain that spewed streams of all different colours into the pond below.

"Wow, this place is almost identical to the gardens on campus," Zahra mused, marvelling at the fluttering, pink leaves of the trees at her side. "I guess they wanted to show off for the visitors."

"You know, a skilled biomancer could kill every person here in a split second," Emilia grinned darkly. "You morons should consider that before doubting my glorious power."

"You don't even have the right spells for that," James muttered, glancing suddenly to the podium. "Hey, I think we're starting."

There was little point in trying to push their way to Nearchos, who had already plunged deep into the crowd. Instead, they lurked at the back, watching as Lady Amelie Tarantis stepped out to the platform's edge. Despite her small stature and significant age, Lady Amelie always wore a supremely confident smile on her wrinkled, round face. Her hair was wrapped in a tidy bun and an elegant, blue dress wrought with swathes of gold fluttered at her feet.

On either side of her sat much of the College faculty, all but the alchemical tutors and research staff. Each one of them was dressed in flawless formalwear and groomed to perfection. After all, the purpose of the games was to display just that - the utter perfection of the arcane arts.

At the very back of the podium lurked the rest of the Tarantis family. Lord Edmund stood as stiff as ever, watching the crowd through shadowy, grey eyes and with a stern expression on his face. He wore a plain, black doublet over and equally plain, blue tunic, topping a pair of trousers - also totally bland. At his side stood his son, Gerard, a plump man with brown, slicked back hair and dull, muddy eyes. Barely fitting the tunic he had squeezed into, he was the absolute opposite of his sister. Caesia was separated from her family by several feet, her ghostly, green eyes staring vacantly into the distance as she wrung her fingers anxiously. The scrawny girl was already strapped with her College issued combat uniform, an armour of thick, muddy brown leather designed for practical lessons. On such a warm summer's day, she looked moments away from passing out as she swayed in the gentle breeze.

"Ladies and gentlemen, might I have your attention?" Amelie asked, her voice magically amplified by a nearby illusionist. She smiled warmly as the crowd fell silent before her.

"Is there a reason why Lord Edmund isn't giving the speech?" Zahra whispered. "I thought it wasn't customary for women to give speeches here."

"It's not..." James mumbled. "Actually, I don't think he's ever given a speech! Not that I can remember, at least."

"My friends, it is my utmost pleasure to welcome you all to the three hundred and eleventh annual Triarcanum!" Amelie declared, spreading out her arms in celebration. "A whole nine hundred years ago, Artur Tarantis founded the College of Arcana as a centre of all things arcane - a place where knowledge could thrive, a place of revolutionary discovery and exciting innovation, a place where the mages of tomorrow could take their first steps to enlightenment!"

She paused as applause rose from the crowd. Many nobles turned to one another and exchanged handshakes, patting each other on the backs for nothing in particular.

"Since its conception, the College has provided the best and brightest of Elaria's magical community, from acclaimed scholars and cunning advisors to heroic battlemages and brilliant generals. They are the men and women who have guided Verdenheld through the darkness of this world - the Arachni Wars, the Interregnum, the Severin Rebellions, all spurred to glorious victory by the mighty Tarantine army!"

"Didn't half of the battlemage corps die in the Rebellions?" Zahra asked. "That's why so many children were born that year with essence, right?"

"Just roll with it," James sighed. "They're kinda full of themselves."

"And that is why we are here today - to celebrate those who hold the future of the realm in their hands. Lord Edmund and I are very proud to announce this year that our own daughter will be partaking in the tournament. Caesia, would you care to tell our guests about the arrangements this year?"

The crowd exchanged confused glances as they awaited even a single motion from the girl. One could see the sweat drenching her brow as she stood frozen on the spot, staring into the crowd with wide eyes. Hands pattered with hesitant applause as she took a slow first step, quaking violently as she moved to the podium's edge. Lord Edmund rolled his eyes as his daughter came to a stop, making a poor attempt to hide the piece of scrawled upon parchment in her grip.

"Uh... the, um, the tournament will consist of... will consist of three rounds," she mumbled. The audience was baffled at the sight of her screwed up eyes and the sad sound of her coarse, panicked breaths. "I-In the first stage um, the stu- competitors will have to... they'll... they have to..."

With an agonised groan, Gerard Tarantis trudged to her side and whispered into her ear, slowly pulling her back from the edge and sending her back with her head hung low.

"In the first stage, competitors will be tested in not only their combat prowess, but in their quick thinking and tactical know-how," he announced, unbridled confidence in his thick voice. "Using advanced illusion magic and a splash of abjuration and evocation, the arena to our east will soon be transformed into a theatre of battle! Competitors will be tasked with bringing down an array of monsters, large and small, created by our evokers and illusionists to imitate the real things!"

"Monsters...?" James gasped, the thought of taking on a beast with a stick being a rather harrowing one.

"Points will be earned for each monster slain based on not only power and difficulty, but also on the skill and finesse with which they are dispatched. Students will be eliminated if they are knocked unconscious or tossed out of bounds, but their points will still count for their overall team score. The top twelve of the sixteen teams will go through to the next round, the nature of which will be revealed tomorrow for the sake of preventing pre-planning."

"Thank you, Gerard," Amelie sighed, glancing disappointedly over her shoulder at Caesia. "There you have it! The monster stage will begin in fifteen minutes - students should report to their designated starting zones, while the rest of us shall be seated. May luck be with our future leaders!"

Under thunderous applause, the crowd began to disperse. Nearchos slipped back to James' side and five of them rallied at the edge of terrace, overlooking the arena below.

"Alright, real talk - I'm freaking out," James stammered, his speech rapid with fear. "How are we going to fight monsters?!"

"Same way you fight anything..." Emilia growled, trembling with bloodlust. Everybody took a large step back as the girl's fingers fused together, the edges of her hands forming into rigid blades. "You go for the heart!"

"That is *really* creepy," Nearchos muttered at the sight of Emilia's morphed flesh. "But Emilia's right, we shouldn't have too much of a problem if we keep things tactical."

"I guess that'll be up to me," Zahra sighed. "My illusions won't be all that useful against monsters, so I guess I'll try and do strategy."

"Anyone know how big these things are gonna be?" James asked.

"A manageable size, no doubt," Laurent said. "And I'm sure they'll keep the danger level to... a fairly low level."

"I dunno..." Emilia smirked, pointing a hand over the balcony's edge. "That looks pretty dangerous to me."

The rest of her team looked out upon the arena as a wave of purple energy rolled over it, shifting and warping the landscape in its wake. The grass was stripped away and reduced to a soggy mud. The trees sagged and bent as the leaves vanished from their suddenly twisted and lifeless branches. The pristine, white buildings were cloaked with dirt and turned to crumbling ruins. In mere seconds, the once tranquil sanctuary had become a blasted warzone.

"Vera's mercy…" Nearchos gasped. "That landscape won't mesh well with water."

"It's perfect," Emilia grinned. "There will be no escape from their inevitable deaths!"

James' heart sank at the sight of the battlefield - mobility might have been his only chance in this. He just had to hope that Bruno was right, that his team would cover for his weakness.

"I guess we should get down there," Zahra mumbled, stiff with anxiety. "Everyone ready?"

"I need a wee," Emilia smiled, prompting groans from much of her team. "Come, Sir Knight! To the bushes!"

As the girl raced off with Laurent in tow, the rest of the team started down the staircase and down to the arena. They weaved carefully through group after group of nobles, all filing onto the balconies and brimming with excitement at the thought of the spectacle they were soon to witness. The most powerful men and women in the world were watching - the pressure was high indeed.

Chapter Four - Hell on Elaria

"Look at him..." Lucia growled, narrowing her eyes as she watched Reiner wander the wall surrounding the arena. "He thinks he's better than us. Bastard."

Hasso could let slip only a grunt as he supported Lucia's feet on his shoulders. He was grasping her ankles tight as she glared over the top of the thick, wooden gate at the far end of their open-topped changing room. She had been there for a few minutes now, surveying the actions of her most hated opponents.

"Oh, just wait until the combat round," Lucia grinned. "I'll shove his lackey's sword so far up his ass, I could roast him over a fire."

"If he even makes it there in the first place," Isadora smirked. Lucia's eyes darted right and she found herself baffled at the sight of her teammate perched atop the gate, her muscular legs dangling playfully over the gate. "I could kick the ass of any one of those spineless snobs."

"Oh, they'll get through," Lucia said darkly. "I could see it in their eyes - he and that tall bitch are out to get me. Seems they want to teach me a lesson in manners."

"Yeah, what *was* their problem?" Isadora muttered. "Sounded like they were getting seriously personal..."

With a grave sigh, Lucia clambered down the Hasso's shoulders. "Well, they certainly have a bone to pick with House Severin. Nothing new there," she mumbled, toying with a flickering flame in her palm as she paced up and down the room. "Considering how clued up they were, I'd reckon their parents are vassals. My... Lord Viktor screwed them over after the rebellions, gave 'em no credit for liberating Jordenholm and gave it all to House Tarantis. Left a pretty bad taste in a lot of mouths."

"So, they take it out on you?" Hasso scoffed. "How is that fair?"

"The man who wronged them is dead and my brother is untouchable. That just leaves me - They're trying to coax me into doing something I'll regret, banking on my temper to ruin my house's reputation."

"Don't you think you're making a few too many assumptions?" Josef sighed. "Most of what you've said has no evidence to-"

Lucia slammed her foot down on the bench and scorched the wood black with a violent explosion. The planks split beneath her boot and the bench collapsed inwards, sending Josef and Matheas tumbling onto the ground in a heap.

"I don't need evidence!" she spat, drawing a whimper from Josef as she kicked his shin. "It's always the same damn thing - that stupid old man screwed someone over and now I have to pay for it."

She slumped back onto the bench opposite that which she demolished, brooding silently as she stared blankly around the room. It was a dull place - flawlessly maintained, stone walls, a spotless, wooden floor and an open roof that beamed the sun down upon them. Lucia detested how clean and perfect everything was in Abenfurt - it was far too unnatural. Jordenholm might have been dominated by crumbling buildings and shifting tides of filthy peasants, but it at least felt real. This… this was almost alien.

"Well, I guess there's only one thing to do then," Isadora grinned, her eyes alight with excitement as she glanced to Hasso, who returned a shake of his head. "We'll just annihilate them! We'll win the tournament and prove that you don't mess with House Severin."

"*Don't encourage her!*" Hasso hissed.

Lucia smirked as she tightened the slender, leather boots of her combat uniform. "That's the plan… those fools'll regret the day they crossed House Severin."

"Just be careful, okay?" Hasso warned. "Don't let them get to you."

"Hmph, it'll take more than a few petty insults to set me off," Lucia said smugly, her head held high. "Besides, you're suggesting they'll have a chance to get a word in before I turn them to ash."

Hasso groaned beneath his breath as Lucia sprang up from the bench. He knew she didn't mean that, but he feared that such a mentality was a risky one to have. As much as she disregarded the possibility, her anger was likely their team's biggest weakness.

"Alright, you bunch of assholes!" Lucia announced. "Let's talk tactics."

Emilia stalked along the wall, humming no tune in particular. She had sent her faithful servant to join the other liabilities in their changing room while she hunted her quarry. A battered, stone brick in hand, she wandered the battlements taking quick glances into each and every room, a practice that had left her privy to many interesting sights - crying girls, juggling pyromancers, a bench stomped in two. It had also been quite the learning experience - from one look alone, she now knew that Lucia's scars were head to toe, that Hasso was a lot more chubby than he appeared and that Isadora preferred to forgo underwear entirely.

"Come on, Casey…" Emilia whispered as she crept to the edge of yet another room. "Don't be scared, I'll make it quick!"

Gripping the stone wall and peering slowly over, she stared with crazed eyes into the room below. Alas, it was the wrong team once again, though her gaze still darted quickly around the room, taking in every juicy detail. Galen's feet were vastly larger than expected, Brooke was juggling spinning, scarlet discs between her fingers and Ava had a pair of frilly, pink panties on display as she squirmed into her uniform. All in all, a fairly unremarkable viewing.

"Hey, hey! Check this one out!" Brooke chirped, thrusting her right hand high and launching a disc into the air.

Emilia stumbled back as it whipped past her face, while Brooke tipped the other from her left hand and rolled it along her shoulders, round the back of her neck and onto her right hand. She leapt up into the air and caught the other as it fell on her left hand, balancing them carefully as she returned to the ground on one leg. Emilia raised an eyebrow, genuinely impressed, as the rest of Brooke's team applauded her performance.

"Shouldn't we be discussing strategy?" Ava smirked, leaping up from the bench.

"The most fundamental part of a team is keeping morale high!" Brooke sang as she dispelled her discs in flashes of red. "We only have to get into the top thirty, I'm sure we can afford to take it a little easy."

"You know we're fighting monsters, right?" Ava laughed, giving her friend's shoulder a playful shove. "You might be fine, but we can't *all* fly."

"Pft, with your ice and Nicolas' shields, we're untouchable!" Brooke assured her. "This round'll be easy!"

Emilia stepped away from the edge and continued her march. She only wished her team could be so confident and upbeat. James was clearly terrible, Zahra had a completely unfounded inferiority complex and Nearchos... he just needed to pull the stick out of his arse. It was clear that Emilia and her faithful knight would have to carry their team, for only they were without flaw. Of course, Emilia was rather pleased by such a situation - having useless teammates such as those three would surely allow her to shine brighter.

"Competitors, to your positions!" boomed the voice of Gerard Tarantis across the arena. "The first round will begin shortly!"

Strange, Emilia thought - the games had been announced by a faculty member when she had come with her father in 408. She supposed that Gerard's charisma would do the games some good over the dull tones of a sleepy professor.

As the time for battle drew close, Emilia's skipped east along the battlements, catching glimpses of the changing rooms as she made for her own. As a glimmer of green caught her eye, she skidded to a halt, clenching her brick tight as a dark grin spread across her cheeks.

"The important thing to remember that these are more than simple illusions," Caesia explained to her team. "Beneath the surface, their physical forms are made of evoked energy, meaning that we can take advantage of the fundamental flaws of evocation."

59

"That should play well to our favour," Bruno muttered, nodding his head slowly as he racked his brain. "Larger scale evocation is vulnerable to collapse. If a key component is eliminated, it could cause a chain reaction."

"And disperse much of the remaining energy," Caesia grinned, an uncommon sight indeed. "If we can apply enough pressure to a creatures' joints, we should have no problem destroying them."

Emilia slipped slowly around the edge above, drawing close to the bench on which Caesia was perched. She grasped her brick in both hands and raised it up to her chest, her heavy breaths blasting loose rubble from its top.

"I-I think Emeric and I could do that..." Florence mumbled. "I mean, if Emeric is okay with that! I didn't... I don't want to assume, it's just-"

Her wide eyes fluttered as she gazed into the air, fumbling for words. Emilia froze as the two of them stared blankly at one another, slowly withdrawing the brick from above Caesia's head and disappearing back into the battlements. Once out of sight, she tossed her weapon to the ground and scurried back to her changing room.

Damn that spotty, ginger cretin! Her plan was foiled so painfully close to victory, mere seconds away from knocking that girl flat! It would have been perfect - an embarrassment like no other, eliminated from the tournament before the games had even begun. No matter. Her reckoning was inescapable. Soon, the world would understand who truly had the gift, who truly deserved their praise.

"Where in Elarios is Emilia?" Nearchos groaned. "We're due to begin any moment now!"

Emilia wandered to the ledge overlooking her changing room and peered over the edge with a smug grin. She shuffled silently to the wall above their gate and threw her legs over the top, dangling them into the arena and kicking them merrily as she listened in on her teammates.

"My lady assured me that she will arrive before the round's start," Laurent assured him.

"And you believe her?" James muttered. The anxiety that quaked his voice was clear.

"Of course! Lady Emilia is extremely passionate about winning this tournament! She would not miss it for her life!"

Ah, Laurent. As much as she bossed him around, Emilia had a great deal of respect for the man - loyalty like his was hard to come by, especially for somebody with a gift like hers. If her pink essence were to grow and flourish, she would need a noble protector like him to stand at her side.

"Ready yourselves, students!" Gerard announced. "The Monster Round will begin in thirty seconds!"

"Well, *Lady Emilia* had better hurry the hell up," James muttered. "I swear, if she doesn't show up…"

"Oh, don't get all worked up," Laurent smiled. "If she weren't coming, why would she have stopped by for her uniform?"

"Wipe her arse?" James sighed. "What is she even doing?"

"Having a walk, I believe. Clearing her head."

"That's it?" Zahra scoffed. "She could've told us, I can do that for her!"

"I doubt she'd let you," Nearchos smirked. Their faces dropped as the dull sound of a horn rang across the arena.

"Ladies and gentlemen!" Gerard boomed. "Without further adieu, let the first round of the three hundred and eleventh Triarcanum begin!"

Under the thunder of distant applause, the gates began to grind open. Emilia shuffled to her feet and balanced carefully on the edge of the wall, stretching her arms as she listened with a smirk to James breaking down.

"She's not coming. She's actually not coming!" he groaned, his head in his hands. "Of all the damned teammates we could've picked, why did it have to be the crazy one?!"

"James, please, calm down," Zahra urged. "Emilia might have abandoned us, but we can still give it our all."

"But how are we supposed to win with four people?!"

"You weren't seriously expecting to win this, were you?" Nearchos sighed. "Have you even seen the other teams?"

"Come on, guys," Zahra muttered, marching through the rising gate. "Let's go do our best."

The four of them stepped out onto the muddy battlefield, glum in expression but stiff with conviction. Their boots sank into the soil, their every step dragging as they waded out of the changing room.

"*To war, Sir Knight!*"

Laurent shrieked as Emilia plummeted down upon his shoulders, terrifying the rest of his team as he collapsed under her weight. He toppled to his knees and fell flat in the mud, taking Emilia with him and plunging the both of them face-first into a murky puddle. Emilia let slip a feeble wheeze, her legs still wrapped around Laurent's neck as he shuffled from the ground.

"What the- Emilia?!" James scoffed, almost lightheaded at the sudden bombardment of confusion and relief.

"Where were you?" Nearchos asked, his body sagging as the stress of her absence burnt away.

Laurent staggered to his feet, nearly toppling backwards as he wobbled upright with Emilia clinging to his shoulders. The two of them were dripping with muddy water, their faces painted with greys and browns.

61

"Taking in the scenery," Emilia said smugly. "Now, Sir Knight, to battle! Mush!"

"My lady, I-"

"*Mush or I'll mush your head*!"

With a reluctant sigh, Laurent gripped his lady's leg, drew his mace and stormed off, leaving the rest of their team speechless in the dust.

"Wait!" Zahra called, throwing out her hands in desperation. "Where are you going?!"

"Somewhere you idiots won't slow me down!" Emilia called as she disappeared into the treeline. "Good luck, morons!"

"But... but we need to work as a team," Zahra mumbled.

"Then let's get after her!" James snapped. He flung out his left arm and with his right, whipped his hand around in a circular motion. A disc of scarlet light flickered to life on his wrist, encompassing his forearm with an evoked shield.

The three of them raced after their teammates as horns bellowed across the arena. The sky above lit up with hundreds of throbbing lights, some red, some blue. As the echoing horns died down, the lights suddenly plunged, falling upon the battlefield like comets. The trio skidded to a halt as a crimson flare veered towards them.

"Uh... what's that?" James mumbled, raising his shield to his face as they backed slowly away.

"I think that would be a monster," Nearchos stammered. He drew up his hands and tore the moisture from the ground at his feet, the mud around him overflowing with blue-tinted water.

In a blinding burst of vibrant light, the crimson comet struck the ground ahead of them. The last glimpse that James saw of their teammates was of Emilia's foot impacting the side of Caesia's head and battering her to the ground.

"Oh no, you fell!" she laughed, sheer madness in her frenzied growl. "*How unfortunate!*"

The duo disappeared behind the shifting mass of red light, which warped and cracked as it moulded into shape. It was big, several times their size - not a good sign at all.

"Well, I... I guess it's just us!" Zahra sighed. "My illusions are all mental rather than physical, so I'm sorry, but... you two'll have to cover for me."

"You can't do *anything*?" James scoffed. "Surely, there's something you can do!"

Zahra shrank away in shame. "I-I only know manipulation spells! This stage isn't suited to my abilities!"

"Then hang back and deal with tactics!" Nearchos commanded. "James, you can keep the creatures distracted while I pummel them with water."

"Yes, Admiral!" James concurred, thrusting his right hand aside and forming a cylinder of energy in his grip. He drew his baton to his shield and stood ready.

They turned to face the monster as it began to take form, the lashing tendrils of energy retracting into poised legs and clenched teeth. An arched, cat-like body formed at its centre, wielding at its end a slender tail. The head grew rigid and blotted out its shoulders in its sheer width, sprouting a snout that dripped torrents of saliva from its colossal teeth. The tip of its tail widened into a jagged instrument of destruction, a chunk of bone laden with spikes. As the creature took shape and its illusionary skin began to spread, the faces of its opposition dropped.

"Nearchos… did you bring a change of pants?" James mumbled.

The dirt cracked beneath brutal talons as the criox readied for battle. Over its rough, green skin, an armour of rigid bone protected the behemoth. Built in plates all the way across its back, it expanded around the head to create what could only be described as a helmet. The monster's tail lashed the ground, splintering the earth with a smash of its tail-club as it heaved a deep, trembling roar.

"Hey, uh… is running a viable tactic?" Zahra asked, her voice rapid and hysterical.

"Absolutely!" Nearchos cried, stumbling over himself as he turned tail, wading through the water at his feet.

All at once, the three of them swivelled around and ran for their lives. The ground quaked as the criox took a bounding leap and launched into a sprint. The beast was by no means fast with its armour weighing it down, but it was certainly agile. It thundered after them, its every step a tremor.

Nearchos flicked his arm over his shoulder and fired a torrent of water from his palm, blasting the creature's face. It skidded to a halt, shaking itself off and growling with growing impatience. The students darted around a nearby building as the criox recovered and continued its advance.

Zahra lost her footing in the mud and slipped onto one knee, bathing her arms and legs in slimy filth and spattering her face with dirt. "Hide!" she cried as James dragged her along.

The criox's clubbed tail cleaved through the building, shattering the walls and hailing them with shrapnel. James pulled Zahra in and sheltered her beneath his shield, while Nearchos deflected the rain of masonry with a jet of water. As the beast rounded the corner, the trio skidded into cover in a grimy trench.

"Dak'ra!" Zahra gasped as she collapsed to the ground, shivering and caked in mud. "Ala'mir lek temet, Ala'mir lek temet! Se menata jaal xuth…"

"Hey, hey! Calm down, okay?" James whispered, planting his hand gently on her shoulder. "Just stay quiet, it'll pass."

"No… that thing's got our scent, it's not going anywhere," Nearchos said. "Any ideas, Zahra?"

Zahra wiped the dirt from her face and composed herself. As her mind swirled with panic, her eyes drifted to the watery filth that covered her hands. "The mud…" she mumbled. "Waterlog the mud!"

Nearchos leapt from cover and threw out his hands, shooting a deluge of water into the ground at the criox's feet. The beast growled and turned to meet him, its feet sinking further into the ground with every step. While the criox dragged itself through the mud, James and Zahra jumped up with their friend.

"What do we do now?" James asked.

Zahra's face was blank. "I… have no idea," Zahra mumbled, pulling at her hair as distress took over. "Goddess, we have no follow up! Idiot!"

"Zahra, focus!" Nearchos urged. "What do we do?"

Her breaths became panicked as the pressure set in. "I don't know, just blast it!"

Taking a deep breath, Nearchos stepped forward and fired a torrential stream into the criox's face, blanketing the beast in water and suppressing its advance. James and Zahra edged slowly away as the creature continued its march. That march came suddenly to a halt as Nearchos' water began to harden.

"Hey!" Ava called from atop a nearby. "Need a hand?"

Violet ice surged up the criox's legs, overtaking the water at its feet and entrenching the beast in the mud. Ava raised her hand and clenched her fist. A dull humming grew amidst the din of distant battle, drawing ever closer. James barely ducked as a disc of scarlet light whipped overhead. It vanished into thin air and dropped Brooke from atop it, who summoned a smaller disc to her hand as she skidded onto the ice. In a graceful motion, she slashed the beast's leg in two, spraying the ground with crimson sparks as she glided by.

James' mouth dropped open as he stared on in awe. Brooke leapt from the ice and lashed out her arms, forming a large disc at her feet and careening back around. As the monster collapsed onto its front, she soared overhead and summoned a disc to each hand.

Ice sprawled across the criox's hide and consumed its neck. Brooke hurled her discs down, slamming against the creature's head with meteoric wrath. Slashed away like a dead branch, the criox's head toppled from its body and its form dispersed in a shower of red embers.

"Everyone alright?" Ava called, a bright smile on her face.

"Just about," Nearchos sighed as he fruitlessly brushed off the mud from his uniform.

Oblivious to the conversation, James watched with short breath as Brooke skidded onto the ice. He had never thought much of her - a fairly unremarkable girl with shrunken eyes, a plain face spattered with acne and dark, auburn hair that sank in wavy lengths to her shoulders. Now though, as she swept gracefully through the air, that timid girl appeared incredible.

The disc at her feet spewed a hail of ice as she ground to a halt, spraying James with an avalanche of violet flakes and jolting him from his trance.

"Oh, I'm so sorry!" she gasped, her mouth buried in her hands. "The ice, it just- I didn't mean to, um… do that."

"Yeah, n-no problem," James stammered.

"Oh, it's all over you… I-I'm sorry, I can fix this," Brooke urged. "Ava! Ava, I messed up!"

Ava hopped down from her rock and froze the mud beneath her solid upon impact. She was a tall and lanky girl, similar in height to Zahra yet far prettier. Her skin was smooth and rosy, her hair a silken mass of braided, hazel hair. She certainly didn't belong in such a hellhole, but there was not a speck of dirt on her and her violet eyes oozed confidence.

"Oh, calm down!" she laughed, flicking her hand out to James and dispelling the ice that peppered his uniform.

Brooke turned back to James wearing an apologetic smile. "Sorry…" she whispered as she retreated to her friend's side.

"We'd love to stay and chat, but we've got a tournament to win," Ava called as the two of them pranced off. "Good luck!"

"Wow… they're good," Nearchos sighed. "Is something wrong, James?"

It took a few seconds, but James managed to rip his eyes away. "Hm? Oh, yeah. I mean no, no problems here."

"Right… Okay, it's time to get tactical about this. There might only be three of us, but we can still score some points. All we need is a strategy."

Though Zahra simply slumped back against a wall, James clenched his fists and nodded in agreement. Surely, there were other teams that suffered a disadvantage - all they had to do was beat four of them. They could do this, he knew it.

Having sent James and Nearchos off, Zahra sat with her head in her hands, dwelling in the shadow of a looming ridge. The darkness reinforced her glum state, her mind racked by uselessness. Her entire power set was worthless in this challenge, thus she was too.

She glanced up as a rumbling drew close. James skidded from behind a derelict building, the ground at his feet trembling.

"How'd I let you talk me into this?!" he yelled, stumbling over upturned soil as he fled towards her.

"Because you're an idiot!" Zahra called.

The building behind him exploded in a shower of shattered marble. A colossal, chitinous ball rolled into the open, a wheel of natural armour that carved a deep trench through the ground as it tore after its prey.

"Oh my- what part of *small* did you not understand?!" Zahra cried. She scrambled to her feet and bolted from beneath the ridge.

"It followed me, what was I meant to do?!"

The harrog accelerated after them, obliterating rocks and squashing trees. As the beast drew behind them, it unravelled onto its feet. It was not unlike an armadillo - if an armadillo was twelve feet tall, had razor spines the size of a person and bore dripping mandibles that flanked its gnashing maw. The monster screeched and opened its gaping mouth, bearing down upon its helpless victims.

A blast of water sent a sizable rock hurtling down the harrog's throat. Nearchos leapt to the ridge's edge and thrust out his arms, unleashing a torrent of water from his palms and ramming the rock deeper. The harrog reeled back with a defiant shriek, yet its efforts were hopeless. With the creature's throat filled with water, Nearchos dragged his hands apart, rupturing its neck in a hail of sparks. Water cascaded to the ground and the beast dispelled in a flash of light.

"Sorry I'm late!" Nearchos called. "I had to stop and talk to Isadora about rules violations."

"If you weren't our only hope at getting points, I'd punch you so hard!" James growled as he marched around the ridge. "So… one down. Is that good?"

"Isadora said her team's killed eighteen," Nearchos sighed.

"What?!" Zahra gasped. "Oh, this is all my fault…"

"You can't blame yourself for having the wrong powers," James said.

"But I can for my failure as a leader," Zahra mumbled. "I let Emilia run off on her own. If she and Laurent were here, we'd have killed so many more."

Horns blared across the arena as they stepped to the top of the ridge. Innumerable lights flared around them as monsters dispersed into the wind and silence hung suddenly over the venue.

"I-Is it over?" Zahra scoffed. "No, no, it can't be over!"

"Ladies and gentlemen, I present to you the finale of this incredible stage!" announced the deafening voice of Gerard Tarantis. "A beast of incredible size and strength is arriving in the arena! The stage will end once the monster is felled... or once all students have been eliminated."

"Did he- what?" James mumbled, his mouth falling ajar. "He's not... is he serious?"

"Without further adieu, good people of noble Verdenheld, I give you a beast of legend! A scourge upon the realms of men once thought extinct, now returned through the glorious might of magic! I present to you... a reaper-class dragon!"

Their faces dropped as a blue light flared in the sky, bright as a second sun. Growing steadily in size, it plummeted to the ground and began to take shape.

"Ala'mir, se cafala..." Zahra gasped, her eyes fixed wide.

From a titanic torso burst a neck that shot far into the air, crowned with a maw of teeth the size of man. Jagged spines emerged down its length, to the very tip of its winding tail, which formed into a colossal scythe of pure bone. A pair of leathery wings burst from its sides, blotting out the sun as the beast rose and loosed a terrible roar. It was a sound that quaked bone, that shook the mind. Its cry was death.

"James..." Nearchos whispered, backing slowly away. "What does reaper-class mean?"

"How should I know?!" James snapped. "It probably means *run for the fucking hills*!"

As dull, green scales began to sprawl across the creature's form, James and Nearchos darted for cover, stumbling down the ridge as fast as their legs could carry them. Zahra however, remained frozen, rooted to the spot and shaking with fear.

"Zahra, we gotta go!" James urged. "Zahra?"

Growling under his breath, he hurried back to her side and grasped her wrist. As he dragged her down the ridge, his gaze locked with a serpentine eye. Drool exploded from the dragon's maw as it let slip a bone-rattling roar. It's mouth fell open and a blue glow surged up its winding neck. As blinding light beamed from the back of its throat, James grabbed Zahra by the shoulders and yanked her to the ground.

A wave of blue mist avalanched down the ridge, blasting over them and chilling them to the core. The mud froze solid and the rocks turned white. Zahra shrieked as the sting of frost swamped her leg, glancing back to see it locked to the ground by ice.

"Leave me!" she begged, falling limp and submitting to her fate. "I'm useless anyway..."

"Are all you Novekhiri so dramatic?" James snapped. "Get up!"

James summoned his shield back and hammered it against the ice, which hissed and melted away under the heat of its energy. He dragged Zahra from the remaining puddle by the scruff of her uniform and hauled her onto her feet.

She tried desperately to escape James' grip as he pulled her along by her wrist. The ground trembled beneath them as they fled, the sound of crumbling rocks and crashing trees drowning the panicked shouting of students.

"No, what are you doing?!" Zahra cried. "You don't need me, I'm slowing you down! I can- you can use me as bait! I'll distract it while you-"

"Will you cut it out?" James growled. "You're not useless and I'm not leaving you behind!"

They looked back as a pair of titanic claws split the edge of the ridge. The beast's head slithered over the top and bore its dripping teeth, wrenching its mouth wide open. A frigid breeze blew over the students as they dove for cover, sliding down the muddy slope and towards a formation of rocks.

"Out of the way!" Nearchos commanded, dragging his hands up and drawing the moisture from the earth.

James leapt aside and pulled Zahra with him, leaving an open slope between Nearchos and the dragon. Flicking his hands into the air, Nearchos pulled the water into the air and sent it forth. A column of water exploded from his position and met the dragon's icy breath. The collision spawned a wall of crumbling ice, blockading the slope and severing the dragon's line of sight.

Nearchos waved his teammates along as he made for a nearby building. The blasted ruin was a feather touch away from collapse, but it was cover all the same. They ascended the crumbling steps and skidded behind whatever remnants of walls they could find. The ice wall came crashing down as the dragon battered it aside with a sweep of its snout. Its eyes narrowed, surveying the area before it. After a time that felt like an age, its neck whipped around and its attention turned to another unfortunate group.

"I think it's leaving," Nearchos sighed, squirting his cheeks with water from his fingers.

"Yeah... Zahra, what the hell was that?" James muttered. "It was like you were trying to get yourself hurt!"

"I just didn't want you to waste time worrying about me," Zahra mumbled into her knees as she pulled them close. "Whatever time you spend saving my skin, you're not scoring points. I'm just a liability."

"Nobody's a liability," Nearchos said. "Look, we don't have time to sit around. We need to do something."

James glanced over his shoulder and out of cover. "Dragon's still out there," he sighed. "God, why did there have to be a dragon?"

"These games are all about the spectacle," Nearchos sighed. "Conjuring up an extinct creature is bound to turn some heads."

"Dragons are extinct in Athaea?" Zahra gasped.

"Wait, what?" James scoffed. "Whatever. How are we gonna get past that thing?"

"How about we just run in the opposite direction?" Nearchos suggested.

James peered out of cover and watched as a group of Class C students was swamped in a column of icy mist. "Works for me," he said, springing from cover.

The three of them hurried out the back of the building and as they fled, crimson lights began to hail from the sky once again.

"Why are there more?" James moaned as the monsters made landfall.

"Probably to root out those who try to hide," Nearchos said. "Just ignore them and run!"

They leapt and stumbled through the mired trenches as projectiles hailed around them and hideous screeches echoed in the air. The ground trembled as the dragon stomped across the arena, blasting students with ice as it wrought its path of destruction.

As Team al-Masir passed beneath a crumbling watchtower, the dragon turned upon a new prey. Its dragon's tail whipped around and shaved the base of the tower, knocking James to his knees with a spray of debris. Zahra yelped as the building began to tip towards them and cast them into shadow. She shoved Nearchos along and they sprinted for safety. James stumbled to his feet, slipping again and again in the mud as he tried to regain his footing. Zahra skidded to a halt beyond the tower's shadow, her eyes growing wide in horror.

"James!" she cried, watching as a hail of rubble cascaded between them.

An arrow struck the ground before him and exploded with a pulse of wind, blasting him off his feet and onto his back. The tower came crashing down and bathed him in a cloud of debris, painting his armour white. He peeled himself slowly off the ground, wiping off his eyes and gazing upon the crumbling wreck that lay mere inches from his feet.

"Damn, you nearly died," Isadora said as she wandered to his side. "You really ought to be more careful."

"Died?" James gasped, scrambling to his feet. "How? It's just an illusion."

Isadora smirked. "No, the buildings are real, just with illusory coat of paint. That thing would have crushed you *flat*."

James stared blankly as Isadora scurried over the shattered tower like a spider up a web. As the harrowing realisation sank into his mind, his train of thought was shattered by an echoing voice in his mind.

"James? James, can you hear me?"

"Zahra? Yeah, yeah, I can hear you… how can I hear you?"

"I'm in your head, you idiot," Zahra hissed before retreating into a gentle tone. "Are you okay? You're not hurt, are you?"

"No, I'm fine," James sighed, looking the steep rubble up and down. "Can Nearchos get this rubble out of the way?"

"I don't see why-" A colossal roar boomed across the arena and the dragon's neck began to careen towards the fallen tower. "Goddess… James, I'm sorry, we have to go."

"Wait, what am *I* meant to do?!" James snapped, receiving nought but silence. "Zahra? For the love of…"

He looked around in distress, finding himself alone. The thunder of the dragon's footsteps sounded nearby, serenaded by the distant shouting and screaming of students. Was this the College's idea of entertainment? Traumatising its students with life threatening situations? He supposed that this was the kind of danger that a battlemage had to expect - but perhaps with less dragons.

"Damn it," he growled.

Summoning his baton to his right hand, he set off running. His course was directionless - either he bumped into his friends or he survived long enough for the dragon to be taken down. Provided, of course, that the dragon could even be brought low.

He darted in and out of cover, searching for a place to hide. Through the means of cowering behind rocks and waiting for other students to distract the monsters, he wormed his way far away from the centre.

The ground began to rumble as he ran into the open. He watched as a trio of Class A students came storming out of the twisted treeline, mere metres ahead of a bounding criox. Sucking in his breath, he leaped for cover and threw himself into another shattered building.

"Ah, welcome!"

James jolted in terror, his heart racing as he span around to the smiling face of Brooke. She was huddled tightly into the corner of the room, obscured in shadow, her red eyes glowing in the darkness.

"Sorry, sorry!" she cried. "I didn't mean to scare you, I just… I thought…"

"Brooke?" James gasped, slumping against the wall as his head went light. "What are you doing here?"

Her welcoming smile returning to her cheeks, Brooke bum-shuffled into the light and sat with folded legs beside James. "Hiding, same as you," she smiled. "Flying is hard work, I needed time to recharge my essence. Where's your team?"

"I don't know, we got separated by the dragon," James muttered. "What about you?"

"Ava sent me out to hunt some weaker targets. I can fly, so it's pretty easy for me to hunt some down and pick them off."

"Sure wish I could fly," James sighed. "Wait, yes! This is perfect, um… if it's not too much trouble-"

"Help you find your friends?" Brooke smirked. "Sure thing, but we might have to make a few stops on the way. Can't be slacking this close to the end!"

She leapt onto her feet and slammed her foot down, emitting a pulse of scarlet light that solidified into a disc of shimmering energy. Planting both feet firmly in its centre, the energy slipped around her toes and locked her in place.

"Now, you're going to have to pull a bit of weight yourself here," Brooke explained. "With two people onboard, I'm less manoeuvrable. We'll be more vulnerable to projectiles, so I'll need you to catch them for me."

"Projectiles?" James scoffed. "What's been shooting projectiles at you?"

"Oh, all sorts. There's been spikes, explosives, projectile vomit… it's kinda nasty, but it's a whole lot worse for whoever's standing under me at the time."

James took a deep breath as Brooke waved him along. He shuffled hesitantly onto her disc, his boots hissing as he planted them behind hers. The energy slipped around his toes and locked him in place, though it felt like nothing was even there.

"Just grab my shoulders and hold on tight," Brooke smiled. "I must warn you - once you've flown, you'll never look at birds the same way again."

"Okay… you know, if you think this is too risky…"

"Don't be silly!" Brooke chirped. "I'll be just fine!"

"Wait, what about-"

Brooke threw back her arms and the disc launched into the air. James' breath rushed to the back of his throat and his tangled hair was blasted back. He dared not look down, clinging to Brooke with all his might and squeezing his eyes shut. As Brooke straightened them out metres above the ground, James peeled his dry eyes slowly open.

Though they glided only metres above the ground, the view was stunning. Beyond the chaos of the battlefield and the rolling canopy of the Abenwood, he could see the glistening ocean, the magnificent white peaks of the Bulwark Mountains and even the distant speck of Aldreichen amidst Unity Bay. The touch of the wind, the glory of the view, the rush of excitement - it filled him with pure glee and drew a childish giggle.

"Amazing, isn't it?" Brooke yelled over the muffling wind. "Incoming!"

James gasped as a pack of four yacti skidded to a halt beneath them and slung a hail of spines from their pincushion tails. He raised his shield, barely catching the razor shards as a few of their number whipped past Brooke's disc.

"Keep that shield up," Brooke commanded. "I'm going for the kill."

She hovered slowly to a halt and thrust out her arms, summoning a disc in either palm. Raising them overhead, she hurled them down upon her prey. The discs sliced through their targets like water through parchment, dicing a pair of yacti in two. With a flick of her wrists, they deflected off the ground and careened into the other two, beheading them in a swift motion and dispersing their forms.

"Holy crap…" James whispered, watching as the discs swooped back into Brooke's hand.

"What was that?" Brooke asked.

"I said good job!" James smiled as they moved on. "That was smooth."

"Ah, um… thanks," she laughed. "So, how is your team doing?"

James took a deep breath and pulled himself together. "Not that great," he sighed. "Zahra's powers are useless for this and mine aren't powerful enough to fight monsters."

"Oh, that's awful," Brooke gasped. "I wouldn't mind lending a hand. Th-that is if you want, I don't want to intrude… I'd rather lose a few points myself than let you get ruined by luck."

He could scarcely believe what he had heard. Brooke's kindness had always seemed unnatural, like an act for the sake of appearances. He had assumed it fake, a means to cosy up to the influential students, but it was real.

"I… you don't…" He took yet another deep breath. "Thanks, but I don't think that's allowed. We're probably pushing it with you giving me a lift."

"Yeah, of course…" Brooke mumbled. "Anyway, you've still got Laurent and Emilia!"

"Who barely have half a brain between them," James muttered. "Look, don't worry about me. I'll be fine."

"Are you sure?"

"Not really, but I'm willing to believe."

Brooke smiled sweetly. "That's the spirit. Oh, you might want to hold on tight."

They plummeted suddenly to the ground, trailing sparks and skidding into a trench. Like a blur, they whipped down its length and past Reiner's group, who did battle with an enormous bear. Brooke stuck out her arm and slashed the beast's knee with a disc as they slid by.

"No hard feelings!" she called, hurling her other disc backwards.

The disc sailed back down the trench and through the bear's gut, shattering it into the wind before returning to Brooke's hand. They slid around a bend and out of the trench, where Brooke deflected her discs off a wall and destroyed a pair of airborne drakes. She launched back into the air, returning her discs to her hands and swiping another drake in two.

James couldn't wipe the smile off his face. Even with such little participation, he was having the time of his life. Just watching this all unfold was exhilarating, a rush like no other. He could already feel the addiction coming on.

"Um, Brooke?" he whispered. "This is really fun, but… I need to get back to my team."

"Oh my- of course!" Brooke gasped. "Sorry, sorry, I get carried away. We'll go find them right now!"

At that, they sailed across the battlefield in search of Zahra and Nearchos. A glimmer of pink lit up in the corner of James' eye, but he opted to ignore it for his own safety. Eventually, Brooke glided to a stop, peering down upon the rampaging dragon that still barrelled across the arena. Over her shoulder, James could easily spot Zahra, unmistakable by her skin, taking shelter with Nearchos. They were huddled in the shadow of a crumbling verge, hidden from the searching beast that roamed above them.

"There they are!" Brooke chirped. "I'll set us down nearby and you can- duck!"

The dragon's tail cleaved through a building and bowled it down, scattering debris into the air. Brooke swerved aside, but a chunk of marble struck James in the side, winding him and setting them off balance.

"Oh, I'm so sorry!" Brooke cried. "I didn't- I messed up! It's really, really hard flying with two people and I thought I'd be better than I was! Now you're hurt because I'm stupid and I couldn't-"

"Focus on flying!" James snapped, whipping out his hand and readjusting her head frontward. "I'd rather be hurt than dead!"

"Okay, I'm sorry, I'm sorry," Brooke mumbled. "Oh God!"

The tail struck the disc at their feet with colossal force and shattered it into sparks. The sheer amount of backlash left Brooke limp and the two of them spiralled out of the sky. Their leather armour took the brunt of the friction as they struck the ground and skidded over mud and rock. Wheezing for air, James watched as the dragon began to turn.

"Goddess!" Zahra gasped as she jumped from cover and hurried to his side. "Are you alright?"

"I'll live," James spat, taking her hand and staggering to his feet.

As they led him away, he looked over his shoulder. The dragon's eyes fell upon Brooke, who had barely begun to stir from the ground. She scrambled desperately in the mud, her fragile arms unable to support her weight. James slammed his foot down and skidded to a halt, clenching his fists and gulping down his terror. Zahra and Nearchos could scarcely believe their eyes as their friend turned tail.

"What are- James, no!" Nearchos yelled as his friend stormed towards the dragon. "She'll be knocked out at worst, it's not worth it!"

As a shard of ice glanced worthlessly off the dragon's hide, the beast turned its attention to the west. James slid through the mud and to Brooke's side, sinking his baton into the ground and dragging himself to a halt. His eyes widened as the jagged tip of a leathery wing cleaved towards them, ripping up the earth.

"James? What are you doing?!" Brooke cried, staggering onto her knees and coughing up dirt from her throat. "Run!"

"James, now isn't the time for heroics!" Nearchos growled.

His shield raised, James leapt into the path of the wing. He dispelled his baton in a flick of his wrist and dragged Brooke behind him. She shrieked with terror as, in an explosion of mud and moisture, the wing swept from the ground and smashed with titanic force into James' shield. It shattered in an instant. With a visceral crack, the shield exploded into sparks and blasted the two of them off their feet. They tumbled into a crumpled heap, Brooke gasping for air and James cradling his left arm as it burned with agonising pain.

"You... what are you... why?!" Brooke growled, whimpering as she shoved James off her.

"It- it worked, didn't it?" James spat, his voice strained by pain. He glanced up from his quaking arm and froze at the sight he beheld. "Oh…"

The dragon's neck curled away from its assailant and its gaze fell upon them. Icy, blue mist wept from its maw as it bore down upon them and swung its jaw wide. James and Brooke lay motionless as the monster's frigid breath blew over them like a lashing wind, projecting upon them a blinding, blue spotlight as the back of its throat lit up.

"Heads up, Serith!"

James had not a moment to glance over his shoulder before he and Brooke threw themselves flat in the mud. A column of yellow flame exploded from behind them, consuming the dragon's maw in fire and sweeping away the icy breeze. The beast reeled back, letting slip a fearsome roar as it staggered back and shook of the flame.

A scorched boot fell upon the mud beside James' head, followed closely by a demeaning chuckle. He pulled himself from the ground, his hair dripping with filth, and stared up at his saviour. As his gaze followed the length of her body, a pair of rolled up sleeves revealed a familiar pair of blotched, red arms.

"You must really like the taste of that mud," Lucia sneered, thrusting out her hand to him. "Get the hell up, you sorry excuse for a mage."

He glanced aside to see Brooke already running. With a reluctant sigh, he reached for Lucia's hand, only for her to clench his wrist and yank him violently onto his feet. They had barely exchanged a glance before she shoved him behind her, nearly knocking him back to the ground.

"Now, get out of my way," she growled, thrusting out her arms and igniting them with flame. "We don't want to risk you dying before I can kick your ass in the combat stage, do we?"

"Wait, you're not going to-"

Lucia span around, slammed her foot down and detonated an explosion between them. Swamped by the heat of the blast, James staggered back to his team and left the girl standing amidst a column of billowing smoke. The fire that cloaked her arms spread across her body, encompassing her legs like a suit of blazing armour. Before anyone could warn her otherwise, she broke into a sprint and charged the dragon, trailing fire in her wake. It seemed like madness, but the conviction in her eyes said she had a plan.

"Isadora, boost me!" she commanded as the dragon gritted its teeth and poised for battle.

As if summoned by Lucia's words, Isadora emerged atop a shattered building and loosed a glowing, blue arrow towards her leader. Lucia leapt into the air as the arrow struck the ground beneath her, a blast of wind exploding from its end and propelling her into the air. A field of vibrant purple light flashed into reality behind her and with a swing of Hasso's arm, smashed against her back and sent her soaring after the beast.

James watched with his mouth ajar as Lucia sailed through the air like a blazing comet, thrusting her arms over her head as the dragon turned to meet her. Its razor maw swung open, its throat aglow. With a ferocious roar, the beast lunged, its jaws snapping down upon her. An explosion lit up its mouth and propelled the girl aside. She cleaved her fists down upon its snout and with a deafening crack, a colossal blast swamped the battlefield with yellow light.

"Goddess above..." Zahra gasped, shielding her eyes from the blinding nova.

The trio simply stood and watched, marvelling in awe as Lucia floated elegantly to the ground. She swivelled around, casting up her arm as the maw of an enraged dragon swung open before her, flaring with light. A torrent of ice erupted from its throat and slammed against a pair of barriers, purple and red, that flashed suddenly into reality only inches from Lucia's face. She glanced back with a grin at Matheas and Hasso, who strained and gritted their teeth as they struggled to resist the incredible force of the dragonbreath.

"Isadora!" Lucia snapped as she stepped back from the beast. "Light up that mouth!"

The Thyresian sprang from her perch and loosed a wind arrow into the ground below her, cushioning her descent and bouncing her nimbly onto the ground. She drew another arrow and ignited it with flame. As the monster's breath died away, she loosed it into its maw. The dragon convulsed as the arrow slammed into the back of its throat, yet it simply growled and prepared once again to attack. A flick of Isadora's wrist soon changed the beast's tone, as the arrowhead detonated in an explosion of shimmering flame and erupted from the dragon's maw like an arcane volcano.

"Hasso, you're up!" Lucia growled, a wide smile on her face.

At her command, Hasso flung up her arms and warped the air above him. A slender, wedge-shaped shard formed above him, akin to the tip of a gigantic spear. As the dragon reeled back and roared with agony, Hasso thrust the shard forth and propelled it towards the beast. Lucia cackled triumphantly as it streaked through the air and slammed the back of the dragon's throat, punching through the back of its head with a visceral crunch. The monster keeled over, the tip of the shard jutting from the back of its head, and with a boom that echoed all throughout the Abenwood, exploded in a shower of icy, blue sparks that hailed the area like a gentle snowfall.

A silence hung over the arena as students crawled from hiding and slipped out of cover. Lucia threw back her head and let the hail of essence simmer against her raw skin, throwing her arms wide and taking in a deep breath of the frigid air.

"The dragon is vanquished!" cried Gerard, his booming voice drowning the distant cheers of the spectating nobles. "What a glorious show! Team Severin claims first place!"

Lucia gazed into the crowd with a smug smile plastered on her face. She wiped the simmering sweat from her brow and sidestepped Hasso as he tried to place his hand on her shoulder. From beneath her blackened fringe, she smirked at James and slapped his back hard as she passed.

"Hey, don't look so down!" she smiled, her voice choked with sarcasm. "There's always next year…"

James screwed up his fists as he watched the girl strut off towards her changing room, the rest of her team in tow. Josef and Matheas laughed and jeered amongst themselves, while Isadora flailed around excitedly as she sang Lucia's praise. Team al-Masir on the other hand, stood in silence, put completely to shame by the spectacle they had just witnessed.

"So… that it," Nearchos sighed. "It's over."

"Nearchos, could you give us a moment?" Zahra muttered, darkness in her tired eyes.

"Um, sure. I'll meet you back at the changing rooms."

James shrank back as Nearchos wandered off, leaving him under the spiteful glare of Zahra.

"What were you thinking?" she growled, clenching his shoulder and spinning him to stare into his eyes. "Why did you do that?"

"She was going to be crushed!" James insisted.

"Look, I appreciate you wanted to be helpful and all, but you should be looking at the bigger picture!" Zahra hissed. "We have our own team to worry about!"

"But, what if she'd been hurt?"

"Oh, don't give me that - what if *you'd* been hurt? If it weren't for that shield, you'd have broken half the bones in your body!"

"That's what it's for!" James snapped. "I wouldn't have done that if I didn't know we could make it out!"

"Whatever, it doesn't matter anyway…" Zahra sighed, looking shamefully to the ground. "We've probably been eliminated. We killed what - two monsters?"

"Maybe that's good!" James smiled.

"James. That is *not* good," Zahra moaned, her lips trembling as she drew her hands to her head. "I can't believe this… I don't want to. It- it's not fair!"

James bit down upon his lip as Zahra teared up, her voice growing hysterical as they waded back to the changing room.

"I couldn't do anything that round! I just had to stand there and watch us lose!" she sobbed, weeping tears into her palms. "I was meant to be perfect… I was supposed to represent my country and show everyone how great we are! A-and… and now, I won't even get the chance. They'll ship me back off to Novekhir and send someone who isn't a sad, stupid failure."

"Zahra, I-"

"It's not your fault," she mumbled. "I just… I'm going to go cry myself to sleep. Sorry I shattered your dreams."

He watched speechless as Zahra trudged ahead, snivelling quietly and wiping down her face to no avail. He did just as terribly as her, only he had no excuse but his own incompetence. Brooke alone had proved the usefulness of evocation in the challenge, but James had done nothing but stand with his shield in the way. It was wrong that Zahra was blaming

77

herself, but James found himself lost in how to make that right. Instead, he just followed in her shadow, watching her with a heavy heart.

The walk of shame back to the changing room was one of deathly silence. Most of the teams they passed were elated - Isadora was hailing Lucia with praise, Bruno was attempting to wrangle his team in a group hug and Reiner's team were bad-mouthing every person that passed them by. It was nice to see everybody so happy, yet it was equally as depressing.

James raised an eyebrow as he peered into the room, where Nearchos stood looking a sheet of parchment up and down. The look on his face was one of sheer disbelief, his eyes wide and mouth ajar. As his teammates stepped indoors, he turned to them and lifted it for them to see.

"Hey, um… you might want to see this," he smirked.

Zahra tried for a moment to ignore him, but eventually took a glance. Her body drooped as she loudly exhaled, slumping onto the bench as she broke down once again into tears. James peered at the parchment as she collapsed out of his way - it was a summary of their team's scores and finishing position.

"Wait… holy crap!"

They were fifth. Nearchos sat at a mere twenty points, while James and Zahra sat at a tragic zero. Laurent had scored forty-two. Emilia had scored two hundred and five.

"Two hundred and sixty-seven?!" Emilia growled. "What the hell were you idiots doing the whole time?"

The trio span around to find Laurent and Emilia, both covered head to toe in dirt. Laurent's golden hair was dulled and ragged, the purple in his eyes flickering as he panted for breath. His mace was as caked in dirt as his face and covered scratches and scuffs. Emilia on the other hand, was an utter wreck. Her hair had regressed from cutesy pigtails to a sprawling, ashen mop. Her glasses were bent and cracked, sheltering her sagging, raw eyes that had barely a speck of pink in their dull, green pupils. Her combat uniform was a tattered ruin, shredded and sullied, its sleeves torn clean off to make way for her flesh-blades.

"You scored two-hundred and five points?!" Nearchos scoffed. "What the- How?!"

"Why so shocked?" Emilia sneered, wiping down her glasses on her scuffed trouser leg and dirtying them even further. "I told you I was amazing, didn't I?"

She glanced up at Laurent with an eager grin. The two of them had spent the entire week together, easily allowing them to synergise their abilities against the targets. Even so, he had barely kept up as she swept from monster to monster, dicing them apart in a manic frenzy.

"Fact is, we've just been training hard," Emilia said smugly. "Fighting, thinking, strategizing..."

"And your strategy didn't involve *us*?" Nearchos hissed. "Or even telling us your plan?!"

"Pft, dead weight," Emilia smirked. "You losers would've just slowed me down. I mean, seriously? Twenty between the three of you? Disgraceful..."

It was true - twenty points was pathetic, especially between the three of them. They had done nothing but panic and run, relying on Nearchos as their only hope. Each one of them was ashamed of themselves, brooding in a sad silence.

"You're right..." Nearchos sighed. "We can do far better than that - we were disorganised, incoherent and totally directionless."

"No thanks to dumb and dumber..." James muttered. His words were followed quickly by a violent punch to the gut.

"*Show some gratitude, John!*" Emilia growled as she withdrew her hand from her winded ally. "I'm glad to see at least one of you have some sense - we need to work as a team if we're going to win this."

"You ran off on your own!" James snapped.

"And you didn't follow me!" Emilia growled. "I made my own plan because our *team leader* didn't have one at all!"

Zahra buried her face in her hands and whimpered quietly under her breath. She had failed - as a mage, as a leader and as a representative of her people. If Emilia hadn't made up for her mistakes, she would have soon been on the boat back Novekhir. She had to do better.

"What's her problem?" Emilia smirked, only smiling wider as James shot her a dirty look. "Fine, fine, I won't pry..."

"Look, finger pointing aside, we made it," James said, a smile wavering on his face. "From here on out, we need to work together, especially if we want to even come close to Lucia's team."

"Indeed!" Laurent boomed, making Nearchos jump with his sudden burst from silence. "My lady and I have proven well enough that our team has the fight it needs, now we just need the coordination."

"We'll only have a day to prepare..." Zahra muttered. "And we don't even know what's coming up tomorrow."

"Then we'll plan on the spot," Nearchos said. "If we put our heads together, we should be able to adapt pretty quick."

James grinned with newfound courage as Laurent nodded in agreement and Emilia returned no backtalk. It had been a rough round, but the worst was surely out of the way. They still had a chance, he was sure of it.

"Come on, team leader," he smiled, placing his hand gently on Zahra's shoulder. "There's no time to lose."

Zahra dragged her hands from her face and stared up at him. Her eyes were bagged and raw, glistening with the dwindling remnants of tears. "You still want me as leader?" she mumbled. "Even after that... that disaster?"

Nearchos' hand clenched over Emilia's mouth as she raised a hand in objection. "Just because you got no points, doesn't mean you were useless," he assured her. "What little we did do, it was all down to your quick thinking."

Emilia glared up at Nearchos and spat into his hand, forcing him to retract it. "For your information, Water Boy, I was going to agree," she sneered. "Now that I've felt the rush of battle, I've no desire to fill any sort of leadership role. Zahra is a terrible leader, but it should be quite easy for her to improve."

"Was that an insult or a compliment?" James asked.

"Both."

"Alright... alright, I can do this," Zahra said, taking in a deep breath and composing herself. "We'll get out of these uniforms and go grab something to eat. We can talk strategy then."

"Improving already!" Emilia grinned, droplets of drool slipping from her mouth. "I could eat an entire adolescent, Thyresian male right now!"

At that, the group stripped themselves of their uniforms and got comfy in their own clothes. With the help of Nearchos, they took it in turns cleaning themselves of grime, though Emilia denied his service and remained filthy, insisting that washing herself in front of older students was creepy. So did the first round of the Triarcanum come to a close - while many teams spent much of the afternoon in celebration, Team al-Masir retreated back to campus and spent the day strategizing. It was time that they acted like a real team, so they did exactly that.

Chapter Five - Ahead Full

Laurent took in a hearty breath of fresh air as he wandered the path to Gladewatch's west wing. From atop his shoulders, Emilia hurled stones at the twittering birds and occasionally, at other students. He had at least convinced her not to bombard visitors.

"Bird?" Emilia scoffed, raising another stone. "More like *turd*!"

The stone whipped through the air at breakneck speed, missing the innocent woodpecker and obliterating the branch beneath it.

"My lady, if you'd indulge me, is this what you normally do for fun?" Laurent asked.

"Of course not," Emilia muttered. "I'm simply passing the time… and it sounds to me like you're being judgemental."

"Never!" Laurent laughed. "I'm just curious."

"Well, if you must know, I dabble in acrobatics and I'm quite partial to music. Father got me my own violinist so I could listen to it whenever I want. I used to play with my cat a lot too, but… he's dead."

"Oh dear, what happened?"

A flicker of sadness dwelled in Emilia's eyes. "I was still getting used to my powers and I kind of… I turned him inside out."

Laurent nearly choked on his own breath. "Ah… I, um, I see. That must have been tough…"

"Sunshine was my only friend," Emilia sighed. "But now I've got you! And you're not going anywhere."

"I wouldn't dare," Laurent smiled. "You missed a bird."

"*What?!*" She span around and growled at the sight of an unsuspecting pigeon. "You sneaky, little rat!"

Emilia paused suddenly, lowering her stone and darkening her gaze. She glared ahead, contempt burning in her eyes.

"Is something wrong, my lady?" Laurent asked.

"To cover, Sir Knight!" Emilia barked, leaping from his shoulders and landing on her hands and knees behind a bush. "The enemy is ahead…"

Laurent stared down the path as he hurried into cover with his master. Some distance aside from the west wing's gate, Edmund Tarantis stood looming over his daughter. He had a foul look on his creased face and whipped his hand back and forth in a series of aggressive gestures. Caesia stood before him, a precious few tears trickling into the hand that held her glowing cheek, yet she held a glare of pure contempt upon her father.

"Hmph, look at that little worm," Emilia sneered, crushing several branches in her hands. "She's probably crying about having to face my glorious self in competition! She knows just how much I'm going to show her up!"

"Forgive me, my lady…" Laurent mumbled, hesitant to defy such a merciless master. "But is your ire against Lady Tarantis truly necessary? Can you not co-exist?"

Emilia glanced up at him in silence, a smile growing slowly on her dimpled cheeks as she broke into a manic chuckle. "I shouldn't be surprised that you're so blind to the injustice," she sighed. "That girl was treated like a god when she was born - they said her gift was revolutionary, that she marked the beginning of a new age. You know what they said when I was born, Sir Knight? They called me a mutant. They said my gift was nothing, called my father a madman!"

"So, you seek to prove that you are equal to the girl," Laurent mused. "That your gift is just as legitimate as hers."

"Well, yes… but why stop there?" Emilia grinned darkly. "I'm going to be *so much* better. I'll be so vastly superior that the fools who denied me will weep at my feet! They'll understand that they were foolish, that they were wrong to scorn father, to scorn me! They'll see that *I* am the future of Verdenheld, the future of human evolution! I will be their-"

"What are you doing?"

Emilia turned slowly around, her eyes twitching as she glared up at Nearchos. Their teammate stood with his arms folded, staring at them in a mix of confusion and disappointment.

"Are you spying on the Tarantis girl?" he sighed. "I can't even begin to tell you the amount of legal and moral implications-"

Like a feral beast, Emilia leaped upon him and wrapped her legs around him, increasing her density and toppling him to the ground. She pinned him down behind the bush, breathing erratically as Laurent tried to wrench her from atop him.

"You're ruining my attempt at stealth, you soggy, brown twit!" she growled, fighting Laurent for control over her clenched fist.

"She's gone, you madwoman!" Nearchos cried. "There's nothing to hide from!"

Emilia released her grip immediately and poked her head up from behind cover. Watching as Caesia trudged through the gate, she span back to Nearchos with a burning fury in her eyes.

"You scared her off!" she roared, hardening her hands as she raised them over her head. "You walking skid mark, I'll rip your-"

"Sleep," Zahra sighed, planting her hand against the back of Emilia's head and knocking her out cold.

Nearchos shoved the girl flat onto the grass and scrambled to his feet. Laurent scooped her into his arms and the two of them turned to meet Zahra, who was closely shadowed by James.

"Ahem… thank you," Nearchos mumbled, brushing himself off.

"What in the Goddess' hallowed name did I just walk into?" Zahra scoffed. "It looked like she was trying to… you know…"

"Emilia was trying to kill me for a reason about as irrational as you'd expect," Nearchos muttered. "I found her spying on the Tarantis girl and tried to explain to her the error of her ways."

"And she attacked you for blowing her cover?" James smirked, chuckling at Nearchos' confirmation. "How can someone so crazy be so predictable?"

"That out of the way - How are you, Laurent?" Zahra smiled.

"I'm feeling tip-top!" Laurent declared, springing to his feet. "A long bath in the morning and I'm loosened up, fresh as a daisy and ready for a good bit of competition in the sun!"

"That's 'yes' in normal-speak," James said. Laurent hauled Emilia over his shoulder and they set off towards the stands. "So, what do we think this round'll be?"

"Hopefully, something less physical," Zahra sighed. "If I have to fight anything else before the combat stage, I might cry."

"They wouldn't do three highly physical rounds in a row," Nearchos said. "Right?"

"You'd think not, but I wouldn't say it's out of the question," Laurent muttered. "Academic competition would hardly be entertaining to most audiences."

Zahra cringed at the very idea - he wasn't wrong, not one bit. These games were purpose-built to show off, there would be no tests of mind. Still, she held hope that the College would not be so cruel.

Her mouth dropped open as they stepped through the gate. Past the wooden ramparts of the improvised west wing lay a podium overlooking a large seating area. Beyond the crowd of nobles that inhabited the area, a wide set of steps led down onto the dusty racetrack that surrounded Gladewatch. Many of the competitors already stood in waiting behind the starting line, though Bruno was busy shovelling down refreshments

"A race?" Zahra gasped, her heart sinking as she stared across the scene before her. "But I… I don't… why?!"

"Hey, it's alright," James smiled. "You can still shine in the combat stage. So long as we get through, you'll get your chance."

"I guess…" Zahra sighed, dragging her fingers through her hair. "This is terrible. This is utterly, absolutely, so completely unfair!"

"That's… not exactly the spirit."

They wandered onto the track and joined their fellow students behind the starting line. Some teams talked tactics, while others stood idle and vacant eyed. Bruno was trying to teach his uninterested team a variety of stretches. Hasso was watching with his face in his hands as Lucia kicked

Matheas repeatedly in the shin. Isadora was on her knees praying, Brooke and Ava were warming up with some kind of dance routine and Reiner was glaring as usual at Team Severin.

"Ladies and gentlemen!" boomed Gerard from atop the stage. "I bid you welcome, on this fine summer's day, to the second stage of the three hundred and eleventh Triarcanum!"

"As you can no doubt tell, today's event will be a race. Students must complete one full length of the track and will be awarded points based on their position in the race, with first place earning double points for the victor! A few rules for our competitors to keep in mind - You cannot physically harm other students, nor can you stray out of bounds. Lastly, any spells that allow perpetual flight are barred from this activity."

"I feel attacked," Brooke muttered.

"The race will commence when the tenth horn sounds. Competitors, on your marks!"

While the audience scrambled to their seats and the horns began to blare, the sixty remaining students took up positions behind the starting line. Zahra followed the strip of white paint until the found her name and her team filed up behind her.

Emilia turned around to Nearchos, who stood at the back between Galen and Caesia. "Water Boy. I demand that switch places."

"Um... why?"

"Why ever not?" Emilia smiled.

Nearchos rolled his eyes and shuffled around her, falling into line behind Laurent. He raised an eyebrow as Laurent drew the silvered mace from his side and wiped it down with a handkerchief.

"Laurent, are you sure you should be running with that?" Nearchos asked.

"Of course!" Laurent laughed. "It's sure to come in handy for tackling obstacles."

An anxious silence was cast over the mob of students as the final few horns rang. As the ninth echoed across the venue, James furrowed his brow and peered over Zahra's shoulder.

"Wait a minute," he hissed. "We don't have a plan!"

The sound of the final horn was barely audible over the din of magical spells that responded. Where many simply took off running, there were those who summoned transport or blasted themselves off the mark. While the rest of the team launched into the race, Emilia swung suddenly around and kicked out Caesia's legs from under her, cackling as the girl fell on her face with a pathetic wheeze.

"Oh no, I tripped you up!" she growled, practically frothing at the mouth. "*How unfortunate!*"

She sprinted after her team, catching up quickly. They were in the midst of the majority of the competitors, those who were equally unathletic and without any manner of mobility powers.

"This isn't fair at all!" Zahra hissed, watching as several students sailed into the distance. "Nearchos is the only one here who can use his powers to get around. What are the rest of us supposed to do?"

"I guess... I guess we'll just have to hope we're better suited to the obstacles," James sighed, trying his best to hide the fact that he was already running out of breath. "Nearchos, you should go ahead and score us some bigger points."

"Those points won't be worth much if you four are lagging so far behind," Nearchos said. "The other teams seem to be sending people forward in twos or threes, so we need to move multiple people at once."

"That should be no problem," Emilia said smugly. "Sir Laurent and I will have no problem keeping ahead of this rabble."

"So, what? Me and James just... try our best?" Zahra sighed. "This is so-"

"Coming through!"

James and Nearchos leapt aside as a sheet of violet ice blasted across the ground beside them. They looked over their shoulders as a scraping sound drew ever closer. Their feet firmly planted on a disc of scarlet energy, Brooke and Ava skidded past, surfing along the ice and waving as they went.

"You're doing great, guys!" Brooke called as she slid into the distance.

A smile grew across James' face as he watched Brooke and Ava speed away. "I've got an idea," he grinned, skidding to a halt and thrusting out his left arm. "Emilia, Laurent, you two go ahead. The three of us will stick together."

"Aren't we meant to be working as a *team* now?" Emilia sneered.

"We work as a team by not working as a team," Laurent smirked. "There will be plenty of time for teamwork in the combat stage."

"Hmph, no teamwork means more me-work," Emilia chirped. "Sir Knight, let us depart!"

While James summoned his shield to his arm, Laurent cast his mace over his head. The weapon powered up with an intense whine and surged with purple light. Emilia leapt onto his back as he span around and skidded to a halt.

"Laurent, are you sure that's wise?" Nearchos called.

"Perfectly! My lady can lower her density and slow my descent!"

Many students around them dove out of the way as Laurent slammed his weapon down. With a deafening bang, it unleashed a blast of purple light that brought with it a heavy wave of wind. With Emilia strapped around him as a human parachute, he soared overhead and sailed off down the track.

"Wow… does that count as flying?" Zahra asked.

"It's not perpetual, so it's legal," Nearchos said. "So, James, what's this plan of yours?"

"Well, we're kinda stealing Brooke's idea," James mumbled, an awkward smirk on his face. "We can hop on my shield and ride your water like they're doing Ava's ice!"

"That thing will barely fit two of us!" Zahra said. "What about me?"

"You can climb on top!" James smiled. "You're pretty skinny, I'm sure we can handle your weight."

"I'm not skinny, I'm tall…" Zahra muttered under her breath. "Alright, I guess we're doing this. I hope you know what you're doing."

"So do I!"

James planted his shield on the ground and stepped carefully on. It rocked back and forth as he pressed down his feet, but he was quick to find a balance. Nearchos followed suit, hopping on behind him. While James locked their feet into place, Zahra approached from behind, analysing how she would pull this off.

"Okay… Nearchos, can you just crouch down a moment?" she asked.

Lifting her left leg high, she slipped over Nearchos' back and shuffled onto his shoulders. Most of the students passing them by gave the trio a myriad of confused looks as Zahra wrapped her legs over his chest and grasped James' shoulders as she was lifted up.

"I'm not sure I like this," Nearchos mumbled, his head being crushed between Zahra's legs as she held on tight. "Can we switch positions?"

"Too late," James smirked. "Get us going, Water Boy!"

"Please, not you too," Nearchos groaned.

He raised his hands carefully and drew them slowly up. The arid dirt at their feet slowly began to darken as droplets of water began to slip from the cracks. Watching with increasing boredom as tiny puddles began to form at their feet, Zahra glanced down at Nearchos with an impatient sigh

"Nearchos… What are you doing?"

"I'm drawing water from the ground," he said through gritted teeth.

"What- it's dry as a Dareshi drought!" Zahra snapped. "There is a river right there!"

"If I draw water from the river, I'll waterlog the grass between there and the track. The resultant quality of the grounds would reflect poorly upon the College and myself in turn."

"We don't have time for this…" Zahra groaned. She looked around quickly before drawing her hand to Nearchos' head. "Submit," she whispered, her palm glowing subtly with golden light.

Nearchos' eyes fluttered and flashed momentarily yellow. "Good idea, I'm on it."

As his friend threw out an arm and reeled in a clenched fist, James glanced to Zahra with an eyebrow raised. "You know mind control is illegal, right?"

"Not in Novekhir," Zahra grinned.

"That's… not how it works," James mumbled. "Whatever, let's go!"

A torrent of water surged onto the track and gathered beneath them, rocking them back and forth as the shield was undercut. Nearchos flung his arms out ahead of him and they shifted suddenly into motion. James toppled forwards as the force of the gathering wave tipped them forth, yet he was yanked upright by Zahra. After a turbulent few moments, the wave reached its peak and flattened out the shield.

"Not too fast now," Zahra warned, relaxing her arms. "Shouldn't be hard to catch up at this speed."

"You know, this is pretty fun!" James laughed as they cruised down the track. "We should do this more often, maybe down the canal… Can he hear me?"

"I think he's concentrating," Zahra said. "Is there anything I can be doing? I feel kind of bad…"

"I dunno, just be the leader, I guess? You can figure out how to get us through the obstacles."

"Obstacles?"

"Yeah - like that."

Zahra looked ahead, over the fencing and around a bend. Lashing vortexes of wind roamed the track, picking up students and hurling them about like ragdolls. Many desperately navigated the cloud of dust left in their wake, some with speed and others with caution. Several had already made it through - she could barely see the unmistakable shape of Laurent and Emilia, who were walking out of a vortex and into open air as if it were not even there. Emilia's density manipulation was obnoxiously versatile.

"Vortexes…" Zahra mumbled. "I can get us through here."

"You can?" James asked.

"Yes. Essence can't pass through other essence, it's a basic magical principle. By releasing illusory pulses, I can stop them momentarily while we pass. I'll have to apply more power than usual, but I think I can handle it."

The trio shielded their eyes as they skidded into the surrounding dust cloud. The thunderous rushing of wind overwhelmed all senses as it grew ever louder. The water shifted and the shield rocked, tossing them about under the force of the gale. Coughing up dirt and wheezing for air, James peered around his arm to see the writhing face of a vortex careening towards them.

"Zahra…" he spluttered.

"Pulsing!" she snapped, closing her eyes and taking a deep breath. The incoming vortex arched overhead and steadily diverted its course, skidding along an invisible barrier.

"Uh, did you do it?" James asked.

"Yes!" Zahra smiled. "The pulses are just invisible, for the sake of not blinding people."

"We're already blind!" James laughed.

"Well, we would be blinder. Full speed ahead, Nearchos!"

They weaved nimbly through the midst of the roaming vortexes, ducking and darting up and down, left and right as they made for the exit. Zahra tracked their progress from Amani's eyes and soon enough, they burst out of the dust cloud and skidded back to safety. Choking on particles and gasping for air, the first obstacle was easily cleared. The track ahead was all but clear - it seems they still had some catching up to do.

"That was so easy!" James gushed. "We're already frontrunners! Zahra?"

Zahra's eyes were squinted in confusion, staring ahead. "My pulses are picking something up, but I don't see anything," she mumbled. "It's like… I don't know, a wall?"

"A wall?" James scoffed. "Hey, Nearchos, maybe we should slo-"

The three of them were jolted suddenly into the air, the water beneath them dispersing as they floated upwards. Nearchos gasped as he released his concentration and looked around, completely baffled.

"Nearchos, tell me this is you," Zahra urged, tightening her grip around her friends as they began to tilt forwards.

"This… this isn't me," Nearchos said. "I think we're caught in some kind of… floating field?"

"You can blast us out of here, right?"

"Of course. It'll take a few bursts, but we'll get there," Nearchos assured her. "Hold on-"

"Guys…" James mumbled. "What are those?"

As James' shield tipped down, the three of them stared into a massive, flat pit, hidden from afar by illusions. The expanse of dirt was swarming with creatures no bigger than a dog, scorpion-like beasts coated in off yellow, chitin armour. Orange flame spilled from between their plates and wept from the jagged brazier at the end of their tails. The triplet red eyes of the arachnids homed upon them, serenaded by a chorus of screeches.

"Ectaclists?!" Zahra gasped. "Those are meant to be native to Novekhir!"

"Never mind that, someone do something!" James snapped, thrusting out his arm as the first ectaclist whipped back it tail.

In a swift motion, the creature slung a bolt of fire into the air. Nearchos slipped a hand beneath James' arm and propelled a jet of water from his palm. James summoned a second shield to his wrist and the two of them took up arms against the incoming storm. A hail of fire lit up the air, glancing of James' shield and simmering away amidst Nearchos' water.

While her friends flailed around in a frenzied defence, Zahra gazed down upon the battery of ectaclists below. The ground beneath them was scarred with scorch marks, blackened gashes that still glowed with yellow embers. She had not noticed in the fray of panic, but upon closer inspection, the shrivelled husks of many ectaclists littered the pit.

"Wait, they're *real*?!" Zahra scoffed. Her horror at the cruelty of their fates was soon dulled by realisation. "They're real… I can use my magic!"

"Can you get 'em to stop firing?" James asked.

"I'd need training to communicate with them, but I could stun a few. They'll keep firing, but only in the same direction."

"Do it!"

Peering around James' shield, Zahra extended her hand to a group of ectaclists and squeezed her eyes shut. "Demekhstratza," she whispered, filling their mind with a choking static. "Get us out of their firing lines!"

Nearchos drew back his other hand and blasted a torrential jet from his palm, propelling them slowly forwards. Even as they drifted away, the storm of fire continued to rain upon their original position. Zahra smiled proudly as Nearchos edged them along, yet her work was not done. More ectaclists took aim and reeled back their tails, met swiftly with a debilitating static. Zahra's breath grew heavy as she moved from one group to another, disabling one before moving to the next while the last recovered. A headache was quick to manifest in her mind, but she forged on.

As they reached the end of the pit, she turned to another group, where one ectaclist had wrapped itself around another's tail. Before she could shake herself of her confusion, Zahra watched as the former was catapulted from the ground and came hurtling through the air towards them. James shrieked as it slammed against his shield with a crack and latched itself around it, drawing back its tail and surging fire into its chitinous brazier.

Zahra whipped out her hand and planted her fingers against the creature's head. "Demekhstratza vakani!" she cried, shrinking away as the ectaclist fell limp and slid away.

The ectaclist plummeted to the earth as the trio cleared the pit. The gravity field eased away and deposited them on the ground, where Nearchos reached out to the river and drew more water to their feet.

"What did you do to that thing?" James gasped, still panting for breath after their surprise visitor.

"I-I applied more mind-static and disabled its movements," Zahra mumbled. "I hope it's okay... runes!"

"What?"

The ground beneath them detonated, shattering the shield at their feet with a deluge of crimson flame. Nearchos toppled back and plunged to the ground, taking Zahra with him, whose grip dragged James after them. The three of them collapsed into a pile, hailed with dust by their impact in the dirt.

"Se da'kra..." Zahra groaned, her voice muffled by James' back. "You can get off me now."

"Sorry," James muttered as he rolled onto his hands and picked himself up. "The hell was that?"

"A fire rune," Zahra sighed, rubbing the back of her head. "Hold on." She thrust out her arms and loosed an invisible pulse of energy. "Ala'mir akantse... it's a runefield."

"A runefield?" Nearchos moaned. "Ivarrion's light, what are we meant to do about that?"

They looked ahead, across the vast expanse of track that lay before them. Several groups were still navigating the area - a group of Class A students shuffled step by step through the maze, while a couple of Class C students were building a bridge of ice. Bruno, Harmodius and Florence marched upon a pale green barrier, projected by Caesia from atop Bruno's shoulders. On the other side of the runefield, Emilia glanced over her shoulder and waved smugly to her teammates. Her uniform was painted black, her sleeves crumbling and her boots reduced to ashen particles.

"Did she..."

"Yeah, I'm pretty sure she did," James muttered. "Zahra, you can detect the runes, right?"

"I can, but we'll be overtaken in no time if we try to go around. Can't Nearchos just blast them?"

"The more I destroy, the less essence I'd have left to move us about," Nearchos said. "We need an alternative."

"Zahra...?" James asked. "If your pulses can detect runes *without* setting them off, could you make it so that-?"

"Intensify the pulses," Zahra grinned. "That's brilliant! Right, everybody stand back."

James summoned his shield and dragged Nearchos behind him as Zahra closed her eyes and outstretched her hands. A light flickered to life amidst the right-hand side of the runefield, growing larger and brighter with every second that passed. She took a deep breath and threw out her arms. A wave of golden light exploded from the epicentre and spread metres across the track, triggering a chain of detonations that lit up the ground ahead. Blinding red light bathed their bodies as a deafening thunder rang their ears and shook the trees around them. The shockwave of the explosion left them weak in the knees, yet they stood unscathed before the inferno that remained.

"By the gods!" Nearchos gasped, looking around at the blank faces of many gawking students.

"Es ghar!" Zahra spat as she shook herself off, cringing at the beating headache that assaulted her. "Come on, before they reform!"

Following her lead, James and Nearchos charged across the devastated track. Nearchos whipped out his arm and sprayed a deluge of water over the flames, snuffing them out and drenching Zahra's boots.

"Do you mind?!" she snapped.

"Sorry!" Nearchos cried, throwing out his hands to his side. "James, we need the shield."

"On it."

James ripped the shield from his arm and planted it upon the gathering water, hopping on while Zahra clambered onto Nearchos' back. They were reassembled in no time and with a thunderous crash, Nearchos propelled them onwards.

"Alright," Zahra muttered as she got comfortable on Nearchos' shoulders. "Looks like everyone's running this part and recharging their essence. If we can catch up with Laurent, he could give us a boost and get us closer to first place."

"Doesn't Laurent's blast only work on him and Emilia?" James asked. "She's resistant to the shockwave and he can't be hurt by them, but I'm pretty sure they'd snap us in two."

"Not if he hits it right," Zahra said. "If he can get it beneath the shield and detonate a compressed blast, he can boost the shield without striking us."

"Let's just focus on getting there first," Nearchos growled.

"Agreed. Amani, aftul jisaf!" Zahra commanded, closing her eyes and peering through Amani's.

"What's she doing?" James asked as Amani spread her wings and darted ahead.

"Scouting ahead. I'm not being caught off guard by anymore obstacles."

"Right. You see anything?"

"Be patient…" Zahra warned. "Is- that's a wall."

"A wall?" James smirked. "What's the catch?"

"I'm not sure there is one," Zahra said, watching as Brooke and Ava soared over it uncontested. "There's a bunch of people standing at the base, they probably don't have a means to bypass it."

"It's simple, but not something people think about going into a race," Nearchos muttered. "They probably put it there just to catch people off guard."

"Huh, that's kinda mean," James smirked. "We can clear that, right?"

"We might struggle on our own, but like Zahra said, using Laurent could be a good idea."

"Then, let's go!" James bellowed.

Zahra chuckled at his intense enthusiasm, pumping a fist into the air and roaring as Nearchos accelerated them towards their teammates. The obstacle came quickly into sight and it was no garden wall - it was ripped straight from the fortress, a monolithic slab of stone that towered over the group of desperate students beneath it. As they drew close to their allies, Zahra leaned forward and tried to signal Laurent.

"Laurent!" she called, waving her arms back and forth. "Can you give us a boost?"

Laurent took a double take as he looked back, a grin emerging on his face. He ducked down and checked with Emilia for confirmation before positioning his mace over his shoulder. As his teammates streaked past, he heaved it down upon the ground behind James' shield and unleashed an explosive blast of wind. Nearchos' water was all but vaporised as they were sent rocketing into the air.

"I regret this completely!" Zahra cried, holding her hands over her eyes as they soared metres over the wall.

James laughed hysterically as the breeze battered his shield and blasted his hair - there was no greater feeling in the world than flight. Nearchos threw out his hands and summoned water from the river, building a writhing ramp upon which they skidded to the ground. All that remained between them and the finishing line was an empty length of track, inhabited solely by Lucia, Isadora, Brooke and Ava.

"Alright, Nearchos, let's give these ladies a taste of our dust," James grinned.

The water beneath them surged forth with greater force than ever. Brooke glanced over her shoulder as they closed upon her, narrowing her eyes and smirking as she gazed upon their copycat strategy. Isadora also turned around, pointing towards them as she mumbled to Lucia behind her.

"Uh oh…" Zahra gasped as Lucia looked back and ignited her arms.

Driving her hands down at her sides, Lucia lit up the ground beneath her with flame. A massive explosion quaked the ground and swamped the width of the track. Brooke skidded to a halt, grinding onto the dirt and collapsing onto her face, Ava falling on top of her. Far enough away to avoid the blast, Team al-Masir streaked through the veil of lingering smoke, blasting it apart with an illusory pulse.

As they neared the end of the track, the finishing line came into sight, swarmed by7 cheering nobles applauding their approach. First place was in sight - they had the speed, it was a simple matter of covering the distance in time. As daunting as the race had seemed, glory was truly in sight.

Laurent and Emilia slowed as they approached the looming wall, staring up at it with confident smiles. Emilia chuckled at the gaggle of worthless students gathered around its base - some simply stood around, accepting defeat, while others tried to burrow through the stone with feeble magic. Pathetic.

"Shall we vault it?" Laurent asked, flourishing his mace dramatically and nearly taking off a boy's head.

"We could..." Emilia sighed with a darkening smile. "Or, we could show these weaklings the *raw power* we wield!" She stopped in her tracks before the wall, throwing out her arms as she stood before a mob of inferior fools. "Sir Knight, battering ram me!"

Laurent reeled back his mace and charged it with energy, swinging it around and smashing it into Emilia's hardened back. Launched like a ballista bolt towards the wall, Emilia hardened herself head to toe and impacted the stone with a chilling crack. It was thankfully hollow on the inside, a pair of parallel layers connected by a wooden rampart - little more than parchment before scissors. Laurent slipped into the crumbling, Emilia-shaped hole, bashing its edges aside with his weapon as he squeezed through the tiny gaps and out to the other side.

"Oh, what a rush!" Emilia growled, stumbling out of a shallow crater and shaking herself of dirt like a wet dog. "Now, we'll see about taking first place..."

As they set off running again, Emilia surveyed the track ahead. It was a straight line from where they stood, all the way to the finishing line. Brooke was still picking herself up off the ground, barely standing as Ava eased her gently to her feet. Ahead of them was the rest of Team al-Masir, following in the wake of Lucia and Isadora.

"Ha! Look at them go!" Laurent laughed. "They're a mere few metres from first place!"

"If they're behind, they're not in front!" Emilia snapped. "I say we change that."

"Indeed," Laurent grinned, lifting his weapon. "Ready when you are, my lady."

"Good... let's win this race."

Laurent clenched his weapon in both hands and tensed his arms as he channelled energy into the mace's head. The silvered metal was overtaken by purple light, flaring ever brighter as he pumped more and more into it. He gritted his teeth, clenched his eyes shut and swung the weapon over his head. They skidded to a halt and as Emilia shifted her density, Laurent brought the mace down at her feet.

"Cower before me, mortals!" Emilia growled. "Your saviour has arri-"

A colossal blast of purple light flooded the track, sending Emilia soaring like a streaking comet through the sky. In but a few seconds, she was barely a speck in Laurent's vision. As he started off jogging again, he raised his hand in salute.

"Godspeed, my lady."

Another explosion rocked James' shield as Lucia blasted herself further forwards. They were lucky enough to still be upright, but they would never catch up with such an obstacle in their path. James was happy enough to place second - he would have taken eighth with a smile - but with first place so painfully close, he couldn't help but lust for more.

"Hey, Nearchos, how easy would it be to shoot us over her head?" Zahra asked.

"Not happening, I'm afraid," Nearchos mumbled, his head hanging low as his mind ached. "I'm pretty tapped, reckon I can barely get us over the finishing line as it is."

"Right… *akh-seht*," Zahra growled. "I don't think we're getting past her anytime soon. Guess we can settle for second."

"Come on, there's gotta be *something* we can do!" James moaned. He paused and looked back as a distant, manic laughter grew rapidly more intense. "Do you guys… what the?"

A blur whipped overhead, cackling maniacally and trailing pink light. Zahra nearly lost balance as the three of them stared up, watching Emilia glide over Isadora's head.

"Is that Emilia?" Nearchos scoffed, trying to peer past Zahra's stomach.

"Goddess above, it is!" Zahra gasped. "Come on, Emilia!"

"She's not going to make it," James said. "Nearchos, can you send her further?"

"Not while I'm sustaining this wave."

"Forget the wave, we're getting her to first place!" Zahra snapped.

James' shield skidded onto the dirt as the water gave way and sank into the ground. Hopping into the puddle that remained, James dispelled his shield and stepped out of the way as Nearchos raised his hands.

"You two keep going," Nearchos commanded. "This is a risky one for me and there's a chance I won't be able to go on once I'm done."

His friends nodded and stormed on, leaving him in the dust as he drew columns of water from the ground. The blast would have to be a powerful one if it were to reach Emilia - he had to put all he had into it. He pulled back his arms and thrust them forth with all his might, unleashing a violent jet of rushing water from the ground and blasting it into the sky. He collapsed to one knee, blood erupting from his nose, watching as the gushing torrent smashed into Emilia's back.

"A fine bit of spellcasting, my friend!" Laurent called, who was trailing slightly behind Brooke and Ava. "Care for a lift? I've become adept in the art of carrying people."

Utterly drenched and quivering at the touch of the wind against her wet skin, Emilia glided at incredible speed towards the finishing line. She closed her eyes and relished the caress of the breeze that blasted her hair and flapped her cheeks. As she soared over Lucia's head, she flung out her hand, two fingers raised, grinning at the blurred sight of the girl's glare.

Lucia stared for a moment in total disbelief, yet her mood quickly turned foul. "That tiny bitch..." she growled. "Isadora, give me a wind arrow!"

With an eager grin, Isadora ground to a halt. Whipping an arrow from her quiver, she skidded to one knee and channelled power through its shaft. As her teammate took aim, Lucia thundered ahead and set her feet ablaze.

"*Now!*" she bellowed, igniting her arms and legs as she leapt into the air.

With a piercing crack, Isadora sent her arrow sailing after Lucia. The head slammed into the dirt beneath Lucia's heel, its flaring blue light swamped by vibrant yellow. A pulse of wind blasted her from the ground in a hail of dirt, followed swiftly by an explosion that combined, sent the girl soaring after Emilia with a trail of smoke and fire billowing in her wake.

The frontrunners watched with wide eyes as the frenzied madwoman descended upon Emilia with her hands alight with flame. Emilia - who had been sailing quite peacefully towards the finishing line, a smug grin on her face - glanced over her shoulder as the sound of an animalistic roar drew suddenly close.

"*Out of my way, Short Stack!*" Lucia barked, her burning hand cleaving down from above.

Emilia barely had time to gasp before Lucia's fist hammered down and with a flash of light and a thunderous crack, propelled Emilia straight into the ground. Both teams winced as Emilia's face slammed with brutal force into the dirt and spat a shower of jagged shrapnel into the air, while Lucia pulled her flames back and glided elegantly over the finishing line.

Emilia's limp body rolled after her, tumbling over the line and coming slowly to a rest.

Lucia threw out her arms and embraced a silent, shocked crowd, her eyes narrowing as not a cheer rose from their midst.

"Disqualified!" yelled a College official, standing with a clipboard at the line. "Emilia Arrenni claims first place!"

As a hesitant cheer rose from the crowd, Isadora stormed across the finishing line, followed closely in tow by James and Zahra. Brooke and Ava were next to stumble across the line, a few metres ahead of Laurent, who hauled Nearchos over the line on his back. As happy as they all were, the lot of them stood in silence, watching fearfully as Lucia growled with seething rage.

The girl was stiff with anger, the veins in her arms bulging as she clenched her scarlet fists tight. Yellow embers floated from her simmering skin, flames flickering around her hands as she fought to suppress her seething rage.

"My lady!" Laurent cried, hurrying to Emilia's side. "Are you alright?"

Emilia slowly peeled herself from the ground, her ragged, ashen hair dragging through the dust as she lifted her swaying head. "Of course, I am," she muttered, coughing up a mouthful of dirt as she raised her quaking hand to her face. "I won, didn't I?"

She glanced down as she found her eyes naked, gazing with a sigh upon the twisted frame of her glasses, the glass splintered into shards. Laurent looked down upon them gravely - had his lady not hardened her skin for impact, those shards could have found a home buried in her skull. Nonetheless, Emilia staggered to her feet groggy yet fairly unscathed, her rigid skin sagging back to normal as she breathed a heavy sigh.

"Well… we did it," Zahra smiled, wiping her sweat-drenched brow as she stiffened herself upright.

"But at what cost?" Nearchos wheezed, slumping to the ground as he panted breathlessly.

While Team al-Masir chuckled amongst themselves, Isadora slowly approached her leader, careful yet barely hesitant.

"I guess we're in something like third place now… not bad!" she smiled, sighing as Lucia remained in a dark silence. "Hey, we might not be first, but we're still through to the next round. It's no big deal."

Lucia glared up at Isadora, her very gaze drawing sweat from the girl's brow. "No. Big. Deal?" she growled. "Get out of my sight… horrific burns won't do you any good in the combat stage."

Lingering for but a moment, Isadora eventually shrugged and wandered off. "Good race, guys," she chirped, frightening Nearchos as she smacked him merrily on the back.

"Should... we do something?" Zahra asked, still watching Lucia carefully as the girl stormed off, leaving behind a trail of black footprints in the dirt.

"Definitely not," James smirked. He took a satisfied breath as the bulk of the competitors arrived, proud in knowing that they had done something amazing. "Now, can we just talk about how hard Emilia is carrying us?"

"Well, I wasn't going to bring it up," Emilia said smugly. "But, now that you mention it... I'm kind of incredible."

"Hey, that was as much Laurent and Nearchos' doing as yours," Zahra said. "But, I guess that was still a masterstroke on your behalf. I'd never have thought of using biomancy to fly."

"Mm, you can do just about anything with biomancy - there's a reason why it's easily the greatest magical school... Just be glad I didn't use the alternative method of flight. Once you've seen those fleshy wings, you can never unsee them."

"Oh God," James scoffed. "Are we talking like, dragon wings or..."

"More like a flying squirrel. It's *really* freaky," Emilia grinned. "Anyhow, I imagine you've re-evaluated your opinions on my gift. No doubt you can finally see the error in your assumptions."

James, Zahra and Nearchos looked back and forth at each other with doubt in their faces. Even Laurent sighed and looked away, though he was safe in his position behind Emilia.

"You three really try my patience, you know that?" Emilia hissed. "Fine - deny it all you want. I'm sure I've changed plenty of minds today and I intend to change the rest tomorrow!"

"And there we have it, ladies and gentlemen!" boomed Gerard's echoing voice across the fortress. "The race is officially over, so let's take a look at the scores. In first place by a sizable margin indeed, is Team al-Masir scoring three hundred and forty-two points! Coming in second, we have Team Trausch with two hundred and twenty-one and in third, Team Severin with one hundred and eighty-three."

A chill shot down James' spine at the very thought of it - to have scored nearly twice the points of Team Severin. It was gratifying as it was terrifying - Lucia was sure to be angry.

"As for those who were not so fortunate, Teams Eisner, Verrani and Dossen have been eliminated with the lowest points. Joining our frontrunners in the combat stage will be Teams Lechner, Nikostrakis, Von Schirtz, Rouselle and Escerich. Tomorrow, the eight remaining teams will battle for supremacy and display the full extent of their incredible abilities. For now though, let us give a round of applause for the talent we have seen here today!"

Zahra looked to James with a bright smile, sucking in their pride as the crowd before them roared with applause.

"You did great!" she yelled.

"Are you kidding?" James laughed. "I barely did anything, just summoned a glorified circle!"

"Are *you* kidding? That whole plan was yours!"

"That whole plan was stolen from Brooke."

"You were still amazing," Zahra smiled, patting him on the back. "We couldn't have done it without you."

James went red with embarrassment. His heart couldn't help but reject the idea that he was useful, but he knew in his mind that he wasn't as worthless as he told himself.

"You know I'm still screwed in the combat stage, right?" he said. "A baton won't get me very far."

Zahra looked him up and down, her eyes narrow in assessment. "I might have an idea for that," she whispered. "I'll get back to you tomorrow."

"Okay… Hey, where's Emilia?"

He followed Laurent's suspicious gaze to the edge of the crowd, where Emilia stood with her hands on her hips before an aged man. He was a large fellow, yet neither fat nor muscular. His creased face was worn and scarred beneath a layer of frayed stubble. The dull tunic squeezed tightly around his body was a relic, weathered and pocked with holes. Compared to the nobles around him, he almost looked homeless.

"That is all incredibly impressive, but I'd like to know more about this gift of yours," he said eagerly, his voice a thick mire. "What can it do? What makes you so special?"

"Ha! A better question would be, what can't it do?" Emilia sneered, turning with a sweet smile to her friends. "Ah! Lord Mortan, allow me to introduce to you my faithful servants. Observe, my friends, what a level-headed individual looks like."

"Harald Mortan, Lord of Vandal's End," the man smiled. "It's a pleasure to meet you all. You put on a fine display."

Zahra reached hesitantly to shake his hand. "Thank you… my lord."

"Harald here is capable of seeing what you morons cannot," Emilia said. "I was just telling him about how I single handedly saved your worthless selves in the monster *and* race stages."

"Mm, Miss Arrenni has quite an impressive set of abilities, especially for someone of such a young age," Mortan said. "She was just about to tell me what makes her tick."

"Interesting," James smirked. "Go on, Emilia. Tell him what makes you *so* special."

"Well, where to begin?" Emilia sighed. "To put it simply, I am vastly superior to any mortal being that inhabits this laughable world."

"She has no idea," James said. "Maybe because she *doesn't have a-*"

Emilia span around, her hand glowing pink, and slapped him across the face. He collapsed into Zahra's arms, eyes vacant and drooling like a baby. Zahra's gasp turned into a giggle and she planted her hand on his forehead.

"Wake," she said, smirking as his eyes fluttered drunkenly.

"Ahem... if you truly don't know the extent of your gift, perhaps I could be of service," Mortan smiled. "I know some people who would *love* to meet you. They could help you."

Laurent narrowed his eyes and edged closer to Emilia, his hand drifting to his mace.

"Help me?" Emilia scoffed. In an unsurprising turn, her chipper mood became dark and foul. "I'm not some needy freak of nature like that Tarantis bitch. I know my power! I am a god amongst you pathetic creatures! You can take your help and choke on it, you tiny, miserable insect!"

Zahra and Nearchos stared with horror at Lord Mortan as he reeled in shock. They gulped as he composed himself and returned Emilia a stern glare.

"I see. That is a shame," he said, turning to Zahra. "Best of luck."

Much of the group breathed a sigh of relief as he turned his back. Emilia stirred her saliva in her mouth and spat a hail of the stuff all over Lord Mortan's back. He paused for a moment, growling under his breath before marching off.

"What in the Abyss was that?" Nearchos snapped.

"Yes, I can't quite believe it myself," Emilia mused. "The audacity!"

"*I mean* what do think you're doing, disrespecting and literally spitting on a lord like that?!" Nearchos hissed. "He could have your head for that!"

"Hmph. I suppose I can forgive you for being out of the loop," Emilia said smugly. "House Mortan has about as much power as you idiots have talent. House Severin destroyed Vandal's End and salted the earth - that fossil is the last of his line."

"You sure have a way of attracting the strangest people," James sighed, dodging Laurent's curious glance. "Whatever... good work team. I'm off."

"Not without me, you're not!" Zahra demanded, hurrying after him.

Watching his friends depart, Nearchos turned to glare at Emilia. "Look, I don't have much riding on this tournament, but they do. If you don't start behaving yourself, I'll-"

"You'll what?" Emilia laughed. "Rain on me? I appreciate you're trying to grow a pair, but I think you're short a bit of fertiliser."

"What is that supposed to mean?" Nearchos growled.

"It means *fuck you*."

Nearchos clenched his fists and turned his back. "You are one sick little girl…" he muttered.

Emilia waved him off with a wide smile on her face. She glanced up at Laurent, who folded his arms and tilted his head in a motherly fashion.

"Yeah, yeah. No more abusing visitors," Emilia sighed. "That *was* pretty satisfying though… what do you make of that Harald Mortan?"

"I don't know," Laurent said, his voice strained by concern. "Just be careful, okay? I know you scarcely need protection, but disable your powers with sladium and you're just a girl."

"I'll have you know, this girl has claws!" Emilia smiled, planting her hands triumphantly on her hips. "Besides, I'd never go anywhere without my faithful knight. He'll always be there for me."

Laurent took a deep breath, staring into the crowd. He had never considered that some might believe in Emilia's gift, especially someone powerful. There could have been hundreds out there who sought a power she did not have, who had been fooled by her father's desperate fantasy. It would be no small task defending his charge, but he was prepared. He was made for this.

"Of course, he will," he smiled, shuffling to one knee. "That's what friends are for."

Chapter Six - Hope

With the race over, many students retreated back to Abenfurt to enjoy their free time, while others remained at Gladewatch to indulge in the festivities. Emilia and Laurent had done just that, while Zahra and Nearchos scattered across the campus to train, leaving James to study in his lonesome. As much as he wanted to train, he barely even understood the fundamentals of evocation - books were his only hope at having a chance in the combat round.

The afternoon crept slowly by and after hours of soul-crushing boredom, it was time for dinner. As the sun began to dip behind the looming towers, James made his way to the dining hall.

"Hey, James!"

Pausing as he approached the towering door, James span around to the patter of footsteps. Waving excitedly and panting for breath as she ran after him, Brooke was wearing a wide smile as always. She stumbled to his side, sweat pouring down her brow, and brushed aside her tangled fringe.

"You... you won the race!" she stammered, shaking herself off as they continued into the dining hall. "I mean, you totally ripped off my idea, but you won!"

"Oh, uh... yeah, sorry about that," James smirked.

"No, no, it's fine! Really!" Brooke urged, suddenly panicked. "I'm joking! I-I would never... I don't- I... You looking forward to the combat stage?"

"I guess?" James muttered. He was totally screwed. "You're still in the running too, right? You came third?"

"Yeah, but... well, I'm a little scared," Brooke mumbled. "I don't suppose you've looked at the match-ups?"

"I didn't know they'd been decided. You're not against-"

"Lucia?" Brooke smirked, her smile plastic. "Yeah. I'm not so worried about myself, but Ava... with her ice, she'll be easy prey for Lucia. I'm afraid she'll get hurt, or worse."

"She'll be fine," James smiled. "After today, I think Lucia'll be a lot more careful about keeping to the rules."

Brooke took a deep breath and returned a full smile to her face. "You're right," she chirped. "It'll be fine. I mean, these games are just for entertainment anyways, right?"

Frankly, James had no idea what Brooke's team were in for. Lucia could tackle the combat round in one of two ways - as a normal person... or as herself. He didn't want to admit to her how high the chance of injury was, but it was high. Still, after seeing Brooke in action during the monster stage, it seemed like anyone's game.

They stepped between the colossal double doors and into the dining hall. Within its mahogany walls swarmed every one of the College's seventy-five magic students, while most of the alchemists and scholars had returned home for the summer and left their table deserted. The other four tables that stretched down the length of the room were marked with coloured tablecloths that matched their assigned essences and were laden with readily prepared meals that glowed with warming enchantments. Meanwhile, a tiny, sixth table was set up in the far corner of the room and marked with a swathe of green paint, where Caesia sat stirring her soup glumly.

"Serith!" Bruno boomed from afar. "Get over here and save me from this freak!"

"*You dare speak of a lady in such a tone?!*" Emilia growled, clenching the table's edge as she leant across it with gritted teeth. "I'm not sure you understand who I am, you diminutive cretin!"

"For the last time, I know exactly who you are!" Bruno groaned. "And I'll say it again - being loosely related to Lord Arrenni doesn't entitle you to execute people for no reason!"

"I have a perfectly valid reason!"

James glanced hesitantly to Brooke, who was already skipping over to the table. He followed suit, reluctantly taking a seat beside Emilia, whose head snapped immediately to the side with a wide grin. Despite having acquired a new pair of glasses, she had removed none of the dirt from her face nor hair.

"Ah, Jeffrey!" she chirped. "I was just regaling the fat man with the tale of my glorious victory."

"I told you, it's muscle!" Bruno growled.

"I can't hear you, you're too fat!" Emilia sneered. "Anyhow, thanks to my ingenious plan of propelling myself over the finishing line and inciting the explodey girl to disqualify herself from the race, we've now landed ourselves a most interesting match-up!"

James raised his hand in objection. "You didn't even-"

"*I'm talking!*" Emilia hissed. "We're against Team Nikostrakis, bunch of Class A pushovers. They've got an abjurer, a biomancer, a pyromancer and an electromancer."

"Wait, that's only four-"

Emilia's hand lashed out and fell upon James' mashed potatoes, splattering them across his tray and all over his face. He stared blankly into the decimated remains of his food as Emilia withdrew to normality with an innocent smile.

"If we've all gotten our interruptions out of the way, I would continue," she muttered. "Fifth on their team is a curious one - he's an alchemist."

"What? Is that allowed?" Bruno scoffed.

"Oh, I heard about that!" Brooke chirped. "Since there's only seventy-five students, the alchemistry students were offered a place in the competition. I guess he was the only one up for it."

"Either he's mad, or he's got some serious tricks up his sleeve," Bruno mused. "You don't just walk into a magical tournament with a bunch of bottle unless you've balls forged of tricinium."

"What about you?" James asked him. "You know your match-up?"

"I do, and it's a bloody weird one," Bruno sighed. "*Five* hydromancers."

While James and Brooke sat frozen in disbelief, Emilia threw her head back in a hearty cackle. "That's ridiculous!" she laughed. "How dense must you be to make such an inflexible team?"

"They're a one trick pony, sure, but that trick is no doubt blasting the enemy team out of the arena within the first few seconds," Bruno explained. "We've got the electromancy to deal with them, but it'll be a matter of keeping them on the field long enough to do their thing."

"Mm, you'll just have to hope that Caesia can keep up a good defence," Brooke said. "Can she do that?"

"Yes, do tell, my obese friend," Emilia hissed, leaning in close. "Have you figured out the Tarantis girl's capabilities yet?"

"I guess you'll have to find out," Bruno smirked, prompting a darkening of Emilia's eyes. "The mystery about her is an advantage I'm not quite willing to give up."

"Fair enough," Brooke smiled, watching Emilia fearfully as the girl seethed with rage. "Well, I guess none of us have it easy. No matter what happens tomorrow, I'll be proud I made it this far!"

"Oh yeah, you're up against Team Severin tomorrow," Bruno muttered, his words cutting short Brooke's breath. "How you feeling about that?"

"I just hope everyone has fun," Brooke mumbled. The terror in her eyes was unmistakable.

"Ah, speak of the devil!" Emilia grinned, sending a visible shiver down Brooke's spine.

James glanced hesitantly over Brooke's shoulder, his heart beginning to pound as he saw Lucia circling around the yellow table. His eyes darted to Zahra, who watched the girl with concern and pursed her lips apologetically as she and James exchanged a look of fear. With Hasso and Isadora stalking in tow, she wandered over to the red table and stopped behind Brooke with a smug grin plastered on her cheeks.

"Well, Serith... looks like you made it to the combat stage after all," she smiled, striking James off guard with her laid back tone. Was she not seething with rage?

103

James glanced to his friends for aid, yet he was found alone in this conversation. Brooke was nearly face-down in her food trying to avoid Lucia's attention, Bruno was searching the room for nothing in particular and Emilia was watching James squirm with an unnerving smile.

"Maybe I was wrong about you… or maybe, your team's just been carrying you," Lucia mused. "Sure looked to be the case from where I was standing. You barely cast a spell the whole race!"

"There wasn't really anything for an evoker to do…" James muttered.

"Is that right?" Lucia smirked, slamming down her hand upon Brooke's shoulder, who whimpered in fright. "I understand that Team Trausch took third place, and that Brooke here was their front runner."

"It suited her specialty more than-"

"Face it, James," Lucia sighed. "You're helpless. The combat stage will destroy you. If you don't want to get seriously hurt, I suggest you sit it out. It uses a two versus two system, so there's a good chance you can get to the final without getting blasted apart."

"Is that advice or a threat?"

"You people really do think me a monster, huh?" Lucia chuckled. "I'm telling you the facts - your team is pretty good, but there's never been a link weaker than you. Let them take this one."

"And why are you telling me this?"

"That's a good question, isn't it?" Lucia smiled, her eyes darkening and voice shifting to a growl. "I'm telling you this because I *want* you in the finals. And then I'll obliterate each and every one of your pathetic friends for showing me up."

His shoulders stiffened as his body quivered with fear. He knew that she would not take her embarrassment lightly, her broken personality had simply hidden her burning anger. For Lucia, the Triarcanum had just become personal. That thought alone was one to bring nightmares.

"And it'll look good for the crowd!" Lucia chirped, suddenly bright and chipper. "Imagine their excitement when I single handedly hospitalise five students - what a spectacle it will be!"

At that, she turned her back and strolled gently away, her hands clasped behind her back as she swayed merrily.

"And if you *are* fool enough to fight, I hope you've got some real good tricks up your sleeve. You're going to need more than a sparkly stick to beat… anyone, really."

James buried his hand in his cheek as he sank into a state of shameful brooding. Emilia snorted with laughter, yet her piggish snigger saw Lucia stop suddenly in her tracks. With a glance to Hasso and a deep sigh, she swivelled back around.

"One more thing," she groaned, leaning over the table and slamming her hand down before Emilia. "Sorry I broke your glasses…"

Emilia glanced down blankly at the small stack of coins planted before her. With a sweet smile, she swept them eagerly off the table. She had several spare pairs, but money was money.

"Don't think this means I won't hit you any softer," Lucia spat, spinning back around and storming back to Hasso's side. "And I'll see *you* in the first round, Circles."

Brooke shrank back as her company watched Lucia march off. James turned back to Emilia, his eyes wide in a mix of shock and confusion. Every one of them was baffled at her sudden act of kindness. Kindness by her standards, at least.

"Did that just happen?" James scoffed.

"She didn't seem too happy about it," Bruno smirked. "I'm sure it was Hasso's idea."

"And since when does Hasso hold any sway over her?"

"I dunno," Emilia grinned, counting her hard earned riches. "But I got free money!"

"You all give Lucia a hard time," Brooke sighed. "She's intense, but she's got a heart… it just takes a lot for her to use it."

James and Bruno paused for a moment, their eyes fixated on Brooke's. Her eyelids shimmered in the light, painted with a finite number of tears that trickled slowly down her rosy cheeks.

"Are you crying?" Bruno asked.

"Am I?" Brooke laughed, her voice the slightest bit hysterical. "I just yawned is all… yeah, I'm going to bed. Bye, guys!"

She scrambled to her feet, spattering the table with soup as she whipped her tray away. The rest of the group watched as she hurried for the door, depositing her plate and wiping her eyes as she disappeared into the corridor.

"What was that about?" Emilia muttered through a mouthful of potato.

"She's scared," James sighed. "I don't blame her… I wouldn't wish that match-up on anybody."

"People give Lucia too much credit," Bruno said. "She's not nearly as unstoppable is people say she is."

"Then how would you stop her?" James asked.

"Yet another advantage I intend to keep quiet," Bruno grinned. "But let me tell you - Caesia is *smart*. She's figured out a strategy for almost every student in the tournament, ourselves included."

"Hmph, I'd like to see that stupid nerd counter me!" Emilia laughed. "My defences are impenetrable!"

"Sure…" Bruno smirked.

105

"Well, I'd better go get some rest," James sighed, casting down his cutlery and slipping from the bench. "Good luck tomorrow, Bruno."

"Careful what you wish for, Serith," Bruno chuckled. "If we both win our first round, you're up against me."

That was unnerving. Bruno's team was not the scariest, but it seemed incredibly well rounded. They were far more coordinated than most and were likely able to synergise their abilities well. That was a thought for later however, as he first had to worry about Lykinios and his team, and about surviving a single round with a stick for a weapon. The very thought of the combat round terrified him, but he had to do his best.

"Well, my flab-ulous friend, looks like it's just you and me," Emilia grinned. "Say, did I ever tell you about the miraculous circumstances surrounding my conception?"

With an agonised groan, Bruno slammed his cutlery down and kicked his legs over the bench, marching off without a word and leaving Emilia alone at the table.

"Hey! I'm talking to you here!" Emilia snapped, before returning to her cold dinner with a feral growl. "Ah, they're just jealous…" she muttered under her breath. "Bet they wished they were cool like me. I've got pink essence, what do they have? Nothing, just a bunch of regular nobodies is what they are…"

She glanced up, narrowing her eyes as Florence and Emeric stared back in confusion from some way down the table.

"What're you looking at?" Emilia growled. "Eyes down or I'll rip them out!"

As the two of them retreated back to their food, Emilia emptied James' tray onto hers and steepled her fingers in contemplation. There was much for her to prove and little time to do so. If she were to make those fools believe in her gift, she would have to go all out. And so would she do exactly that.

Thus did the second day of the Triarcanum come to a close. The night rolled by, accommodating many a student rushing to fit in some final practice. The coming day would be merciless, for the combat stage allowed for all but the most lethal of spells.

The hammering of James' door shook him suddenly from his slumber. He jolted up, his eyes barely open as he stared across his room and into the dull light breaching his curtains. It was barely morning - so much for a good night's sleep. He slipped with a drunken slowness from beneath his duvet and trudged to the door, nearly tripping over several items of discarded clothing as he went. He yanked his door open and stared tiredly into Zahra's bright, yellow eyes.

"Put this on, we've got work to do," she demanded, thrusting a weighty box into his chest.

"Wha...?" James mumbled. He glanced down blankly at the box and as he looked up at his friend, he realised that she was outfitted rather unusually.

A beige shawl was draped around her shoulders over a weathered, brown tunic, which topped a battered skirt that sank to her knees. The veil of fabric gave way to slender, black leggings that stretched down to her rugged boots. As one would expect, she looked straight out of the Novekhir Desert.

"I couldn't help but overhear that you were a little underequipped," she smiled. "I ran into town last night and commissioned a few bits and pieces for you. Let me tell you, overnight production is *expensive*."

Suddenly wrested from his groggy state, James' eyes lit up and he peeled the box open. Cluttered into its depths was an assortment of scuffed, steel plates of varying shapes and sizes, all crude and misshapen from a race against the clock. They looked terrible, but they were armour all the same.

"Wait, you... spent your grant on me?" James gasped, his mind bouncing between guilt and delight.

"Of course!" Zahra chirped. "I already have what little gear I need from my time with Al-Acazar Academy. I figured since it was there to spend, I may as well put it towards someone who needs it! It's not very good because of time and all that, but it should do."

James was utterly astonished. The equipment grant required an extra investment, one that his parents could never think to make after spending all they had on his tuition. Never in his life had he expected this, it was like a dream come true.

"I-I don't... thanks!" James laughed, picking carefully through the box's contents.

"Well, don't just stand there!" Zahra snapped. "Put it on! We've got a good hour and a half before we set off and we're spending every minute in that training yard."

The widest grin on his face, James charged back into his room and dumped the contents of the box onto his bed, marvelling at the torrent of metal that toppled out of it.

"You've got shoulder plates, elbow pads, shin guards and gauntlets," Zahra called after him. "Sorry I couldn't get you a helmet... there wasn't really time."

"Don't apologise for being the best person in the world," James laughed.

Zahra blushed with embarrassment as she leant back against the wall. She waited patiently while James squirmed into his gear, smirking at the crashing and clattering of steel that rang almost constantly from around the corner. She glanced around the room, counting the items of clothing strewn across the ground - fourteen in total, counting two for the underpants crammed precariously into a shoe.

"Would it kill you to clean this place once in a while?" she groaned, prodding a crumpled shirt with her boot.

"Come on, it's not that bad!" James called.

"Is that right?" Zahra sighed. "No offence, but this place stinks like a hasati's snout."

"Meaning?"

"Like those 'pig' things, only they live primarily off each other's waste."

"Oh… you wanna help me clean up then?"

"No."

James chuckled quietly as he strapped his final shin guard around his leg and hobbled back around the corner. Over his sleek, leather combat uniform were a number of crude and uneven plates that covered most of his joints. They were rather unwieldy, but serviceable all the same.

"How do I look?" he asked, bracing for the worst.

"Well, you don't look terrible," Zahra mused. "It's rough around the edges, but you'll look good from afar!"

"Good enough," James grinned. "So… training?"

"Indeed," Zahra smiled, waving him along. "And there'll be a surprise waiting when we get there…"

After all that she had done for him, James could hardly refuse. With a willing smile, he followed her out into the silent hallway and started out for the training yard. The campus was in complete tranquillity, only the whistling breeze and twittering of birds to be heard. The icy touch of the morning air was still so alien to Zahra, a cooling stream that kept her awake at such an early hour.

Beneath the dull light of dawn that broke between the spires above, they stepped into the empty training yard undisturbed. Zahra span around with an ecstatic smile and raised her hand into the air.

"Amani, jabal!"

At the flick of Zahra's wrist, Amani came gliding overhead, a long rod in her mouth. As the drake skidded to the ground between them, James staggered back and caught a better glimpse at the object trapped between her jaws. It was no rod at all - it was a crimson, leather sheath slathered across the middle with drool and protruding a battered iron hilt from its end.

"Your blade, Sir James," Zahra grinned.

James' eyes fluttered in disbelief as he stepped hesitantly towards Amani, who extended her neck to meet him. He took the cold grip in his hand and lifted the weapon from the drake's maw, looking it up and down while his mouth struggled for words.

"Uh, this- this is amazing but… what do I need a sword for?"

"There's your answer," Zahra smirked. "You see, I figured this might be the case. You're looking at evocation like it's abjuration, as creation rather than replication."

She sighed glumly at James' blank stare. The boy had not been kidding about the state of his evocation studies.

"Alright, allow me to explain - The difference between abjuration and evocation is subtle, but significant. Barrier spells focus on creating static shapes that serve no other purpose than to simply sit there, but are very simplistic and easy to form. Evocation is about recalling a shape from memory and replicating it to the exact detail, allowing for the creation of more intricate shapes and designs that can interact with the world around them and be moved at will."

"You want me to replicate this sword?" James scoffed. "Zahra, I can barely make a stick! How am I meant to learn that in an hour?!"

"You don't have to remember every detail, just the important ones," Zahra insisted. "Just the blade and the hilt, that's why I got you a simple one."

"I don't even have the skills to do *that*!"

"You do, I promise," Zahra smiled, grabbing him by the shoulders. "What you've done so far is wrong, but it still puts into practice all the fundamental magical concepts you need for replication. If you use the sword as a shape guideline, you can project the energy around it with ease. Repeating that process enough times should give you an idea of how to form it without aid."

"Zahra, I… there's no way!"

"Some might say there's no way we're winning this tournament," Zahra grinned. "But you're still going to get out that sword and give it your all. Come on, we'll start with a basic edge and ease you into some more advanced shapes. You'll have a proper weapon in no time!"

Chapter Seven - To Battle

Two hours passed and with the sun high in the sky, James and Zahra found themselves crossing the bridge into Gladewatch. Much to James' dismay, Zahra had insisted that they jog there, though they had still failed to beat the rest of the participants. That appeared as more of a boon than anything, as they passed along the trodden path unimpeded, the breeze in their hair and sweat on their brows.

"I really wish I'd seen you in action sooner!" Zahra laughed, glancing over her shoulder with a smirk. "We could've worked on your stamina."

James looked up from the ground, panting desperately for breath as he fought the pain in his chest. "I... I thought you were one of us! Since when were you so athletic?"

"I can stay fit *and* be a loser!" Zahra chuckled. "Fitness is an important part of anyone's lifestyle - a healthy body is a healthy mind."

"You sound... you sound just like my mum," James gasped.

"Then your mother is a wise woman," Zahra chirped. "Do you seriously not exercise?"

"I... just never really want to," James muttered. "It's one thing talking about it, but..."

"You can't be bothered?" Zahra smirked.

"Well, yeah," James sighed. "I just have a hard time doing things I don't want to do."

"What's not to like? The wind in your hair, nature all around you, freedom the likes of which one can never quite replicate!"

"And sweat. And chest pains. I really don't see the allure."

"Oh, you're such a pessimist!" Zahra laughed, watching Amani dart through the trees with a mischievous grin. "Here, I'll give you a break. Amani, qinat!"

"Qinat?"

James gasped as Amani dived upon him. His attempt to duck was found futile and the drake's claws clenched around his collar and yanked him off his feet. Zahra giggled with glee as her friend was suspended in the air, flailing worthlessly.

"Zahra, this isn't funny!" James stammered.

"Humour is a matter of perspective," Zahra chuckled. "And I for one, think you look ridiculous."

"Put me down!"

"Is it not the custom in your land to say please?" Zahra grinned. "You know what rudeness gets you? Another five minutes in the air."

James growled impatiently as he hovered down the path. Once he was over his proximity to the drake's serrated maw, it was almost a relief to be off the ground. Alas, his clothes were chafing and Amani's melting breath was toasting his neck, so it wasn't exactly the most comfortable of positions.

Without James slowing her down, Zahra sprinted the rest of the way around Gladewatch's circumference and soon found herself approaching the north wing of the fortress. Similar to the south wing, the area comprised mostly of stands, built amidst a grassy clearing and around a large, rectangular arena.

Amani deposited her cargo a short walk from the entrance, where Zahra stood stretching beside a hunched tree. She gave James a devious smirk as he glared at her, waiting patiently as his plastic anger broke down into a smile.

"I expect that sort of pettiness from a lot of people, but you?" he laughed. "Zahra, I'm disappointed."

"Not as disappointed as *I* am in your poor physical health," Zahra said, shaking her head in shame as she stretched her biceps. "Once this tournament is through, we're going for a run every morning."

"What?! No way!" James scoffed. "I don't- you can't force this on me!"

"Yes, I can," Zahra grinned darkly. "And I don't think you're going to resist. Because you enjoyed it."

"No, I didn't!"

"Oh, you did," Zahra chuckled. "Go on - look me in the eyes and tell me you won't do it."

James stared into her eyes speechless, evaluating the myriad pros and cons that laid before him. The idea was one he had always resented, one that had always seemed so agonising yet now appeared suddenly appealing. It would certainly help him improve, for he would need to be fit if he were to be a battlemage. Plus, spending more time with Zahra was never a bad thing.

"Six o'clock, Isoriday morning," she whispered, nudging him along. "Come on, we'd better find the others before Nearchos is killed."

Four sets of stands lay ahead, strewn down the eastern side of the arena. They were marked A, B, C and D, all reserved for College students. As James and Zahra rounded the side of B, an unmistakable voice piped up.

"James?" Lucia laughed. "Guess you took my words to heart!"

James turned with a pained sigh to meet Lucia, who was wandering up from the lake and dragging Hasso in tow as always. She was clad head to toe with tightly fitted armour, split down the middle between a sinister black and a fiery orange. The burning, white stallion of House Severin crowned the centre of her chestpiece. Her head however was bare, exposing two streaks of black paint smeared across her eyes and a smug grin plastered on her face.

"You're looking pretty good, Serith," she smirked. "Got a little foreign aid?"

James glanced to Zahra, who smiled back warmly. There was no shame in accepting a friend's aid, he knew that. "Yeah. Zahra already had gear, so she spent her grant on me."

Lucia chuckled quietly to herself. "Cute," she smiled, the suggestive tilt of her head painting Zahra's face red. "Maybe you'll have a chance at the final after all. Surely, even you clowns can handle Bruno and his band of rejects."

James was often taken aback by how cool and calm Lucia could be, sometimes even a little pleasant. The girl was cruel and vindictive to be sure, but she had her moments of peace.

"Then I guess we'll see you in the final," James grinned with fake confidence.

"I guess you will," Lucia said sinisterly. "And now that you've got gear, I don't have to feel bad about blasting you into oblivion."

Zahra sighed as James shrank away. "Well, we'd best not keep you," she smiled. "After all, you're up first."

"That we are!" Lucia grinned, grabbing Hasso by the wrist and tugging him along. "Enjoy the show, Serith. Try not to piss yourself when I blow Ava's head off."

James watched with fear as Lucia dragged Hasso through the gate. The rules were obviously against lethal spells, but one could never be too sure with Lucia. All it took was for her to snap, then there was every chance that a student could be violently vaporised. Between her fire and her volatilis disorder, she was terrifyingly unstable.

"Worry about her later," Zahra said calmly, placing her hand on James' shoulder. "We need to keep our heads."

"Yeah…" James sighed, stiffening himself. "She thinks we have a chance against Bruno's team. You reckon she's right?"

"I don't see why not," Zahra smiled. "They've got some talent, but as far as teams go, I'd say they're pretty middle tier."

"Have you seen the size of Bruno?"

"Bruno is only one man. The rest of his team are far weaker - Caesia and Emeric don't seem interested in being here and Florence is a gibbering wreck half of the time."

"I guess…" James sighed.

"Look, let's not get ahead of ourselves just yet. We have to beat Team Nikostrakis first."

They stepped around the stands and to the arena's edge. It was far less terrifying than the terrain of the monster round, a rectangular area of grassy plains, battered trenches, jagged rock and a couple of trees. As for the

112

stands, theirs comprised four rows of five seats each and on the second sat Nearchos, alone.

"Morning," he called, waving awkwardly as his friends ascended to their row. On his lap sat a bronze Thyresian helmet - a slender bowl of metal split by a T-shaped slit and protruding two blade-like prongs at the chin.

"Where are they now?" Zahra groaned.

"Don't know. Hopefully, they'll be here shortly," Nearchos said, glancing to James. "Looking good."

"Thanks," James smiled. "Not sure how much use this'll all be, but I'll at least get points for style."

"Which could mean the difference between victory and defeat!" Zahra said. Her eyes narrowed as she peered over Josef's head and to the foot of the stand. "What the…"

James and Nearchos turned as the clatter of metal heralded the arrival of a silver clad warrior. They glanced up at the fortress of metal that gazed down upon him - his armour was sleek and clean, a flawless, pearly white. A golden tabard fell down his front, displaying at its centre the black shadow of a duck. Purple eyes dwelled within the darkness of his grated visor, shining the same colour as the dull glow that throbbed around the ornate, silver mace hanging at his belt.

"Greetings, fellow teammates!" declared the knight, his hands planted heroically on his hips.

"Laurent?!" Nearchos gasped. "What in Perinax's name are you wearing?"

"Tis my armour!" Laurent declared. "As an enchanter, I am allowed to bring any equipment I desire to the battle, so long as it is enchanted by yours truly!"

"You're a walking lightning rod," Zahra sighed.

"Nonsense!" Laurent laughed. "My enchantments will protect me from all harm, I assure you!"

Following loosely behind him came Emilia, stumbling about as she wrestled with her chafing leggings. Everybody's jaws dropped at the sight of her.

"Nepheratae take me…" Nearchos gasped.

Every inch of Emilia's combat uniform was drenched with congealed, hot pink paint. Aside from her head, only her forearms and feet were spared from the dazzling eyesore, both completely bare to be sharpened at will. Her ashen pigtails hung from beneath a massive sun hat that cast a shadow over her smug face.

"I know, I know," Emilia smiled. "I look amazing."

"What have you done?" James moaned.

113

"It's called having a theme, Jacob!" Emilia hissed. "And mine is pink!"

"Where are your shoes?" Zahra asked, glancing with concern at the jagged terrain of the arena.

"Don't need 'em," Emilia said smugly. "Long as I harden my feet, I've got more durability and better grip than any mere shoe!"

"And what's with the hat?" Nearchos smirked.

Emilia shrugged. "It's... my hat. My neck got burned in the sun yesterday, so I'm wearing this today."

"It doesn't look burnt," Nearchos said.

"Because I 'de-burned' it, you half witted nincompoop. Are we all done with questions?"

With not a word from her teammates, Emilia slumped into the seat beside Zahra. Laurent waddled after her and slowly bent his knees, his armour banging and buckling as he touched down upon his chair.

The first two teams were already preparing and it was looking to be an explosive first round. Lucia paced up and down before her bench at the arena's end, yelling loudly at her teammates. Team Trausch sat in silence on the far side of the battlefield, with Ava notably absent.

"*Kas*, Zahra!" Ava called, hurrying up the steps. She giggled quietly as Zahra raised an eyebrow. "That was wrong, wasn't it?"

"You called me a man," Zahra laughed. "It's *ka*."

"Oh, well ka, Zahra," Ava smiled. "Could I talk to you for a moment?"

Zahra glanced to James, who shrugged in return. "Of course," she said. "Emilia, could you..."

"Nope."

Groaning in pain, Zahra jumped up from her seat and shuffled past Emilia, who sat with her legs fully stretched. Laurent wrenched himself from his seat in a series of sharp clatters and clangs.

"Thank you," Zahra sighed as she wandered to the bottom of the stands with Ava. "Something must be seriously wrong for you to come to me."

"It's nothing drastic. Brooke is just worried I'll get hurt," Ava said. "I figured some reassurance from the smartest girl in the class would do her some good."

"You want advice?" Zahra scoffed. "I don't really know much about cryomancy..."

"I just need something basic, anything! Make it up if you need, I don't care."

"Suppose I can do basic," Zahra muttered. "If she's worried about your ice being melted, it won't be as bad as she might think. Cryomancy might adopt the properties of ice, but essence is essence - pyromancy, cryomancy, it's all just energy."

"You think it won't be as reactive?"

"Count on it," Zahra smiled. "It'll melt, but I think you'll have to worry more about the explosions."

"I guess you're right..." Ava sighed. "Were there people like her where you come from?"

"Like Lucia?" Zahra smirked. "Not even close. Everyone at the Academy was all business - they were as level-headed as they come, but *ghar* were they boring. The people here are... interesting, but there's no place I would rather be."

"Hm, that's sweet," Ava chirped, patting Zahra on the shoulder. "I'll see you on the other side then."

"And I'll be rooting for you. It's about time someone put that monster in her place."

"Welcome, ladies and gentlemen, to the third and final stage of the Triarcanum!" Gerard announced. "As you know, this will be the long awaited combat stage! Competitors will split their teams into two pairs, each of which will participate in a tag-team battle against their assigned opponent. In the event of a tie, the remaining members of the teams will fight a tiebreaker battle. First up, we have two incredibly promising groups - Team Severin and Team Trausch!"

Ava took a deep breath as the crowd erupted with applause. The gravity of where she stood rushed through her mind as she hurried back to her team - a lowly groundskeeper's daughter, battling the most talented of mages before a crowd of nobles. It was a terrifying thought.

"There you are!" Brooke gasped, springing up from the bench. "You had me worried."

"Nothing new here then," Ava sneered, chuckling as Brooke tilted her head and pursed her lips. "I talked to Zahra - she said there's nothing to worry about. The ice shouldn't melt that much."

"It's not the ice I'm worried about," Brooke sighed. "What if you get hurt? You've seen those explosions, she could kill you!"

Ava planted her hands firmly on Brooke's cheeks. "You're getting worked up over nothing," she smiled. "Lucia'll respect the rules, same as anyone. We might be burned here and there, but it'll be a small price to pay for victory."

"You really think we can do this?" Brooke mumbled, peeling away Ava's palms.

"Of course, we can!" Ava chirped. "We beat them in the last round, could have beat 'em in the first if they hadn't killed that dragon. What's stopping us from finishing the job?"

Brooke smiled and nodded, but the conflict in her eyes was clear to see. Ava patted her friend on the back and span around to her team, puffing out her chest and holding her head high.

"Alright, team, it's go time!" she declared, clapping her hands and summoning them to attention. "I know you're all… a little on edge about our matchup, but I know we can do this."

"Yeah," Brooke smiled. "We take out Lucia, the whole team falls apart."

"That said, we shouldn't underestimate the rest of them," Ava warned. "Lucia is the most powerful offensively, but they all have their own merits."

"And how are we actually planning on taking Lucia out?" Galen asked.

"Leave that to us," Ava said. "Lucia will want to set a precedent, so she'll take the first round. Brooke and I will meet her."

"We will?" Brooke mumbled.

"Of course, we will," Ava smiled, grasping Brooke's wrist. "You can distract her with apologies, while I freeze her solid!"

"Very funny…" Brooke smirked. "Okay. Okay, we can do this! Let's put that monster in her place."

As they marched into the arena, Gerard Tarantis stepped up to the podium at the arena's edge. He seemed to have become less and less scruffy by the day, his clothes far tidier and his moustache finely trimmed.

"This is looking to be an exciting battle, my friends," he declared. "With three stand-out competitors on the field, this might be a hard act to follow! On Team Severin's side, we have none other than their pyromancer and leader, Lucia Severin, fighting alongside their electromancer, Josef Duffant!"

One could discern no emotion from Lucia's dead expression. She simply stood there, her eyes an empty void, glaring across the length of the battlefield. Was it contempt or calculation? Or was she trying to psyche out her opponents? Brooke shook herself off. It was best not to look, nor fuel her inner panic.

"And fighting for Team Trausch, we have a pair that may as well be joined at the hip - their cryomancer and team leader, Ava Trausch, and their airborne evoker, Brooklyn De'Claire!"

Brooke went red as she watched many of the students scoff and snigger. She locked up as the horns began to blare, the moment of reckoning drawing closer with every mind-quaking blast.

Ava place her hand on Brooke's shoulder and squeezed it tight. "We can do this," she smiled. "*You* can do this."

A gaze into Ava's bright, violet eyes was enough to wipe Brooke of doubt. "I know," she whispered, raising her fists in readiness. "Let's get this bitch."

Emilia shrieked with giddy laughter as the ninth horn sounded. James rolled his eyes and fixed his sight back upon Brooke. There was little sign of the hysterical wreck he had encountered last night - she stood tall, her fists clenched and hair lashing in the breeze.

"Come on, Brooke," he whispered.

"Hold on to your seats, my friends," Gerard warned. "This battle might literally blow you away! Combatants… begin!"

An explosion of yellow flame drowned out the final horn. Trailing smoke, Lucia propelled herself halfway across the battlefield and skidded into cover. Brooke summoned her discs and deflected a bolt of lightning before a cascade of violet ice severed Josef's line of sight with an enormous jagged wall.

"Lucia?" Josef called.

"Yeah, yeah…" Lucia moaned. She jumped up and sidestepped an incoming disc, cupping her hands together and igniting them with flame.

The trees shook and stands rattled as a behemoth explosion sent of lance of flame streaking across the battlefield. It punched through the ice like a foot through an anthill, shattering the wall in an avalanche of shards. The blank look on Ava's face said it all, but Brooke was unmoved.

While Ava desperately reassembled her wall and cut of Josef once again, Brooke sent her discs hurtling after Lucia. A jet of flame consumed one immediately, the other breaking through and grazing her ear as she dodged aside. It careened around and smashed into her shoulder, tripping her up as it returned to Brooke's hand.

"Piss off!" Lucia growled, thrusting out her burning hand and blasting Brooke with a gout of flame.

Brooke lashed out with her remaining disc and flicked her other hand to the side. The disc grew suddenly in size, shielding her body as she ducked behind it and let the flames wash over her. Ava raised her finger, drawing an eager smile from her ally.

"Here we go…" Emilia grinned, leaning forward in her seat.

The disc left Brooke's hands, pushing back the fire and slamming into Lucia's face. Summoning another pair of discs, Brooke took to the skies atop a third and hurled one to the ground. It streaked past Lucia's head and slammed into the ground, spitting a hail of sparks as it accelerated across the arena. Lucia merely laughed as it bounced into the distance, returning fire with another gout of flame.

"Brooke's attacks are powerful, but you can see them coming from a mile away," Nearchos muttered. "If her opponents pay enough attention, they're remarkably easy to dodge."

"Well, they're in pairs for a reason," Laurent grinned. "Observe."

All eyes fell upon Ava as the girl leapt from cover, thrusting her hand aside. While Lucia continued her charge and Josef slung lightning at Brooke, a wall of purple ice exploded from the ground at Team Severin's end. Many in the held their breath as Brooke's wayward disc skidded onto the ice and tore along the towering mass, hissing with steam as its course was diverted.

Lucia looked back with wide eyes to see a scarlet blur streak from behind them and slam with an explosive crack into the back of Josef's head. He toppled forward and fell face down upon a waiting bed of ice that shifted beneath him and tossed him over the battlefield's edge.

"*Idiot!*" Lucia growled, the flames around her hands spreading down her arms as she turned back upon her foes.

James tensed at the unbelievable sight before him - her skin scuffed and worn and blood pouring from her mouth, Lucia appeared outmatched. With Brooke in the sky and Ava backfield, she would surely struggle to counter them with her short-ranged pyromantic abilities. Was it possible that this was Team Severin's end?

Jagged ice burst from the ground ahead of Lucia as she charged Ava's position, creating a looming ridge that cast her into shadow. With an enormous crash, Lucia blasted the mass with a violent burst of fire, shattering the wall into crystalline shards and belching fire across the arena. She leapt from the inferno and consumed her right arm in flame, whipping it out and blasting an incoming disc into oblivion with a fiery jet. While Brooke cringed at the backlash of its destruction, Lucia reeled back her left hand and gathered a ball of crackling flame in her palm.

Brooke had little time to dodge the incoming fireball, leaning back and letting the disc at her feet take the brunt of the blow. The explosion split its scarlet face in two. Brooke squealed in terror as she was thrown backwards and plummeted suddenly to the ground.

The audience went silent as the girl fell upon the rocks, flailing helplessly. Violet ice surged from below and reached into the air, forming an elegant ramp and sliding Brooke to safety. Cold but alive, Brooke regained her bearing as she skidded down the ramp and onto her behind. With a nod to Ava, the ramp's end extended upwards and sent Brooke flying into the middle of the arena. Lucia stopped in her tracks as the girl came hurtling towards her, conjuring a pair of discs in either palm. Brooke skidded along the dusty ground and dug her discs in deep, grinding to a halt between Ava and Lucia.

"Yes... Glorious single combat!" Emilia growled, her eyes lighting up with bloodthirst. "Gore that pathetic little goblin!"

"What's wrong with you?" Nearchos scoffed.

In a shocking move, Brooke charged Lucia head on. Lucia threw up her flame cloaked arms and stumbled back as the cleaving discs glanced off her wrists, spraying sparks of red and yellow as Brooke slashed through her defenses. Dazed by her opponent's sheer aggression, Lucia swiped erratically back and forth and deflected one attack after the other.

"Out of my way, Circles!" she hissed, sidestepping another swing and striking back with a right hook.

They hacked and slashed, thrust and jabbed, sparring back and forth in clashes of orange light. Though her flames had barely wavered, Lucia's flame cloak was simply inferior to Brooke's evoked weapons. She could not sustain a close quarters fight.

As another volley of strikes battered her arm, she clenched her trembling fist and funnelled as much energy as she could into her hand. Brooke threw up her discs as a glowing fist plunged for her chest and braced as Lucia's punch detonated upon her defences. The blast glanced off her discs and sent her skidding back onto a waiting expanse of violet ice. She sprang to her feet and flicked her hands aside, conjuring scarlet blades on the soles of her boots. Lucia's eyes fluttered as Brooke glided past on a pair of magical skates, ice spreading ahead of her as she ran circles around her opponent. The flames that consumed Lucia's arms burned ever brighter as she took helpless swings at the evoker, whose fast and fluid movements made her nigh unassailable.

Brooke dipped beneath a firebolt and skidded up a rocky ridge, launching herself overhead and cleaving her hand down upon Lucia. Barely grazing her opponent's elbow, the disc in her palm smashed the ground and shattered in a violent discharge of energy, blasting Lucia back as Brooke lunged after her. She summoned another disc and swung both hands down, smashing Lucia's shoulder and sending her reeling.

"By the gods, Brooke is incredible!" Nearchos laughed.

"Isn't she?" James grinned. "She's totally destroying her!"

"No... Lucia's just playing defensively, letting Brooke tire herself out," Zahra observed. "Look - she's slowing down."

It was true, Brooke's movements were becoming sluggish. She ducked around Lucia's fists and skidded around with her arm reeled back. As she struck for Lucia's face with an overhead swing, she found her wrist locked in a burning grip.

Her gasp was cut short as Lucia blasted the ground and ripped the both of them off their feet. Strafing towards the battlefield's edge, Lucia swung Brooke around and let her slip, sliding to a halt and watching as her opponent sailed over the boundary. A wall of ice erupted from the ground and barely contacted Brooke's boots, cutting her momentum and smashing her into the grass. Much of the crowd winced and Ava cupped her mouth in horror, yet Brooke rolled groggily onto her back and stuck up her thumb with a feeble wheeze.

"If I were you, I'd step out of bounds," Lucia yelled as she span back around. "You don't want to risk pissing me-"

Ice exploded from the ground ahead of her, a cluster of jagged shards that sent her staggering back at its approach. Her foot dug deep into the dirt, shifting the boundary line as she skidded to a halt at the very edge. The ice began to sag as Lucia extended her hand, billowing with steam as she carved a path through its centre.

"What do you think, Zahra?" Nearchos asked.

"It's anyone's game…" Zahra muttered. "This may be a matter of essence management - both of them have expended a fair amount, so it's possible that someone might run out."

"Or… someone dies!" Emilia grinned, her legs kicking hyperactively. "This is getting me so *pumped*! I-I need to fight something! Hey, Water-"

Zahra clamped her hands around either side of Emilia's head. "Sleep…" she whispered, her palm emitting a golden glow that saw the girl sag immediately onto Laurent's shoulder, sound asleep.

They returned their attention to the battlefield, watching as Lucia waded out from amidst the towering column of steam. She barely caught a glimpse of Ava gliding by before another wall of ice erupted in front of her. Lucia roared as she slammed her hand into the ice, detonating it in an explosion of glistening fragments. Narrowing her burning eyes as Ava skated past, she flung her arm over her head and hurled a ball of flame into her path. Another ice wall surged from the dirt and splintered at the meteoric impact of the attack, while Ava skidded along its side and span herself back upon Lucia.

Flames had begun to spread across Lucia's body, creeping down her back and igniting her legs. A wave of explosions cascaded across the arena, yet they were dulled as Ava kicked a shield of ice into her path and darted left. Lucia growled with rage as another wall of ice burst from the smoke and smashed her jaw, sending her stumbling back and toppling her over a scorched shrub. Landing on her backside, she searched the battlefield with short breath, her vision shrouded by the smoke that billowed from the many craters around her. She whipped around and scrambled to her feet as a ramp of violet ice shot overhead.

It twisted suddenly and stretched into the air, carrying Ava upside down over Lucia's head. A flick of the girl's wrist saw a hail of icicles fall upon the pyromancer, who leapt out of the way as they crashed to the ground and shattered into a shower of violet sparks. Lucia had barely stood up straight when a bolt of ice slammed into her shoulder, blasting a jagged mass of ice across her left arm.

The roar she bellowed was fuelled by hate, her shoulders igniting with flame that spread across her body like a raging wildfire. The ice melted away in an instant and the burning girl turned her attention upon Ava. The very sight of the cryomancer gliding effortlessly around her boiled her anger to a critical level. As Ava rounded a bend and prepared another icebolt, Lucia thrust her arms into the sky with an animalistic growl.

The ground surrounding her lit up with yellow flame. Ava continued still as the world around her was swamped in fire, easily trampling the inferno with her ice. She skidded around another bend, searching for Lucia amidst the blaze, and slid right into the path of a waiting fist.

Lucia's hand flared with blinding light as her whole arm exploded violently into flame and rushed towards the girl's face. A thunderous crack plunged the arena into silence, a flash of light marking the explosive contact of the fist against Ava's face. The controlled yet potent explosion blasted Ava off her feet, the sheer force sending her sailing metres across the battlefield.

The mouths of the crowd fell ajar as the flames died out and Ava's limp body rolled to a halt, steam billowing from her scorched face. James' trembling eyes fell upon Lucia, who stood staring darkly at her blazing fist. The look on her face was almost emotionless, an unexpected combination of anger and disappointment. With a pained sigh, she dispersed the fire from her palm and looked upon the crowd.

"Oh my... um, victory to Team Severin!" Gerard stammered.

The crowd slowly began to applaud the brutal display as Ava was hauled onto a stretcher and carried away. Lucia did not embrace their praise - her face was grave and empty even in the face of glory. She trudged to the battlefield's edge and was met by Hasso, who placed his hand gently on her shoulder as they wandered back to the stands. On the other end of the field, Brooke was in hysterics, bawling her eyes out beside Galen. Leopold and Nicolas were in uproar, demanding a disqualification. Alas, any manner of brutality was tolerated so long as it was not lethal.

"By the gods..." Nearchos scoffed. "What did I just witness?"

"I'm... not sure," Zahra mumbled. "But I don't think Lucia liked it anymore than we did."

James was silent, watching with a heavy heart as Brooke lay down on her bench, weeping into her hands. As bad as he felt for her, he was just as scared for himself, scared that he or any of his friends could meet the same fate as Ava. It was clear to see that Lucia had demons, but that did not change the facts - she was a monster and a danger to everyone who stood in her way.

The mood surrounding the arena was one of anxiety as the next pairs took to the battlefield. A morbid silence hung over the venue as they did battle, every aggressive motion flinching the audience as they awaited another brutal display. Thankfully, no such display came.

The crowd had begun to perk up and let slip a hesitant cheer as Isadora socked Leopold in the nose. He collapsed backwards and toppled out of bounds, drawing a delighted giggle from his opponent.

"Where's Galen?" she called to Matheas.

"I don't know…"

"What do you mean, you don't know?" Isadora scoffed. "It was your job to keep an eye on him!"

"He disappeared! I haven't seen him in ages," Matheas said. "Maybe he's hiding behind-"

Matheas convulsed and staggered backwards. An invisible force struck his chin and he fell flat on his back. Isadora simply watched with a growing grin, slowly sliding an arrow from her quiver.

"I see…" she smiled. "We've got an invisible man on our hands."

She raised her bow and in a lightning motion, loosed the arrow across the arena. It struck the ground at Matheas' side and unleashed a blast of icy mist, painting the area around him blue. Galen glanced down at his icy hands, jolting in terror and turning tail. Isadora laughed as he fled, picking out a blunt-tipped arrow and firing it into his back. A pulse of wind blasted him off his feet and sent him spiralling out of the arena.

"Victory to Team Severin!" Gerard declared. "With a score of four to two, give it up for our first semi-finals team!"

Isadora slung Matheas over her shoulder and skipped back to her team, where Josef and Matheas reluctantly applauded their return. Lucia glanced up at Isadora, who stood proudly before her, and grunted before burying herself back into her hands.

Emilia's eyes drifted open as the audience applauded Team Severin's victorious march back to the stands. She looked around in confusion and wiped the drool from her drenched chin.

"Huh? What happened?" she mumbled, swaying drunkenly back and forth. "Did I win?"

"Team Severin has won, my lady," Laurent whispered. "We are up next."

"And I fell asleep halfway through?" Emilia scoffed.

"Um… yes! Yes, you must have been quite tired after chasing that rabbit earlier."

"That stupid rat had it coming," Emilia sighed. She glanced to the foot of the stands, where Team Trausch trudged back to their seats, Nicolas dragging Galen in tow. "Say, what happened to the pretty one?"

"Ava? Well, she... she was quite badly-"

"Liar!" Brooke wailed, summoning a disc and hurling at Zahra. The weapon whipped narrowly past her and struck Emilia square between the eyes, slicing her glasses in two yet barely flinching the girl. "You said she couldn't melt the ice!"

"I-I never... I said it would melt slowly!" Zahra cried, throwing up her hands as another disc warped into Brooke's palm. "I didn't think Lucia would apply so much power!"

Galen grabbed Brooke's wrist and lowered it to her side, gently moving her along. "Leave it, she was only trying to help."

"No, get off!" Brooke cried, shaking off his grip and shoving him away. "I- I don't..."

With her head in her hands, she fled back down the steps and disappeared behind the stands, the faint sound of her weeping still audible in the distance.

"Hmph, no need to apologise," Emilia muttered, discarding her glasses deliberately into Emeric's face.

"You gave them advice?" Nearchos hissed. "Zahra, the rules quite clearly state that you cannot confer strategy with your opponents."

"It wasn't strategy, I just explained a basic arcane principle," Zahra urged. "But I'd never have expected Lucia to overcommit her essence like that. By all means, she should have run out by the time she'd beaten Brooke, never mind Ava!"

"There's something seriously wrong with that girl..." James said gravely.

"That's quite enough moping, chaps!" Laurent declared, his armour rattling as he sprang to his feet. "We're up!"

"Yes!" Emilia growled, tumbling from her seat. "The time has come... time to kill!"

Nearchos rolled his eyes as they filed out of their row and started down the steps to the arena. "Zahra, I'm a little concerned about Emilia," he whispered. "How she is... it's beginning to seem less and less like an act."

"I know, but she's probably the best mage we have," Zahra sighed. "Will she hurt someone? Probably, but she won't kill. Not if that means disqualification."

"But anything else goes," Nearchos said. "She could slice someone's arm off and get away with it."

"Exciting, isn't it?" Emilia chirped, grasping his arm and gazing up at him. "I can only imagine the fun I'll have with such *tender* victims..."

123

Nearchos yanked his arm away as she caressed it with manic obsession. She cackled at the startled look that plastered his face.

"I'm just messing with you!" she laughed. "God, you're so gullible. What cause would I have for severing someone's limbs when I can so easily go for the head?"

She giggled at the shiver that shot through his body. Prancing ahead, she leapt onto the bench at the arena's end, her legs vibrating in a surge of giddiness. The team took their seat on the bench and huddled together.

"Alright," Zahra sighed. "This time, let's make a plan *before* we start."

"I'm going to come out and say the obvious," Emilia said. "The baton baby should be left for the tie breaker. We'll have far more success without him."

James raised his hand as Nearchos prepared to refute her. "She's right. I'll probably be better when I can focus on one target. Against two, I'll be wiped out in no time."

"It was my understanding that James cannot stand up to many of the other students," Laurent said. "No offence, of course."

"You're not wrong…" James sighed. "But if I'm in a pair, we'll be more likely to lose than reach a tie breaker."

Zahra took a deep breath, reluctant to discourage James after doing so much to support him. "You're sure?" she asked.

"Positive," James smiled. Lucia was right in her assessment - he was a liability. It was nothing that he was ashamed of, but it was a reality that he had to work with.

"Fine," Zahra groaned. "So, anybody have an idea for the plan?"

"For the love of God…" Emilia muttered. "You're the *team leader*!"

"But- But I don't-"

"You are leagues smarter than anyone else here. Now get your bloody act together and for once in the damn tournament, think for yourself!"

Everybody paused in concert and stared blankly at Emilia, who rolled her eyes and looked away.

"Did you just compliment her?" James laughed.

"I will rip you two," Emilia warned.

Zahra sat in silence while Emilia threatened him, rubbing her arms as she mulled over Emilia's words. The girl was right - this was on her. As daunted as she was by her previous failures, she would never grow as a leader by dwelling on the past. She took a deep breath as her teammates fell silent

"Alright. Alright… I think Nearchos should go with me. I can use my illusions to disable any threats to him, like Catelyn's electromancy. That should give him free reign to do some serious damage."

"Smart," Nearchos smiled. "I can deal with Meridian and Lukas no problem, so long as Catelyn and Lykinios are out of the way."

"And I guess that puts me with my faithful servant," Emilia chirped, slapping her knight on the back.

"You two have a solid combination of damage, speed and durability," Zahra said. "So long as you can close the distance, I doubt you'll have many problems… and that just leaves one more thing."

"Um, would that be me?" called an approaching boy. He was a short thing with topped with a head of frizzy, chestnut hair. His dull, blue eyes were alight with excitement and an eager grin stretched across his narrow face. "My name is Franz Holtz, I'm the alchemist with Team Nikostrakis."

All at once, Team al-Masir raised their heads and narrowed their eyes.

"An eavesdropper…" Emilia growled. "Let's get him disqualified!"

"No! No, I swear, I barely heard a thing," Franz urged. "In fact, Lykinios barely lets me in on the plans anyways, says I'm too obsessive! Bah."

"Yes, you're clearly very… normal," Zahra mumbled. "Is there something we can do for you?"

"There is, if it's not too much trouble," Franz said. "I was hoping you might lend me a favour."

Zahra glanced to her team, who were each painted with suspicion. "What kind of favour…?"

"Oh, nothing scandalous, I assure you," Franz smiled. "I simply wish for you to give me a bit of feedback. I believe I've ironed out most of the side effects in my potions, but it's quite hard to tell without a wider sample of human specimens."

"What did he just call me?" Emilia hissed.

"It would be wonderful if, in the unlikely event that you experience any unwanted effects, you would let me know after our battle."

"Uh… what kind of side effects are we talking about?" Zahra asked.

"Theoretically, none! Though, you should be prepared to experience something in the realm of nausea, blackouts, loss of eyesight, projectile vomiting… oh, and permanent loss of motor function."

"Are you sure-"

"Any feedback would be greatly appreciated," Franz declared, rushing back to his team. "Preferably, in a non-physical format!"

They watched with blank faces as he ran down the length of the arena.

"Is anyone else terrified?" James whispered.

"Very," Zahra said. "How do we deal with him?"

"Assuming he'll be throwing chemicals at us, we can probably just knock him out," Nearchos suggested. "He's got no superhuman abilities, what's he going to do about it?"

"Maybe he'll drink some crazy concoction and go all big and stuff!" Emilia hissed. "You know, like super strength or something."

"Potions can't do that, Emilia," Zahra sighed. "Their mostly medicinal… or acidic."

"Then he'll be no problem!" Emilia smiled. "So, who's up first? Personally, I'd like to go second so I can show you all up."

"No argument here," Nearchos said, strapping on his helmet. "Ready, Zahra?"

Zahra took a deep breath and drew a long strip of brown cloth from her pocket. "As I'll ever be," she sighed, wrapping it over her eyes."

The rest of her team watched cluelessly as she tied the blindfold around her head and stepped into the arena.

"Is seeing not a little important?" Nearchos called as he jogged after her.

"I can see just fine," Zahra said. "The blindfold hides who I'm targeting while I use detection pulses to build an image of the battlefield. Only flaw is I can't see colour or any kind of gas."

"That's… impressive," Nearchos smirked. Now he knew how James felt, dwelling in the shadow of those more talented than himself.

They came to a stop amidst a patch of grass, renewed after being burned black by flame. Across from them stood Lykinios, the opposition's skin-headed leader, alongside a giddy Franz. The alchemist wore a long, beige trench coat, dozens of colourful vials glinting within. Nearchos hardly feared the boy - he could be taken out with ease.

Nearchos glanced back to Zahra, who was mumbling erratically in her native tongue. "Nervous?" he grinned.

"You can tell?" she laughed anxiously. "All these people… I don't know how you stay so calm."

"I've trained for years to deal with high stress situations," Nearchos said. "Things change fast when you're at sea - a good leader has to keep a level head."

"Lucky you… I've had nothing of the sort," Zahra sighed. "People underestimate just how stressful the role of ambassador can be."

"Mm, one wrong move and you've changed history for the worse."

Zahra gulped down her fear. "I'm glad you understand, but please don't say that," she hissed. "My nerves *do not* need this right now."

Nearchos retreated into silence and Gerard stepped up to the podium and spread his arms wide.

"Apologies for the wait, my friends," he smiled. "Our experts had plenty to repair after Team Severin's explosive first round. Without further adieu, let us move on to our next matchup! We have Team al-Masir versus Team Nikostrakis! Fighting for Team Nikostrakis will be abjurer Lykinios

Nikostrakis and alchemist Franz Holtz! I'm sure you're as curious as I am to see what he can bring to this fight."

Franz nodded to Zahra as she glanced across at him. She dreaded to think what hell he had in store for them.

"As for the victors of yesterday's event, Team al-Masir will be fielding their hydromancer, Nearchos Phokinas and their illusionist, Zahra al-Masir!"

The curious stares of the crowd put her terribly on edge, not helped by the counting of the horns. She was an alien to them, an unknown. Some looked upon her with disgust, others with terror. Nearchos was right - the future of her people depended upon the impression she made that day.

"With such oddities on the field, this truly could be anyone's game!" Gerard said. "Let's see what surprises they have in store for us. Combatants, begin!"

The final horn sounded and Zahra reached for Lykinios' mind. A golden barrier rolled between them and both Lykinios and Franz stepped smugly behind it.

"I need that barrier down!" Zahra yelled.

"On it," Nearchos said, raising his hand and firing a stream of water across the arena. It hissed as it struck the barrier, blasting steam into the air.

While Nearchos hammered the barrier, Zahra could do little but stand there. She stiffened at the growing anxiety, standing useless before the eyes of the crowd. As she considered the situation, a terrible fear grew in her heart - What if Nearchos broke the barrier and blew them away? What if she didn't even get a chance to display her power? She couldn't let that happen, her whole purpose in life depended on it.

Suddenly, her pulses picked up an incoming projectile. She leapt back as a vial of clear liquid plummeted to the ground a mere metre in front of her. In a flash of light, the chemicals ignited and exploded from the vial, bathing the surface in a blanket of flame.

"You see that?" she called.

"I did. I think Lykinios is using a second barrier to catapult them."

Lykinios' barrier shattered. Their opponents leapt to the ground and scurried out from beneath the jet of water overhead. In the split second that Zahra could reach Lykinios' mind, another potion slammed the ground before her, destroying her concentration and belching fire over her feet.

She had barely finished screaming by the time Nearchos had hosed down her legs, but it had given Team Nikostrakis enough time to reposition. Another barrier flickered in and another potion was slung high into the air.

"Damn it," Nearchos growled, ducking behind a tree. "They're making this a battle of attrition."

"It doesn't help that this is essentially a two versus one," Zahra sighed. "I'll bring in Amani. She can flank the barrier and chase them out of cover."

"Where I can blast them," Nearchos grinned. "Sounds like a plan. I'll keep up the pressure."

While Nearchos returned to firing, Zahra reached into the sky. As she sank into concentration and tracked Amani's mind, she was oblivious to the vial that struck the ground beside her. A yellow mist seeped from its shattered remnant, rising into the air as Zahra found her friend.

"Amani, vas-"

Her next breath was cut short as her throat clenched tight. A burning sensation spread from her mouth to her chest, growing more intense with every second. Her arms locked up as she grasped desperately at her neck. She looked with horror to James, who stared wide eyes as she began to violently choke.

"Zahra?" he gasped, jumping from his seat. "Oh my God... Nearchos!"

She collapsed to her knees, tears pouring from beneath her blindfold as she gagged on her own throat. Cackling deviously amongst one another, Franz and Lykinios jumped from cover, moving towards her behind a moving barrier.

"Bastards," Nearchos growled. He threw out a hand and blasted Franz' flames with water, pumping a cloud of rolling steam across their end of the arena.

Lykinios' barrier was a beacon amidst the veil, beaming golden light in every direction. He and Franz advanced carefully towards Zahra's position, watching the steam around them with bated breath.

"There!" Franz cried, shoving Lykinios in front of him.

A jet of water exploded from the mist behind them and slammed into Lykinios' gut, blasting him into his own shield and knocking him out cold. As the steam seeped away and the barrier flickered out, Franz yanked a veil from his coat and threw it to the ground. A clear, blue liquid blanketed the ground between him and Nearchos as he leapt behind a rock.

Nearchos stepped forwards, only for the pool before him to light up with electricity. He dispelled his water as it arced towards him and began to circle around.

Franz leapt up and, as Nearchos fired another jet, hurled another vial. It struck the water head on an unleashed an explosion of white mist, freezing stream solid.

"Ha! Your magic is worthless against the power of alchemy!" Franz laughed, drawing two more vials from his coat. "Cower before me, mage, as I put an end to your miserable-"

A blast of water propelled the cluster of ice into his face, smashing him over the head and knocking him flat. The ice shattered against the ground and drenched his limp body in frigid water.

"Victory to Team al-Masir!" Gerard declared.

Nearchos breathed a deep breath as the crowd began to applaud and trudged back to Zahra's side. She lay beside a puddle of red-tinted vomit, wheezing for air and staring emptily into the sky.

"I'm sorry," she said, her voice an abrasive whisper, no louder than the breeze. "I… I'm sorry…"

"Come on," Nearchos urged, grabbing her feeble arms and dragging her to her feet. "You need help. I'll get you to a biomancer."

The rest of their team watched in silence as Nearchos led her away. The way Zahra hobbled, the way she clutched her stomach and coughed blood into the grass - for James, it was more than enough to draw tears. Even Emilia had a look of pure shock on her face.

The moment Franz was on his feet again, he came frolicking over, dripping a hail and smiling widely with beaming glee. "So! While we wait for the subjects, what did you think?" he asked. "Pretty impressive, right?"

James clenched his fists and rose from the bench to meet him. "What the hell was that gas?!"

"I call it 'vortic grasp'! A bit of water, a dash of vorticath saliva, the smallest drop of-"

In a lightning reflex, James smashed Franz as hard as he could in the nose. Emilia shrieked with laughter as the boy staggered back, clutching his face in his hands.

"Argh! You bloody madman," Franz cried. "I hardly think that was-"

Emilia grabbed Franz' wrist as he raised his finger. "Bored!"

She slung him by the arm into the stands, sending him flying several metres and bowling down a trio of audience members. James eased himself back into his seat and winced as she slapped him on the back.

"I'm impressed," she smiled, signalling Laurent to attention. "Proud, almost… Come, Sir Knight! We have work to do."

James was left in his lonesome as he watched his teammates march off. Cradling his head in his hands, he expelled his stress and a long, drawn out moan. After the monster stage, the race had made the whole tournament seem like such a novelty, so much that he had forgotten its true nature. This was a deadly game, one that had just gotten all the more dangerous.

Emilia's every stride oozed swagger as she and Laurent strutted onto the battlefield. The smile on her face was as blissful as it was manic, her whole body trembling with excitement as the cheering crowd sent her ego rushing to her head. While she threw her arms wide in embrace, Laurent flourished his mace and drew his shield from his back. He set down the silvered slab and leant casually against it as they took in their audience's praise.

"Mm... you hear that?" Emilia sighed. "They adore me."

"And why wouldn't they?" Laurent laughed. "Few in this tournament have stood out quite like yourself."

"Like *us*, Sir Knight," Emilia smiled. She tried to place her hand on his shoulder but reeled back at the sting of its heat. "You're... a little on the warm side. Not gonna die, are you?"

"Well, um... it does seem that my cooling enchantments are a fair bit less effective than anticipated," Laurent mumbled. "But, I'm not quite cooked alive yet, so I should be good to go!"

"If you say so," Emilia smirked. "Oh, this is going to be *so* much fun. The last time I was this excited, I pissed myself twice!"

"Yes, well let's not try to break any records."

"No promises. Bad bladders run in the family."

They stood to attention as a horn blared across the arena. The crowd fell silent once again and Gerard stepped up to the podium.

"Well, while I can't say that was the most thrilling of matchups, I think our next competitors can surely guarantee us a glorious display! Fighting for Team Nikostrakis, we have electromancer Catelyn Stahl and pyromancer Meridian Engel!"

Emilia narrowed her eyes and growled at the very sight of them. She hated pretty girls and the College was festering with them. Catelyn was one of those dull, makeup slathered brunettes - the ones who thought their illustrious hair gave them superiority, but were as dense as an anvil. Meridian looked like a ghost, even with her thick blusher. Fair haired and pale skinned, she was a haunting sight - That, and Emilia thought her name was stupid.

"And on Team al-Masir's side... well, this is where things get interesting! We have enchanter Laurent Bouchard and - one you know well from yesterday's outrageous overtake - give it up for al-Masir's biomancer, Emilia Arrenni!"

Emilia giggled childishly as the crowd roared with applause. Her skin lit up pink as it hardened into a rigid hide. Her hair became motionless, her pigtails sitting idle in the breeze. As the horns began to count down, she raised her hands and cemented them into blades.

"Do try to remember, Sir Knight, that right now you are a honey-soaked child punching a beehive. I don't want to see you go anywhere near that electric girl."

"You needn't worry, my lady!" Laurent assured her. "My shield is specially enchanted for just that!"

"Wonderful," Emilia smiled. "Let's show these ladies what power looks like."

"Brace yourselves, ladies and gentlemen!" Gerard boomed. "This is shaping up to be an intense fight indeed! Combatants, begin!"

Laurent raised his shield as a bolt of blue lightning streaked across the arena. It shot straight beneath the shield and into his foot, sending energy surging through his armour. Emilia watched with a widening grin as he quaked on the spot and collapsed into the dust. Frozen on the spot, she glanced to a startled James before erupting into a piercing cackle.

"Oh, I… I can't… I can't breathe!" she stammered through hysterical laughter. A lightning bolt deflected harmlessly off her arm as she staggered about in a daze. "I just- just give me a… I'll just-"

"Damn it, Emilia, concentrate!" James yelled.

"Uh, yeah… yeah, I'm on it," Emilia sighed, still giggling quietly as she span around. She barely flinched as a ball of fire exploded against her forehead, stepping out of the resulting smoke with a dark grin on her face. "Run, you fools… run while you still can!"

She launched into a predatory sprint, bent almost onto all fours. Fire and lightning hailed her approach, yet found no effect. Bolt after bolt struck the landscape around and as she ducked, dived and weaved across the battlefield and what little hit her glanced worthlessly off her armoured hide.

"Are you even aiming at her?!" Meridian growled.

"She's too small, I can't land a good hit!" Catelyn cried. "Just use the beam!"

Meridian too a deep breath and cupped her hands. Tracing Emilia across the battlefield, she held her aim ahead of the girl's path and lit up her palms with divine, yellow light. A beam of fire erupted from her hands, cleaving rocks apart as she swept it left. Emilia did not stop - she skidded under the beam as it swept through her cover and as it careened back around, she leapt onto a fallen tree and gracefully somersaulted over it.

"What's the matter?" she sneered. "Can't even match my skills as an acrobat?"

"Meridian!" Catelyn shrieked as Emilia broke cover and lunged towards her.

No amount of fireballs could stop the girl, exploding worthlessly around her and painting her pink uniform black once again. Catelyn screamed as

Emilia grabbed her arm and span her around. A rigid elbow slammed into her gut, bending her over and smashing her chin against Emilia's knee.

"You should have run while you had the chance!" Emilia roared. The audience cringed as she stamped down on Catelyn's knee, the incredible density of her foot inverting the leg with a brutal crunch.

Catelyn's wailing was silenced by colossal punch to the jaw, knocking her flat on her face. Springing to her feet, Emilia looked smugly upon her mangled opponent as another fireball exploded against her shoulder. She glanced up at Meridian, whose fair skin had gone a deathly white - even her blusher looked paler.

"Go on, run," Emilia grinned, pacing slowly towards her. "It'll look better for the crowd if you cry."

Meridian took a deep breath and stood straight, prompting a demeaning chuckle from her opponent.

"Do you know how much trouble you're in? How much I'm capable of?" Emilia hissed. "The audience knows it. As will the world, soon enough! Finally, they'll love me. They'll love me like they always should have! *Like I deserved!*"

Flames burned in Meridian's palms, even as she trembled before her advancing foe. Such silent defiance, it only fuelled Emilia's anger. She clenched her fists and gritted her teeth, growling like a wild beast as darkness overcame her.

"You'll see… you'll seem I'm not a mutant, not a freak! You'll understand-"

"We're in different classes! W-We've never met!" Meridian cried. "I don't even know who you are!"

Her words left Emilia stunned. Tears slipped from Meridian's eyes as Emilia descended suddenly into a fit of manic laughter.

"Oh, I'm going to enjoy making an example out of you," she grinned, bloodlust in her eyes. "Consider it your honour to introduce me to the world!"

As Emilia took her first step, Meridian lashed out with her hand and projected a fiery beam. Grinning as it scythed towards her, Emilia grabbed Catelyn by the neck and raised her body in front of her. Meridian yelped in fright and dragged her aim low, slicing a black line across the ground at Emilia's feet.

"Ha!" Emilia scoffed, reeling Catelyn's body behind her back. "You weakling!"

She slung the girl over her shoulder and sent her hurtling across the arena, bowling Meridian into a crumpled pile. A fireball exploded against Emilia's face to no effect. She burst from the smoke in a thunderous sprint, barrelling towards Meridian at terrible speed.

Meridian screamed as she staggered to her feet, ducking beside a meteoric punch that shattered the bark of the tree behind her. As Meridian fled, Emilia slammed her foot against the crumbled trunk and with a series of cracks and crunches, sent the tree careening to the ground. It crashed down before Meridian, drawing from her a desperate yelp as her escape was cut off.

A torrent of flame burst from her hands, engulfing Emilia in a golden inferno. Meridian gasped as a blazing foot burst from the fire and slammed into her gut, smashing her to the ground. Emilia stepped out from the flames, her uniform on fire, and planted her foot upon her opponent's chest.

"What is my name?" she hissed, grabbing her by the scruff of her armour and pulling her close. "Say it!"

"E-Emily Arrenni?"

Emilia's hand clenched around her throat and dragged her off the ground. "My name is Emilia. Elizabeth. Arrenni!" she declared, presenting herself before the crowd. "And I... I am this kingdom's future!"

She span around and in one meteoric throw, hurled Meridian out of the arena. The crowd erupted in ovation as the girl slammed against the arena's invisible barrier and fell face down in the dirt. Emilia sucked in her breath and took a graceful bow.

"A truly incredible show!" Gerard declared. "Victory goes to Team al-Masir! Give it up, ladies and gentlemen, for our second round of semi-finalists!"

Throwing out her arms once again, Emilia span slowly on the spot, her breath growing ever harsher as she surveyed the chanting crowd. "Yes..." she hissed, the widest smile on her face. "You see it now, don't you? You wretched fools finally understand!"

After a whole minute of bliss, the referee eventually forced Emilia off the battlefield. Her chin in the air, she grabbed Laurent by the foot and marched triumphantly back to her bench.

The thunder of the crowd eventually died away and James was treated to a terrible screeching as Emilia dragged Laurent back to the bench. His armour buckled as she cast him to the ground at James' feet, glancing up at him with her smuggest smile yet.

"You're a psychopath," he groaned.

"I prefer sociopath," Emilia smiled. "Sounds more sophisticated. What matters is that I won. I'll forgive your lack of praise, given your mood, but I'm getting rather fed up of your aversion to recognition."

James took a deep breath and hopped to his feet. "You're right. Despite the atrocities, we won... and I guess I'm in no position to judge."

"No, you're not. Now what do we say?"

He looked at her for a moment, the confidence in her eyes deeply annoying him. Emilia muttered inaudibly under her breath as he wandered off. She grabbed Laurent by the visor and pulled him along as they marched back to the stands.

"You know, insolence like that won't get you far as a battlemage," Emilia said. She grinned at the startled look on his face. "Yes, it didn't take much working out. You don't have the connections to secure a high end job, so you've clearly no choice but to sign on with the dregs of the magical community."

"Dregs?" James sighed. "Do you have to be an ass about everything?"

"Okay, firstly - I am only an ass about *most* things. More importantly though - you're missing the point. I don't know what childish fantasies you've dreamt up about heroic crime fighters and cunning detectives, but to be a battlemage is to be a soldier. It's not a pretty life."

"Oh, because you're one to talk about childish fantasies," James snapped.

"Do yourself a favour and wake up," Emilia sighed. "We might have freaky, supernatural abilities, but our kind doesn't define this world. There's a thousand of us and millions of them... and they're all *so* very jealous."

James was at a loss for words - he could never quite manage them when Emilia got this way. Her shifts from crazed and manic to calm and intellectual were jarring.

"James!" Nearchos called. "Over here!"

He and Emilia turned to see Nearchos and Zahra standing at the foot of Class A's stands. Zahra's eyes hung barely open as she sipped a bottle of frothed, blue liquid and she barely acknowledged the arrival of her teammates.

"You're back!" James laughed, hurrying to Zahra's side. "I... figured you'd be out of action for a while. Are you okay?"

His mind went heavy as her voice projected into his head. "Of course not," she sighed, her tone truly morbid. "My entire throat has been corroded inside out. Drinking this stuff will make it better, but my voice is wrecked."

"It doesn't sound that bad," James smiled.

"Because I'm talking to you with my mind, you moron!"

"Well, I'm sure you sound just fine."

"You think?" she hissed for all to hear. Her voice was a gravelly wheeze, like she had smoked several lifetimes of tobacco. "I'm not fine, James. I never will be."

"Master Benett said the damage is largely permanent," Nearchos sighed. "It'll get better, but her vocal cords are seriously messed up. They'll never fully recover."

Emilia dumped Laurent to the ground and rushed over to Zahra, catching everyone off guard by throwing her arms around her leader's chest.

"I'm sorry, Zahra," she mumbled. "I can beat him up if you want…"

"No…" Zahra growled. "Leave this to me."

The rest of her team followed her dark glare to Franz, who was hurrying over as they spoke. He leapt to their sides, only to flinch as James and Emilia turned to meet him.

"Now, now, there's no need for any violence!" he urged, raising his hands into the air. "All I need is a bit of feedback - any unusual sensations, emotions, reactions…"

Zahra looked him dead in the eyes, not an ounce of emotion on her face. He held a nervous smile as everyone held silent stares upon him.

"Surely, despite your woes, you can understand the necessity of your feedback… you know, for the advancement of science!"

"Can I- Can I ask you something, Franz?" Zahra smiled, choking on her own raspy voice. "Have you ever tried these concoctions yourself?"

"Well, I… none of my offensive mixtures, no."

Her hand clenched tight upon his shoulder. "Perfect. Maybe you can give *me* some feedback."

Franz' eyes widened as he gulped his last breath. He grabbed his throat as he wheezed for air, coughing and spluttering as he sank to his knees. Zahra watched with a sinister smile as he collapsed to the ground, clawing at her feet as he curled up into a ball. Staring down upon him as he wept into the grass, she turned her back and marched off without a word.

"Oof, that was intense," Emilia whispered, following her leader at a distance. "And here I thought you were all a bunch of cowardly nerds. At least I was right about one of you…"

"Be quiet…" Nearchos muttered.

"Wow, talk about self-incrimination, I didn't even say anything!" Emilia laughed. "You remain as gullible as the day we met, Water Boy."

"That was less than two weeks ago."

"Yes, and you were boring for every minute of it."

While Nearchos and Emilia entered into a routine argument, James groaned as he began to reach his breaking point.

"Ugh, I need some air," he moaned. "You all go ahead, I'll be right back."

"You're leaving me with her?" Nearchos hissed.

"You've got Zahra!" James called as he marched off. "Just put her to sleep."

Emilia's eyes darkened as a wave of realisation washed over her. "That was you?!" she growled. James looked away as Zahra shot him a glare. "You're meant to be my friend, you backstabbing little..."

James slipped around the back of the stands and slumped against the supporting beams. How was it that he was the only fazed by the events of the tournament? Between the terrible violence and the brutal injuries, he was struggling to stay calm - If they got to the final, they would undoubtedly be pitted against Team Severin. After what happened to Ava... James feared to imagine what could go wrong.

"James?"

His terrified yelp was mirrored by a shriek from beneath the stands. He span around to the glowing, scarlet eyes of Brooke, glimmering in the shadows. She sat with her knees to her chest and her head hanging low. Tears had painted black streaks down her leather uniform and worn her eyes red and raw.

"Sorry... I didn't mean to scare you," Brooke mumbled into her knees.

"Brooke!" James gasped. "I-I thought you'd gone back to campus. What are you doing down there?"

"I just needed to be alone for a bit..." Brooke sighed. "Not that I mind the company! It's just, nobody else came to see me. Guess they don't care."

"Why wouldn't they?"

"Because they're not my friends. Not many people are," Brooke said glumly. "I try to make people like me, but most of them just think it's an act. People might act nice back, but they don't really care."

"I know that feeling," James smirked. "It's not easy finding friends with all the two-faced assholes roaming this place."

Brooke giggled quietly, a smile wavering on her lips. "I guess so... well, feel free to join me," she said. "Good thing about loneliness is it's in the shade."

After a moment of hesitation, James sucked in his gut and clambered into the shadows. He planted himself in the cold grass beside her, breathing a sigh of relief as the cool touch of the shade washed over him.

"I heard your team won," she smiled. "Sounds like Emilia blew the audience away."

"Yeah, turns out they're big fans of senseless violence," James sighed. "But I'm sure not they liked it when she bent Catelyn's leg backwards."

"Oh my God, that's horrible!" Brooke gasped. "This whole tournament is... it's hell! Did you hear what happened to that group of Class C students in the monster stage?"

"No…"

"Dragon froze them completely solid. A couple of them lost limbs."

"What?!" James hissed.

"The real monsters are the people who run this place," Brooke sighed. "How can they pit innocent students against people like Lucia for *entertainment*?"

"Hey…" James whispered. "You don't have to answer if you don't want to, but-"

"I'm sure Ava is just fine," Brooke smiled. "It totally freaked me out, but I know she'll get back up with a smile. She always does."

"Guess you rub off on her," James smirked.

"Other way around. She has a way of bringing out the best in people… seeing that explosion hit her face, all I could think about was how much I'd failed her, what little I'd done in return for so much."

"You didn't fail her," James said. "You fought Lucia as hard as you could and… and it was amazing!"

"Really?" Brooke mumbled. "I mean, it wasn't that good. If I'd been more defensive-"

"No, Brooke, it was incredible," James urged. "*You're* incredible! The way you use evocation, it's- it's just mind blowing!"

Brooke stared at him in a frozen state, barely a breath slipping from her mouth. A quivering smile spread across her face as she broke into timid laughter.

"I- Wow… thank you," she chirped, her tired eyes springing suddenly open. "Honestly, it's not as complex as it looks. I just apply small amounts of aeromancy to direct the course of my discs and keep up their momentum. It's really basic stuff."

"I know what basic looks like," James grinned. "And that is *not* basic."

Wearing a shy grin, Brooke smeared her hands over her eyes and untucked her legs. "I guess it's not…" she smiled, shuffling to her feet. "I'd better get back to the stands. Wouldn't want to miss anymore than I have to."

James nodded as she slipped into the sunlight. She span back around, a bright smile on her face and a newfound glee in her eyes.

"You going to be alright now?" James asked.

"Yeah, I think so," Brooke sighed, pulling back her tangled mop. "Thanks for cheering me up… at least now I know I've got *two* real friends in this stupid place."

She skipped off towards the arena, leaving James to scramble out from the shadows. He took a deep breath of fresh air as he jumped to his feet, stretching his stiff spine.

"Wow. That was *so* cute!"

James' heart almost exploded within his chest as he jumped in fright. His gaze eventually found the smug face of Emilia smiling down upon him, cupped in her hands as she leaned over the guardrail above.

"I didn't think you had it in you," she smirked. "What a fool I was."

"Wait, I- no! I'm not... y-you're delusional!" James stammered. "I would never-"

"You're totally crushing on her!" Emilia laughed maniacally. "And here I'd expected Zahra to be the object of your affection."

"You're being ridiculous," James muttered. "Zahra has an arranged marriage back in Novekhir, I wouldn't want to intrude on that."

"You're dodging the point," Emilia grinned. "Our useless, little evoker has gone and got himself lovestruck. It's a good thing Lucia destroyed them - that would have been an awkward final..."

"Oh, just shut up, you tiny freak!" James snapped. "You're just too young to understand that a boy and girl can talk about emotions *without* being in love!"

"Ah, the defensive fangs of denial," Emilia sighed, looking dramatically to the heavens. "If you don't want to admit it, that's fine by me. Personally though, I think you'd make a great couple - the two of you are so extraordinarily plain."

James growled quietly as Emilia drifted slowly out of sight, a smug grin on her face all the way. Unwilling to even entertain the notion, he clenched his fists and marched back around the stands.

"Victory to Team Lechner!"

The grass squelched beneath James' boot as he stepped up to the arena's edge. The battlefield was drenched, choked with sprawling puddles and dripping water from just about everything. Harmodius stood at the far end, his blonde hair painted brown and sagging over his face, which wore an expression of incredible discomfort. Bruno was half the arena away from his friend, standing over one of his opponents. There was barely a droplet on his body, emitting such heat that the soil at his feet bellowed steam into the breeze. He was clad head to toe in vibrant, red armour, rigid and crude in appearance yet protective all the same. As the energy cloaking his body warped and fizzled away, he extended his hand to the boy at his feet.

"A valiant effort, my good man!" he roared as his opponent received his meaty hand. "You had me on the ropes there. I'm impressed!"

Bruno glanced up at James and nodded his head in acknowledgement, before retreating to his team. They were surely thinking about the same thing - the semi-finals. James had been intimidated by the concept of going up against Bruno, yet he had only ever seen individual pieces of his armour. Now, seeing him fortified fully in his impenetrable suit, it was a truly harrowing event to imagine.

While Bruno squeezed a fleeing Harmodius into a hearty bear hug, James ascended the stands and returned to his team, where Laurent was nowhere to be found. He slipped into his seat beside Nearchos, trying his best to avoid the knowing stare still beaming from Emilia's face.

"All freshened up?" Nearchos smiled. "Laurent left to make some adjustments. As for the battle, you only missed the first round and it wasn't anything too spectacular. Team Rouselle led with a cascade of water that flooded the battlefield. Harmodius was pinned down behind his shield the whole time, but Bruno just waded through it and beat them senseless."

"What, he just walked right up to them?"

"Pretty much. He's a big man."

That was a startling thought. Clearly, Nearchos would be useless in a fight against the goliath, which took away a great deal of their offensive capabilities. At least they had the saving grace of Emilia - judging by her fight against Catelyn and Meridian, she could pack a serious punch and would no doubt be their best shot at breaking Bruno's armour. That however, relied upon the two meeting in battle at all.

Emilia suddenly jumped to her feet. "Wait, is that- yes!"

She clambered onto the bench, pulling at Zahra's hair as she used her leader to prop herself up. Zahra, still sulking, made no attempt to fight back and simply whimpered quietly in pain.

James and Nearchos followed Emilia's excited gaze to Team Lechner's bench, where Emeric and Caesia were preparing for battle. Caesia's mouth was moving like a blur as she spouted tactics into Emeric's ear, who barely seemed to register her presence as he stared tiredly into the distance. He had the grim face of a person who seriously didn't want to be there.

"Oh, I see," Nearchos sighed, his voice hushed. "She's excited about the Tarantis girl."

"I thought she hated Caesia," James muttered.

"Exactly. If Team Lechner gets through to the semi-finals, there's a chance that they'll face off," Nearchos explained. "And I think Emilia really wants that to happen."

"What did the poor girl ever do to her?"

"Probably nothing. I imagine Emilia sees her as competition, what with all that nonsense about her 'pink essence'."

"If you idiots are trying to be sneaky, you ought to quieten down," Emilia sighed as she shuffled back into her seat. "You're practically whisper-screaming."

"You're not going to scold us for denouncing your-" Nearchos wheezed as James jabbed him in the side.

"You think I could care less about your worthless opinions?" Emilia sneered. "I won't have to once I've killed that nutrient deficient bitch. Competition is no problem if you cave its head in."

Nearchos looked to James with terror in his eyes and the two of them retreated into silence, watching as the combatants stepped onto the field. At Team Rouselle's end stood a pair of boys - Nearchos had studied this team with intrigue and knew them as Maxime and Fernand. They were fairly archetypal of College students, with slicked hair and sculpted faces, looking awfully uncomfortable in their combat uniforms.

At the other end, Caesia had given up on trying to breach Emeric's state of carelessness. He was little different from his opponents in appearance - groomed, caramel hair and perfect skin, though his face was sagged and grim. Caesia seemed far more invested, but not in a particularly positive way. She was stiff with anxiety, staring blankly at the ground as she hopped up and down on the spot. The look on her face was one of terror, but equally one of conviction.

"How does this matchup look, Zahra?" Nearchos asked.

"Huh?" Zahra blurted, followed by a fit of coughing. "Oh, the battle… well, I guess it's pretty straight forward. Emeric is an electromancer, so it'll be his job to counter their spells and take out their opponents. He'll be priority number one for the other team, so Caesia will have to protect him."

"She'd be pretty hard pressed to block two water jets at once," Nearchos mused. "She might be overwhelmed."

"Yeah, and Emeric doesn't look all that into this either," James said. "If either of them don't put their back into this, they'll be blown away."

"I'm so excited, I'm gonna burst!" Emilia squealed.

"And now, my friends, for a round I know many of you have been waiting for!" Gerard triumphantly declared. "This round, Team Rouselle will be fielding two more hydromancers, Fernand Rouselle and Maxime Leroux! At the other end, alongside their electromancer, Emeric De Sardou, Team Lechner will be fielding their much anticipated abjurer, Caesia Tarantis!"

Caesia froze on the spot as the crowd roared, a mix of avid cheering and curious chatter. She looked mortified, in no state to fight, yet her fists still clenched and arced with energy.

The horns counted down amidst a deathly silence until Gerard shattered the silence. "Ladies and gentlemen, are you ready?" he boomed, drawing a colossal cheer from the audience. "Combatants, begin!"

As the words slipped from her brother's mouth, Caesia thrust up her arms and projected a pale green barrier in front of Emeric, just in time to catch a column of rushing, red water. It slammed against the shield with a crack, hissing as it billowed away as steam. As Caesia clenched her eyes shut and braced against the impact, Maxime raised his hands and unleashed a barrage of his own. The blast undercut Fernand's and punctured the already flickering shield. The barrier exploded into sparks and in a split second, Emeric was gone.

"No!" Emilia growled. "You idiot, you're meant to win! How are you so weak?!"

Caesia staggered back, whimpering as her arms trembled in agony. The hydromancers turned to her as she watched Emeric wash up before their bench, laughing between themselves as she cowered in fear. She threw herself to the ground as a deluge of water surged past, dragging herself desperately into cover.

"Oh, I can't watch," Zahra mumbled coarsely into her hands.

Water breached the ground at the hydromancers' feet, spilling puddles onto the grass that grew and convulsed at the motions of their hands. Caesia huddled up behind a rock and cast a barrier over her head, waiting for the inevitable wave.

"They're going to flush her out," Nearchos said gravely. "Literally."

With a coordinated thrust of their arms, Fernand and Maxime sent forth their accumulated water. A tide of blue and red crashed across the battlefield, pulling down trees and shifting rocks with its terrible force. Much of the crowd winced as Caesia was buried in an avalanche of water, only the dull glow of her submerged barrier left to evidence her survival. The audience watched with bated breath as the water reached the other end of the arena, yet Caesia was nowhere to be seen.

"Oh my God, is she okay?" Brooke gasped.

"Maybe green essence lets you breath underwater," Galen smirked, receiving a dirty look back from his teammate.

As the onrush continued, the barrier lit up and lashing, green tendrils crept across the water. Fernand and Maxime barely registered it in their confidence, but the colour soon left their faces. Lightning exploded from the barrier's face, lighting up the arena as it surged through the tide. Electricity climbed their bodies, wrapping them in writhing energy as they convulsed at the shock. Quaking violently, they collapsed into the sodden mud and suddenly, the water subsided and sank into the ground.

"Holy- Ahem... Victory to Team Lechner!" stammered Gerard, himself overcome by disbelief.

While the audience cheered and chanted, much of Class B sat in a shocked silence. They watched as the barrier flickered away and Caesia dragged herself to her feet. Her skin was painted brown with mud and every inch of her body dripped water like a localised storm. She swayed back and forth as she trudged back to her team, barely standing and unable to escape as Bruno marched out with Harmodius and Florence captured in one arm. He squeezed the three of them tight, potentially snapping several of their bones as he roared with laughter.

"I... didn't see that coming," James smirked. "I thought she was an abjurer."

"She is..." Emilia mumbled, her fingers burrowed deep into the frame of her seat. "And that tricky, little skeleton knows electromancy too! She thinks she can one-up me by knowing *two* schools of magic?! I'll show her! I'll show them all! She may have won this battle, but once I get my hands on-"

"Sleep."

Emilia face-planted the back of Lucia's seat, whose glare Zahra desperately avoided as she retracted her hand from Emilia's head. She pulled Emilia back and rested her gently on Laurent's seat, groaning as her nasally snoring commenced.

"So, who's next?" James asked.

"It'll be Team Escerich versus Von Schirtz," Nearchos said. "You'll probably remember the former from the festival."

"Oh yeah, the jerks who were trying to screw with Lucia," James muttered. "What about the other team?"

"They're from Class A," Zahra said, her abrasive voice dull and morbid. "Their leader, Gunter, is an evoker, as is Stefan. Phoebe is a cryomancer, Klaus is an abjurer and Ambrosia is an enchanter."

"There any reason you know so much about that team?" James asked.

"I sit with Phoebe at lunch," Zahra said, receiving astonished looks from her friends. "What? I can have friends outside of you two."

"You always said we were your only friends," James said.

"You are... I just talk to other people while you're not around," Zahra mumbled, her voice becoming more and more strained. "Don't get too worried, a lot of people still talk to me like I'm a child."

"Right... are you sure you should be talking so much?"

"I'm fine. My throat doesn't hurt much after that potion, it'll just be a while before I *don't* sound like I'm the ripe age of ninety."

James nodded and returned his attention to the arena, where Team Escerich and Von Schirtz were lining up before their benches. This would be an interesting battle - not because of those who fought it, but because those who won would face Team Severin next. James was intrigued to see whether they had what it took.

Chapter Eight - An Infernal Reckoning

The next battle of the combat round was nothing to write home about, yet it was a respectable fight nonetheless. Team Escerich fielded Arnvald and Marie, cryomancer and abjurer respectively, against Gunter and Ambrosia. It had been a battle of attrition, each contender being defensively oriented, each focused on wearing down the opponent's essence and cracking their fortifications. Having an abjurer gave Team Escerich the edge they needed, allowing for far more efficient defence that would see them outlast their foes. Arnvald had gone on the offensive with his ice and the battle had been swiftly won.

As for the next fight, Klaus and Phoebe found themselves up against Reiner and Summer. That battle had been far more one-sided, with Team Von Schirtz barely having moved from where they began under the constant barrage of wind. Summer had been propelled into their end of the field and was charged with rooting them out of cover. The following events had been amusing to watch, yet equally sad.

"Oh no..." James mumbled as he watched Reiner levitate Phoebe's body and sling her out of bounds.

"Poor girl," Zahra whispered, sinking back into her hands as she hung her head.

"Victory to Team Escerich!" Gerard announced. "And with that mighty victory, the first leg of the combat round comes to a close! As it stands, Teams Trausch, Nikostrakis, Rouselle and Von Schirtz have been eliminated. Facing each other in the next stage will be Team Severin versus Team Escerich, then Team al-Masir against Team Lechner! We'll give our audience a few minutes to catch their breath before we move onto the semi-finals!"

While Teams Escerich and Von Schirtz returned to their stands, many students from every class sprang up and fled to food stands and outhouses. Aside from Emeric, the rest of Team Lechner filed away to get some food, while most of Team Trausch went back to campus and left Brooke sitting alone. Teams Severin and al-Masir remained in their entirety, though Laurent was still nowhere to be seen.

"I hope Laurent gets here soon..." Nearchos muttered. "We might survive with just four, but I'd rather not risk it."

"Ah, what use is he anyway?" James sighed. "You saw what happened to him - he got totally fried! And as it turns out, Bruno's team has *two* electromancer!"

"True... I supposed we'd best hope that his 'precautions' are up to scratch," Nearchos said, glancing aside to Zahra, who was peering over her shoulder. "Something wrong, Zahra?"

"Brooke looks kind of lonely," Zahra whispered. "Do you think we should offer her Laurent's seat? I know we'd risk waking Emilia, but I just feel so sorry for-"

"Ava!" Brooke gasped, launching from her seat.

"Never mind."

The heads of all but Lucia turned to the bottom of the stands as Brooke waded to the staircase. Ava had barely rounded the corner before her friend fell upon her. In the moments before Brooke's hug made impact, one could perfectly see the burns that swamped Ava's face beneath a shell of ice. All the way from her chin to her forehead, the left half of her face was painted scarlet by warped blotches of raw skin. Her swollen left eye hung barely open and her hazel hair was blackened by flame.

"I was so scared," Brooke mumbled into her shoulder. "Your face…"

Ava managed a feeble smile, stopping Brooke's hand before it touched her burns. "The biomancer says it'll heal poorly… and that my eye is permanently blinded," she sighed, her words slurred by her bloated cheek. "But hey, at least it's got a good story behind it. How many burn victims can say they got their scars from fighting mages in gladiatorial combat?"

"Yeah… you look great," Brooke smiled, slapping her friend on the back and moving her along. Ava's legs trembled with every step as they ascended the steps and slipped into their seats.

"Damn, Lucia didn't hold back on her," James muttered.

"Did you expect any less?" Nearchos sighed. "That girl leaves a path of destruction everywhere she goes. I'm surprised she didn't do the same to Brooke."

"Brooke didn't give her the chance," Zahra said. "I gave Ava false hope - that made her vulnerable. Lucia took advantage of that and won. We may not like it, but she's doing what it takes to win this."

"And dealing grievous wounds in the process," Nearchos growled. "You know, part of me wants to lose the next round."

"Wait a minute…" James muttered, narrowing his eyes at the two empty seats in front of them. "Where *is* Lucia?"

The grass shrivelled and blackened as Lucia collapsed to the ground, her skin simmering as she stared glumly into the lake ahead. As much as she detested water, the anxiety of being near it helped to take her mind off her wrongdoings. Her heart pounded at the mere caress of the stuff against her boots and her raw skin began to itch wildly. It was an awful feeling, yet it was preferable to the alternative.

"Lucia?" Hasso called, stepping carefully out of the treeline.

"Go away," Lucia growled as she launched a stone into the lake. "Just let me be alone for once…"

"When you're alone, you only get yourself more worked up," Hasso sighed. "And I don't think you want that right now."

Lucia stared glumly into the pond, narrowing her eyes at her reflection. "I... I don't know what to do. I can't keep hurting people like this."

"You're getting better," Hasso smiled. "You'll have control in-"

"I'm not though, am I?" Lucia snapped, burning a patch of weeds to a crisp as she clenched her fists. "Look at me, Hasso! I just melted half of that girl's face - the punch wasn't even meant to explode! I-I can't control it... I just get so angry!"

Hasso looked upon her gravely as yellow embers began to fall from her skin. Lucia's anger issues had never meshed well with her disorder, but she had done well to come so far, to become as strong as she had - Hasso had not a doubt that she could someday overcome this.

He wrapped his arm around her with a warm smile, staring into her trembling eyes. Lucia never cried - the few times she had tried, the tears had evaporated before they even left her ducts. She simply sat in a brooding silence, flames flickering down her arms and lashing Hasso's skin.

"We'll get through this, Lucy," Hasso whispered. "I promise."

Lucia glanced up from the water and began to slowly compose herself. "I told you... don't call me that," she smirked, glancing over her shoulder. Between the stands, she could spot Isadora waiting by the bench. "I think we're up."

"You sure you're up for this?" Hasso asked.

"Course I am," Lucia grinned, flicking her wrist and igniting it with flame. "I've been looking forward to putting my fist through that wind bending bastard."

"Figuratively," Hasso warned.

"Oh, right... yeah," Lucia mumbled. "Come on, let's go win."

Zero to one hundred - Hasso was well acclimated to Lucia's rapidly shifting mood by now. He knew that Ava would dwell on her mind for time to come, but he imagined that a good thing. It would humble her, inspire her to better control her anger. He hoped so, at least.

Lucia marched back into the arena, pushing and shoving her way through the crowd, Hasso following in her wake. Her team perked up as she shoved a pair of bystanders aside and burst from the audience's midst, approaching the bench with a confident smile.

"Vera's blade! Where have you been?" Isadora hissed, toying impatiently with one of her arrows.

"Taking a walk," Lucia muttered. "Everybody ready?"

"So long as you don't incinerate anyone this time," Josef muttered. Lucia could have set him alight with the glare she shot him. "What? I don't want to be disqualified!"

"Yeah, yeah, I'll dial it back," Lucia groaned, pretending she didn't see Hasso's encouraging grin. "Any more of you idiots want to complain?"

Matheas hesitantly raised his hand. "Actually, I'd really-"

"Alright, let's talk teams," Lucia snapped. "Hasso's with me for the second battle, Isadora and Matheas will be our first team. Josef, you're our tie breaker."

"And I assume you've a strategy behind this?" Josef sneered. "Or are you just thinking about what's best for yourself?"

"*You're on thin ice, Sparkles,*" Lucia warned through gritted teeth. Why did everybody think her so self-centred? "Of course I have a strategy! Hasso and I can lay down enough firepower to overwhelm them easily. You all have crowd control and area denial abilities, which combined will totally cut them off from most of the battlefield."

"Surely, it would be a good idea to mix and match?" Isadora suggested.

"They'll expect us to do that, so they'll split their teams to tackle both offence and defence. We do the opposite and they won't have enough on either team to handle us."

"Makes sense, I guess," Matheas muttered. "But I doubt it'll be that simple."

"We're adaptable," Hasso smiled.

"That we are," Isadora grinned. "I trust Lucia on this."

Matheas and Josef glanced to one another for reassurance and slowly began to nod their heads. An eager smile on her face, Lucia glanced across the battlefield and scanned the enemy team.

At the head of the opposing group stood Vivienne, explaining strategy to her allies and pointing with her rapier at Lucia's team. Reiner wore an eager grin on his face, while his teammates all listened to Vivienne's words intently. Lucia wished that her team could have the respect that Reiner's had for each other, though she supposed that her attitude was probably half the problem.

"Isadora, Matheas, you're up," Lucia commanded as she slumped onto the bench. "If you end up fighting the aeromancer… make sure he knows whose team just kicked his ass."

A wide grin spread across Isadora's face while Matheas rolled his eyes. "Not sure he'll hear me through his concussion…" she chirped. "But I'll see what I can do."

Lucia's eyes lit up with murder as a smile graced her cheeks. At least one of her teammates had a pair. She watched with pleasure as her teammates marched off, penting her fingers in cunning.

"Are you sure that they can handle him?" Hasso asked, slipping to her side.

"They won't have to," Lucia said. "He's made it quite clear that he wants to take me on himself. He expects that I'll go second due to my ego, because I'll want to make up for my team's mistakes but not risk a loss of glory in the tie-breaker spot."

"If you're so sure, why not switch it up?"

"Because the rest of our team is ill suited against him. Isadora's arrows and Matheas' abjuration will be ineffective against wind. Josef could do it, but much of the opposition is capable of countering his abilities. You and I are the only ones who can take on an aeromancer to any degree of success."

Hasso nodded in agreement as he returned his gaze to the battlefield. Even for him, it was easy to forget that Lucia was no less clever than the rest of the students.

"Do you two actually love each other, or is it all just business?" Josef groaned. "Because I haven't seen a single splinter of affection between-"

"I will snap you!" Lucia warned with fists clenched. "Weedy little freak…"

Chuckling quietly to himself, Hasso assessed the scene before him. While Matheas jumped up and down on the spot, Isadora was sat peacefully on a tree stump, whistling merrily as she carved the shaft of an arrow with her knife. She was utterly unfazed by the pressure of the situation, off in her own little world. It was admirable, yet fairly concerning.

At the other end of the battlefield stood Arnvald, the towering, shaggy maned Nord, and Summer, the foundation-coated blonde with a bowl for hair. Reiner was confined to the bench, just as Lucia had predicted. Still, they were a formidable team - Summer could disable a target and allow Arnvald to easily eliminate them. It would be a matter of defence and manoeuvrability, avoiding a clear line of sight with Summer while avoiding Arnvald's ice. It would be difficult, but not impossible.

"If Isadora has half a brain, she'll use her arrows to obstruct Summer's vision," Lucia said. "Matheas is an excellent defence, but it'll be up to Isadora deal with them for good."

"That's a lot to put on one person…" Hasso muttered.

"She can handle it," Lucia said confidently. "She's the most versatile student in our class and I hear that the Veranians are pretty good under pressure."

"Your attention, my friends!" boomed the voice of Gerard across the arena. "Now that we are all refreshed, let us move onto the second stage of glorious combat! It looks like we have our two most controversial teams facing each other on the field today - Give it up for Teams Severin and Escerich!"

Lucia furrowed her brow as the crowd hesitantly cheered. How was her team receiving less applause than Zahra and Bruno's worthless gaggles?

"For the first battle, Team Severin will be fielding their abjurer, Matheas Berwalder, alongside their outstanding enchanter, Isadora Astraeanos!"

Isadora blew a kiss into the crowd as they cheered the mention of her name, some on their feet singing her praise.

"Wow, they really like her," Hasso observed.

"Of course, they do," Lucia said. "Have you ever heard of a bow-wielding mage? She's one of a kind."

"Against them, Team Escerich will be fielding their biomancer, Summer Holtz, and their cryomancer, Arnvald Ivarsen! Not often you get to see a Nordic mage, hm?"

Hasso rested his chin in his hand as the horns began to count down. "Are you nervous?"

"I don't get nervous," Lucia muttered. She sighed at his doubtful stare. "Don't you insinuate… I picked this team out because I know they have what it takes. I haven't a doubt in my mind."

Their attentions were snapped back to the battlefield as combat commenced. Isadora had Matheas had already flung themselves into cover, while Arnvald and Summer poised in readiness for their foes to make a move. Isadora turned to Matheas and uttered a series of unintelligible words into his ear.

"This should be good," Lucia smiled, shifting hyperactively in her seat as she leant forwards.

Matheas leapt to his feet and thrust up his arm, raising a shimmering barrier between the two of them and Summer. At the moment of its completion, Isadora sprang from cover and slid three arrows simultaneously into her bow. Sidestepping a hurtling shard of ice, she raised her weapon and loosed the arrows high into the air, arcing them over the barrier and hailing them upon Summer. The girl hardened her skin with a confident smile, but had not expected smoke to explode from the arrow's tips, swamping the area around her in a rolling blanket.

"Keep her suppressed!" Isadora demanded as she vaulted cover.

"Good…" Lucia growled.

They watched as Isadora sprinted after Arnvald, who turned his focus to her and pushed his hands high. With a piercing crash, a wall of jagged ice surged from the ground ahead of her, towering twice her height. Isadora slid an arrow from her quiver and leapt against the wall, springing nimbly off it and loosing an arrow into the ground below. A pulse of wind blasted her several feet into the air just enough for her to grasp the top of the wall and clamber to its peak. Arnvald, who had returned his attention to Matheas, jumped in fright as Isadora fired a crackling arrow into the ground at his feet. Lashing tendrils of lightning surged from its head and into Arnvald's body, convulsing him violently as he fought against its disabling effect.

Lucia cackled maniacally as Isadora leapt from the wall, her bow swung behind her head like blade. That laughter suddenly subsided as Isadora froze on the spot, her weapon inches from Arnvald's face.

"What is she doing?" Hasso hissed.

"Biomantic paralysis..." Lucia muttered. "Matheas let the girl slip."

The boy could scarcely be blamed. He had kept Summer within Isadora's smoke for ample time, but it was impossible for him to control such a large cloud. Summer scrambled from cover nearby and darted for Arnvald, placing her palm against his skin and hardening it instantly. With nothing to conduct it, the lightning simmered away and he slowly began to recover.

Shaking himself off, the Nord glanced up at Isadora's wide eyes with a grin and cloaked his arms with ice. Hasso buried his face in his hands as Arnvald reeled back his frozen fist and plunged it into Isadora's face, yet it found nought but a crackling barrier.

Arnvald glanced up at Matheas, who swept another barrier between Isadora and Summer and severed the biomancer's magical grip. Isadora slumped to the ground with a breathless gasp, while Summer turned with darkness in her eyes to Matheas. The abjurer manipulated his shields and morphed them into one, reinforcing it and cutting off Summer from her foes. Isadora sprang to her feet, casting down her bow and sliding a pair of arrows from her quiver, while Summer barrelled after Matheas as he ducked into cover.

"Good save," Hasso observed.

"Mm, but he's totally changed the nature of the battle," Lucia said. "This long ranged fight just became close quarters..."

While Matheas ran circles around Summer, forcing his barrier into her face, Isadora set her arrows alight with blue flame and charged Arnvald head on. She fell upon him like a whirlwind, bombarding his armour with a hail of blows. His sweeping blows found nought but air as she ducked and dived around him, jabbing and slashing at his carapace like a wasp. Several precision strikes saw the ice on his back cascade to the ground, followed by a final, cleaving blow. She jammed an arrow into his shoulder blade, his roar of agony quickly snuffed by the energy that surged through his spine.

Grabbing the arrow, she pulled herself up and tumbled over his shoulder. In one swift motion, she grabbed her bow, drew an arrow and loosed it into his chest. The blunt tip found his chest, unleashing a blanket of ice and engulfing his whole torso in a glacial prison. As he twitched and writhed to little effect, Isadora shoved him to the ground and turned to Summer and Matheas with a smug grin.

"I like her…" Lucia grinned darkly. "Come on, crack her bowl-head!"

"Figuratively!" Hasso yelled.

Matheas turned his head as Isadora charged his position, stepping back as she raised her arrows over her head.

"Hand!" Isadora cried.

Looking at her baffled, Matheas turned back to his shield, only for Summer's hand to erupt from the other side. Just as Isadora's arrow sent a surge of electricity through her forehead, Summer's hand took hold of Matheas' face. The two of them collapsed on top of each other and the crowd went wild. The look on Lucia's face however, was grave indeed.

"Victory to Team Severin!"

Isadora slung her bow over her back with a prideful smile, staring off into the crowd as they roared for her victory. However, the attention of her team hung not on her deeds, but on Matheas, who had already snapped awake and was trudging back to his potential doom. Lucia slipped slowly from the bench and heaved a deep breath, a quaking smile on her face. She tilted her head innocently as Matheas wandered shamefully to meet her.

"Can I just say-"

"*Idiot!*" Lucia roared, lashing out her hand and smacking Matheas across the face with a violent crack. "We could have had it so much easier! What the hell were you doing?!"

"Come on, it's only one point!" Josef urged.

"Did I ask for your input?!" Lucia growled. "We were *this* close to making a loss nigh impossible, but you just had to get the glory, didn't you?"

"I-I didn't think!" Matheas cried. "I had no idea that Isadora was coming, I… I just…"

"Leave it, Lucia," Isadora called as she stepped out of the arena's bounds. "So what if we're a point down? It's not like you won't crush them into the ground."

With a begrudging sigh, Lucia shoved Matheas back and folded her arms tight. Of course she would crush them, those uppity Class D snobs. They were nothing compared to her, nor the rest of Class B. This fight would be easy.

"Yeah…" she muttered. "Well, good job out there. I'm impressed."

Isadora smirked as Lucia grasped Hasso's wrist and dragged him along. Words of praise from Lady Severin seemed hard to come by - she was more amused than honoured.

150

"Oh, one more thing," Isadora smiled, whipping the carved arrow from her quiver. "Reiner wasn't there to receive this, but I gave Arnvald a good blast with it."

The arrow's shaft was elegantly carved with the word 'Severin', an ample means of letting the enemy know whose team crushed their hopes and dreams. Lucia grinned at the sight of it, smacking Isadora on the shoulder as she marched for the battlefield.

"I'll be sure to rub it in," she sneered, loosening her body as she marched on.

"Try not to blow off anyone's face this time, will you?" Josef sneered as she went. "I'd rather not be disqualified at your-"

Lucia span around and smashed her fist straight into his gut, detonating a compressed explosion that blasted Josef back into the bench, which caught his feet and sent him toppling backwards. While Lucia marched off without a word, Hasso looked back at his limp teammate with a sigh.

"Well... let's hope we don't need a tie breaker," Isadora smirked, parking herself on the bench beside the clobbered boy.

"We seem to have quite a matchup for the second round!" Gerard announced as the contenders stepped onto the field. "Team Severin is going all out, fielding their second abjurer, Hasso Kassenberg, along with their leader, Lucia Severin! I needn't remind you of her field of expertise..."

The air was thick with anxiety, cursed with an unnatural quiet that made Lucia's blood boil. They were afraid of her - what else was new? For years she had known her fate, to be shunned by every man, woman and child in the kingdom. For her name to be that of a boogieman, a subject of dark tales, a weapon to scare the children. All that she could do was avoid being a villain in the history books.

"At Team Escerich's end, we have a staunch opposition indeed. I think expect quite the show with *both* leaders taking to the field - give it up for aeromancer, Reiner Escerich, and his illusory ally, Vivienne Beau... God, that's a mouthful. Vivienne Beauvillier!"

Vivienne. Lucia hated Reiner enough, with his slicked, blonde hair and picturesque face, but that pointy-nosed snob really pissed her off. The way she held herself, so high and mighty, as if she were perfection incarnate. They were all the same, these groomed, little princesses - egocentric jerks living their perfect lives with their perfect faces. It was people like her that sickened Lucia to the core.

The final few horns slowly shook her from her trance of hatred. She clenched her fists, igniting her hands with flame as she stared directly into Reiner's eyes.

"Remember, they're looking to embarrass me," she said. "Either they'll draw this out or end it as soon as it begins. Be ready for both."

"I hope you're ready, ladies and gentlemen, because this is looking to be our most explosive matchup yet! Combatants, begin!"

Lucia looked down in confusion as the flames on her arms were dragged forwards. The air around them rushed to the opposite end and gathered before Reiner in a swirling vortex. Hasso raised a barrier as a funnel of gale force wind exploded across the battlefield. The shield was shattered in and instance and Vivienne thrust out her hand. Lucia's attempt to react was thwarted as the wind diverted to her, snuffing her flames and blasting her back.

She glanced aside to Hasso, who was reeling with his head in hands, fighting a mental war with Vivienne. This was a clever move, Lucia though - both her and Hasso were powerful with momentum, yet initially weak. Alas, it was also a particularly foolish move. They invested a lot of essence into the attack, it would surely have been a shame were it to fail…

Flames erupted from Lucia's feet and lashed across the battlefield, subducting the wind and setting the ground ahead of her ablaze. Her mouth became a smug grin as the force of the wind wavered, the heat of the fire sending it rising into the air. She whipped her right hand out and sent a bolt of crackling flame streaking towards Vivienne, who shrieked as her eyes slipped open. A jet of wind snuffed the firebolt with ease, but Vivienne's concentration had been momentarily shattered.

"You like to start big, huh?" Lucia laughed, her right arm exploding into flame. "Hasso… rain fire!"

A grin spread across Hasso's face as his hands throbbed with energy. While Lucia hailed firebolts upon Vivienne and kept their opponents occupied, he thrust his hands high and materialised a shard of light above his head. He took a deep breath and spread out his hands, splitting the projectile into two, then into four, then into eight. Lucia giggled maniacally as Reiner's jaws dropped, his smugness wiped away as he witnessed the dozens of head-sized blades arrayed against him. He loosed a blast of wind towards him, clashing against a torrent of flame. Lucia turned slowly to Hasso, her blazing fists raised.

"Focus down the girl!" she growled, launching into a sprint towards her panicking foes.

"Vivienne, stop him!" Reiner hissed as he conjured a swirling vortex of wind around him.

"I can't concentrate!" Vivienne cried, staggering back as another firebolt smashed the ground before her. She gasped as the shards of purple light shifted into motion, flicking out her hands .

Like a deluge of hail, Hasso unleashed his shardstorm with a thrust of his hand. One after another, they streaked across the battlefield and hurtled towards Vivienne's position. Though a tunnel of wind surged to meet them, it could destroy but a few. The first shard broke through and whipped past Vivienne, easily sidestepped. Alas, the projectiles reacted - they suddenly dove, slamming the ground before her and exploding with pulses of light that ripped up dirt and blasted Vivienne from her feet. The repeated explosions rang the ears of the crowd and blasted a veil of smoke across a fraction of the arena. As the last shard touched down, Hasso gasped for breath, his eyes flickering and nose dripping blood.

Reiner watched with his mouth ajar as the shroud began to clear, his teammate nowhere to be seen. His eyes darted into the smoke, where a yellow light began to flare in its midst. It soon became apparent that the encroaching shadow was *not* friendly.

"Your turn, Airhead!" Lucia roared, bursting from the smoke with her right arm ablaze.

The girl fell upon him, trailing fire as she cleaved her blazing hand towards him. A flick of Reiner's wrist saw the air around him rush into her path, slamming into her gut and driving her momentum to nought. He pushed out his hand and with a pulse of wind, sent her spiralling back from whence she came. A purple barrier materialised at her back and travelled with her, gradually slowing her descent until she slumped onto the ground.

"You really are mad, aren't you?" Reiner chuckled as Lucia scrambled to her feet. "I expect nothing less from a Severin - no strategy but raw aggression. It's no wonder your house was crushed by rebellion!"

Lucia winced at his words. "Big words for someone whose partner was just blasted to pieces," she sneered. "Hasso, let's kill this stuck up bastard!"

Her words were met with nothing, yet the audience gasped and gawked. The look on Reiner's face oozed cunning and deceit, his smug glare hanging upon her with unwavering confidence. Lucia glanced over her shoulder, where she watched Hasso's body fall limp, slender fingers pressed against the side of his head.

"How embarrassing!" Vivienne grinned as she withdrew her hand and let the boy sag to the ground. "You've so much bravado packed into that thick skull that you've barely any room left for brains!"

Lucia stared wide eyed at Vivienne as she drew her rapier. The girl that Hasso attacked must have been a decoy. Damn illusionists...

"You're as much a disgrace as the rest of your house," Vivienne sneered. "House Severin - nought but a gaggle of warmongers and psychopaths."

"Are you assholes going to fight me, or are you just here to make witty comments about my house?" Lucia growled.

"Nothing but violence on the mind…" Reiner smirked. "Of course, we'll fight you - we'll give our audience the entertainment they came for and crush your pathetic ego to dust!"

Lucia rolled her eyes. "God, you're dramatic… let's get on with this."

She whipped around and blasted Vivienne with a burst of flame. Her form warped and vanished as the flames washed over her, a smug smile on her fading face. As the doppelganger faded, Vivienne leapt from cover and lunged at Lucia with her rapier, its electrified tip gliding barely past her neck.

"Nice try!" Lucia laughed, flinging out her hand and firing off another blast. Her face dropped as her opponent's form vanished once again. "You little bitch…"

Vivienne skidded from behind a tree and made a thrust for Lucia's gut. Lucia grabbed the rapier, only for it to vanish in her grip. With an impatient growl, she planted her hand on the double's face and blew its head clean off.

"Someone's angry…" Vivienne sneered.

Lucia yelped as a prick in her back sent a jolt of electricity shooting through her body. She swung around and caught Vivienne's wrist in her grip, twisting her hand and forcing the rapier from her grasp. Pressing her palm against the girl's chest, Lucia detonated a compressed explosion that sent her flying back.

"You're fucking right, I am," Lucia spat, stamping down upon the rapier's blade.

"That sword was my father's!" Vivienne hissed. "You… you…"

A firebolt exploded from Lucia's hand and slammed into Vivienne's chest, toppling the girl onto her knees. As the wind began to pick up, Lucia turned to Reiner and raised her hands, meeting the incoming funnel of wind with a stream of fire. Stepping through the flames, she unleashed a fiery beam upon his position, chasing him into cover as she scythed it across the width of the arena.

"Yeah, run you bastard…" she muttered, wiping away the blood that slipped from her nose.

Reiner leapt from cover, gathering the air around him. As a thumping headache overcame Lucia's mind, she slid into cover and threw her back against the rocks. She buried her head in her hands as the wind passed over her, lying in wait while her essence recharged.

"Is it too much to ask what the hell your problem is?" she yelled.

"You're as ignorant as you are arrogant," Reiner sneered. "Does House Escerich not ring a bell?"

"Not in the slightest," Lucia groaned. "Why? What did the great Lord Viktor do to wrong yet another house?"

"This has nothing to do with your degenerate father," Reiner growled. He unleashed a blast of wind that smashed against the rocks, hailing Lucia with debris. "Lars and Juna Escerich. Remember them?"

"No!" Lucia snapped.

"Really? Because I vividly remember you *personally* executing them! Right before ordering a massacre of our garrison!"

Lucia's eyes shot wide open. "Shit…"

"But your men didn't stop at the garrison, did they?" Vivienne hissed from a concealed position. "You wanted to know what our problem is? Maybe the Butcher of Serren's Pass just needs to look herself in the mirror."

A wave of darkness overcame Lucia. She dug her fingers into the dirt, her breath becoming heavy. There were plenty of things in her life that she was not proud of, that she had shafted away into the depths of her mind. Serren's Pass was one of the worst.

"I was fourteen!" she insisted, leaping from cover and blasting another of Vivienne's doubles. "Your parents antagonised me and I lost control… I didn't mean for innocents to die!"

"You had no reason to take even one life!" Reiner spat, narrowly missing her with another blast. "But still, you set your dog of a captain on us!"

"He took advantage of me!" Lucia cried, her voice becoming slowly hysterical. "He knew I couldn't control myself and he used me!"

"It was your choice. *You* gave the order," Reiner growled. "Even without an ounce of your father's blood, you're still just the same as him."

"Shut up!" Lucia roared, throwing out her hands and firing off a colossal blast.

Reiner leapt from cover as an enormous gout of flame engulfed his position. Flames began to creep up Lucia's arms and embers drifted from her face.

"It always comes down to fire, doesn't it?" Vivienne grinned, strolling from behind. "The poor, little psychopath can't face her problems without trying to blow them away…"

Lucia whipped around and blasted her with flame, shattering the doppelgangers form.

"I'm afraid this is one you just can't hide from," Vivienne sneered, emerging from behind a distant tree. "You're stuck here with us. Trapped until you recognise the terrible sins you've-"

Another fiery blast obliterated the girl's form, only for another to step out of a nearby trench.

"Leave me alone!" Lucia begged, her legs beginning to quake. "I'm... I'm not a-"

"A monster? No, you're so much worse," Vivienne hissed. "Monsters kill out of necessity, to feed. You hurt people because it's the easy way out, because you're too scared to face the consequences of your own heinous actions!"

"No... you're wrong," Lucia mumbled, blasting the double with a feeble gout, barely shifting its form. "You're wrong!"

"You can't deny who you are," Vivienne smiled. "Nothing more than a twisted bastard, drunk on power and blood. You're not a monster - you're a murderer."

Lucia could feel her skin simmering, her mouth drying, her body trembling. Her breathing became ragged, strained by panic as it slowly became a fearful whimper. They were getting to her - it was exactly as they wanted but she was powerless to stop it. The anger that boiled within her was uncontrollable, completely unstable. She would have wept if she could have, for the thought of losing control truly terrified her.

"Stop... please, stop!" she cried, the confidence stripped from her voice and replaced with a fearful desperation.

"Look at her, Reiner. She's pathetic," Vivienne smirked. "Strip away all that ego and she can do nought but cry."

The ground at her feet began to blacken. Her armour began to hiss and whine, her skin to flicker with fire. She wrapped her hands around her head, shaking it back and forth in denial, yet only furthering the terror she felt. She didn't want to hurt anybody, not again. She didn't want to be the monster.

"I don't want to... please..." she mumbled, her body quaking as it began to ache and sting with pent up essence. "No... no, no, no!"

"She truly is insane!" Reiner laughed at the sight of the hysterical girl, reduced to a husk of her usual self. "It's no wonder her mother couldn't cope!"

Dragging her fingers through her hair and scorching it black, Lucia threw back her head and shrieked a scream of pure rage. Her whole body lit up with yellow light, blinding the audience as she flared bright as the sun itself. The ground set ablaze with lashing flames, spreading like wildfire across the battlefield. As her scream reached its peak, a storm of flame exploded from her body, tearing across the landscape in a gigantic, infernal cloud. The grass and trees were reduced to husks and the ground was upturned and scorched as her opponents scrambled desperately for cover.

And then, all was smoke. A choking cloud of dark smoke hung over the battlefield, yellow flames throbbing in its midst as they burned the scenery to ash. Vivienne staggered to her feet, her breath hoarse and her clothes sullied with soot. Her eyes widened as the crack of an explosion sounded amidst the veil.

"*Die!*" Lucia screamed as she exploded from the smoke, her whole body engulfed with vibrant flame.

She skidded to the ground and flung her arms overhead. Vivienne had barely a chance to move before Lucia's fists impacted the ground and swamped the two of them in a colossal blast, sending Vivienne flying off her feet and flinging her several metres over the arena's edge. Amidst the sound of crackling flame, Reiner could hear Lucia's manic breaths, her voice tortured by anger and pain. The girl's gaze snapped to him, her throbbing pupils like blazing stars amidst the fiery veil that cloaked her.

"You *are* a monster," Reiner gasped as he stumbled back, readying his spells.

"I know…" Lucia growled. Her contorted face was barely visible amongst the fire that engulfed her head, yet the violent lashing of the flames was enough to convey her fury.

She raised her hand, her whole arm aglow with white flame. With a crack that shook the Abenwood, she fired a ball of flame into his chest, faster than any arrow and hard as a falling boulder. No amount of wind could stop it. Reiner was engulfed in a blinding flash and hurled metres across the battlefield, slammed against the arena's invisible barrier and left smouldering in the grass. A silence hung over the battlefield as the thunder of Lucia's attack still echoed in the distance.

"Is that a disqualification?" Gerard whispered, seemingly forgetting the audibility of his voice. "Really? If you say so… Victory to Team Severin!"

Not a single person clapped. The audience simply stared down upon the battlefield, its surface torn almost completely asunder. Everything flammable was blazing with fire and much of the ground was scorched and warped by smoking craters.

Lucia stumbled to her knees, the flames flickering from her body as her anger slowly began to simmer away. Her veil of fire cleared and her eyes faded to an icy blue as she stared down upon the scorched bodies of her opponents, their skin wrought with burns and their clothes reduced half to ash. The flames around her face slipped away and revealed her grave expression, her mouth trembling as she breathed tortured and hysterical breaths. As the heat died away, blood finally began to flow from her nose and tears found their way out of her dry eyes. She buried her head in her palms as she snivelled and wept, consumed by a dark shame that sank her heavy heart. Her head hanging low, she scraped herself off the ground and trudged back towards her team.

Her anger was getting no better - if anything, it was getting worse. No matter how hard she tried, no matter how many times Hasso held her and told her it would be alright, she could never control it. It was hopeless. She was a monster.

Under the grim silence of the shocked crowd, she passed Josef and Matheas, who were retrieving Hasso from the arena. She could feel their eyes watching her - they feared her, just like everyone else. As for Hasso, Lucia was glad that he didn't have to see that. He had so much hope for her, it would have been a shame to see it go up in flames.

"Damn, you're intense!" Isadora laughed, leant eagerly forward on the bench. "I mean, I already knew that, but... wow!"

Lucia glanced up from the ground, utterly taken aback. "What?"

"What do you mean, *what*?" Isadora scoffed. "You blew up the entire arena! It was amazing!"

"You're... not scared?" Lucia mumbled.

"Nothing scares me," Isadora grinned smugly. "All these prissy nobles might be afraid, but I'm just impressed. You are *seriously* talented."

Lucia wanted to believe that, but there had been no talent in what she did. Hatred had given her that power, pure anger born of petty words. She stared for a moment at her admiring teammate, before storming off into the crowd, hiding her tears beneath her charcoal fringe.

"I can't believe they let that maniac in..." Josef sighed as he dumped Hasso onto the bench.

"I like her," Isadora smirked, slinging her bow over her back.

"You kidding? She's insane!" Matheas hissed. "You saw what she did to Ava! She's a danger to everyone here."

Isadora stared off into the crowd, a knowing smile plastered on her face. "Yes, she is... and that's why we're going to win."

James had not thought it possible, but he and everybody else had been stunned even more than the last time Lucia took to the field. The blast they had witnessed had been of unimaginable scale, the sheer intensity of Lucia's every move leaving the audience shaken to the core. It had been as terrifying as it was exciting, yet far more intimidating for James' team given the possibility of fighting the girl.

"Ahem... I, um... guess we're up," Zahra mumbled, rising slowly from her seat.

"We're dead," James sighed. "We're actually dead."

"Let's worry a-" Zahra broke suddenly into a fit of coughing, grabbing her potion and taking another swig. "Ahem. Let's worry about our inevitable deaths later, okay? Nearchos, can you get Emilia?"

Nearchos shook himself from his empty state of staring. "Huh?"

"Can you carry the child?"

He took a deep breath and glanced to Emilia, who had been dislodged by the quakes of Lucia's blasts and lay face down on the floor. Shuffling to his feet, Nearchos rolled her over with his foot, peeling her head from the puddle of drool beneath it.

"Do I have to?" he moaned, receiving dead expressions from his friends. "What if she wakes up?"

"Run," James smiled.

Nearchos reluctantly shovelled Emilia off the floor and they started down the stairs. They turned as thunderous footsteps shook the stands, watching as Bruno marched down the opposite steps to meet them.

"Zahra!" he boomed. She shrank away as he loomed over her, his shoulders stiff as he thrust out his hand. "May the best team win!"

Zahra stared blankly at his hand, fumbling for words. "Wh-what?"

"She doesn't do handshakes," James smiled, leaning around her and gripping Bruno's hand. "I'll go easy on you."

Bruno roared with hearty laughter as he marched back to his team. "Thank God! You had me quaking in my boots!"

James laughed anxiously and turned to Zahra as they continued on. She appeared utterly baffled.

"Handshake?" she asked.

"Yeah, you grab the other persons hand and shake it up and down," James explained. "It's, uh… it's like a show of respect. Or agreement. Or a greeting, I guess. Damn, handshakes are complicated…"

"Wouldn't a simple bow suffice?"

"Well, yes… but handshakes are more intimate. They're like… I don't know, do I look like a professor of culture?"

"With hair like that, a little," Zahra smirked.

Nearchos glanced down as a wave of warm air washed over his face. He jumped at the sight of Emilia's opening eyes, tripping on the arena's border and watching in horror as she toppled from his hands. James and Zahra stared blankly as she landed face down on the ground, limp and motionless.

"Oops…" Nearchos mumbled, wearing an apologetic smile.

"Um, is she okay?" James asked. "She's not moving."

Zahra buried her mouth in her palm. "Nearchos, I swear to the Goddess, if you just knocked her out…"

"I-I didn't… this wouldn't have happened if you didn't keep putting to sleep! Mind control is illegal for a reason!"

"Do you even know what mind control is?" Zahra hissed. "Wake her up or I'll give you a first-hand example!"

Nearchos took a careful step to Emilia's side and bent over her, gently grasping her shoulder and tipping her onto her back.

"Emilia?" he whispered. "It's time to wake up…"

As his hand drifted to her neck, her eyes snapped open. He shrieked as her foot lashed out and slammed him between the legs. Bloodlust in her eyes, she grabbed him by the shoulders and dragged him to the ground beside her before jumping up in a frothing frenzy.

"I knew it!" she growled, whipping her finger towards Zahra. "Who do you think you are?!"

"Tired," Zahra groaned. "Complain all you want, it was for the greater good."

Emilia watched with her mouth ajar as Zahra continued on, pulling James along with her.

"Hey! I'm talking to you!" Emilia yelled. "Don't you ignore me!"

Growling under her breath, she booted Nearchos' shin before trailing after them.

"Stupid losers…" she muttered, dragging her every step and flattening every flower she could. "Maybe, Emilia, this is why people don't like you… No. No, they're just jealous. They just wish they could be as perfect as me… Yeah. I mean don't I have? Gorgeous eyes, the most beautiful hair, power like which the world has never seen… They'll see. They'll all know how great I am once I gut that little swine of a-."

James and Zahra sniggered as Emilia slammed her forehead against the tree beside their bench. She staggered back and after a brief few moments of collecting herself, punched a hole through the trunk and slumped grumpily onto the bench. Nearchos limped behind her, collapsing at her side with an exhausted gasp.

"So, um… what kind of plan does our mighty leader have in mind?" James asked.

"Well, we'll hold off on our decision about the second round until Laurent gets back, but it doesn't look like we'll be seeing him for the first," Zahra said. "As for the first round-"

"I'm going first," Emilia hissed. "The Tarantis girl is mine."

"We don't even know if she's up first," James said.

"Yes, we do," Emilia sneered. "Why else would she be standing up?"

It was true - she and Harmodius were on their feet before their bench, where the rest of their team remained seated. Nearchos followed her vacant gaze to the podium, where Gerard conversed with the rest of the Tarantis household.

"Is anyone else a little on edge about taking her out in front of her entire family?" Nearchos asked.

"Leave that to me," Emilia grinned darkly. "I'll put that little runt in the ground!"

James chuckled quietly at the irony of her words. "Little ru-"

Emilia smashed the back of her hand across his face and with a gasp from Zahra, sent him toppling backwards off the bench. "Cram it!" she snapped, intensity in her voice the likes of which even she had never mustered. "I'm gonna show that stupid old man who's *really* got the gift! I'll tear that girl limb from limb and then... then everyone will have to believe me!"

Everybody turned awkwardly away as Emilia descended into a fit of maniacal laughter. James glanced across the arena at Caesia, concerned for her safety. The poor girl had no idea what she was in for.

"I'm not sure we should let Emilia fight her," Nearchos whispered.

"For her sake, I'd agree..." Zahra said. "But I don't think there's a person in the world who could fuel Emilia as much as her."

"You want to field her because she'll perform better?" Nearchos scoffed. "Zahra, think the ethics here! She'll destroy that girl!"

"If we can take anything away from the last round, it's that you don't win battles by playing nice. Emilia knows the rules and she wants to win - she's not going to kill anyone."

"Of course not!" Emilia smiled. "Not literally... does brain death count or will I need to stick to full body paralysis?"

"Just behave yourself," Zahra groaned. "Please."

"Yeah, yeah, of course..." Emilia chirped. "Now - if my knight in shining armour isn't here, I'll be needing a new mode of transport." She sprang to her feet and beckoned to Nearchos as she wandered into the arena. "Come, come, Water Boy..."

"You want *me*?" Nearchos scoffed.

"I need someone to propel me across the battlefield. You are the only one capable of this. You are coming with me."

Nearchos turned to Zahra with the deepest sigh. "Zahra?"

"She's right," Zahra said. "You might not like it, but you're the only other person who can get Emilia to the opposite end of the field."

"Judging by her last performance, I'm not sure if she needs the help," Nearchos muttered.

"The longer I endure their attacks from range, the less I can take it up close," Emilia said. "I might look invincible, but I have a limit. I don't expect to reach it, but it's a risk I'm unwilling to take."

It felt unnatural to hear Emilia admit her own mortality, but that did not change the truth of the matter. "Fine," Nearchos sighed, picking up his helmet and strapping it tight. "If she kills me, Nepheratae be my witness, I will haunt you all."

"Oh please, you don't have it in you," Emilia smirked. "You'd just follow them around and demand that they pick up litter and respect their elders."

The two of them marched onto the battlefield, leaving Zahra and James to chuckle amongst themselves.

"Nearchos!" Zahra called, her abrasive voice barely audible. "Keep in mind, Caesia has electromantic spells."

"Yeah, don't want you going the way of Laurent," Emilia laughed.

Nearchos nodded to Zahra and as his eyes shot past Emilia's he had to make a double take. "Wait, where are your glasses?"

"On the floor somewhere. That girl with all the spots cut them in half, remember?"

"Don't you need them?"

"No, they're purely for reading," Emilia said. "And the only thing I'm going to be reading today is the terror on that girl's face."

A horn sounded and plunged the site into silence as Gerard returned to the podium. "Hm… we have some interesting talent in this matchup," he mused. "It's Team al-Masir versus Team Lechner, two teams whose journeys have not been the smoothest, but have been fruitful all the same."

"Good thing I carried you all, huh?" Emilia whispered, jabbing Nearchos' side as he tried to ignore her.

"Team al-Masir is fielding a combination that we have not yet seen in action - their hydromancer, Nearchos Phokinas, and their biomancer and star teammate, Emilia Arrenni. This girl is certainly one to watch, totting the highest scores in both the race and monster stages *and* sporting perhaps the smoothest round of the combat stage thus far! With such an impressive track record, I'm sure we're all eager to see her in action."

Nearchos could feel Emilia's ego expanding, the look on her face becoming more and more smug with every word in her favour. It was annoying, but she had somewhat earned it.

"Standing against Team al-Masir, Team Lechner has chosen a curious duo - one of their evokers, Harmodius Alexidas, and their abjurer, Caesia Tarantis! With a pairing focused so heavily on defence, Team Lechner clearly knows what they're up against."

"Alright, let's do this, Water Boy!" Emilia growled, hardening her skin as the horns began to count down. "Keep the girl suppressed while I kill the shield guy."

"You know killing is against the rules," Nearchos sighed, unsure of whether the girl was joking.

She placed her hand on his arm and smiled up at him. "Don't you see I've got this tournament on my strings? I can do whatever I want…"

Withdrawing from his side, she glanced down into the pool of water gathering at his feet. He groaned as she warped her hand into the shape of a hairbrush and began carefully assessing her reflection.

"Oh, and if you eliminate the girl before I get to her... I'll meld that helmet to your head."

Nearchos shifted his gaze as far from her as possible. There was no point in strategizing, it would get him nowhere. He would simply have to rely on her savagery to win the day. If he could support her offensive well enough, they could come out of this on top.

Gerard's voice echoes across the battlefield as the final few horns sounded. "I know plenty of you are dying to see what these ladies can do, so we shall delay no longer. Without further adieu... combatants, begin!"

Emilia was gone from Nearchos' side in an instant, sprinting like a blur towards Harmodius as he summoned a shimmering, golden tower shield. Nearchos blasted her with a jet of water and sent her soaring across the battlefield, before turning his attention to Caesia. He threw out his arms and unleashed a thunderous lash of rushing water, firing it across the arena where it met a barrier of green light.

Nearchos looked aside as his water hissed and crackled under the heat of Caesia's barrier. Emilia was already upon Harmodius and was performing exactly as expected - the poor boy looked as if he were weathering a storm. Emilia sprang side to side, leaping into the air like a maniac as she cleaved her arms back and forth and rent ragged gashes through her opponent's shield. It was like watching an istrix savage a sheep.

"Caesia, *do something*!" Harmodius cried, not even able to lift his weapon under Emilia's barrage.

"I... I'm rather indisposed right now!" Caesia snapped, barely audible over the sound of crashing water.

Electricity surged into Nearchos' stream as Caesia smashed a lightning bolt into its midst. It travelled with ferocious speed down the jet, but flickered away as Nearchos ceased his blast. Unwilling to give the girl time to breath, he slammed his foot down and spread a new pool at his feet. With his ammunition prepared, he raised his hands and took hold of it. The water split into two streams, each tearing towards Caesia in a cascading pincer. Having barely recovered from the last blast, Caesia shook off her hands and thrust up a pair of shields in defence. The water crashed against them with a deafening crack, one that forced a distant whimper from Caesia as she braced against the impact.

"*Die!*"

Nearchos glanced down the battlefield and barely caught sight of Harmodius' shield before Emilia slashed it in two. The shield exploded into a shower of sparks and Emilia's other hand swept up from below. She battered Harmodius' spear aside and leapt into the air, cleaving her jagged arms over her head and smashing down upon his skull. Blood spattered her hands as they impacted his forehead and sent him toppling backwards, collapsing onto the ground motionless.

"Vera's mercy…" Nearchos sighed. At least Harmodius wasn't dead.

He turned back to his water jets as a crackling sound drew close. His eyes widened at the sight of the arcing green light rushing towards him, surging from the faces of Caesia's shields with terrifying speed. He ceased the blasts and staggered back, but he had reacted much too late. The last he saw of the battlefield, as energy surged into his body and dulled his mind, was Emilia laughing hysterically at him. His legs went numb and he collapsed to the ground, his vision swamped in black.

Emilia slowly recovered from her amusement, wheezing as her lungs ran empty. This was perfect - the girl had been left solely to her, and she got a kick out of Nearchos' elimination! As Caesia dropped her shield, panting for breath, she glanced to Emilia with widening eyes. She could see the insanity in the girl's face, a thirst for blood pulsing in her eyes. Emilia could smell her fear, for Caesia was terrified.

"*Say your prayers, you green eyed-*"

A bolt of pale green lightning slammed into her stomach, barely staggering her as she rooted her feet to the ground. A toothy grin spread across Emilia's face as she raised her jagged hands with an eerie chuckle. She launched into a sprint, leaping and bounding across obstacles as she raced for Caesia's position.

"What's your problem?!" Caesia cried as she launched another bolt to no effect.

Emilia did not answer, far too consumed in her own twisted thoughts. She waded through a hail of lightning as if it were nothing, bolt after bolt glancing off her rigid skin. Despite Caesia's panicked state, her every bolt struck Emilia's chest with pinpoint precision. Though she was hopped up on adrenaline, Emilia could feel her essence waning. Eager to finish the fight quickly, she fell upon her prey, swiping down with her bladed hands.

Caesia threw up her hands, her eyes squeezed shut as Emilia's hands struck her arms. Like nothing was even there, Emilia's fingers glided through Caesia's skin and out the other side, spitting green light and leaving not a scratch behind.

"What?!" Emilia scoffed as Caesia staggered away. "What the hell was-"

A shimmering barrier flickered to life at her feet. Emilia had barely time to register the glistening, green square before it jolted beneath her. The cheering audience paused in silence as she was launched off her feet and flung into the distance, her hardened body shattering rocks upon her impact against the ground. Caesia's arms slumped to her sides as she watched jagged stones avalanche over her motionless opponent.

"Victory to Team-"

The mound of rubble exploded in a shower of fractured stone as Emilia burst from its midst. "You think you're so much better than me?!" she roared, panting like a feral beast. "We'll see who's gifted *when I rip your scrawny, little arms off!*"

"What are- that's what this is about?!" Caesia scoffed, raising her arms in readiness. "Your essence is *red,* you dolt!"

"*Liar!*" Emilia growled through gritted teeth. As a shimmering barrier appeared ahead of her, she flung her hands overhead and with a chilling scream, cleaved them down and tore it in two.

Shield after shield rose in her path, each one shattered with a sweeping blow. Emilia relished the whimpers that slipped from Caesia's mouth with every swing, giggling as blood began to trickle from the girl's nose. Alas, she was blissfully unaware of her own leaking nostrils - each of them was running out of essence.

Such mortal problems were of no issue to Emilia, however. She smashed aside a final barrier and drew back her arm to strike at her prey. A sheet of green light stuttered to life at her feet, yet it was easily shattered with a simple pounce. This was it - victory.

"You little weakling!" Emilia laughed. "You're not worthy of that gift!"

Her fist obliterated the shallow remnant of a barrier and plunged into Caesia's cheek. Her jagged fingers smashed against the girl's face and send her spiralling backwards, a hail of blood spattering the ground before her. She collapsed against a rock and slumped to the ground, wheezing pathetically, while Emilia stood tall with a maniacal cackle. She thrust her arms open and embraced the silent crowd.

"Behold!" she roared, spinning around before them. "Your precious 'miracle child' is beneath me! I am the one! I have the gift! Me!"

They did not cheer... had they not witnessed her majesty? She stood before them in an eerie silence and followed their anxious stares to the ground at her feet, where pink pupils locked with green.

Caesia, barely conscious, raised a single finger, sheer desperation in her face as she charged it with energy. Emilia gasped and reeled back her arm, hardening her skin with all the might she could muster. A meagre lash of lightning spat from Caesia's finger and straight into the back of Emilia's throat, cutting her breath short and sending a surge of energy into her head. She blacked out almost immediately, toppling face-first into the grass with a pathetic thud.

"Victory to Team Lechner!"

James and Zahra watched from the sidelines with jaws dropped. Zahra cupped her mouth in her hands as Caesia's eyes rolled back and she fell flat in the mud. Even the audience hesitated to applaud, the two contenders utterly wiped out.

"That was… brutal!" James gasped, stiff at the tension he had just experienced.

"Yeah, poor girl," Zahra sighed. "She didn't deserve that."

"She still put up one hell of a fight!" James muttered. "I didn't think she had it in her."

"Nor did I, but that doesn't change what Emilia did… do you think we picked the right teammates?"

"Probably not, but we've gotten this far," James smirked. "Hopefully, she's got the killing out of her system."

"Here's hoping," Zahra groaned, burying her face in her palm. Emilia's display had been exhausting to watch.

Nearchos staggered to his feet and surveyed the blasted arena in a drunken daze. Bruno was hauling his teammates back to their bench on his shoulders, while Emilia still remained face down in the mud. He glanced to Zahra and James, who returned him a pair of awkward smiles.

"I suppose we'd better get Emilia…" James sighed, dragging himself from his seat. The two of them jumped up and wandered to meet Nearchos.

"What happened?" Nearchos mumbled, his voice groggy and slurred.

"Emilia went a little overboard," James smirked.

"Overboard is a grave understatement," Zahra muttered. "She was so focused on showboating and bullying the poor girl that she let her damned guard down!"

"Guess I expected nothing less," Nearchos sighed. "I'm… going to sit down. My head is killing me."

He collapsed onto the bench, watching with his head in hands as his friends retrieved Emilia's limp body. That had been an embarrassing round for him - for both of them, it seemed. It was foolish for him to let his guard down like that, he knew better. As someone whose field required quick thinking, such failure was shameful.

James and Zahra hauled Emilia back to their end and dropped her onto the bench.

"Well, Laurent still isn't here," James sighed. "Guess it's us next."

Zahra looked as if she were about to cry. "I guess so…"

"We're a point down, but we're still in this," Nearchos assured her. "If we can take out their next team with no losses, we can win this without a tie breaker."

"Ha!" boomed an approaching voice. "Child's play!"

The clatter of armour heralded Laurent's arrival. His shimmering armour bulged with fur that slipped from every seam, swelling his suit exponentially. One could vividly see the sweat pouring down his face behind the helmet's visor, where his eyes strained in discomfort.

"Fear not, my friends!" he announced, placing his hands triumphantly on his hips. "For I have insulated my armour! No longer will I be at the mercy of the electromancers!"

The three of them stared at him with both faces and minds utterly blank.

"You stuffed your armour with fur…" Zahra groaned. "In the summer?"

"Ha!" Laurent scoffed. "Heat is but another obstacle! I, Laurent of Gerasberg-"

He glanced down to the bench, his gaze hanging on Emilia as he heaved an exaggerated gasp, flinging his hands to his head.

"My lady!" he cried, rushing over and leaving Zahra with her face in her palm. "Oh, cruel fate, why did it have to be her?!"

"She's not dead, Laurent," Zahra muttered.

"Oh. What in Elaria happened to her?"

"She got blasted with lightning while she was busy showing off," James muttered.

"And I was not there to protect her…" Laurent mumbled, hanging his head in shame. "I will not let this happen again! I was negligent and sullied my vow to stand at her side - I pledge that no harm will ever come to her, lest my blood be spilt in her place!"

"You wouldn't have- Ah, whatever," Zahra sighed. "Now that you're here, I think it's best if you two go in as our next team."

"Me?" James scoffed. "Zahra, I suck!"

"You two… you'll do better than me," Zahra said. "Your abilities are so much more practical and I… there'll be less chance of me messing everything up again."

"Are you kidding? Zahra, you've done nothing wrong!"

"James, please, you don't have to lie to me," Zahra mumbled, a gentle smile on her face. "I've been nothing but a liability. You guys go and win this for us."

After a moment of confusion, James slowly began to chuckle, unable to believe what he was hearing. "Liability?" he laughed. "This morning, I could barely conjure a stick. In the space of an hour, you taught me better than any book or tutor ever could have. In what world am I better than you?"

"Okay, maybe I'm book smart, but I can't fight! I-I'm useless out there!"

"Like hell you are!" James laughed. "We'd have gotten nowhere in the race if it wasn't for you! Just use that big brain of yours. If *Lucia* thinks you're the smartest in the class, it's gotta be good for something."

"I-I can't!" Zahra urged. "I don't… I'm not…"

James waited silently as Zahra quickly dug herself into a hole. She had no means to refute him - no matter how much she put herself down, he was completely right.

"I'm not going anywhere," James said, crossing his arms in defiance. "Get out there and win."

Zahra's heart was racing, her mind melting. She stared across the battlefield as she slipped hesitantly from the bench, watching as Emeric trudged into the arena with Florence in tow. She had seen Florence at work in the Gardens - the girl was talented, but her spells seemed basic and fairly weak. Perhaps this wouldn't be that bad…

Bottling her breath, she started slowly towards the boundary, stiffening more and more with her every step.

"Beautiful day for a good scrap, hm?" Laurent bellowed as he jogged to her side, already panting for breath in the searing prison of his armour. "Suppose you're rather used to this glorious weather!"

She barely registered him, far too busy stressing herself out within her own bubble. With a muffled laugh, Laurent withdrew and took up his position, flailing his mace around with a series of heroic grunts and roars. As if the cheering crowds didn't make it hard enough for Zahra to concentrate.

"Moving on to the next round, we have two pairs that haven't quite shown their colours just yet," Gerard announced. "At Team al-Masir's end, we have enchanter Laurent Bouchard and illusionist Zahra al-Masir! We've seen little of them in previous stages and their fates in the last round were quite unfortunate, but I think we might be in for a chance to see them shine!"

"Fighting for Team Lechner, we have biomancer Florence Belveau and electromancer Emeric De Sardou! Another pair with little to boast, we surely have a battle underdogs on our hands! Who, I wonder, will triumph?"

Zahra took a deep breath, staring across at her opponents. Emeric was vacant as ever and Florence was flushed red with bottled breath, seemingly containing a breakdown. Despite having a nervous breakdown, the tiny redhead looked adorable with her puffed out cheeks.

"Now, Laurent-"

Her heart sank at the sight of the knight executing a flawless series of jumping jacks on the spot, warming himself up despite wearing an oven. Zahra sighed deeply and shook her head - this would be painful.

"Now, Laurent, be careful," she warned as she wrapped her blindfold over her eyes. "We're two-one down, but we can still get the win if we both remain standing."

"Worry not, Zahra," Laurent proclaimed, ceasing his warm-up and raising his weapon. "I have this all under control!"

"Combatants, begin!"

A lash of crimson lightning ripped through the air. Laurent threw back his head in a demeaning chuckle and whipped up his shield into its path. Red danced with purple in a violent flash before a bolt of crackling purple exploded back across the battlefield. Emeric barely gasped before it struck his shins, flooding his body with a surge of electricity and sending him toppling to the ground, a quivering wreck.

"To battle!" Laurent roared, raising his mace high and launching into a sprint towards Florence, who was totally frozen in horror.

Zahra watched at a complete loss as Laurent charged off into the distance. Never had she been so utterly blown away, nor had Florence. The girl stood quaking, breathing hysterically as her armour clad foe barrelled after her. Laurent drew close, reeling back his mace over his head, the weapon pulsating with shimmering purple as it accumulated power. This match was going to be over in seconds and Zahra hadn't even moved a muscle!

Florence screamed in terror as the knight fell upon her, throwing her hand aside as she squeezed her eyes shut. The ground beside Laurent shattered as a jagged, brown vine erupted from the dirt and lashed suddenly towards him. Zahra winced at the clang, his armour still ringing as he sailed through the air. Laurent struck the ground with a crash and tumbled out of the arena, wheezing pathetically as he rolled to a stop in the grass.

"Da'kra..." Zahra gasped.

Her head was spinning as her eyes darted erratically around the arena, while Florence slipped into cover behind the rocks, trembling with fear. She was alone, with no offensive capabilities and no defenders to stand between them. Her veiled gaze drifted to the bench, where James and Nearchos returned her reassuring smiles. They had no hope of a win now, but they could at least shoot for a draw - Zahra knew that she had to do this, for her team.

A visceral crack broke her train of thought. She staggered back as a vine exploded from beneath her and flailed sluggishly after her. The ground convulsed ahead of her as another breached the surface, narrowly missing her leg as she leapt out of its path. With not an idea what to do, Zahra ran for open terrain. It was time to reveal her trump card, but she needed to draw Florence out.

"Amani!" she called, much to the confusion of the crowd.

Zahra skidded around a rocky verge and onto a plain straight of grass. She would wait here until Amani arrived, in an open plane where she could remain vigilant and manoeuvrable. As she felt the drake draw close, her focused mind was blinded to the obvious. The grass at her feet lashed around her heels, dragging her to a halt, barely still standing. She glanced down, watching in escalating panic as the blades snaked further and further around her legs, consuming her feet and caressing her knees.

She squeezed her eyes shut, focusing her mind despite her fear. Failure was not an option - she had to persevere.

Her vision was overtaken by vibrant colour and glaring light and she gazed upon the battlefield from on high. From Amani's eyes, she could easily see Florence slowly moving closer, yet she had to keep her priorities straight.

"Mesae, Amani," Zahra smiled, masking all emotion behind a gentle tone. "Akantse."

Amani entered a nosedive, the air surging around her as the drake plummeted towards the grassy plane. Florence squealed and leapt for cover as the golden blur darted overhead, letting slip a high-pitched screech as she swept towards her master. A jet of slender flame erupted from Amani's mouth as she glided by, bathing the grass in melting heat and burning it away in but a second. Zahra leapt free, shaking her feet violently and patting out the flame that flickered on her boots. It was time to turn the tables.

"Amani, hefera!" Zahra barked, watching as the drake swept immediately around and darted towards Florence's position.

"Tha- that's not fair!" Florence cried as she sprang from cover and fled. She span around as the flap of Amani's wings drew close, thrusting up her hand in panic and ripping a vine from the ground.

The drake rolled carelessly aside as it whipped by, spreading its wings and diving upon her. A jet of flame slashed the ground before her, staggering her back as the stone splintered at her feet. Florence turned away, ready to run, yet came face to face with her incoming opponent.

"Sorry!" Zahra yelled as her fist connected with the girl's freckled cheek.

Florence stumbled away, clutching her cheek in one hand as she whimpered like an injured mutt. Zahra hesitated at the sad sight of the girl, tears trickling from her eyes as she gasped in pain. The ground cracked beneath them as Florence stiffened herself and rose upright. Her jaw clenched tight, her hands curled into fists - Zahra had just redefined

Florence's outlook on the battle, and now she would reap the consequences.

Zahra dodged aside as a vine thrashed by, slamming the stone with a brutal crunch. She had little time to recover before the next burst from the stone, glancing against her shoulder and sending her spinning. The first swung around and smashed into her back, jolting a sharp pain through her spine and shoving her back into the second vine, which swept narrowly over her head as she ducked low.

"Ama- Amani!" she gasped. Her breath fell short as a third vine slammed against her stomach, pumping the air from her lungs and battering her to the ground. "Miri vasir!"

In but a few seconds, the vines sagged around her, perfectly in sync with a piercing wail that echoed across the arena. Florence flailed her hands desperately as Amani fell upon her, snapping at the girl with her razor maw. Zahra staggered to her feet, watching with a wavering grin as Amani slipped behind Florence and grabbed her by the collar. With a thunderous flap of her wings, Amani swept the girl of her feet and dived back down, slamming Florence into the stone beneath the drake's full weight.

Coughing and spluttering, Florence tried to peel herself from the ground, only to cease her resistance as a jet of fire pummelled the stone beside her head. As the girl fell limp and buried her face in the ground, Amani reeled back her neck and bellowed a screech of victory.

"Victory to Team al-Masir!" Gerard roared, his words drowned by the erupting crowd.

A daze of swirling emotions came over Zahra as she stared blankly into the cheering crowd, a smile spreading across her face as she descended into a fit of ecstatic giggling. She did it - not only was she useful, but she won! It filled her with such joy, such wonder and excitement! All her hard work had truly paid off. She span around to the southern bench, where James nodded in prideful acknowledgement, knowing full well the doubts she had overcome. This was *her* victory - she had claimed the draw they needed to stay in the fight.

"Wow... y-you... you're really good!" Florence stammered, panting her every word as she scrambled to her feet. The girl was a quivering wreck, her skin blackened by dirt and her hair ragged with sweat.

"Are you okay?" Zahra asked, extending her hand to help.

Florence waved off her hand and wrenched herself upright. "I-I... I'll be alright," she smiled shallowly. Her quaking hand lingered on a bloodied slit that leaked from her forehead, but otherwise she was just absolutely filthy.

"You're sure?" Zahra insisted. "You're breathing a little funny..."

"Oh, I just… I just got a really bad stitch," Florence giggled. "I don't exercise all that much. It hurts my tummy."

"Well, you did a really good job," Zahra smiled. "You burrowed those things through solid rock!"

"Well, yeah, I-I guess… I mean, it's the only spell I know," Florence muttered. "I'm not very good… I think they gave me the wrong school of magic."

Zahra chuckled quietly to herself, taken aback by how Florence could demean herself after her amazing performance.

"And I get scared real easy," Florence sighed. "I'm afraid I'll get hurt and I really don't want to because pain… hurts?"

"You're doing great, Florence," Zahra assured her as she turned her back. "You'll be an amazing biomancer in no time."

Florence stared wordlessly after her as Zahra ran back to her bench. She glanced down at the drooping vines at her feet, contemplating a different outlook on her powers. Maybe she just needed to learn more spells, become more versatile. Maybe she wasn't as bad as she thought.

Blinding colour breached the veil of darkness as Emilia's eyes floated open. Her head was heavy, her thoughts jumbled and her breathing ragged. As the blur of her vision subsided, the figures of James and Nearchos became clear, just in time for Zahra to come sprinting into view and fling her arms around the both of them.

"What did I say?" James laughed.

"I know, I know, you were right!" Zahra cried joyfully. "I thought I- I just- it was… I did it!"

"Indeed, a magnificent display!" Laurent called, trudging back to the bench as stretching his beaten back. "And I do believe the crowd adored your partner."

Zahra glanced to the skies, watching Amani circle overhead. While the people of Athaea had a reasonable understanding of human mind control, it was the novekhiri alone who could touch the minds of animals - finally, she had gotten the display she so desperately needed.

"I do apologise, my friends," Laurent mumbled. "I was overzealous, it was foolish of me to attempt such a reckless charge."

"Yeah, but you also took out Emeric in the first two seconds of the fight!" James laughed. "You guys were amazing."

"And with our teams tied, we've still a chance at victory," Nearchos smiled.

His words sank slowly into Emilia's mind, her eyes widening as the dots connected. If the scores were drawn and her knight had been eliminated in that round, then that must mean... she lost? No. That was impossible, right?

"Tied...?" she mumbled, her voice a raspy whisper in her arid throat.

"Ah, my lady, you awaken!" Laurent said triumphantly. "The scores currently stand at a draw, thus it shall up to James of Abenfurt to win the day!"

Emilia's eyes fluttered while James visibly flinched at the thought. "We... lost the first round?" she stammered, turning drunkenly to Nearchos. "W- What did you do?!"

"What did- *me*?!" Nearchos scoffed. "It was you who was showing off all the damn time!"

"Yeah, you were too busy celebrating to notice you hadn't knocked Caesia out," James smirked. "She blasted you right down the throat, knocked you out cold."

The very concept of failure shifted Emilia's world on its head. She was meant to be gifted, she was meant to be invincible! As her heart sank with shame, all that filled her mind was a mist of pure rage.

"Where is she...?" Emilia growled, leaping up from the bench with a sudden surge of vigour. "*I'll kill that stuck up cretin where she stands!*"

"You will do no such thing, my lady!" Laurent demanded, much to the disbelief of his peers. "Senseless violence will solve nothing. You are better off besting the girl at a later date, in a means that displays more arcane prowess than simple brawn!"

"*NO!*" Emilia roared, grabbing her head in her hands as she twitched and trembled. "She has to die... I have to win!"

Her voice was twisted by desperation, her eyes shimmered with welling tears. It would have been a tragic sight were it not outright terrifying. Met with empty stares and speechless silence, the girl let slip a hysterical gasp and turned tail, scurrying into away with tears streaking down her quaking arms as she hid behind her hands. The rest of her team watched in total confusion and each turned to Laurent.

"You're not going after her?" Zahra asked.

"I believe Lady Emilia would benefit from some alone time," Laurent sighed. "I fear that my company inspires her less... rational side."

"I'm pretty sure Emilia doesn't have a rational side..." Nearchos muttered.

"Ah, you'd be surprised," Laurent smiled.

"Look, psychotic children aside, we've still got a round to win," Zahra said. "James, you ready?"

"Not particularly..." James sighed. "But what choice to I have?"

"That's the spirit!" Zahra chirped. "You can do this, James. Destroy that mass of muscle."

James clenched his fists as he stared across the battlefield, towards the opposing bench. The behemoth form of Bruno stood stretching before it, his muscles pulsing as he flexed his mighty arms. At his side was Caesia, who was barely awake and badly bruised around her right eye,. She stood flicking through a bland notebook, talking endlessly to her leader and pointing occasionally towards James. Despite her dazed state, the girl was strategizing - James needed to counter that advantage.

"Any advice?" James asked.

"Of course," Zahra smiled. "Bruno uses a suit of magical armour. That kind of spell requires a lot of effort to sustain and a fair bit of essence, even in the crude form he uses. You could probably wear him down if you keep up the pressure, perhaps focus on multiple points to strain his attention."

"Like taking out the monsters… you said his armour is crude?"

"It's uneven and rigid, as you'd expect from an apprentice level mage," Zahra said. "If you strike the edges, you might be able to shatter it. Maybe."

"Okay. Wish me luck, I guess."

Zahra took a deep breath as James wandered into the arena. Bruno was a jolly fellow, but he would not go easy. What came next, she knew might be hard to watch.

"Ladies and gentlemen, we have our first tie breaker battle!" Gerard declared, drawing a cheer from the audience. "Fighting on behalf of Team al-Masir is one we haven't yet seen on the field - al-Masir's evoker, James Serith!"

The crowd was almost silent at his announcement. Understandable, yet still a fair bit discouraging. Sucking in his doubt, James checked the straps of his gauntlets in an effort to distract his mind.

"And it looks like Team Lechner is fielding their leader for this fight - Bruno Lechner. We've seen his armour in action and he looks a promising one indeed, but how will his defences fair in this clash of evocation?"

As the horns blared and the countdown began, Bruno stuck up his hand and waved across the battlefield.

"I'll be honest, James, I didn't expect it to come to this!" he called. "Your team has outdone themselves."

"I could say the same of yours," James smiled. "And I didn't expect to see you here, of all people. Figured your place was in a two-v-two fight."

"Well, in the event of a tie breaker, I wanted someone reliable in place to bring it home. My teammates are talented, but they've not got the staying power."

"Fair enough…" James sighed, loosening his wrists. "May the best man win."

Bruno grinned widely, clenching his fists and tensing his muscles. "Indeed."

The crowd fell silent as the blaring horns ceased. Bruno thrust out his hands and James closed his eyes, both waiting for the same two words to sound.

"Combatants, begin!"

While Bruno's body was consumed by red light, James pulled his left arm to his chest and summoned his shield. Whipping his right hand aside, he summoned energy into his grip and warped it into shape. With a determined grin, he opened his eyes and glanced down at his weapon.

"Uh... sword?" He stared blankly at his hand as the crude shape of its blade shifted out of shape and dispersed into the air. "Hello?"

He flicked his hand out again, gathering his essence before watching it vanish before his eyes. Watching as Bruno advance, he growled under his breath and flailed his hand about desperately.

"Come on, come on!" he hissed, staring up at his incoming foe. "Damn it!"

The impact of Bruno's fist against his shield reverberated through his arm, quaking him to the bone as he staggered back. Bruno was cloaked in energy, nought but his eyes and palms exposed by his rigid armour. James was so horribly out of his league.

As the pressure intensified, he had no choice but to fling out his arm and summon his baton, drawing it to his shield as Bruno continued his assault. One blow after another hailed his shield, interweaved with an occasional right hook that was barely fended off with a flail of his baton.

"Wake up, James!" Bruno laughed. "You'll get nowhere hiding behind that puny thing!"

Another strike battered his shield and with a dark growl, James raised his baton high and slammed it down over the withdrawing fist. His attack struck Bruno's gauntlet with a bang, driving it into the ground and barely dulling its glow. While his opponent dragged his fist back, James swung the baton for Bruno's head. A shiver shot up his spine as his wrist landed in a heavy grip. Bruno twisted his arm and locked him in place, reeling back his fist with a hearty chuckle.

The impact of Bruno's punch rang through his forehead, a wave of pain that left behind a swirling daze. James' disoriented eyes drifted across the arena as he stumbled drunkenly about, barely able to stand. Bruno's name was on the mouth of every man and woman in the audience, all cheering for his victory. They loved him, why wouldn't they? He was amazing. James was nothing close.

His attention shifted to his bench, to his friends. Where Nearchos and Laurent sat in anticipation, Zahra stood at the very edge of the arena. The look on her face was one of determination, an assuring smile despite the worry in her eyes. She had worked so hard for this, even taken the time to help James where nobody else cared to. For her sake and that of his team, James had to win this.

He closed his eyes, digging in his feet and pushing his hands together as Bruno charged after him. Energy flowed to his palms and he drew them apart, pushing them out to meet the meteoric descent of an armoured fist.

A loud crack punctuated the connection the blow. Bruno smiled a satisfied grin as he watched his gauntlets grind against the warped blade of a scarlet sword. The weapon flickered and shifted with instability, yet it held fast against the weight of his strike. James slid his blade aside and leapt out of Bruno's path, drawing his sword to his shield and taking in a deep breath.

"Ha! That's more like it!" Bruno laughed, loosening his arms as he readied for a real fight. "Now, we're in for a *real* fight!"

James had no time to be terrified - he had to be smart about this. He quickly analysed his foe, picking out possible weak points and putting together a plan. As Bruno leapt at him, he sidestepped the cleaving blow and thrust his shield up into Bruno's wrist, smashing into the energy field and dulling its glow. A swift follow-up caught James off guard, barely caught with his blade yet clipping his side as the fist careened away.

An uppercut glanced off his shield as he backed off, before following up suddenly with a jab at Bruno's left shoulder. The tip of the blade slashed the armour with a dull crack before an arm swept it aside. Bruno continued his aggressive assault, but the sword gave James the range and agility he needed to ward off his opponent's attacks and slip in the occasional jab and slash, each targeted at the arms. The goliath barely seemed to notice the gradual dulling of his armour around his joints.

After a full minute of sparring back and forth, Bruno grabbed the edge of James' shield and thrust it aside. His left hand swung around to the side, yet his wrist was caught by the edge of the blade. Shoving the arm back, James stepped close and thrust his shield into Bruno's other wrist. He grinned as the dull armour cracked, giving away with a feeble hiss and dispersing his gauntlet into the air. As the goliath staggered back, James flung around his sword and smashed Bruno's left wrist once again, obliterating his other gauntlet. A cheer rose from the crowd as he clenched his sword in both hands and cleaved it down upon the dazed brute. The blade crashed against his right shoulder and in a sudden flash of red light, the armour cloaking Bruno's arm shattered and dispersed, triggering a collapse that saw half of his chest suddenly exposed. As Bruno shook himself off, his helmet began to flicker and warp, fading slowly in and out of reality.

"Ah, there's a lot more to you than meets the eye, James!" Bruno laughed. "Let's see how you handle this!"

Bruno thrust his hands out to either side and dispelled much of his armour in a blinding flash. His helmet became suddenly stable, while the energy that returned from his legs reformed quickly into a new pair of gauntlets, as well as returning to his knees as pads. He raised his fists and advanced towards James, an eager smile on his cheeks.

Once again, he brought down both hands from above. James moved to easily block the strike with his blade, yet he found his sword caught between Bruno's hands and kneepad. In a sudden motion, his foe raised his hands and brought them back down, smashing the blade over his knee. A burning pain shot through James' head as his sword exploded into sparks and he stumbled back. His eyes fluttering, he barely caught an incoming punch inches from his face, pushing it aside with his shield and backing off towards the arena's edge.

With renewed prejudice, Bruno launched a flurry of cleaving punches, hammering at James' shield as he retreated. He could barely keep the thing raised under the volley of colossal blows, but they clearly were not meant for breaking his defences, so much as draining his essence. It was a battle he could not sustain, but one he had no other choice but to fight - with both of his hands reinforcing his shield, he hadn't the time to summon a weapon.

As he took cover behind his shield and weathered another meteoric blow, a series of erratic motions in the audience caught James' eye. He stared blankly at Brooke as she flung her left hand back and forth like some kind of lunatic. After a few moments of failed communication, she rolled her eyes and pointed impatiently at her left wrist. James glanced down at his shield, his mouth falling open as he understood what he must do.

Bruno's next attack found the face of James' shield and was swiftly shoved aside. Before the next hit could land, James slammed his shield into Bruno's chest and staggered him back. Quick to recover, Bruno shook himself off. He gasped as James' shield came hurtling through the air towards him. It glanced off his helmet, shattering it into sparks and sending him reeling in a daze.

James whipped his hand high and summoned his baton, charging after his foe and throwing out his other to return his shield to his wrist. With a bang that echoed across the arena, he slammed the baton against the shield, propelling it into the side of Bruno's head. His opponent stumbled back, swaying groggily as James' shield cracked and splintered into the air. With a defiant roar, James dispelled his baton and lunged at Bruno, flinging his arms around the goliath's waist and barging him back. Like a crumbling tower, Bruno toppled meteorically into the grass, while James fell to his knees and collapsed just short of his enemy's feet. His arms gave out from under him and he fell flat on his face, his hair caressing the arena's edge.

"An astonishing victory from Team al-Masir!" Gerard declared over the victorious blaring of trumpets. "Ladies and gentlemen, we have our finalists!"

James scraped himself from the ground, blood dripping from his nose, and glanced with the widest of smiles into the thundering crowd. His gaze was obscured as Bruno stumbled to his feet, laughing heartily as he stretched his back.

"A glorious battle indeed!" he chuckled, trudging to meet his victorious opponent. "That was some impressive stuff, my friend."

"Thanks," James sighed. "You're not mad about losing to a novice?"

"Pft, novice… talent isn't about knowing the best spells, its about knowing how to use them!" Bruno declared. "And you, my good man, used them to incredible effect." He looked downfield to his bench, smirking at the sight of his sulking team. "Looks like some hugs are in order… good luck in the final - I'll be rooting for you."

With a nod and a warm smile, James watched as Bruno wandered away. He didn't want to think about the final, not yet. What mattered in that moment was that his victory was celebrated. He span around and conjured up what little might he had left to run back to his bench. His team was up on their feet in applause, Laurent in particular raising his hands to the heavens in ovation. As he drew close, his legs went slowly to jelly and he collapsed right into Zahra's arms.

"That was incredible!" Zahra gushed. "You- you actually did it!"

"You doubted me?" James spluttered, watching as blood trickled from his nose and onto Zahra's shawl. "Ugh, I can't feel my arms…"

"Well, this is certainly a cause for celebration!" Laurent declared, throwing his arms wide. "Bring it in, my friends!"

His silvered arms enveloped the rest of his team, pulling Nearchos into a group hug. The moment was fleeting however, as James and Nearchos leapt back at the sting of Laurent's armour against their skin.

"Oh my- get off, get off!" Zahra cried, shoving Laurent away as she stumbled back. "Your armour is boiling!"

Laurent glanced down and prodded his gauntlet. "Ah, so it is. I suppose a simple acknowledgement of our victory will suffice."

"Oh no, we're celebrating alright," James grinned. "How does drinks sound?"

"I say save it for tomorrow," Nearchos said. "As crazy as she is, it would be a shame to celebrate without Emilia."

"I'll ensure she is in tip-top shape!" Laurent declared. "Shall we call it... tomorrow after dinner?"

"I can do that," Zahra smiled. "I don't drink, but I'll be there."

"Then it's settled," James said. Tomorrow was fine - they had the whole weekend to themselves before the final. "So... can someone carry me home? No?"

"No," Nearchos smirked as the group turned their backs.

"That's fine. Totally fine... I'll just stay here for a bit. You know, rest my legs and all that. Don't feel like you have to wait."

Chuckling quietly to herself as they left James in the dust, Zahra glanced back over her shoulder. "Hey," she smiled. "I'm proud of you."

"Right back at you," James smirked, barely lifting his hand as he attempted to wave her off. "See you tomorrow."

Watching his team go, he leaned back of the bench with a deep sigh. It felt surreal, but they had won. He had won. Despite the odds stacked against them, they had triumphed and now, they had a shot at victory. Never had he expected to come close, but here he was. All that was left in their way was Team Severin.

"That was amazing."

James barely flinched at the surprise, having been jumped one too many times over the past few days. He turned with eyebrows raised to Brooke, who had slipped onto the bench in an astonishing feat of stealth.

"Oh, uh... thanks," James laughed uneasily. "You really bailed me out there with the whole... um, shield thing."

"Ah, that was all you," Brooke smiled. "Well, I guess it was me a little. Still, you got him! Honestly, I didn't think you stood a chance."

James looked awkwardly to the ground, chuckling under his breath. He looked back up at Brooke, whose face had dropped and drained of colour.

"Oh no, I didn't mean it like that!" she cried. "I-I don't- you, I just... sorry."

"Didn't mean it like what?" James smirked.

"Oh, I... I thought you thought that I thought you weren't very good... which you are! Very good, I mean, not very not good."

"Okay, let's just start this conversation over. Thanks for the help."

It took a moment for Brooke's mind to process the restart, her eyes staring blankly into the void. "No problem!" she suddenly chirped. "I mean, I'm technically not allowed to help you... but you helped me, so it's fine!"

"Is that how it works?"

"Well... no, but I think from a moral standpoint, the two cancel each other out," Brooke said, her eyes darting about as if distracted. "So, final in two days. You ready?"

"I guess," James sighed. "But, if it's all the same to you, I'd rather not think about it right now. Better I relish the victory."

"Yeah, of course! I'm sorry, I just thought you would… I was trying to… that's fine. I'm sure you'll do great anyways."

"Are you feeling alright?" James laughed. "You sound a little bit… a little…"

"Flustered? No, no! Not me… nope. I-I'm just tired, not thinking straight. I need a lie down! Bye!"

James watched at a loss for words as Brooke slipped from the bench and hurried away. "Uh… bye?" he mumbled. What was that about? She was always weird around people, but that seemed like a whole new level - may she was just tired. The day had been hard on her, after all.

He peeled himself slowly from the bench, surveying the arena as the audience filed back to the festival grounds. To think that only a year ago, merely joining the College seemed an impossibility, yet there he stood. In a place so alien, so out of his league, he had found not only belonging, but purpose. Now, all that was left to do was to take that final leap - to win.

Chapter Nine - The Problem Child

A blast of warm breath shook Zahra from her groggy state as it deflected off the pillow in which her head was entrenched. After the day she'd had, the sleep that followed had been truly euphoric - perhaps a little too much, considering the sunlight that spilled from atop her curtains. She wrenched herself upright, only to notice a weight upon her legs and heaved a heavy sigh.

Merely budging her leg did nothing to shift Amani, who was curled up on her bed, hissing quietly in her slumber. Zahra smiled a sweet smile, but was nonetheless determined to escape. She propped herself up and reached out, running her fingers gently along the drake's golden scales and up her neck.

"Amani… Amani?" she whispered, caressing the drake's head in her glowing hand. "Skei."

Amani's eyes fluttered as the slender spikes along her back pricked, her head swaying slowly to meet Zahra's smile. Zahra giggled as the drake stumbled drunkenly to her feet, chirping gleefully at her master's awakening.

"Ka, Amani," Zahra grinned. Her voice was still gravelly and her throat sore, but it at least didn't hurt to talk. "You mind getting off me?"

With a reluctant whine, Amani leapt off the bed and beat her wings, sailing gracefully to the top of the wardrobe, where she perched in waiting. Zahra swung her legs out of bed and yanked open a drawer, scraping up a hakhmat fruit. She toyed with the soft, green ball for a moment before tossing it to Amani, who caught it in her jaws and ravenously gulped it down, spewing yellow droplets of hakhmat juice all over the wardrobe doors.

While Amani guzzled her food, Zahra jumped out of bed and threw on her shirt as she wandered to the window and flung open the curtains. The sun was already sinking in the sky, about halfway to the horizon.

"Ala'mir, how long was I out?" she groaned, glancing to Amani. "What happened to waking me up at six?"

Amani tilted her head and chirped quietly. Shaking her head, Zahra looked herself in the mirror with a sigh. Her hair was a frizzy mess, draped over her face and down to her shoulders. Her eyes hung barely open, choked with sleep and red around the sockets.

"Amani, fetch some water, will you?" she mumbled, waving her hand in the drake's direction.

She smiled as Amani sprang from the wardrobe, clenched her claws around a bucket and darted out of the window. Zahra slumped back onto the bed, her gaze drifting lazily around the room as she awaited her drake's return. The dorm had become a bit of a mess lately - relative to usual, at least. Books on arcane theory and illusion magic had piled up in stacks upon every item of furniture, towers of battered tomes and loose parchment. The variety of plants that littered her room were sagging from neglect, their vibrant petals dulled and leaves shrivelled. The hakhmat bush was fine at least, perfectly acclimated to months without rainfall.

The hammering of a fist against her door snapped her out of her trance. Sliding hesitantly to her feet, she clawed her trousers off the back of her chair and hopped into them as she edged towards the door.

"One minute!" she called as the door thundered once again.

She grabbed her hair in her hands and dragged it back into a crude ponytail, wrapping it tight as she jammed a foot into one of her boots. Stumbling to the door with her right foot stuck halfway into her boot, she swung it open with an awkward smile.

"Laurent!" she chirped, leaning against the doorframe and obscuring her foot behind the door. "You checking to see I'm alive?"

"No, I… I need your help," Laurent mumbled. She had never seen him so tense, nor with such conflict in his eyes. "It's Emilia."

"Se gaal tagar…" Zahra groaned. "What has she done now?"

"That's just it - I don't know," Laurent said gravely. "I can't find her anywhere."

"She's probably just off having a tantrum somewhere," Zahra sighed, edging slowly back into her room. "I wouldn't worry about it."

"Zahra, please," Laurent urged. "I just… you'll understand if you see for yourself."

Sagging in defeat, Zahra wiped her hand down her face and groaned impatiently. "One second," she moaned, slipping behind the door and slamming it shut. "Why me…?"

She slumped back against the door and stared emptily to the heavens. She had barely woken up and suddenly, she was tied up in another episode of Emilia's antics. Amani fluttered through the window, sloshing water onto the carpet as she lay the bucket down on the ground and looked up at Zahra with her teeth bared.

"Ugh… could you water the plants while I'm gone?" Zahra muttered, adjusting her boot and wiping her eyes. "Please?"

Amani narrowed her eyes and hissed venomously, yet she quickly relented and began nudging the bucket towards the nearest plant pot. A smirk on her face, Zahra whipped open the door and stepped out into the hall.

"Alright, let's go," she sighed. "You think Emilia's missing?"

"I'm positive," Laurent said. "She wouldn't just disappear like this, not so close to the finals."

Zahra buried her head in her hand, still half asleep. As much as Laurent partook in Emilia's childish behaviour, he took his protection of the girl very seriously. She supposed that his radical assumption would likely not be baseless. Thus, they set off for the red dorms and Laurent explained to Zahra the questionable situation at hand.

"And just because Emilia has trashed her room and wasn't there when you turned up, you think she's missing?" Zahra smirked as they ascended to the second floor. "Don't you think you're overreacting?"

"I assure you, I am not," Laurent muttered. "Whether she has ran away or... worse, something is afoul."

"I still think you're being irrational," Zahra sighed. "Even if Emilia *has* ran away, she'll be back before you know it."

Laurent was eerily silent as the approached Emilia dorm. The door was bent and fractured, hanging barely on its hinges. As Laurent swung it open, Zahra stared with horror into Emilia's devastated room.

The walls were wrought with gashes, rent through the brickwork like butter. Shredded clothes and splintered wood littered the carpet, cluttering the ground surrounding a toppled wardrobe. Her bed was in two halves, cleaved straight down the middle, its torn bedding cast to the ground.

"Goddess above..." Zahra gasped. "As bad as this looks, Laurent, I'm pretty sure this is all Emilia's doing."

"Of that, I have no doubt," Laurent sighed. "But Lady Emilia goes nowhere without me, or without me knowing at least."

"I think you're being a little paranoid," Zahra muttered, picking up and assessing a small portrait of a white feline creature.

"I am not," Laurent growled. "Something is afoot, Zahra, I'm certain."

"Alright, well... say that she has gone missing - are we thinking she ran away or...?"

"As distraught as my lady was at her defeat, I simply can't see her running away," Laurent muttered. "This tournament means too much to her, she would never miss the final."

"Fair enough, but let's not jump to any conclusions," Zahra said. "We'll have a look around, see if we can find anything. If something does come up... I don't know what we'll do."

She glanced around the room, baffled by the thought of where to begin. Few objects lay unbroken, most buried beneath shattered furniture. As she wandered the room, struggling for analysis, she came to a stop before a massive string instrument.

"That's a big lute..." Zahra muttered, brushing dust from its mahogany hide.

"*That* is Lady Emilia's cello," Laurent said. "It's fortunate that it survived her tantrum, I understand they are rather expensive."

"How... isn't she a bit small for that thing?"

"She does require a stool," Laurent muttered. "You see, there it is. Right by... the window."

The two of them glanced to one another, both struck by a gentle breeze as they edged towards the window. They had barely noticed at first, but the window was empty of glass. Zahra slid the stool aside with her foot and crouched by the windowsill, where a sparse layer of glass shards sprinkled the brick.

"This wasn't broken out of rage," Zahra mumbled. "Looks like Emilia left through here."

"But why go through the window?" Laurent asked. "What was stopping her from leaving out the front gates?"

"I might put it down to paranoia," Zahra mused. "She is a bit... deranged."

"My lady is... unstable, but she is no fool," Laurent insisted. "I dare say, we might have a kidnapping on our hands, or an attempt at the very least."

"I suppose you could be right... maybe she escaped. Either way, she's probably long gone."

"Zahra... I-I have to find her," Laurent urged. "If she is in danger... then my honour is too. I made a vow to protect her and damn it, I won't let her come to harm! I can't."

"Look, let's not get too hasty," Zahra insisted. "We should alert the faculty. They'll call in the battlemages and have this dealt with in no time."

"And what if the perpetrator is a member of College staff? We have no idea the nature nor motive of the situation - we have to treat this with utmost care."

"Seriously now, you're being irrational," Zahra sighed. "Why would a member of the College faculty want to abduct Emilia?"

"Lady Emilia has made a fair few enemies in her time here, not to mention the thousands who have been wronged by House Arrenni. I can think of a great deal of people who might have a bone to pick."

Zahra buried her face and groaned into her hand. "We'll run it be the others. Nearchos is pretty rational, he might know what to do."

Laurent pursed his lips. "Don't you think Nearchos might be a bit *too* rational."

"Oh, absolutely," Zahra muttered. "Still, we need to talk to them. You and I shouldn't be doing this alone."

With a reluctant nod from Laurent, the two of them made for the dining hall, where they would no doubt find their friends.

Nearchos sat twiddling his fork, staring blankly at the red tablecloth as James chattered away. It seemed a boon when they had been allowed to mix essence groups in celebration of the upcoming final, but he had found himself sidelined even by his friend. Brooke had been the centre of James' attention for the last half hour - the two of them seemed to have become fast friends since the week began.

"Honestly, it's way more straight forward than it looks," Brooke insisted.

"You fly around on a disc while throwing two smaller discs that you can control with your mind, concentrating on both flying and perfectly deflecting them off surfaces!" James laughed. "How is that straight forward?!"

Brooke giggled behind her hands. "Okay, okay, maybe it's not *that* simple..." she chuckled. "But each little bit is really easy. There's just a lot of moving parts."

"Okay, then teach me," James said.

"You want- It's not that simple."

"Now see, you keep telling me it's easy... and then you say it's complicated."

A blank look on her face, Brooke took a deep breath and gathered herself. "Right, let me explain - it's not hard to make the disc levitate, nor to make it move. Everything is really easy to do, but the hard part is making it all work at the same time."

"Because you've got to cast like... ten spells at once?"

"Eh, six or seven," Brooke muttered. "It takes a lot of practice. I've been working on this and nothing else for years."

"And how hard will it be for me to learn this?"

"Very. Especially starting from such a low level," Brooke said. "No offence, of course! Y-you're doing great for someone... for a person who..."

"Can you teach me or not?"

Brooke stared at him through wide eyes, her mouth ajar. "What?"

"I want you to teach me," James smiled. "I mean, who else is going to do it?"

As Brooke fumbled for an answer, she glanced over his shoulder, where Zahra and Laurent came marching into the hall.

"James, Nearchos!" Zahra called, hurrying to their sides. "We need to talk."

"About what...?" Nearchos asked. "Is something wrong?"

"There's a problem with Emilia," she whispered. "I'd rather keep it private."

185

James made a deep sigh as he began to shuffle along the table. "Sorry," he said to Brooke, who simply smiled and stared down at her food.

He and Nearchos moved to the very end of the table, where Laurent and Zahra joined them. Zahra nodded to Laurent, who sucked in his gut and clear his throat.

"Gentlemen… we believe that Emilia may have been kidnapped."

"Theoretically!" Zahra interjected.

"Kidnapped?" Nearchos scoffed. "That's… that's a wild conclusion to jump to."

"She's vanished without a trace, seemingly out of a broken window," Zahra said. "Laurent is adamant that she can't have run away. He thinks that this might be an attack on House Arrenni."

"If I wanted to attack House Arrenni, the cousin of a cousin wouldn't be my first choice," Nearchos muttered. "If someone has taken her, it must be for a reason specific to Emilia herself."

His eyes widened as he exchanged glances with the rest of the group. "You don't think…"

"Her essence," Zahra groaned, burying her face in the table. "Ala'mir, some idiot must have fallen for that stupid act!"

"We should report this to the guard," Nearchos said.

"No way," James warned. "If this has to do with her essence, the person responsible must still be in the city. Hell, they could even be part of the College faculty!"

"Exactly," Laurent said. "We need to proceed with caution, see what we can figure out on our…"

He trailed off, sighing as Lucia stalked over to their table, the rest of her team following loosely in tow. The rest of Team al-Masir collectively groaned at her approach, drawing from her a patronising snigger.

"Well, well… having a little team meeting, are we?" Lucia sneered. "I've gotta say - I'm almost impressed. You lot are probably the last team I'd expected to reach the final."

"Not now, Lucia," James moaned.

"What, would you rather I wait till the short girl is here?" Lucia chuckled. "Surely, she's not still crying over that embarrassment of a fight."

She grinned ever wider as Team al-Masir tried to ignore her, leaning further in and planting her hands on the table.

"I wouldn't blame her. To win so much glory and be beaten by, of all people, Caesia Tarantis," Lucia laughed. "You could kill that weed with a feather."

"Seriously, piss off!" James hissed.

Lucia was visibly taken aback by his outburst. "God, what has you so riled up?"

"We've lost track of Emilia," Zahra groaned. "Laurent can't find her anywhere and we think there's a chance she's been taken. Now, if you would kindly leave us alone and let us deal with this, that would be *wonderful*."

"So, what you're saying... is you're a teammate down," Lucia mused. "We can't be having that now, can we?"

"Wait, you're not-"

"I am," Lucia said, turning to the team at her back. "If you jokers don't want a part in this, scram."

Josef glanced to Matheas, the two of them exchanging pained sighs. "Lucia, we have a final to plan for," Josef hissed. "You can't just go off and-"

Lucia waved her hand and watching smugly as Josef's food caught fire. He dropped his tray to the ground with a frightened gasp and, grabbing Matheas by the sleeve, stormed off.

"Cowards!" Lucia barked after them. " Isadora, you onboard?"

"Sure, sounds fun," Isadora chirped.

Lucia nodded and turned back to the others. "Shove it, Lightning Rod. I'm sitting down," she growled, pushing Laurent along the bench. "Go on, what happened?"

"We think Emilia has been kidnapped," James said. "Problem is, we have no idea where to start looking."

"We don't want to go to the battlemages or the faculty incase the kidnappers have ears on the inside," Zahra said.

"Smart move," Lucia muttered. "But it sounds to me like there's a quite obvious conclusion here - Shorty practically tortured the Tarantis girl right in front of her father. I've met the man and let me tell you, he takes no prisoners."

"You think House Tarantis orchestrated this?" Zahra mused. "It makes some sense, but Lord Tarantis didn't strike me as the type for this sort of thing."

"You're right, disappearances isn't really his style," Luca said. "But it does happen to be *Lady* Tarantis' style. That woman has a ruthless side, believe me."

"And... how do we get her back?" James asked.

"That's a good question..." Lucia smirked, glaring across the room. "I'll be right back."

"Lucia, wait!" Hasso snapped, scrambling to his feet and hurrying after her as she marched towards the door.

"Here we go..." Zahra muttered. She slipped from the bench and gestured the rest of the group along. This would at least be worth spectating.

Lucia stormed across the hall and ground to a halt before the rickety, green tea table in the darkest corner of the room. Her shadow fell across Caesia Tarantis, who glanced up from her notebook and sighed longingly. Half obscured beneath her wavy bob, a blotch of swollen, purple skin throbbed around her left eye.

"Hey, Tarantis!" Lucia growled, skidding to a halt and raising her clenched fist. "Tell me where the girl is or I'll put a hole in your head."

Caesia stared at her blankly for a moment, utterly taken aback. "Uh... what?"

"*Don't play stupid with me, you scrawny twig!*" Lucia spat, hammering her hands down upon the rickety table. "Emily Arrenni - your bastard parents kidnapped her, didn't they?"

Hasso approached gently from behind and reached for Lucia's shoulder, only for it to set alight and send him reeling back. Caesia simply smirked.

"Assuming you mean the lunatic who tried to kill me in the tournament, I haven't a clue what you're talking about," she muttered. "Black eye or not, I still won the round - my parents have never been less disappointed in me."

"Come on, Lucy, just calm-"

"*Don't call me that!*" Lucia hissed, drawing muted laughter from her audience. "Who do you think you're fooling? The girl gives you that shiner and suddenly, she's turned up missing. I know how your mother operates - that's just her style."

"As is recruiting children as spies," Caesia sighed, slumping back in her chair. "Look, if my parents are involved in this, I'm none the wiser. Though, I can say with utmost certainty that they could not care less about my injury."

Hasso caught Lucia's fist as it raised at her side. "She doesn't know anything," he whispered, slowly lowering her arm. "So, what do we do now?"

"I don't know," Zahra sighed. "I could try and get Amani to track her scent, but..."

"It's Zahra, isn't it?" Caesia asked, flicking to a new page in her notebook. "Can I ask you something?"

"I... suppose so."

"When you're wearing that blindfold, how is it you see? I'm guessing you use illusory pulses, like a changeling." She smiled as Zahra nodded, taking up her quill and scribbling in her book. "And have you considered the utility of the pulses in identifying essence colouration?"

"What?"

Caesia smugly raised an eyebrow. "And I heard your people knew it all about illusions. A simple modification to your casting technique can have your pulses mark different colours of essence. It's rather handy…"

Laurent turned to Zahra, his eyes brightening. "If you could do that…"

"I could locate Emilia," Zahra gasped. "Caesia, I-"

"You can thank me by leaving me alone," Caesia muttered. "And Lucia? Please start wearing perfume, I could smell your sweaty musk from across the hall."

"You little fucking-"

"Time to go!" Hasso yelled, dragging her off by the arm. "We'll meet you by the canal!"

Zahra nodded and turned to the rest of her team. "Sounds like a visit to the library is in order," she sighed. "Come on, team, let's get our girl back!"

As the rest of his friends stormed off, James turned awkwardly to Caesia. "You know… we could always use another hand in this."

"Pft, what do take me for?" Caesia scoffed. "No, I think I'll opt out of that one. I'm not exactly suited to danger and all that."

"Understandable," James smiled. As he edged away, a crude drawing in Caesia's notebook caught his eye. It was of a boy with frizzy hair, drawn beside a circle, a cylinder and a sword. The whole thing was covered in paragraphs upon paragraphs of cursive text.

"Is… that a drawing of me?" he asked.

"Hm, I'm surprised you can tell!" Caesia smirked. "I'm not very good… and no, I'm not musing you for any emotional reasons. It's purely for the sake of annotation."

"And why are you annotating a picture of me?" James asked, feeling particularly uneasy.

"If you must know, I'm using the tournament as a learning experience," Caesia explained. "By assessing the strengths and weaknesses of my allies and opponents, I hope to learn from them and incorporate their practices into my own spells."

"You have notes on *everyone* in there?" James scoffed, receiving back an impatient nod. "Do you… have anything on Lucia?"

"I do, but surely revealing such information would be malpractice, no?" Caesia sneered. "After all, I might be out of the running, but I'm certainly not on your team."

"Yeah, yeah, of course…" James mumbled, turning his back.

"Although… perhaps you could sate my curiosity," she smiled. "I haven't had the chance to ask Brooklyn, so do tell me - what is the backlash like in evocation? How does it feel, how does it vary in severity?"

"Well, um, it's based on how hard you get hit," James said. "Whatever damage the creation can't handle spills over into my head. It normally feels like someone stuck a knife in my skull."

"Hm, a crude but informative analogy... not dissimilar from abjuration," Caesia mused, scribbling violently in her notebook. "Thank you, James... and as a friendly piece of totally irrelevant information, volatilis disorder burns essence exponentially faster than average. Bare that in mind."

A wide smile growing on his face, James nodded his head and hurried after his team. Together, the four of them headed for the library to find what they needed to save their friend.

Lucia watched the gates of the College like a hawk as she, Isadora and Hasso loitered by the canal bridge. For about half an hour now they had lurked there, listening to Isadora's stories while they awaited Zahra gang of idiots.

"So, at this point, you can probably guess I'm kinda pissed," Isadora said, kicking her legs merrily over the edge of the canal. "And naturally, I punched him in the face! He was so fixed on taking my sister's lunch that he didn't notice I knocked out one of his gold teeth. I said to him - 'Whatever, keep the food!' and let him run off with his tail between his legs."

"Is that it?" Lucia scoffed. "You just let him go? You should've beaten the shit out of that bastard!"

"Wait, wait, there's more," Isadora grinned. "You see, poor Amphidoros, he was lined up to fight one of the Archon's champions - Kharon, the Crimson Storm."

"That is *so* cheesy."

"I know, right? But damn, is he formidable. I took Amphidoros' gold tooth and used it to bet against him. The odds weren't the best, but let's just say we ate more than just bread that night."

She and Hasso grinned with delight as a fledgling smirk grew on Lucia's face, one she tried desperately to hide.

"Are you smiling?" Isadora laughed.

"No..." Lucia mumbled, her face creasing further as she tried to bury it.

"You're smiling!" Isadora gasped, punching her playfully in the thigh. "And here I didn't think it possible."

"You're delusional. I never smile," Lucia chuckled. "God, where are those morons? It's been... a while."

"Hey, these things take time," Hasso said.

"Please, I cast my first firebolt when I was ten."

190

"Accidentally," Hasso smirked. "And resulting in a fire that destroyed your entire bedroom."

Lucia glared at Isadora as the girl sniggered behind her hand. "We don't talk about that," she muttered. "Ah, there they are. Took you long enough!"

Zahra rolled her eyes as she stepped out from beneath the gate, James, Nearchos and a fully armoured Laurent in tow. "You try reworking the fundamentals of a spell in the space of an hour with no prior knowledge!" she snapped, before taking a deep breath and composing herself. "The spell is ready. I've got the book here for good measure, but I think I've got a... vague handle on it."

"A *vague* handle?" Lucia sneered.

"I can do it," Zahra said. "I'll channel my essence through Amani and release the pulses from the air."

"I get it," Lucia groaned. "Just get on with it, will you? I haven't got all day."

"Yes, we do," Hasso said.

"Quiet, you!" Lucia hissed. "Come on, do it already!"

"Would you let me concentrate?" Zahra growled. "I need quiet while I get to grips."

Closing her eyes, she merged her consciousness with Amani's and commenced the first pulse. She watched from above as a city block materialised as a frame of white lines. Blotches of red, yellow, purple and blue shimmered to life as the pulse highlighted their group, spreading across the College and lighting it up like a starry night.

"Alright, Amani," Zahra whispered. "Find me that girl."

Amani spread her wings and streaked across the cityscape, blasting invisible pulses from above. The rest of the group stood in silence, watching as Zahra stared with closed eyes into the sky.

"Ugh, could you be any slower?" Lucia hissed.

"Se dak'ra!" Zahra moaned. "Please, can you just shut your stupid, blotchy face and let me work?!"

She shrank away beneath Lucia's empty stare, suddenly realising the weight of what she had just done. Lucia took a step back and began to scratch vigorously at her cheek while the rest of the group watched in a startled silence.

"Um, thank you..." Zahra mumbled, closing her eyes. "Now, if I... there she is. I've got her!"

"Yes!" Laurent roared. "Where is she? Is she okay?"

"All I know is she's alive," Zahra said. "She's at a manor not far from here, just a few blocks south."

"A manor?" Lucia smirked. "Maybe she's just visiting relatives."

"Emilia doesn't care much for her family," Laurent said. "I don't see her being there willingly."

"Can we stop beating the bush here?" Isadora sighed. "Let's just accept that Emilia has definitely been kidnapped and think about how we can solve this."

Zahra took a deep breath and put on a mean face. "She's right. We need to go to that manor and see what's going on. Any objections?"

"Not an objection, but can I ask why Laurent is wearing armour?" Hasso asked.

"You can never be too careful," Laurent said, tapping his helmet with his finger. "Now, shall we see what this manor is all about?"

The group headed into the city and in a few minutes, they stood before the looming fence of a grand manor. It was a massive building, worthy almost of a palace, decorated with stained windows and marble pillars. Before it was a vast terrace, littered with exotic plants and gushing fountains. All of this sat behind a massive, barred fence laden with razor spikes.

"Alright, you lot get out of here," Lucia said, marching off towards the gate. "I'll take this from here."

"You'll do no such thing!" Zahra hissed.

"I'm Lucia Severin, I can do what I want," Lucia sneered. "I'll blow this stupid gate open, kill anyone who tries to stop me and get your little runt back before the sun's down."

"You can't do that!"

"Believe me, I can," Lucia smiled, leaning in close. "Now get out of my way."

"Look, maybe you *can* do that, but that doesn't mean it's a good idea!" Zahra urged. "There could be anything in there. I think we can all agree that it would take more than a few thugs to even lay a scratch on Emilia - we have to treat this with caution."

"Okay."

"What?"

"We'll do it your way," Lucia sighed, folding her arms. "And when it goes wrong, I'll do it my way."

"Right... well, the logical thing to do would be to sneak in," Zahra said. "I don't see any security, so we just cut through the fence, slip in through a side entrance and find Emilia."

"How do we know there *is* a side entrance?" James asked.

"Because there's one right there," Isadora said, pointing to a small door at the edge of the west wing. "It's probably a storage cupboard for groundskeeping tools, but we can make it work."

"Great, let's go," Lucia said, wandering off to the western end of the fence.

"Wait, we can't just go breaking into a manor in broad daylight!" Nearchos snapped.

"You'd rather wait until night?"

"No, I- No!" Nearchos scoffed. "It's illegal!"

Lucia span back around and planted her scarlet hand on his shoulder. "*I* decide what's legal," she smiled. "Quit your whining and let's go."

Nearchos looked to Zahra for support, yet he received only a shrug. Lucia marched to the end of the fence, igniting her hands and slashed apart several bars in two clean swipes. As passers by paused and stared, Lucia turned to them with her hands on her hips.

"Official Severin business, go back to your day," she announced before hopping through the smouldering gap.

Isadora sprang after her, followed closely by the rest of the group. James patted Nearchos on the back before hurrying after them, leaving his friend in total conflict.

"Ugh, Isoripes forgive me…" he moaned, trudging after them. "This is the right thing to do. Saving children takes precedence over the law… It doesn't, but… you're doing the right thing."

They wandered along the edge of the silent terrace, hugging a length of bushes as they made for the side entrance. The whole place seemed devoid of life - there was not a person in sight and the interior was lit only by a few flickering candles.

"Should we be worried that there is no security here?" James whispered. "I'm getting a real haunted house feeling from this place."

"I'm more worried about Pots and Pans over here," Isadora smirked, gesturing to Laurent. "He's loud as a pyrewyrm."

"Ah, not to worry," he assured her. "My armour is enchanted to be muffled at will."

"You could do that this whole time…" James sighed. "And you just made a racket anyway?"

"The muffling requires concentration," Laurent said. "It's not easy to sustain, even when merely talking."

"Fair enough."

Lucia ran ahead and melted the padlock in her grip, swinging open the door and letting the rest of the group pile into the storage cupboard. Yellow light unveiled the room before them as Lucia ignited her palm, revealing an abnormal amount of rakes, brooms, and buckets, amongst other things.

"Well… we're in the cupboard," Laurent said. "What do we do now?"

"We go through the wall," Lucia said, her hand whining as flames spread down her arm.

"Can somebody please sedate her?" Zahra asked. "Look, we have to get through this wall without anybody hearing us. That means no explosions, no magic weapons and no angry screaming!"

"Then what are you doing right now?" Lucia smirked.

"This is whisper-screaming, it's different!" Zahra hissed. "Can anyone get rid of this wall?"

Her shoulders slowly sank as she looked around at the room of awkward faces. As Lucia began to chuckle, Laurent hesitantly raised his hand.

"I can," he said. "I might need a bit of space."

"You're not going to…"

"No weapons," Laurent smiled, stepping up to the wall and pressing his hands against the brick. "If I enchant the bricks, I can make them release pulses of wind, which should apply enough pressure to crack the wall. If I can do that across a large area, we should be able to pop this segment out."

Brick by brick, he infused his essence in the structure and shattered part of the wall. The rest of the group watched as he slowly formed a circular crack in the brickwork.

"Isadora, Lucia, I assume you're the strongest people here," Laurent whispered, his voice strained. "I'm going to push this segment out of the wall, I need you to catch it."

Isadora nodded eagerly and crouched readily beside, followed reluctantly by Lucia. Laurent clenched his fist and a dull pulse of wind on the other side sent the circular segment toppling into the cupboard, spraying dust as it fell into Lucia and Isadora's waiting hands.

"That was amazing," Zahra laughed, patting Laurent on the shoulder. "We're headed for the east wing. I should be able to mask our presence from anyone we see, so let's stay as a group."

"If you insist," Lucia muttered. "After you, oh fearless leader."

Zahra led the group through the dimly lit corridors of the manor, maintaining an invisible bubble around them that obscured them from sight and blocked all sound moving in or out. As they passed into the centre of the building, they would encounter the first of many guards - soldiers draped in chainmail, bearing neither colours nor sigil. For such a large building, they seemed few in number and mostly unsuspecting of any trouble.

"Why didn't you do this in the combat round?" James hissed as they piled through a doorway. "I can think of several occasions when this would have been *really* useful!"

"How am I meant to win a fight if I trap myself in a bubble?" Zahra muttered.

"Couldn't you have made this thing a little bigger?" Lucia growled, glaring at Nearchos as his arm dug into her side.

"If it were any bigger, we'd risk bumping into something!"

"Isn't that called having eyes?" Lucia sneered.

"I am trying to concentrate!" Zahra yelled, her voice returning as a deafening echo from the bubble's rippling walls. "Why can't you all be like Nearchos and have nothing interesting to say?!"

"Hey! I'm interesting…"

The awkward silence that followed was interrupted suddenly by Isadora, who reached over Lucia's shoulder and shook Zahra's arm.

"Hey, she looks important," she whispered, pointing down the corridor. "You want to de-cloak and listen in?"

A black robed woman stepped out ahead of them, shadowed closely by a man who stood obscured behind her. Her crimson eyes glared back at him through a featureless mask, her fists clenching around the twin-bladed staff that rested in her hands. Zahra signalled the group and they piled around the corner, taking cover in an empty corridor as the bubble vanished from around them.

"General, I… I don't understand," the man urged.

"How many times do I have to say it?" she spat, her voice mired by a subtle nordic accent. "There is *no such thing* as pink essence!"

"General, the facts are there to be witnessed. Her eyes - the colour is unmistakable."

"Harald, listen to me," she growled. "You know *nothing* about magic, so don't assume to tell me what is fact or fiction. That girl's essence is a mutation. You've put your entire operation at risk for naught."

As she paced along the width of the corridor, the grizzled face of Lord Harald Mortan emerged in her shadow. Zahra ducked around the corner, and glanced to the rest of her group.

"It's Lord Mortan," she whispered. The look on Lucia's face turned suddenly foul, sinking into a dark glare.

Mortan heaved a deep sigh. "How do I fix this?"

"You can't," the woman sighed. "Return the girl and she'll know too much, brainwash her and her novekhiri friend will figure it out eventually."

"So, what do we do?"

"We? I don't have time to worry about your problems. Find a way to deal with this or we will have no choice but to cut ties. I can't allow you to jeopardize our plans."

"Of course, General," Mortan mumbled, turning to a pair of his men as the woman stalked off. "Hans, Torben… I… kill the girl."

Laurent jumped up as Mortan marched off, while his soldiers shuffled hesitantly in the other direction. "Zahra-"

"I know, I know," Zahra hissed. "Wait. Where is… oh no."

James and Nearchos looked over their shoulders to find only the four of them remaining in cover. Lucia, Hasso and Isadora were nowhere to be seen.

"Dak'ra…" Zahra spat. "Okay, okay, this is fine. James, Nearchos, go after them. Laurent and I will get Emilia."

James took a deep breath is she and Laurent marched off. "Zahra?" he called. "Be careful."

"What kind of idiot do you take me for?" Zahra smirked. "I'm out of here. This one's on Amani."

Nearchos glanced to James as their friends disappeared around the corner. "We shouldn't be-"

"Yeah, yeah, I know," James groaned, setting off running. "Sorry to offend your sensibilities, but I've got my orders."

"James- Ugh, Diannis protect us…"

Zahra slipped out into the street and leapt into the air, grasping Amani's feet as the drake swooped down upon her. Beating her wings with all her might, Amani dragged Zahra onto the nearest balcony, where she huddled up and merged her consciousness with that of her pet.

Meanwhile, Laurent pressed on through the manor, his shield raised and mace poised to strike. Four soldiers had already crossed his path, all cast low with overwhelming zeal. He grunted with his every step, trying to ignore the sting of the gash in his thigh, rent by a wayward blade.

"Laurent? Can you hear me?"

"Zahra?" he whispered. "You could have asked before invading my head."

"Given the situation, I'm sure you can let it slide. I've tracked Emilia to the east wing, in a cellar beneath the kitchen. You're not far, just take two rights and a left."

"Right, right, left. Got it."

"We'll get her back," Zahra whispered. "I promise."

"I haven't a doubt in my mind," Laurent growled. "On my way."

Laurent stormed ahead, charging around the first corner and smashing an unsuspecting soldier with his shield. Another strike to the forehead bludgeoned the man unconscious.

"You're *good*," Zahra laughed. "Shame you never got to hit anything in the combat stage."

"I thought I'd go easy on them," Laurent chuckled.

He leapt around the next corner and charged a pair of startled soldiers. Their first strikes were easily blocked, leaving them open as Laurent cleaved his mace overhead and slammed it into the ground. A blast of wind

196

blew them off their feet, sending them skidding down the hallway. Laurent leapt to their sides as they recovered, smashing one of the head with his shield and kicking the other in the chin.

"You've got five round the next corner," Zahra warned. "I'll move Amani to support, but you'll have to do most of the smashing."

"I can do that. Let's go."

Rounding the final corner, he stood before a patrolling unit of five soldiers. With no questions asked, they charged him head on, three running ahead while the rest stayed in the back.

The first of their number laughed as Laurent's mace glided past his face, yet quickly changed his tone when an explosion of wind blasted him straight through a window. The next two staggered back, but soon recovered and lunged at him together. The first strike glanced harmlessly off his shield, but a failed attempt at a parry saw the second blade slice between the armour of his gauntlet. Laurent stumbled back, cringing at the intense stinging of the gash and watching as his four assailants approached.

A jet of orange flame burst from the window, slicing the hallway in two and cutting off the soldiers in the rear. Laurent grabbed the arm of his assailant and slammed him in the side, battering him into the wall beside them. The next soldier made a thrust for Laurent's gut, his sword glancing worthlessly off the armour. Drawing his shield back, Laurent threw down his mace and took hold of his opponent's hair, bashing him repeatedly with the shield's face until he eventually collapsed to the ground. He picked up his mace and stood ready as Amani's flames began to flicker.

"Let me get that for you," Zahra chirped.

Amani exploded through a window and latched onto a soldier's head, dragging him through the flames and into the path of Laurent's mace. A slam to the gut sent him crashing through another window, while Amani wrapped her neck around the last man's sword arm and pulled him out of that which she entered through.

"Still in one piece?" Zahra asked.

"Just about," Laurent sighed, brushing his hand gently over his throbbing wrist. "Are we close?"

"The cellar should be just up ahead. You'll have to take this part alone - Amani doesn't cope well with confined spaces."

"Of course... Thank you, Zahra."

"No need. If you have any problems, I'm here - Good luck."

Laurent marched into the kitchen and swung upon the cellar door. A set of crumbling stone steps descended into a dimly lit basement. Flickering torchlight revealed towering stacks of crates and barrels, cluttered with a variety of food and drink.

Every step was an explosion as Laurent's armoured feet clattered against the surface and echoed throughout the cellar. He advanced through the looming shadows, the muffled sound of voices becoming ever quieter as he approached a thick iron door - a vault.

"Are we really doing this?" asked a young soldier from behind the door. "I mean, the girl looks... I don't know, eleven?"

"My friend, this is no girl," an older man growled. "From what I hear, she's a monster."

"She's still a child," hissed the younger man. "I can't do this. You're on your own."

"Suit yourself!"

The younger soldier stepped out of the vault and slammed the door shut behind him. As he turned around, Laurent unstrapped his shield and hammered his mace against its edge. The soldier shrieked as the silvered slab shot across the cellar and slammed into his face, knocking him out cold.

"Alright, girl," the older soldier growled, accompanied by the scraping of a leather sheath. "Let's get those restraints off you. I've always wanted to kill a monster."

Laurent scraped his shield from the ground and ran for the door, raising his weapon over his head and slamming it against the door. The dull ring of his blow was echoed by a loud crashing on the inside. From the other side of the door, the soldier roared, followed a bloodthirsty growl from a very angry girl.

Again and again, Laurent struck the door, the crashed and grunting from within growing ever quieter with every swing. As all fell silent, he detonated a final blast against the door, blasting it open and sending it spiralling off its hinges. Emilia glanced up from the corpse beside which she lay, her white dress soaked in blood and a dripping knife in her quaking hand. She stared at Laurent as he approached, tears rolling down her cheeks from her wide, empty eyes.

"Laurent?" she whispered, her knife clattering to the ground as she rose to her bare feet.

"My lady," Laurent smiled, himself tearing up.

Emilia ran to him and cast her arms around his stomach, squeezing him with abnormal strength. "The- The woman in the mask," she cried, pressing her face against his cold silver plate. "She put my essence in a crystal and... and... and it was red! It was red... I'm a worthless fraud. I'm a stupid, stupid idiot and nobody likes me!"

"I like you," Laurent whispered. "And I'm here now. Like I should have been."

Emilia stared up at him, desperation in her eyes. "I'm scared," she mumbled. "I want to go home."

"We will," Laurent assured her. Her face brightened as he took her by the shoulder and led her from the room. "Though, we might run into a bit of resistance."

"Good," Emilia smiled, a flicker of pink returning to her eyes. "I have a lot of stress to work out."

A flick of Lucia's wrist detonated the wall before her. She marched through the smouldering hole and into an empty bedroom, Hasso begging behind her and Isadora searching with her bow drawn.

"Lucia, please," Hasso urged. "Just take a minute and-"

"Quiet," Lucia growled as they came to a stop in the empty chamber. "Footsteps behind."

Isadora span around, electricity surging through her arrow, and drew her weapon to James' face.

"No, it's us!" he gasped, staggering back to Nearchos' side.

A roll of Lucia's eyes complimented her pained groan. "For the love of... what are you idiots doing?"

"Following you," James said. "Zahra figured you need backup."

"Backup?" Lucia smirked. "Is that what you call yourself? You and your pathetic twig of a sword?"

James gritted his teeth as she turned her back on him. "At least I don't burn innocent people."

Lucia stopped in her tracks, loosening her fingers as her arms tensed. "I don't need your help, nor do I want it," she hissed, setting her hands alight. "Piss off."

She cleaved her hand down upon the hinges of the door before her. Slamming her boot against it, she toppled it to the ground, stepped through and blasted a startled soldier in the face with a bolt of flame.

"Sorry," Hasso sighed. "Just, um... follow at a distance. She doesn't mind *that* much."

Nearchos leant into James as Hasso hurried away. "Why do I get the feeling that she *does* mind that much?"

"Because she does," James sighed.

"Maybe we should just leave this to them," Nearchos suggested. "I'm sure Lucia can deal with Lord Mortan just fine."

"And what if she runs into that lady with the mask?" James hissed. "You saw how scary she looked - I know Lucia's talented, but we don't know what that woman can do."

Nearchos planted his hands on his hips, shaking his head as he paced up and down the room. "We shouldn't be here..."

"Look, I know you don't like this and I get it," James urged. "We're way out of our depth here. We're doing something so completely illegal that it could ruin our lives forever… but Emilia's life is on the line here. You might not like her, but you know we can't just let her die."

"And Laurent and Zahra are handling that. What Lucia's doing, what you want to do, we don't have the right!"

"If we don't catch that man, this could happen again. Someone could die and that blood, Nearchos, it would be on our hands."

Nearchos stared down upon the floor, his eyes alight with conflict. He stiffened himself and stood straight, trying to keep his face from dropping. "Fine… but we take him alive."

"If you manage to talk down Lucia, I'm all for it," James said, waving his friend along. "Just don't push her too hard. I'd rather preserve our own lives than his."

Lucia threw open a pair of double doors, thrusting out her blazing hands as she scanned the orange-soaked hallway. Evening light beamed through the windows, through which she beheld the sprawling terrace of the manor's garden. Vibrant trees and bushes ran rings around a marble gazebo that stood at its centre, where Lucia's eyes fell upon Harald Mortan.

"I want to know how many men are in that garden," she demanded. "Isadora?"

"On it," Isadora chirped, scurrying into a nearby stairwell.

Watching with a sinister grin as Isadora scampered off, Lucia turned her gaze back to the garden. Hasso raised an eyebrow as she took a double take.

"Hasso…" she whispered, stepping closer to the window and narrowing her eyes. "Are you seeing what I'm seeing?"

Hasso slipped to her side and peered across the garden. Beneath the gazebo at its centre, Lord Mortan stood with several crossbow wielding soldiers. At Mortan's side was a navy-robed man, twiddling a slender, wooden staff. Before the two of them stood a familiar goliath, looming over those around him.

"Is that… Bruno?" Hasso hissed. "What's he doing here?"

"Nothing good," Lucia growled, marching for the stairwell. "Let's go fry him."

"Figuratively?"

Lucia turned back to him with darkness in her eyes. "Not this time."

Hasso took a deep breath and ran after her as she thundered down the steps and towards the back door. She shoved James onto his back as he ran out in front of her and raised her fist in Nearchos' face.

They watched as she stormed onwards without a word, booting open the back door and stepping out onto the terrace. She glanced up to the nearest tree, where Isadora smiled back from atop a branch.

"How many?" Lucia asked.

"No guards outside of that gazebo. I count six men, all with crossbows."

Lucia nodded her head and continued her advance. While Isadora repositioned to atop a greenhouse, Hasso caught up with Lucia and grabbed her by the shoulder.

"Lucy, stop!" he hissed. "What's going on?"

"House Mortan were vassals of House Severin. My brother took care of them when they tried to oust us from power, but he was fool enough to let old Harald live. It was meant to be punishment, but I knew it would come back to bite us."

"You can't just walk up there and-"

"I can, actually," Lucia said, clenched his wrist and dragging his hand off her. "And don't even think about getting in my way."

James wandered to Hasso's side as Lucia stepped into the open, facing down Mortan and his men as he returned from the gazebo. "Don't worry," he smiled. "I'm sure she's a plan."

"Harald Mortan!" Lucia boomed.

"Oh no…"

"I never thought I'd see the day you crawled out of your wretched hole," Lucia sneered, shooting the man a smug grin as his face dropped. "What, surprised to see me?"

"Shit," Mortan spat, turning to the mage at his side. "Euric, kill her."

The mage glared back at him. He was a middle-aged man, his brown hair greying and his back the slightest bit hunched. Clenching his staff tight, he loosened his navy robe and stepped hesitantly forward.

"I'm not your bodyguard, Harald," he groaned, his weapon weeping an icy mist.

"Yes, but you have magic!" Mortan hissed. "Quit complaining and kill the damn girl!"

Lucia grinned darkly as Euric spilled an icy mist from his hands, hesitant yet full of conviction.

"After all these years, you're still hiding from me," Lucia laughed. "Fine. I'll just have to destroy both of you."

Her body burst spontaneously into flame and fire exploded from her palms, swamping the gazebo in a colossal inferno. The fire died away and the ice wall behind it collapsed, unveiling an unscathed gazebo surrounded by blazing foliage.

"I don't want to kill you," Euric sighed. "Leave. Turn back now and-"

Another explosion erupted from Lucia's hands, blasting the gazebo to exactly the same effect. She growled as the flames parted and channelled her fire into her hands as she advanced upon the mage.

"Lucia, you can't beat him!" Hasso hissed. "We need to go!"

"Maybe she can't on her own," James said, summoning his sword and shield. "But she's not alone."

"James…" Nearchos warned.

"This is a chance we can't pass up," James insisted. "We can't let these bastards get away!"

As James drew up his shield and charged in, an arrow streaked over his head, bathing Euric's feet in a prison of ice. Euric created ice of his own to meet the incoming torrent of flame, using his cover to release himself from Isadora's snare and turn upon James. His staff slammed against a purple barrier as he swung at the boy, opening him up for James to smash him in the gut with his blade.

The staff struck his shield and detonated an explosion of purple flame, knocking him away in time for Euric to catch another storm of fire. Flame lashed his skin as he threw up his defences and as he span back around, a jet of water hammered his chest and cast him flat on his back.

"What are you doing?!" Harald growled. "Stop screwing around and kill them!"

"You are insufferable…" Euric groaned.

Freezing solid another blast of water, Euric sprang to his feet and knocked aside James' sword. He planted his staff against James' shield and shattered it with a compact explosion, before sweeping his weapon over his shoulder and smashing the boy over the head. As James toppled to the ground, Euric turned to Nearchos, firing a surge of electricity into an incoming jet. Nearchos ceased his attacked as the energy lashed his feet, only for a rush of gale force wind to launch him off his feet and into the bushes.

Deflecting a hail of arrows with a blast of wind, Euric turned back upon Lucia. She drew up her arms and with a defiant roar, unleashed an avalanche of flame. Her magic broke against a barrier like waves against rocks, leaving her frozen in a state of shock. Euric flung out his staff and blasted her with ice, swamping her legs and rooting her to the ground.

"Mortan, you bastard!" Lucia growled, clawing at the ice to no avail. "I'll kill you where you stand!"

A torrent of flame spilled from her palm and surged towards the gazebo. Mortan, a smug grin on his face, flung out a dull, white crystal in front of him. The flames parted around him, vanishing before the sladium in his grip. Lucia dropped her hands as he signalled his crossbowmen, who levelled their weapons towards the girl.

"Harald…" Euric hissed, deflecting another arrow with a flick of his wrist.

"Believe me, Euric. I'm doing the world a favour."

Euric thrust his hand aside and blocked an incoming water jet with a barrier. Casting out his staff, he blasted Isadora's position with ice and encircled her in a jagged prison. As James staggered to his feet, he took a deep breath and summoned his shield once again.

"James, no!" Nearchos snapped as his friend charged into the open, raising his shield in front of him and darting to Lucia's side.

Mortan took a deep breath and held his hand over his head. "You know, Miss Severin, I have been looking forward to this for a long time," he grinned, clenching his fist. "Fire."

Lucia watched with wide eyes as the crossbows unleashed their payload. Hasso leapt in front of her and raised a barrier of purple light before them. The sladium tips of their bolts parted the magical field and half a dozen projectiles slammed into Hasso's chest.

An eerie silence hung in the air as all came to a standstill. Mortan glanced to Euric and together, they beat a hasty retreat. James and Nearchos watched from a distance as Hasso toppled to the ground before Lucia, blood pooling around them. What little fire flickered on Lucia's skin was snuffed. She simply lay there, her expression empty, staring into the lifeless eyes of her love.

Laurent fell against the wall with a tremendous crash, panting breathlessly as he watched Emilia slam another soldier through a table. She prodded the man with her foot before wandering back to Laurent's side.

"You doing alright?" she asked, looking him up and down. His armour was dull and scuffed, many plates rent asunder and spilling trickles of blood down his silver hide.

"Well enough," he growled, staggering upright. "We can't be far now. I wonder how the others are coping."

"Others?" Emilia scoffed. "You mean… you all came?"

"Of course. Last I saw them, they were chasing down Lord Mortan. No doubt they're dragging him to the battlemages as we speak."

They skidded around the next corner, where Laurent peered past half a dozen soldiers to behold a wooden door at the end of the corridor. Light beamed through its glass and bathed their destination in fiery, orange light.

"There - that's our exit," Laurent said, readying his weapon as the soldiers turned to meet them.

"Then what are we waiting for?" Emilia grinned.

She charged headlong down the corridor, smirking as a sword glanced off her face before sending its wielder through the ceiling. Laurent followed suit, charging in after his ward and engaging the soldiers. He barely had the essence left to fuel his weapon's abilities - so did the mace crash against an iron blade with barely a gust of wind.

Emilia punched a hammer wielding soldier in his gut and threw him to the ground. While she kicked him repeatedly in the face, Laurent clobbered his assailant over the head. Another soldier charged him from the right, his blade scything across Laurent's arm and cutting the shield loose from his gauntlet. Laurent staggered back as it tumbled to the ground, reeling before a flurry of violent swings.

As the blade slipped between his plates and narrowly sliced his arm, Laurent reached over his shoulder, grabbed Emilia by the scruff of her dress and swung her around. The sword smashed into Emilia's forehead to no effect and sprang from the soldier's hand. A smug grin on her face, Emilia struck his face with a right hook and knocked him flat on the ground.

"Toss me!" Emilia growled, curling up into a ball.

Laurent shifted his grip to her neck and hurled her down the corridor, bowling down two more soldiers like wheat before a scythe. She tumbled over them, onto her knees and slammed down her fists upon their faces.

As Emilia sprang up off the ground, her eyes shot wide, watching as one of the soldiers staggered to his feet. "Laurent!"

He span around to his right, only for a sladium hammer to careen from the left and smash meteorically into his spine. Emilia shoved a recovering soldier through a wall and charged Laurent's assailant, catching his weapon and snapping the steel shaft over her knee. Laurent collapsed to the ground, gasping in agony, while Emilia grabbed the soldier by his leg and slammed him through the floor.

"Don't just lie there!" Emilia hissed, running to Laurent's side. "Get up and walk it off."

Laurent rolled onto his back, wheezing every heavy breath and staring emptily into the ceiling. "I… I can't," he gasped. "Emilia, I-I can't feel my legs."

"What? Don't be silly!" Emilia laughed, her voice thick with anxiety. "Come on, we can't be wasting time like this."

"Please, Emilia, you have to go," Laurent begged, caressing her face in his bloody hand. "Run. Save yourself."

"Laurent… Laurent, that's not funny…" Emilia growled. "I'm serious, cut it out!"

His hand slipped from her cheek and crashed to the ground. "Please… I can't… I…"

"Laurent? Laurent?!" Emilia cried, shaking him desperately by the shoulder. "Oh God… Oh God, oh God, oh God!"

She slipped her fingers beneath his helmet, where she found the faint beating of a pulse. Scrambling to her feet, she took hold of his arms and dragged him down the corridor, limping as fast as she could towards the door.

"Come on, stay with me," she begged, wearing a trembling smile. "You're going to be just fine."

Emilia's foot slammed against the door and she staggered out into the street with her friend in tow. Laurent slipped from her feeble grip and crashed to the ground at her feet, where she collapsed onto the steps beside him. Swaying back and forth as her nose poured with blood, Emilia placed her quivering hand gently on his chest, tears running down her cheeks.

"You idiot..." she growled, resting her head upon his bloodied chestpiece. "Why did you do this? You shouldn't have come!"

She sat for a moment in silence, a part of her waiting for an answer. Her scarlet hands caressed his helmet, gently pushing open the visor so that she might gaze upon his delicate face.

"I wasn't worth it," she moaned. "My gift is a farce... a lie. I'm nothing! Who would want to save nothing?!"

Withdrawing onto the steps, she tucked her knees into her chest and buried her face between them.

"This is my fault..." she mumbled. "I'm sorry. I'm so, so sorry."

"Emilia?"

Zahra's voice echoed down the street, the pattering of her feet drawing ever closer. Emilia took a deep breath and smeared her hands over her eyes. She wiped the blood from her nose, brushed the tears off her dress and straightened out her hair. As Zahra skidded to a halt before her, she folded her arms and put on a mean face.

"It's about time you showed up!" she snapped, her voice quickly growing hysterical. "I had to drag this useless... this good for nothing... this..."

She toppled onto her back, tears bursting from her eyes as she wailed with agony. Zahra slowly approached as Emilia curled up on the cold ground, snivelling and whining into her quaking arms.

"Just put me out of my misery," Emilia moaned. "I'm better off dead."

"It's okay," Zahra whispered. "It's not your fault."

"Yes it is... I let myself believe I have some stupid gift, told everyone I was special when I was nothing. It's my fault I got taken and it's my fault he came to save me. He wouldn't even be here if I hadn't lied to him about having-"

"Emilia, listen to me," Zahra urged, grabbing the girl by the cheeks and staring into her dull, green eyes. "We don't have time to wallow in self pity

- We need to get Laurent back to campus, he needs a biomancer. Can you carry him?"

"I can't do anything…" Emilia mumbled. "I'm worthless."

"You're not worthless."

"Then why did he save me?" Emilia whispered. "Why save what's already lost?"

"Because you're his friend," Zahra smiled. "You're *our* friend. That's why we came, all of us - because friends look out for each other."

"I'm… your friend?" Emilia gasped. "B-but why? I've been nothing but a jerk to any of you."

"Friends are mean to each other all the time," Zahra smirked. "You're not worthless, not to us."

With a desperate gasp, Emilia flung her arms around Zahra and buried her face in her shoulder. Zahra smiled shallowly, running her fingers through Emilia's hair as they knelt in silence. Gently pushing away her snivelling friend, Zahra rose to her feet.

"Come on," she whispered, extending her hand. "Let's go home."

Chapter Ten - Retaliation

James sat twiddling his thumbs at his desk, staring emptily into the wall. Even as noon approached, his mind was still processing what had transpired that night. After rushing Laurent to the biomancer, they had done nothing more than return to their dorms. What else were they to do? How else would they react? What happened had happened - maybe they just had to live with that.

His door trembled under the force of a hammering fist. He stared across his room, flooded with paranoia as he slipped carefully from his chair. Making an effort to muffle his every step, he moved towards the door, readying his hands to summon his weapons.

A circular, scarlet blade erupted from the doorframe and scythed down upon the latch. As he threw out his arm to summon his sword, a foot slammed against the door and battered it open with a deafening bang.

"James! Wake u-"

Brooke froze on the spot, staring blankly into James' tired eyes. The two of them stood for a moment in silence as Brooke's discs fizzled away and an apologetic smile grew across her face.

"I- I'm so sorry!" she gasped, gripping her head in her hands. "Your door, it-it wouldn't… I had to- you weren't answering, so I… I just…"

She flinched as James' hands grabbed her shoulders. "Okay, Brooke, just calm down," he urged. "What's going on?"

"Th-there's a fire! On the second floor!" Brooke stammered. "I noticed some people were missing, so I flew up here to evacuate them."

"Oh my- is it spreading?" James gasped, running for his shoes.

"They should have it under control before it reaches the fourth, but better safe than sorry, I guess."

"Okay… okay," James murmured, sighing in relief. "How are we getting out?"

"Straight down the middle," Brooke said as she marched into the hallway. "The first floor is clear enough so that we should be able to…"

"What?"

Brooke stepped back from the guardrail and back into James' dorm. "So, it's gotten a little worse since I came up here…" she sighed. "How, uh… how much do you value your window?"

"Not as much as I value my life," James muttered, smiling at Brooke's quiet giggling.

His face quickly dropped and his cheeks went a rosy red as he watched her step precariously over the piles of dirty clothes that cluttered his room. Luckily, she barely batted an eye, far too busy staring emptily at the carpet.

"One emergency exit, coming right up!" Brooke declared.

She stepped up to the window and flicked her hands aside, summoning a pair of discs in flashes of scarlet light. In a swift motion, she sliced vertically down the sides of the window frame, spitting sparks onto the ground with dull whine. Flipping the discs horizontally, she pushed them through the top and bottom, cutting through them like hot butter. She backed slowly away, the window pane captured between her discs, and precariously deposited it onto James' bed.

James simply watched her in awe as she reached outside and summoned a larger disc. She was incredible, a thrill to see in action. The sheer skill and grace with which she wielded her discs was exhilarating, a sight that had his knees weak and his heart throbbing.

"James?" Brooke called from outside. "Is... everything alright?"

"Um, yeah! Yeah, on my way," James stammered, hurrying to the window ledge.

He took her hand and let her haul him onto the disc. The sight of the rooftops around them urged him to look down upon the distant paving stones, where a swarm of students gathered around the tower's entrance. At such an incredible height, nausea struck, a wave of dizziness that shook him from balance.

Brooke gasped as he collapsed into her, rocking the disc almost onto its side as he pushed himself upright. He looked up at her panicked, red face and laughed anxiously. Stepping apart, the two of them chuckled awkwardly as Brooke began to sink her disc to the ground.

"Sorry, I, uh... I looked down," James mumbled.

Half giggling and half breathing heavily, Brooke composed herself. "Yeah... bad idea," she sighed, shuffling onto her behind.

Three stories passed by with not a word between them. Brooke stared blankly at her feet while James looked around aimlessly. After opening and closing her mouth a number of times, Brooke finally managed to utter some words.

"You know... I realised yesterday that I never thanked you for, um, for saving me. From the dragon," she smiled, her gaze still elsewhere. "After what happened to Ava, I kinda realised how big a deal it really was. I mean, I know it wasn't the real thing, but I could've been seriously hurt."

"Oh, well, no problem," James muttered. "Anyone would've done it..."

"Not for me," Brooke sighed. "Even Nearchos was telling you not too."

"Don't take that personally. Nearchos is a man of cold logic."

"I know... still, I'm... I appreciate it. The people here aren't nearly that nice."

"Yeah, Abenfurt sucks," James smirked. "You from around here?"

"No, I'm from the Arrenni side of the Heartland. Grew up at the family estate just off Unity Bay... which also sucked."

"Let me guess - no friends?"

"I had Ava," Brooke sighed. "But, she's the groundskeeper's daughter, so we weren't technically allowed to... well, interact. We had to sneak out in the night, had this nice spot on the beach where we'd play."

"Ava is lowborn?" James scoffed. He never would have thought it of such a pretty girl.

"Yeah, my parents sponsored her tuition," Brooke said. "You're lowborn, right? Who sponsored you?"

"Uh... nobody," James mumbled. "Honestly, I don't know how my parents could afford it. They saved for years, but I swear only a few months ago, my mum thought it was impossible."

"Maybe, they took out a loan?" Brooke suggested. "Or made some kind of deal?"

"Ah, it doesn't matter," James smiled. "What matters is that I'm here."

Brooke glanced up, into his bright eyes. "Yeah..." she sighed, smiling widely.

The disc jolted as it touched down upon the ground. James hopped off and surveyed the crowd of students around them, some bawling their eyes out and others tapping their feet impatiently.

"I'm gonna go check for more people," Brooke said, scrambling to her feet.

"Awesome," James chirped as he wandered off. "Good luck."

"James?" Brooke called. "I... I... I'll see you later."

He watched with narrowed eyes as she floated into the sky, shrinking into cover atop her disc. "Okay..." he mumbled, turning to the crowd and searching for a friendly face. As he wandered through their midst, he noticed a group of College faculty members standing at the entrance, waving about their hands as they barked at Bruno and Lucia. A glance through the open doors revealed a wall of lashing, yellow flame within the tower being desperately doused by hydromancers.

Lucia looked a complete wreck. Her skin was glossy with sweat and her eyelids were painted a dark crimson. Blood was smeared across the lower half of her face and her hair was let down into a greasy, tangled mop. The look on her face was one of total emptiness.

"Ah, you're alive," Emilia sighed. If not for the stool on which she stood, she would have been invisible behind her cello. "I suppose that's something..."

She ceased her sad tune and withdrew the bow, hopping down from the stool and easing her instrument back into its case. James joined her as she slumped to the ground, her head sunken in her hands.

"Fifth floor, huh?" she muttered. "Lucky you."

"Never felt that way until now," James said. "I guess you're second floor?"

"Yep. Now, all I've got to my name is a cello, three pairs of glasses, a portrait of my cat and the clothes on my back. I'd slap that bitch if she weren't in enough pain."

James glanced with a sad sigh to Lucia. "What happened?"

"Dunno. Sounds like they had a fight - Lucia's probably looking for stuff to punch after last night."

"I don't think so," James mused. "From what I've gathered, she hates being seen as the violent one. She wouldn't have attacked him unless it was for a good reason."

"Or, she's just pissed... Ugh, this is all my fault," Emilia groaned, grabbing James by the arm as he opened his mouth. "Don't even think about telling me otherwise. If I hadn't flaunted the fake, stupid gift so liberally, Hasso would be alive, this fire would never have happened and Laurent would still be able to walk."

"What?" James scoffed.

"Yeah... the biomancers say he'll never move them again," Emilia said, her grim expression sinking. "He was an amazing knight. He was going to the best... and I took it all away from him."

"He swore an oath, Emilia, it was his choice," James whispered. "You shouldn't blame yourself."

"Well, I'm going to anyway," Emilia growled. "And I'm going to make it right."

James sucked in his gut and nodded back, drawing a grin from his glum friend. The two of them turned as Zahra came running, Nearchos in tow, both panting for breath.

"Goddess, are you two okay?" Zahra gasped, staring up at the myriad windows that belched yellow flame.

"You want a picture of my cat?" Emilia asked.

"What's a cat?"

Emilia's face was suddenly warped by a tangled mess of emotions, from disgust to pity. James glanced up at Zahra and shook his head, commanding her not to persist.

"We heard there was a fight going on," Nearchos said. "They say Lucia attacked Bruno."

"Apparently, yeah," James sighed. "I'm not convinced."

"Nor am I," Zahra said. "The last thing she'd want to do is cause *more* harm."

"Maybe we should ask her," Emilia muttered, pointing to the entrance as the faculty began to depart.

"She looks terrible…" Zahra said. "We'd probably be better off leaving her alone."

"We can't," James insisted. "There's more to this than mindless violence. We need to find out what happened."

Emilia sprang up from the ground. "Let's go, then!" she snapped, spinning around and pointing to Florence. "Girl! Watch my stuff while I'm gone!"

James watched as she stormed off towards Lucia, followed by the rest of his team. Emilia was on a warpath. As much as her ego had been pummelled into the ground, it had been replaced by a burning conviction to make up for her failure. It was a worrying thought, but it was perhaps the drive that they needed in these bleak times.

Lucia stared through squinted eyes into the tower, watching the hydromancers extinguish her flames. The yelling of the staff fell largely upon deaf ears, for she barely able to concentrate as her vision swirled and shifted. She simply stood in silence, toying with the dull, brown bottle in her quivering hands.

"We've tolerated your insolent behaviour for far too long, Miss Severin," growled Headmaster Levette. "It is getting out of hand. Either you need to change your attitude or we need to have a talk with your brother about terminating your-"

"Shut the *fuck* up!" Lucia moaned, her words raspy and slurred. "Do what you want, I don't care…"

The headmaster stared for a moment into her dark eyes, puffing out his chest. "One chance. One more incident and you're gone. Damn your brother, damn House Severin, the College will not endure your rampant misbehaviour!"

He turned to Bruno, whose vacant stare returned after a moment. He had barely partaken in the conversation, for it had mostly descended into a shouting match.

"Mr Lechner, you can be on your way," Levette sighed. "On behalf of the College, you have my apologies."

"Thank you, Sir," Bruno mumbled, hurrying away. He rubbed the back of his neck as Lucia's glare burned it red.

"I don't want to hear a word about you for the next two years," Levette spat. "Get out of my sight."

With a venomous growl, Lucia shoved him aside and marched away, dragging her feet as she stumbled to the nearest wall. She gave up a metre away and collapsed onto her back, staring up at the grim, clouded sky as she raised her bottle and let the beer avalanche into her mouth. She groaned with agony as stepped to her side and snuffed the light with her shadow.

"Fuck off," Lucia spat, rolling over in the pool of beer around her head. "Let me die in peace."

"Not a chance," Emilia said, grabbing Lucia by the arm and yanking her onto her feet. "We need your help."

Lucia stared at her for a moment, akin to a lifeless husk, before suddenly breaking down into hysterical laughter. "You... you're funny!" she laughed. The smile on her face shifted suddenly to a frown. "Never talk to me again."

"Lucia-"

"*What did I say?!*" Lucia snapped, swinging her fist clumsily at Emilia.

The girl hardened her face just in time, before an explosion detonated against her head and blasted her glasses into tiny shards. Lucia looked to their remains, then to Emilia and then to her smoking fist. Her face shrivelled up and she whimpered with shame, weeping pathetically as she stumbled back.

"Gods," Nearchos sighed. "You are... *so* drunk."

"Of course, I'm fucking drunk!" Lucia spat. "Fuck you!"

She swung back her head and gulped down a mouthful of beer, staggering back until she reached a wall and collapsed onto it.

"Lucia, please, you need to focus," Zahra urged. "We just want to know why you attacked Bruno."

"Y-you stupid bitch... you just think I'm a fucking psycho, don't you?!" Lucia growled. "Do you think I *like* hurting people? You think I do it 'cause it's fun?"

"No, I-"

"Well, I don't! Every damn time, I try and I try to stop myself, but I just... I can't!" Lucia cried, tears suddenly flooding from her eyes. "I'm a freak... I'm a fucking monster! You're better off without me, 'cause I'll probably kill you all myself."

The group looked to each other in distress, unwilling to do nothing but afraid to make the wrong move.

"Lucia... nobody here thinks you're a monster," James said gently. "Just calm down and-"

"Piss off!" Lucia wailed, slamming her hands down and igniting the wall beneath her with flame. "I'll... I'll... leave me alone."

Her head sank into her hands as she shrank into a glum sulk. Tears leaked from between her fingers and simmered away as they ran down her scarlet skin. Emilia stepped slowly forward, staring gravely upon her.

"Look, you've lost more than any of us, I get that... and it's all because of me," she whispered. "It's my fault Hasso died and it's my fault that

Laurent will never walk again. I have to fix this and I need you to help me."

"If I help, will you fuck off?" Lucia groaned, rolling her eyes as they nodded eagerly. "Fine… I saw that bastard last night, reporting to their leader. Figured I'd confront him about it."

"Seriously?!" James gasped. "You're sure?"

"Of course, I'm sure, you bloody prick…" Lucia muttered. "When I asked him about it, he acted like he knew nothing. When I didn't back down, he went berserk and attacked me."

"*He* attacked *you*?"

"Yeah, I bet that's so hard to fucking believe, isn't it?!" Lucia snapped. "Maybe you shouldn't assume, you weedy piece of shit!"

"Lucia, please," Zahra urged. "If there's anything you learned-"

"Leave me alone!" Lucia moaned, cradling her head in her hands as she returned to weeping. "I've told you what you want, now get the hell out of here. I never want to see any of you again…"

"Lucia…"

"I said fuck off!" Lucia cried. "You… you…"

They reeled away as watery vomit dribbled from Lucia's mouth. She slumped over, coughing and gagging, before hurling a torrent of beer onto the paving stones. The others stepped slowly away as she wheezed and spluttered, her crying becoming ever more hysterical.

"Maybe we should let her be," Nearchos muttered. "Nobody's getting through to her in that state."

"Poor thing…" Zahra sighed as they wandered away. "I guess we'd better have a word with Bruno."

"I don't understand, why would he work with them?" James scoffed. "He's such a nice guy!"

"It certainly seems off," Nearchos mused. "Maybe, Lucia's just had a bit too much to drink."

"No, that was far too coherent for drunken ramblings," Zahra said. "We need to talk to Bruno."

"What if he attacks *us*?" James asked.

"There's four of us and one of him," Emilia growled. "And if he tries anything, I'll send him through a wall."

"Let's just start things off slow, alright?" Zahra warned. "We don't need to go in swinging."

"Of course, of course…" Emilia mumbled. "Let's go rumble this bastard."

With the fires snuffed, they followed several glum students into the tower. The halls were practically monochrome. Much of the furniture had been reduced to ash and the walls were scarred black by flame. Several walls and pillars were sundered ruins, still smouldering with yellow embers. Those who lived on the tower's lower floors wandered the wreckage like lost souls - some mourning their most prized possessions, while others lamented the inconvenience of it all.

They headed up to the second floor, where the damage was worst. The carpets had been disintegrated, the windows shattered and the floor sunken. Just beside the stairwell was Bruno's dorm and the scattered shards of its door.

"James, you should take the lead," Zahra said. "He might be a little touchy after… losing all of his worldly possessions."

"Good idea," James sighed as he stepped over the rubble. "Bruno?"

Bruno placed the ashen remains of a book down upon his scorched desk, spluttering as a cloud of soot was cast into his face. "Oh, James," he mumbled, far less enthusiastic than usual. "Is your room still standing?"

"Yeah, I'm on the fifth floor, so… I'm good," James smiled. "I heard what happened."

"Nasty piece of work, that girl," Bruno smirked, glancing over James' shoulder to the rest of the group. "Come in, come in! Plenty of room without… any salvageable furniture."

"You seem to be taking this on the chin," James observed. "You sure you're okay?"

"I'm unbelievably pissed, but I'm otherwise alright," Bruno grinned. "I didn't have too much of importance here, apart from a few gold's worth of books. I just feel bad for the others…"

"I'll be wearing the same panties for the next few months, but I'll live," Emilia sighed. "All hard feelings will be directed towards the aggressive party."

"There won't *be* any hard feelings," Zahra hissed. "Bruno, we were hoping you could tell us more about what happened with Lucia. She was a little… nondescript."

"I… I'm not entirely sure myself," Bruno sighed. "She barged into my room, spouting some drunken nonsense about evil mages or something. I told her I didn't know what she was talking about, but she wouldn't believe me. Then… I don't know."

"You don't know?"

"It's like… like a blank spot," Bruno muttered. "Next thing I knew, half the tower was on fire and she was trying to kill me. Kept shouting stuff about Hasso, I think, but I could barely hear her over the explosions."

"So, you have no idea what Lucia was on about?" Zahra asked.

"I knew what she was accusing me of, but she sounded delusional," Bruno said. "She was drunk, that's for sure."

"Maybe we should explain," Nearchos whispered.

Zahra looked to him and back to Bruno. "Yes… Look, Lucia came with us last night to find Emilia - she'd gone missing. We had a run in with… some pretty shady people. Lucia thinks she saw you there."

"What? That's ridiculous!" Bruno scoffed. "Who were these people?"

"We don't really know. Lucia identified one of their leaders as some ex-vassal of House Severin, but we don't know what they wanted."

"They took me because of the gift I thought I had," Emilia said glumly. "But, I wasn't the reason they were here."

"So, Lucia is convinced that I am in league with kidnappers?" Bruno smirked. "How much has she been drinking?"

"Probably a lot, but she was completely sober last night," Nearchos said. "And after what she's been through, I think she remembers every detail of what happened."

"Wait, you're saying you believe her?" Bruno growled. "James, you know me. I'd never consort with bastards like them!"

"Not by choice," Zahra said. "We know you were there last night. Please, tell us what's going on."

Bruno planted his hands on his desk, shaking his head as he gripped the wood tight. His breath grew heavy as he stared into the wall, his body becoming stiff and his teeth clenched. Zahra stepped slowly back as he began to grunt in pain, raising his hand to his head.

"Bruno?" she mumbled.

He span around. A sleek armour of red light flashed into being around him as he raised his fist to Zahra's head. Her mouth dropped open, her eyes wide with terror as she stood frozen on the spot.

James leapt between them. Bruno's fist smashed into his forehead, slamming his head into Zahra's and toppling the two of them to the ground. Nearchos thrust out his hand and blasted Bruno's gut with a torrential jet of water. The goliath did not flinch as it slammed against his armour and dispersed into the air, advancing forwards with his armoured fists raised. Nearchos stumbled back and tripped over his recovering friends, collapsing on top of them as they writhed in panic. He span around to Emilia and cleaved his gauntlet down upon her.

A deafening bang left their ears ringing. Emilia smirked, clenching her hand around his fist as she held it effortlessly in place.

"Someone hasn't been paying attention," she said darkly.

Smacking his other hand aside, she raised her foot and hammered it into his gut. Its meteoric impact flung Bruno off his feet, across the room and straight through the opposite wall, taking half of the brickwork with it. Zahra shoved her friends aside and scrambled to her feet, running out into the hallway as Emilia marched out of the crumbling breach. Emilia planted her foot on Bruno's chest and pressed it down, the immense density of her leg shattering his armour in an instant. Avoiding his swings as he thrashed about, Zahra skidded to his side and reached for his head.

"Sleep!" she gasped, wincing at the friction of the carpet against her legs.

His eyes rolled back and his head slumped to the ground. Zahra breathed deeply as James and Nearchos staggered through the breach.

"Damn... that was intense," James panted, rubbing his swollen forehead. "What do we do about this wall?"

"Nothing," Zahra said, lying back on the dusty carpet. "Anyone who finds it will think it was caused by the fight."

"And what do we do with him?" Emilia asked, wiping the gushing blood from her nose.

"We can't keep him here," Nearchos sighed. "James, can we..."

"Use my room? Absolutely," James smiled. "Emilia, can you carry him?"

"No, I... I put a little too much into that kick," Emilia mumbled, swaying drunkenly. "I need a sit down."

With a reluctant sigh, James dug into his pocket and produced a key. "Take this and head up to room nineteen," he said. "We'll try to drag him up the stairs."

Emilia took the key and scurried away, while the others dragged Bruno gradually up the stairwell. As they turned onto the fifth floor, Zahra stumbled as she walked backwards into someone. The trio looked up with blank faces at a baffled Josef.

"Wow... Lucia really laid it on hard," he muttered. "Is he okay?"

"Yeah, yeah!" James assured him. "Just a regular bit of unconsciousness."

"Mm, nothing to worry about," Nearchos smiled.

Josef watched as they shuffled past, narrowing his eyes. "You wouldn't happen to know what's up with Lucia, would you?" he called. "I saw the short girl, so you obviously found her, but Lucia's come back... a mess. Did something happen?"

"No," Zahra chirped, smiling widely. The suspecting look on his face sank her heart. "Hey, can we just back up a little?"

They edged to Josef's side and Zahra laid Bruno's legs gently to the ground. She looked Josef up and down and sighed affectionately. "I'm going to be straight with you - I have a crush on you."

Josef choked on his breath as she drew her hands to his head. "R-really?" he gasped.

"No," Zahra grinned. Her fingers pressed hard against his temples and his eyes glazed over. "Forget *everything* you just saw and return to your dorm."

With a nod of his head, Josef turned and retreated to his room. With a smug giggle, Zahra swivelled around and grabbed Bruno's legs again.

"Damn, that was smooth," James laughed as they continued down the corridor.

"What use is illusion magic if you don't know how to get in people's heads?" Zahra said, her head held high with pride.

Rushing Bruno into James' room, they slammed the door behind them and hauled him onto James' bed. Emilia turned away from the window with a clueless look on her face.

"What happened to your window?" she asked, pushing her hand outside.

"Brooke did that," James said as he stepped back from the bed. "We had to float down to avoid the fire."

"That's sweet," Emilia sighed, tilting her head with a smile.

James growled under his breath as Emilia giggled quietly to herself. The group gathered around his bed, gazing with concern upon Bruno.

"So... anyone have any thoughts?" Nearchos asked.

"Well, that clearly wasn't Bruno," Emilia muttered. "It might not have looked like it, but that armour took a serious amount of pressure to crack. It was far more powerful."

"And more streamlined," Zahra said. "Either he's has been hiding a greater understanding of evocation... or it was someone else casting the spell *for* him."

"Come again?" James scoffed.

"Mind control. The mage we ran into last night used an illusion spell on us, so it's not impossible that he might have been influencing Bruno, using him as a spy of some sort."

"Is there any way we can find out for sure?" Nearchos asked.

"I can probe his mind for manipulation," Zahra said, shuffling to her knees. "Athaean illusion magic is far weaker than the novekhiri stuff, so I might be able to remove it altogether."

"Be my guest," James said, stepping back and giving her space.

"If I'm lucky, the intertwining of our minds could leave an imprint," Zahra muttered, met with an audience of blank faces. "An imprint. Residual memories that can linger for a while after mind-altering powers. I get them a lot with Amani."

"That's... weird," James muttered. "Useful, but weird."

"You know, I thought I never owned a zi'skemeht," Emilia laughed. "You have some *seriously* unusual tastes."

"Not a word," Zahra growled. "Now, everyone be quiet. I need to concentrate."

She closed her eyes and rested her hands gently on Bruno's forehead. Barely seconds later, she was thrust suddenly out of her trance by a colossal burp that echoed through her mind and quaked her body with backlash.

"Sorry, sorry," Emilia giggled.

"Ala'mir! Se gaal fas tagar…" Zahra snapped, clenching her head in her hands as her mind burned. "Do you know how much that hurt?!"

Emilia shrank away as Zahra composed herself and returned to her work. Pressing her hands against Bruno's head, she delved into his mind. It did not take long for the tendrils of her essence to strike a blockade of energy. Though it sprawled throughout his mind, it was spread thin - weak and incoherent. Applying pressure to the mass of purple essence, she quickly began to breach its structure and tear it asunder. As she played havoc upon the mage's spells, trickles of information filtered into her mind and enlightened her of their contents.

As the last strand of purple essence shattered, Zahra's eyes snapped open and she gasped for air, collapsing back onto the carpet. She waved off James' hands as he hurried to help.

"I… I think I got them!" she laughed through heavy breaths.

"Them?" Nearchos scoffed. "There were multiple?"

"Th-There were two - one was a direct control spell, it would have allowed the caster to take over Bruno's body like he did back there. The second was a basic brainwashing spell, forced his mind to prioritise key information."

"And… any imprints?"

"I don't think so, but I got the gist of the brainwashing," Zahra said. "Athaeans must not have figured out illusionary defences, because I could intercept it with no problems. The command was too track all students that suffered serious injuries and would be present on campus tomorrow."

"That's it?" James asked. "Why would they want to know that?"

"Sounds like we could be dealing with more kidnappings," Nearchos mused. "Can't say why, but that seems like the only explanation."

"The command also contained two locations," Zahra said. "The first must be the place where Lucia saw him, but the other is an address - 128 Dawn Street."

"Dawn Street…" James muttered, racking his brain. "Could that be Revani Tower?"

"Go on…" Emilia said.

"It's a building just off Falion Square, surrounded by this massive compound full of warehouses and stuff. It had been abandoned for a while, but it was sold last year. Think I heard it was being renovated for a new museum."

"I'll check," Zahra smiled, wandering to the window. "Amani, jabal!"

Amani swooped down to the ledge and nestled her head in Zahra's hands. The rest of the group watched in an awkward silence as Zahra ruffled the drake's spines and uttered a series of joyous, alien words.

"Hey, can we move this along?" Emilia groaned.

"Yeah, yeah, of course," Zahra said. She turned Amani away and planted her hand on the drake's forehead, taking control and sending Amani fluttering into the distance.

"So…" James sighed. "Wherever this place ends up being, what do we do now?"

"Isn't it obvious?" Emilia sneered. "We go there, beat the crap out of everyone and turn them over to the guards."

"Or, we could just report it," Nearchos suggested.

"Haven't you been listening, you watery turd?!" Emilia snapped. "We can't afford to tell *anyone*. Even if the battlemage guard aren't involved, this illusiony mage guy could find out that we know using his magic! He could have ears anywhere!"

"She's right, we have to deal with this on our own," James said. "But, we'll discuss that when the time comes."

"That's it," Zahra announced. "Revani Tower. I didn't stick around for long, but it's crawling with unmarked soldiers."

"How many, exactly?" Emilia asked.

"Can't tell, I imagine most of them were inside," Zahra said. "But it looked like they were shifting *a lot* of sladium. Weapons mostly."

"Sladium weapons… in Abenfurt," James mumbled, his heart beginning to pound. "You don't think they're going to…"

"Attack the city?" Nearchos suggested.

"Or the College," Emilia said. "Either way, you'd certainly need a lot of sladium."

"If they have sladium weapons, then there's nothing we can do," Nearchos demanded. "We have to report this now, there is no other choice."

"Not necessarily," Zahra mused. "Look, whatever we do, we can't do it in broad daylight. You three should take some time for yourselves, prepare, make sure you're okay with this."

"What about you?" James asked.

"I'm going to stay here. I think we owe Bruno an explanation," Zahra smirked. "We'll meet at… eight. At the Cauldron, that tavern across from the Citadel."

"We can't do this," Nearchos insisted. "We shouldn't!"

"You don't have to," Zahra sighed. "Sit this out if you want, but we're doing this. I'll see you tonight."

Grumbling under his breath, Nearchos marched off. James followed reluctantly and Emilia skipped away on her own, while Zahra slumped back onto the bed and wringed her finger anxiously. As much as she understood the necessity of what they were about to do, she feared it all the same. Alas, she had to be strong - she was their leader, after all.

Lucia gazed out from the connecting bridge between the yellow dorm tower and the library. The dark sky cast a grim veil over the grey spires, barely a ray of light slipping from amongst the clouds. She grasped the guardrail tight in her quaking grip, her every anxious breath convulsing her arms, which lay stiff as she endured a beating headache. Her eyes shot up from the pavement below as the snap of a latch echoed down the silent bridge. Isadora slipped from the dorm tower and breathed a sigh of relief.

Narrowing her eyes, Lucia began to back away. "How did you…"

"I'm a good tracker," Isadora smiled, wandering to her side and leaning back against the rail. "What do you think you're doing?"

"I… I was just wondering whether it's worth living," Lucia sighed. "Maybe I should've stayed in that river and boiled to death…"

Isadora stared for a moment at her friend, her heart sinking. Lucia was shaking from head to toe. Her face was twisted by the pain in her head and her clothes were stained with dried up vomit. Never had Isadora seen somebody sink so low.

"Don't talk like that," she urged.

"Why not?" Lucia spat. "It'd be a mercy - Think of all the people I'd spare."

"You're not a monster, Lucia. Monsters don't feel."

"Neither do I!" Lucia cried. "Not when it matters… I cry and I cry, but every time I hurt someone, there's no hesitation, no remorse until it's too late."

"You can still fight it! There's time for you to change!"

"Hasso thought I could fight it… and he's dead now," Lucia mumbled. "He's dead because I failed, because I couldn't stop it! He was the only one I didn't scare away, the only who gave a damn about me! I-I can't… I can't live without-"

Lucia whimpered as Isadora threw her arms around her. She buried her face in her friend's shoulder and what little grasp she had of her emotions slipped away. Isadora smiled softly as Lucia wailed in anguish, tears avalanching down her cheeks and evaporating before they reached her chin.

"I don't know what to do…" Lucia moaned. "I need him!"

"You'll just have to move on," Isadora whispered. "He's not coming back. There's nothing we can do about that."

"He made me think I could be more than... than *this*. It was the only thing keeping me from hurting people and now, I'm a danger to everyone around me."

Isadora sighed quietly, unwilling to emphasise the sweat that Lucia's heat had drawn from every inch of her skin. "Look, I didn't want to say anything before because I figured it would set you off, but you're looking at that disorder all wrong."

"Not now..."

"Yes, now, because it's exactly what you need to hear. You need to accept that you can't get rid of it, but I'm sure you've always known that. It's a part of you forever."

Lucia glared at her, hating the truth that she knew too well.

"You've always focused on suppressing it, even though you can't," Isadora said. "So, why bother? Why not learn to master it instead?"

"Do you think this is just some power to be harnessed, some gift from your stupid gods?!" Lucia growled, shoving Isadora back. "This is a fucking curse!"

"A curse that you'll always have to live with," Isadora insisted. "I say you make the most of it."

"Or maybe, I should just die," Lucia hissed, backing slowly away. "That's one way, right? It's not a problem if I'm dead!"

"But, you don't want to die, do you?" Isadora said calmly. "You want to overcome this, because you're a fighter. Because you're a Severin."

"I'm not a Severin!" Lucia snapped, edging closer to the rail. "I'm a filthy bastard... and a disgrace. I don't deserve my name."

"Lucia," Isadora urged, slowly extending her hand. "Come inside, please."

"Why?" Lucia mumbled. "What's the point?"

"Hasso saved your life for a reason," Isadora smiled as she stepped closer. "If you jump off this bridge, you prove that everything he believed about you was wrong and he dies in vain."

Lucia stared at her, tears flooding from her eyes as she collapsed against the rail. Her gaze drifted to the grim skyline and fell to the ground so far below.

"We still have a chance to make things right," Isadora whispered. "Please. Come down."

They stood in silence as Lucia's heavy breathing slowed. Her shoulders sagged and her legs went numb. As she wiped away her tears, she reached out with her trembling arm and surrendered her hand to Isadora, who led her gently away.

"You're going to be okay," Isadora assured her as they stepped indoors. "We'll get you through this. I promise."

Emilia whistled a discordant tune as she wandered through Falion Square. Beneath the twilight of the sinking sun, the vast expanse of parks and markets sat in an eerie silence. She came to a stop in the shadow of the Arcana Citadel, beneath the creaking sign of The Cauldron. It was a fairly unassuming place, built of a beautiful mahogany and laden with stained glass and vibrant bushes.

She slipped through the door and with a deep breath of choking, warm air, took in the sights and sounds of the establishment. Under the fiery light of the chandeliers, nobles enjoyed drink and company, serenaded by the soothing tune of a lone violinist. From a table in the far corner, Zahra beckoned her over. Along with the James and Nearchos, Bruno joined them at the table, swigging away at a bottle.

"Bruno?" Emilia smirked. "What a surprise!"

"Well, I wasn't about to miss a bit of payback, was I?" Bruno laughed. "Sorry about attacking you back there, didn't exactly have a choice."

"In that case, *I* am sorry for kicking you through a wall," Emilia smiled. "Though, I hope you'll take it as a valuable lesson."

"I've filled in Bruno on the details," Zahra explained as Emilia took a seat. "The general consensus is that we need to prioritise retrieving any students they have at the tower. Destroying the sladium would be nice, but we're in deep enough as it is…"

"We were in deep enough when we set foot in that manor!" Nearchos hissed. "Seriously, do you hear yourselves? This is getting *way* out of hand!"

"Yeah, we're having trouble selling Nearchos on the whole idea," James sighed. "He thinks it's too dangerous."

"Which it probably is," Zahra muttered.

"Pft, don't be ridiculous!" Emilia sneered. "We're *mages*. There's a reason why House Tarantis uses our kind as super soldiers."

"They have sladium weaponry," Nearchos insisted. "What do we do about that?"

"We take their weapons away," Zahra said. "Carrying unauthorised sladium weapons is illegal, so they must store them somewhere, right?"

"And without those weapons, they won't stand a chance," Bruno grinned. "Even James' baton can slice through steel if he wills it."

"So, you're saying we sneak into the compound, destroy their weapons and take out a legion of trained soldiers, just like that?" Nearchos scoffed. "Does nobody else see the absurdity here?!"

"Of course, I do," James sighed. "And as crazy as this sounds, I think it might work."

"Even if we pulled this off, it would be... *beyond* illegal," Nearchos growled. "We can't just go taking the law into our own hands."

"Unless we're under orders," Zahra grinned, staring across the room.

James followed her gaze over his shoulder and yelped as his beer was whipped out from under him. In one mighty swig, Lucia gulped down the remainder, spilling half down her combat uniform, and hurled it over her shoulder.

"Evening, pricks," she groaned, jolting the bench as she slumped onto her behind.

"Lucia?" James scoffed as Isadora perched beside her friend. "What's with the change of heart?"

"None of your business," Lucia muttered. "So, what's the plan?"

"No offence, but... are you sure you're in a state to be doing this?" Zahra asked.

"I've sobered up now... mostly," Lucia said, followed swiftly by a loud belch. "Okay, I might still be a *little* drunk, but I'll be fine."

"Do you want a splash of my water?" Nearchos asked. "That should wake you up."

Lucia bolted up from table and grabbed Nearchos by the collar. "If so much as a droplet of that shit touches me, I'll turn you to ash!"

"Yeah, best keep these two apart," Isadora smirked, easing Lucia back into her seat. "Lucy doesn't cope well around water."

"*Don't call me that!*" Lucia snapped. Isadora barely flinched at the impact of girl's punch.

"Okay, everyone just cool it," Zahra demanded, turning to Lucia and Isadora. "Look, Lucia, is there any way you can legalise an attack on this compound."

"Legalise... not exactly," Lucia muttered. "But if I'm there, I guarantee the city guard won't fuck with us."

"Good enough," Bruno smiled. "Any other complaints, Nearchos?"

"I suppose not," Nearchos sighed. "Look, I... the fact is, I'm not sure I can go through with this. It's not just how wrong or stupid this feels. After what happened to Laurent and... and to Hasso... I'm scared."

"Wow, you're pathetic," Lucia spat. "Might as well drag yourself home, you useless piece of-"

"Lucia!" Isadora hissed. "Play nice."

"Nobody's making you do this," Zahra said to Nearchos. "I'm sure... *most* of us will understand if you want no part in this."

"Yeah, it's a lot to ask," James said. "We're putting our lives on the line here."

223

Nearchos buried his mouth in his hands, his eyes erratic with conflict as he looked around the table. He closed his eyes and sighed deeply, slumping back in his chair.

"I can't just sit by and do nothing… if any of you were hurt, I'd never forgive myself," he said, glancing shamefully to James. "If I'm going to come along, I'd prefer a less dangerous role, if that's okay."

"That's perfectly fine," Isadora smiled. "Right, Lucy?"

Lucia glared at her with contempt. "I hate you."

"That's a yes," Isadora laughed.

"I'm sure we can find you a purpose," Zahra assured him. "Maybe dealing with hostages?"

"Then, I guess I'm in," Nearchos sighed, his voice strained by doubt.

"I should think so," Lucia muttered. "Now, I'll ask again - what's the plan?"

"We don't have one yet," Zahra said. "I'll use Amani to scout the compound, then we'll figure it out from there."

"And then we blow it up," Lucia grinned darkly.

"Possibly, I guess," Zahra sighed. "It depends on what we find."

"Then, what are we waiting for?" Lucia boomed, sending the bench skidding back as she leapt up from the table and laughing as James fell backwards onto the floor. "Let's blow shit up!"

Once again, the group marched into the city, crossing the square to Dawn Street where the looming spire of Revani Tower came into view. Its stained windows were cracked and filthy, the stone crumbling and seeping moss. In such disrepair, one could almost mistake it for a ruin.

As Lucia stormed ahead, Zahra slipped to Isadora's side, watching their ticking time bomb with incredible caution.

"Isadora, can I ask you something?" she whispered.

"Is it about Lucia?" Isadora smirked.

"Yeah… I need to be completely honest, okay?" Zahra said. "Is she *really* up for this?"

"Count on it," Isadora grinned. "Lucy is pissed on a level I never thought possible, but she's got her head on straight. She wants to make amends."

"That's what I'm worried about," Zahra sighed. "Lucia's definition of amends probably sounds a lot like vengeance."

"It does, which is exactly what we need right now."

Zahra watched for any hint of doubt in the girl's face and found none. As great as it was that Lucia had someone to confide in, Isadora was seeming more and more like a bad influence. The last thing that Lucia needed was someone to encourage her violent tendencies.

"Just try and keep a leash on her, alright?" Zahra urged. "I'd rather keep casualties to a minimum."

"No promises!" Isadora chirped, skipping ahead to Lucia's side.

"Ala'mir..." Zahra groaned. As interesting as the Athaeans were, there were some truly problematic people amongst them.

The group assembled on the flat rooftop of a ballroom, overlooking the compound that surrounding Revani Tower. Most of the group managed to make their own way up, while Bruno was tossed by Emilia and poor James had to cling to Isadora's back while she clambered to the top. The seven of them fell into cover behind a golden six-pointed star that crowned the face of the building.

"There are guards patrolling all around the courtyard," Zahra said as she released her control of Amani. "Forty, I'd say. Maybe more. Seems like there's a lot more of them sleeping in the main tower."

"How much is a lot?" Nearchos asked, anxiously clenching his fists.

"I can only see through the windows," Zahra said. "As for the other buildings, I'm seeing piles upon piles of-"

"Interruption!" Emilia announced. "Does anyone else hear that humming?"

The group fell into silence, exposing the dull throbbing of energy nearby. As it began to grow, Lucia rose to her feet and ignited her hands. Emilia sprang up after her, while Isadora slid and arrow from her quiver. Nearchos extended his hands, Bruno summoned his gauntlets and James drew his sword. They trained their sights upon a head of auburn hair that emerged at the other end of the building.

"Wait wait wait!" Brooke cried, cowering behind a pair of discs as she floated slowly up to the roof. "I-I'm sorry, I didn't mean to- well, I did, but I... I don't..."

"Brooke?" James scoffed, dispelling his weapon.

"Explain," Lucia growled as she took aim.

Brooke took an incredibly deep breath as she stepped onto the rooftop. "I'm really, really sorry, but I was eavesdropping on you guys when you were with Bruno and I-I heard what you said about kidnappings and I got- I got really worried, so I went to check on Ava and I couldn't find her and I asked a bunch of other people and... and they hadn't seen her, so I followed you guys out here 'cause I remembered what you said about abductions and I wanted to help because I think my friend might have been taken!"

"Ugh... get up here," Lucia groaned. "Try anything and I'll vaporise you."

Red faced and panting for breath, Brooke shuffled into cover alongside James.

"Hey," he whispered.

"Yes! I mean... hello."

Emilia giggled quietly as the group returned their attention to Zahra, who composed herself and returned to her explanation.

"As I was saying, it looks like the warehouses are stocked with crates, probably all their weapons and equipment. I'm also seeing barrels being moved out of the tower."

"Can you tell what's in 'em?" Emilia asked. "Please be explosive, please be explosive..."

Zahra reassumed control of Amani and dove in for a closer look. "It looks... white. Like milk, but with little, red grains mixed in."

"Sounds to me like cryphactanol," Lucia grinned darkly. "It's explosive as hell, perfect for siege warfare. It blasts buildings apart like they're made of glass."

"What do they need that for?" James asked.

"You idiot, it's obvious," Lucia sighed. "We know these assholes have been abducting students, but it all happened in the space of two days. With their targets out of the way, they're going to go through with the next step of their plan - attacking the College directly."

"What?" Nearchos scoffed. "Why? That would be suicide!"

"Unless most of the College's mages happen to be out of the city for any particular reason... such as the final of a magical tournament."

"Mm, and they'd have a pretty good chance with that much sladium," Bruno growled. "And as to why... sabotage, terrorism, anti-arcanism - the possibilities are endless, but it doesn't matter. What matters is that we stop this."

"Can we really do anything to stop them?" Brooke mumbled. "I mean, we're only... six, seven - eight people."

"A lesser number of mages have turned the tides of wars," Isadora grinned. "Sladium be damned, we can do this."

"And blowing up that tower should even the odds," Lucia smiled. "Light up that cryphactanol and boom!"

"No way!" Zahra snapped. "What happened to 'I don't like hurting people'?"

"*Good* people. People who don't deserve it," Lucia growled. "I've dealt with hundreds of bastards just like these. Sent them all to the headsman."

"You hypocritical- we're not blowing up that tower!" Zahra hissed. "That's final."

"If you say so..." Lucia smirked, glancing mischievously to Isadora.

Zahra rolled her eyes and jumped to her feet, looking over the band of oddities before her. "Okay... I'm going to stay here. I'll relay information and provide surveillance from the air. Emilia, Bruno - Brooke will fly you into the compound and on my signal, you two are going to a *lot* of noise."

"I like this plan already," Emilia grinned.

"Brooke will then return and go with James and Nearchos to recover the hostages. Isadora, Lucia... ugh, I can't believe I'm saying this - you're both on demolition. Destroy as much of that sladium as you can."

"I thought you said *don't* blow up the tower," Lucia sneered.

"What part of that sentence had the word *tower* in it?" Zahra hissed. "For the love of the Goddess, behave yourself. I want to keep casualties to a minimum."

"What's the point?" Isadora asked. "They're going to be executed anyway."

"We don't have the authority," Nearchos said. "We'd be criminals."

"I do," Lucia smiled.

"You've got your orders," Zahra snapped. "Obey them and we come of this alive. This is going to work this time."

"I should bloody hope so!" Lucia laughed, springing to her feet. "Don't suppose you've prepared a speech?"

"Shut up," Zahra groaned, stepping to the rooftop's edge. "Brooke, you're up. As your people like to say, let's get these bastards."

Straining under the colossal weight of her cargo, Brooke panted for breath as she lowered Emilia and Bruno to the ground. The disc beneath them came to a rest and fizzled away, depositing them behind the perimeter wall.

"Oh, this is going to be a blast!" Emilia laughed, stretching her legs and loosening her arms. "Thank you, spotty girl, for the lift."

"My name is Brooke..."

"Wait- Oh! You're *that* girl," Emilia gasped. "You know, I had hardly recognised you without all the tears. I suppose you're not exactly the most... remarkable individual."

"Well, I... I guess I'm not," Brooke mumbled, looking timidly to the ground as she re-summoned her disc.

"Aw, don't look so down," Emilia smiled. "At least you've caught *someone's* attention..."

"Huh?"

Emilia turned her back and skipped away, waving merrily over her shoulder. "Ta-ta!"

"You're a horrible person, you know that?" Bruno smirked.

"I do indeed," Emilia chirped. "It's called having a theme. Mine was pink, but now it's just being a bitch."

"Pretty sure that one's taken."

"Yes, by everyone in this bloody city, but I wasn't aiming to be unique."

Bruno chuckled as he summoned his rigid armour. "You are one *strange* girl, Miss Arrenni."

"Thank you, person whose name I don't think I ever knew," Emilia smiled, hardening her skin. "Sorry, I struggle to retain knowledge about people inconsequential to my life."

"I'm flattered," Bruno groaned. "So, we just have to… beat people up?"

"Sounds fun, doesn't it?" Emilia chirped. "We have to pull the bad guys to one side of the compound while the other morons destroy the supplies, save hostages, et cetera, et cetera."

"Easy enough, so long as we don't die," Bruno sighed, pointing to a wandering soldier. "You want to start with that one?"

Emilia solidified her fists into dull instruments and raised them to her face. "Absolutely."

The following few minutes were ones of total anarchy. As the whole compound was plunged into high alert by a pair of rampaging youths, James, Nearchos and Brooke moved through the compound towards one of the many warehouses, where Zahra had located a group of four students. Meanwhile, Isadora and Lucia breached into building after building, trampling the guards and prepping the sladium supplies for detonation.

"And… done," Isadora chirped, slamming a flaming arrowhead into the floorboards and springing to her feet.

"Can we get out of here now?" Lucia hissed, her eyes screwed up as her head thumped with pain. "All this sladium is pissing me off."

"Sure, I think that was the last one," Isadora sighed. "You wanna blow up the tower?"

"Course I do. Do we have enough arrows for that?"

"No, this part is on you," Isadora said. "Come on, we don't want to linger here too long."

They wandered to the door and peered through a nearby window. The courtyard was luckily rather lifeless, beside a few patrolling guards. However, the front entrance to the tower was surely a no-go, even with little resistance outside.

"Zahra, how are we getting into this tower?" Isadora asked.

"There's an entrance on the west side of the courtyard," said the voice in their heads. "Looks like a cellar, might connect to the basement."

"I hate this," Lucia groaned, shaking her head as she fought a pounding headache.

"Lighten up!" Isadora laughed. "Thanks, Zahra. On our way now."

"Isadora. Don't even think about touching those barrels."

"Of course, of course!" Isadora chirped.

"I don't like her," Lucia muttered as Isadora peered back through the window.

"Really? I think she's nice."

"That's the problem - she's too nice," Lucia spat. "She's so perfect, with her flawless abilities and her stupid dragon."

"Drake."

"Shut up... I just hate it when people have it easy," Lucia sighed. "Some people are just handed their lives on a silver fucking platter."

"Yeah, I get it," Isadora smiled. "My mater's a gladiatrix, has to fight tooth and nail for every coin. She loves what she does, but that woman never shuts up about how much she hates all those aristocrats in the Senate. Paid a fortune to argue, she'd always say."

"I probably look pretty stupid, huh? An heir to a great house, complaining about hardships."

"I think you've earned the right," Isadora said. "You've had a greater fill of pain than an entire house should have."

"I guess so..." Lucia smirked. "You know, I really-"

Isadora flung the door open and leapt outside, followed by a muffled yelp. Lucia's eyes fluttered as Isadora dragged a soldier into the building, her arms around his face and neck. She pulled him to the ground as he thrashed and flailed, his movements slowing to a standstill. As he fell limp in her grip, she let him slump to the ground and sprang up with a smile.

"Sorry about that," she chirped. "We've got a window - let's move."

They slipped out into the courtyard, deserted by the distant commotion. The occasional crunch sounded in the distance as they hurried to the courtyard's edge, falling into cover behind another warehouse and approaching a pair of old, wooden doors.

"This it, Zahra?" Isadora whispered.

"That's it. You can probably expect trouble."

"Now you're talking," Isadora grinned, turning to Lucia. "Ready, Lucy?"

"Ready for you to stop calling me that," Lucia muttered. "Let's get this over with."

She pressed her hand against the latch and set her hand ablaze. The hiss of the heat turned to a whine as she melted through the metal. With a satisfying clunk, the latch snapped in two and the doors jolted out of place.

"Yeah, I can do more than blow things up," Lucia spat, glaring up at Isadora's smile. "Surprised?"

"I didn't say anything," Isadora smirked as they pulled the doors open. "After you."

"Coward."

Isadora slid an arrow into her bow and crept into the darkness of the basement. Yellow light washed the darkness away as Lucia lit up her hand, unveiling an unsuspecting cellar stocked with dripping barrels and massive wine racks.

"Before we go any further," Isadora whispered. "In the event that you get hit hard with sladium, can you put up a fight without magic?"

"Of course," Lucia smiled, crouching down and yanking a slender dagger from her boot. "That's what this is for."

"You carry a knife?"

"I'm the most feared woman in Verdenheld, of course I carry a bloody knife," Lucia muttered. "Besides, you have one too."

"True… heads up."

Isadora drew her bow in a lightning reflex and loosed an arrow into a soldier's chest as he rounded a wine rack. Electricity surged into his body as the projectile deflected harmlessly off his armour. As he collapsed to the ground, Lucia strolled to the rack beside and peered into one of the slots.

"Well, well… isn't this exciting?" Lucia smiled. "You know what they say - when in Abenfurt…"

Isadora snatched the wine from Lucia's hand before it had even left the slot. "We can get wasted later."

Lucia heaved an exaggerated groan. "Promise?"

"Not tonight. Once we've won the final, we'll get *completely* hammered."

A smile on her face, Lucia plucked the bottle from Isadora's hands and slid it back into place. "You're on."

The two of them marched onwards and into a dank passage, wrought with moss and filth. As they approached a bolted, iron door at the end of the tunnel, Isadora turned to a smile to Lucia.

"Jackpot," she chirped. "You know what you're doing once you're in there?"

"Blowing it up?"

"Well, yeah… but we need a plan," "You can control the spread of your flames, right?"

Lucia glared darkly into her eyes. "Too soon."

"Ah. Sorry," Isadora mumbled, turning her head to hide her awkward smirk. "But, can you?"

"Yeah."

"Then this should be simple! Just plant some flames around the basement and when we want to set them off, you let 'em spread!"

She leapt to the door and looked it up and down as she drew an arrow from her quiver and ignited it. Jamming it between the doors, she stepped back and made way for Lucia.

"Alright, you're up," Isadora said. "I'll blow the door and you set some fuses."

Lucia was silent. Isadora looked at her through narrow eyes, watching as her friend stared at the door as if it were a yawning abyss.

"Lucy?"

"There has got to be another way," Lucia mumbled, looking down upon her hands. "If something sets off my disorder, the flames could go out of control, blow the place while we're still inside."

"Or, we could *use* your disorder to blow this place sky high," Isadora grinned.

"What- are you crazy?!" Lucia hissed. "Setting me off is a one way ticket to the grave!"

"Not if you can control it!" Isadora urged. "If you could learn to think straight under its effects, you could use its destructive power as a weapon!"

"Haven't you been paying attention?" Lucia snapped. "I don't want this! I-I need to get rid of it, not accept it!"

"But you can't, can you?" Isadora sighed. "You know you can't, so why keep trying? It'll be with you for life, but that doesn't have to be a bad thing."

"You're crazy," Lucia muttered. "And not just that, you're *stupid*."

"Just hear me out alright? Whenever you start to overload, you try to stop it," Isadora explained, only souring Lucia's mood. "And by doing that, you only make it worse. Don't fight it - let it take over."

"If I do that, I'll kill everyone."

"You won't. It's linked to your emotions, right? So, if you keep calm, you can keep it under control. Just don't panic."

"Just... don't panic," Lucia smirked. "That's it, huh? Oh, why did I not think of that? *Silly me!*" She grabbed Isadora by the collar and pulled her close, darkness in her eyes. "You don't know what it's like! To know what you're going to do but to be so powerless to stop it, for every inch of your body to burn with horrible, horrible pain! Do you think *you* could think straight if your whole body was on fire?!"

Isadora watched as flames raced up Lucia's arm, as her skin hissed and wept sparks. An idea sprung to mind - a cruel one, yet ultimately necessary.

"If Hasso could see you now... he'd be ashamed," she hissed. "Giving up, just like that. Letting him die for nothing."

Lucia stared emptily at her friend and began to slowly back away. "Don't do that," she gasped, panic in her eyes. "Not you. Please."

"He gave you everything," Isadora growled. "He thought you could be more, that there was hope for you! He died for that, for a chance that you're willing to throw away."

231

"Stop…" Lucia begged, grasping her head in her hands. "I don't want to hurt you… please, don't do this!"

"Or maybe…" Isadora took in a deep breath and closed her eyes. "Maybe he just wanted to die so you wouldn't kill him first."

She held her breath as Lucia threw back her head and let slip an agonised wail. Flames burst from her body, spreading ravenously down her arms and legs. Her tortured breathing was drowned out by the roaring of the fire as it crept up her neck and consumed her head. Even as it surged across her shoulders, Isadora planted her hands firmly on them.

"Yes!" she laughed, a bright smile on her face even as her hands burned. "It's okay, it's okay… you can do it."

Lucia clenched her fists and stiffened her back, straining as a dull pain spread throughout her body. Trying to take control was an agony, one that had her whimpering like a frightened child. The towering flames began to recede, taking a shape far less chaotic.

"Calm… turn that anger into passion," Isadora whispered as she withdrew her charred hands. "Just breathe. Let it happen."

As her body was fully encompassed, Lucia's breath began to slow. Her eyes drifted shut, her body loosening. Remorse became desire as hate became conviction.

"Yes… you're doing it!" Isadora laughed. "Lucy…"

Lucia stared down upon her hands, watching as her flame cloak writhed and warped around them. It had been so easy, so simple. It was jarring to think that she had always been capable, held back only by fear. That fear was gone - it was never coming back.

"I'm doing it…" she mumbled, her voice muffled by her fiery armour. Isadora smiled warmly as, for the first time in her life, Lucia broke into genuine, joyous laughter. "I… I… Thank you."

"That's what friends are for, right?" Isadora chirped, sliding an arrow from her quiver. "You wanna blow shit up?"

A devilish grin spread across Lucia's face like a veil of darkness. She raised her blazing palm to the wall and stood ready. "I thought you'd never ask."

One rampage later, Lucia strode out of the tunnel with Isadora in tow, taking a deep breath of fresh air as her burning cloak dispersed. They stood proudly at the compound's edge, staring up at the looming tower at its centre.

"Care to do the honours?" Isadora grinned.

"I'd like nothing more."

Lucia drew her flaming arms wide and closed her eyes, overcome with excitement as she felt her flames crash against the barrels. The detonation shook the city - stone cracked, lampposts rattled and water rippled. The courtyard behind them convulsed, belching white fire from the fractured ground. The base of the tower collapsed into the blinding abyss, an avalanche of stone that crumbled away like dirt against water. In mere moments, the whole thing came crashing down, the sound of its downfall a thunder that quaked bone. The rooftop had barely given way when Isadora raised her hand to her face.

"Best day of my life," she grinned as she snapped her fingers.

Doors and windows exploded with blue flame, lighting up building after building in a chain reaction of bangs and cracks. White light spilled from their midst, blowing out walls and showering soldiers with hurtling shrapnel.

"It's beautiful," Lucia sighed, igniting her hands with flame. "Let's go beat some people up."

"You go ahead. I'm going to sweep the area, check we didn't miss any spots."

"Sure," Lucia said. She gazed across what remained of the inner courtyard, eyeing her helpless prey. "Zahra, have everyone converge on the courtyard once they're done."

Her mind went numb as a seething voice swamped her mind. "What have you done?!" Zahra growled. "You psychopath, there had to be hundreds of-"

Lucia severed the link and continued on her way. Smugness like no other on her face, she gazed upon Harald Mortan with darkness in her eyes.

"Uh... Zahra?" Emilia asked as she watched Revani Tower collapse in on itself. "What was that?"

"*That* was the gracious Lady Severin annihilating hundreds of unarmed soldiers in a gigantic explosion!" Zahra snapped. "Oh, what was I thinking?"

"Aye, maybe we shouldn't have put Lucia and Isadora on demolition duty," Bruno muttered.

"Who else could have done it?" Emilia said. "Don't blame yourself, Zahra. We'll just have to live with her... interesting sense of justice."

"I guess so... you two had better go on the offensive, try and apprehend a few soldiers before Lucia obliterates them."

"We're on it," Bruno smiled. "You ready, Tiny?"

"At least I'm not fat," Emilia sneered.

The two of them shuffled to their feet, peering around the corner and watching the hail of fireballs rain down upon panicking soldiers.

"You know, there was a moment where I thought Hasso's death had changed Lucia," Emilia sighed. "Guess it just pissed her off."

"And made her more powerful, it seems," Bruno mumbled. "You have my condolences for tomorrow."

"You can save them for her," Emilia grinned, fusing her finger into blades and hardening her skin. "Come, my trouser-tearing companion. Let's save some terrorists!"

Harald Mortan stumbled out from the inferno that engulfed Revani Tower, clad in a suit of old, scuffed armour worn a dull black by flame. He threw his tabard to the ground and stamped out the fire, crushing House Mortan's crimson deer into the ashen ground. Taking his sladium crystal in his quaking grip, he staggered into the courtyard and drew his weathered longsword.

"Lord Mortan!" called a soldier, panting for breath as he charged across the courtyard. "Lucia Severin, she's back!"

"Of course, she fucking is," Mortan groaned. "Rally the men and salvage what you can. We make for Strausia tomorrow."

"There's nothing left to salvage, sir!" the soldier cried. "The sladium, the cryphactanol, it's all gone! I don't even know if anyone-"

Mortan leapt back as a chunk of blazing stone struck the boy's head and battered him to the ground. Shielding his eyes, he took a step back, looking in a daze across the world of fire that consumed him. Through the crackling of the flames emerged a high-pitched screech, drawing ever closer as he turned to meet it.

"What the-"

Amani latched onto his helmet and whipped her tail around his sword arm. As he tried desperately to detach the monster, she opened her maw wide and wrenched the sladium crystal from his grip. He watched emptily as the drake flew off, until a group of soldiers emerged atop a nearby building, each wrought with burns.

"Stop that thing!" he growled.

The soldiers jumped to attention. Some turned tail and ran, but three stood fast and drew bows from their backs. Amani ducked and spiralled as the archers took aim, but it was needless - they were swept away by a deluge of yellow flame.

"First kidnapping, now animal abuse," Lucia sneered, emerging on the rooftop and parting the flames that consumed her body. "As always, House Mortan never fails to bring itself shame."

"I should have known you'd be back," Mortan groaned, strapping his blue-tinted tower shield to his arm. "Must you bastards torment me everywhere I go?"

"If the stench of House Mortan weren't so intolerable, we might have left you alone," Lucia said smugly. "You've got a lot of nerve turning your back on House Severin, but to stoop as low as terrorism? I'm disappointed, Harry."

"Turn my back... your brother burned everything I have!" Mortan growled. "And for what? Because I had the audacity to suggest that maybe a brat and his psycho sister don't deserve to rule?"

"Have you seen yourself?" Lucia smirked. "You're talking big words for a man plotting a terror attack on a college."

"The College is just another training ground for the slaves of Verdenheld's war machine," Mortan muttered. "Open your eyes - they're fashioning you into killers to enforce their tyranny."

"Why do think I'm here? The best generals aren't afraid to get their hands dirty!" Lucia declared, her smug eyes darkening. "Speaking of which, I believe I have some cleaning up to do."

"I've been watching my back for eight years, just waiting for your brother to try and finish what he started," "As the last of my house, it'll be my honour to make him the last of his."

"Oh no, this has nothing to do with houses," Lucia growled, flame swamping her body and consuming all but her eyes. "This is *so* very personal."

Firing off an explosion at her feet, Lucia strafed herself into the air. Another explosion sent her streaking towards him, hammering down her hands upon the ground before him. She sprang up to find the scorched face of his shield, reeling back as it rushed after her.

"Don't you think that a little overzealous?!" Harald roared, drawing his shield in front of him and grinning as its arkansteel face set ablaze with yellow flame.

He slammed it down and unleashed a wave of fire that ripped up the ground and blasted Lucia back. Her flame cloak reabsorbed much of the energy that struck, flaring brighter as she charged to meet him. With a feral roar, she cleaved her hands down, swiping back and forth, battering his shield with her blazing hands. The pain that shot through her fingers with each blow was nothing to her, lost in a surge of anger. All that mattered, all that flooded her mind, was vengeance.

Nearchos stumbled back as a ball of white flame exploded against the rooftop above, hailing their scarlet defences with embers. Brooke squealed as they sprayed across her arm and ignited a fire upon her sleeve.

"Fire, fire!" she cried, flailing her arm about. "Do something!"

"Hold still!" Nearchos snapped. He raised his hand and doused her with a jet of water, turning her leathers half black and snuffing the writhing flames.

"Oh God, thank you!" Brooke gasped, slumping against the wall. "This... this cryphactanol stuff is pretty dangerous, huh? What was that maniac thinking?"

"I doubt she *was* thinking," Nearchos growled. "Never mind stopping a terror attack, we're an accessory to one!"

"Nearchos! Focus, alright?" James urged. "Yes, Lucia is a sick, terrible person, but we've got our own job to do!"

"Yeah, we need to get those hostages out of here before they're blown up!" Brooke said, slamming down her foot and summoning her disc. "Get on."

"Won't we be seen?" James asked. "Oh right... I guess that doesn't really-"

Brooke grabbed him by the sleeve and yanked him onto the disc, gritting her teeth and raising them into the air as Nearchos hopped on. They hovered over the rooftop and into open air, every one of them stiff with anxiety as flaming stone hailed from above.

"James... I need you to give me directions," Brooke stammered, squeezing her eyes shut.

"Okay, okay, um... just turn a bit. A bit more. Alright, straight on from here."

She thrust her arms back and hovered them slowly towards their destination. Nearchos whimpered as a blazing chair whipped by, spraying his arm with hissing ember. Before long, Brooke lowered them to the ground and shaking herself off, barged open the doors to the warehouse.

They narrowed their eyes as they looked around the room - it was nothing like they had expected. Warm candlelight illuminated four beds, supplemented with tables covered with crumb-covered plates, well-kept books and jugs of water. Meridian sprang immediately from her bed, an ecstatic smile growing across her pale face.

"Oh my God!" she gasped, burying her mouth in her hands. "They said no-one would come..."

While Meridian limped over to Brooke and embraced her in a hug, James and Nearchos wandered deeper into the room. On one bed lay Catelyn, her twisted leg wrapped in a thick layer of bandages. Vivienne jump up from hers, her skin warped by burns and her hair half shaven. Reiner simply glared at their saviours, his swollen face barely leaving its entrenched position in his pillow.

"Hey Brooke, I don't see Ava here..." James said.

"Oh... heh, must've been a false alarm," Brooke mumbled, a timid smile on her rosy cheeks. She gently eased Meridian onto her bed and smiled down warmly upon her. "It's okay. Nearchos is going to get you all home."

"Home? Are you kidding me?" Reiner scoffed, jumping to his feet. "No, I'm not going anywhere."

"What?" Vivienne hissed. "Reiner…"

"You heard what they said, Vivienne. They're going to destroy the College! The last thing I want is to go back there and die."

James rolled his eyes as Reiner crossed his arms in defiance. "This entire place is exploding!" he yelled. "If we don't get you out of here-"

Brooke punched Reiner in the temple and knocked him flat onto his bed. The rest of the students stared in total shock as she hauled the boy off his bed and dragged him over to Nearchos.

"Get this idiot out of here," she sighed, dumping him to the ground. "Come on, James, I'm sure we're needed elsewhere."

James and Nearchos exchanged blank expressions while Vivienne hurried to Reiner's side.

"Good luck," James said, waving him off and hurrying after Brooke. He grabbed her shoulder as he caught up to her. "What was that?"

"Sorry… I didn't want to waste time," Brooke mumbled. "Every second we were in there, the chance of us being hit by a fireball got higher and higher."

"He was coming around. I think."

"That's a risk I wasn't willing to take. He could have been brainwashed for all we know," Brooke said. "Zahra, the hostages are on their way out. What can we do to-"

The two of them stopped in their tracks as they came face to face with Euric. The mage skidded to a halt metres from them, panting for breath and drenched in sweat. His fingers clenched hard around his staff as he looked upon them with tired eyes.

"You?" he scoffed. "I knew Lady Severin would be mixed up in this, but you? Coming here was a grave mistake."

"It's worked out fine so far," James said. "We've blown up all your stuff and released your prisoners."

"It's over," Brooke urged. "All of it. You can't win."

"On the contrary," Euric growled. "Lord Mortan might be trying to get back at Verdenheld, but I am not so petty. I will bring freedom to the world of magic, freedom from oppressive rules and segregation! Without the College, humanity would flourish - surely, you understand this."

James clenched his fists and gritted his teeth - Of course, he understood that. It was a fact that he had believed all his life.

"You know what?" he sighed. "You're right. Magic shouldn't be hidden behind a wall of coin… but that doesn't mean what you're doing here is right."

"Maybe... but as it would happen, you've given me a far less destructive medium through which to bring this change," Euric said darkly. "How would it reflect upon the College if a group of its students took the law into their own hands and *died* for it?"

Brooke whipped back her hand and launched an energy disk at Euric. It streaked over his shoulder and into the distance, countered swiftly by a stream of ice that drove Brooke into cover.

"It never had to come to this," Euric growled. "What I'm about to do is a product of your own actions."

Brooke fell behind a cluster of barrels and, as purple flame tore into her cover, clenched her fist and recalled her weapon. Euric turned as it approached, lashing out and receiving a crazed girl to the face. Emilia released her grip and dropped from Brooke's disc, latching onto Euric like a feral raccoon.

"Surprise vampirism!" Emilia cried, sharpening her teeth and sinking them into his neck.

Euric roared with pain and released a pulse of wind, blasting Emilia to the ground. He raised his staff over his head and cleaved it down upon her as she rose to her feet. The wooden shaft snapped in two as it collided with her smug face, showering the two of them with splinters as they stared at one another.

"How unfortunate," Emilia grinned.

As Euric tried to withdraw the remainder of his staff, Emilia grabbed its end and bit down upon his hand, tearing bloody gashes through his fingers and disarming him of his weapon. Forcing Brooke and James back into cover with a lash of lightning, Euric turned upon Emilia with a handful of purple mist. A blast from his palm froze her in place as she lunged at him, covering her head to toe in a prison of ice.

"Ah," Emilia sighed, watching as air rushed to Euric's palm. "This is... a less than desirable situat-"

A violent burst of wind blasted her through the wall nearby warehouse, sending half of the building cascading down on top of her. He span around as Brooke descended upon him, dodging a pair of scything discs and stumbling back at they shot up from the ground. Deflecting James' sword with an explosive flick of his wrist, Euric bludgeoned him to the ground with a blast of wind.

"Brooke...!" James gasped as the mage stood over him and ignited his hands.

The incoming discs were shattered into sparks by a gout of purple flame. James shielded his eyes as Euric raised his hands over his head, where they were met by another pair. Soaring overhead, Brooke grabbed Euric by the wrists and pulled him into the air. James watched in awe as

238

Brooke flung him over her head and dragged him meteorically to the ground. The disc at her feet exploded as she struck the ground with a chilling crunch, while Euric smashed into the stone face-first.

"Oh my God," James whispered, rushing to Brooke's side as she rolled onto her back.

While Euric lay motionless in a swelling puddle of blood, Brooke clutched her misshapen arm, whimpering quietly as she stared into the sky. A gentle smile graced her tortured face as James' head blotted out of the stars.

"Did I get him?" she wheezed, closing her eyes and resting her head on the cold ground.

"Yeah…" James smirked, cringing as he glanced up at Euric. "Actually, I think he's dead."

"Better him than you," Brooke sighed. "N-not that killing people is good! No, it's really, really, *really* bad and I feel dirty and wrong, but that's okay because he was going to… he was… I need sleep."

"You and me both," James smirked, extending his hand. "You wanna get outta here?"

Brooke stared for a moment at his hand, her eyes fluttering. She pushed herself off the ground and reached out with her quivering left arm. As their fingers touched, she yelped in pain and withdrew her arm, clutching it to her stomach as she whimpered quietly.

"What's wrong?" James gasped.

"I-I think it's broken," Brooke said. "Actually, it… it kinda doesn't hurt that bad. It just feels really freaky."

"Yeah, we're definitely getting you out of here," James laughed.

"You mean *I'm* getting me out of here," Brooke chuckled as she grasped his hand. "You, uh… want to come with?"

"Someone's gotta keep you from passing out," James smiled.

"Alright," Brooke giggled as her disc formed beneath her. "Hop on."

Lord Mortan struck the ground at Lucia's feet, the remaining half of his splintered shield still hanging from his wrist. His hoarse breaths echoed within his scorched armour as he lay back in the dirt, watching as Lucia stood triumphantly over him.

"You're going to pay for what you did," she growled, her cloak of writhing flame growing more violent.

She planted her foot upon his stomach and reeled back her right arm. Yellow fire turned almost white as she held it against him. Each of her heavy breaths became more and more tortured, not by any physical pain, but by the torment of her own mind begging her to stop.

"You're shaking," Harald wheezed through a mocking chuckle. "You are right to be afraid… I won't be the last to defy House Severin. Soon, the whole world will come crashing down upon this pitiful kingdom."

"Psychopath…" Lucia hissed, her voice warped by agony.

"Oh, I'm the psychopath?" Harald laughed. "Have you looked in the mirror lately? You and your brother, you're nothing more than murderous, hate-filled degenerates."

"Shut up!" Lucia begged, burying her head in her other hand.

"Come on, kill me already! That's what you want, isn't it? To fulfil your sick sense of justice and burn me like you did my family?"

Lucia's arm locked up as it surged with pain, unable to handle the essence that flowed through it. Her breath now turned to agonised whimpers, twisted by sadness and shame. She stared down upon her warped reflection in his chestplate, but it was a monster that stared back. What she saw was not Lucia Severin, but a burning avatar of fire and hate.

Her legs went to jelly as she broke gradually down, weeping without tears. The flames calmed and hissed, simmering away and unveiling her raw skin. Her fiery mask swept away, leaving behind a face tortured by grief. Crackling tears spilled from her eyes as the yellow light left them, returning to a dull blue as the last of the flames died out. She withdrew her hand and stumbled back, collapsing to the ground. Harald looked across at her with a mixture of shock and confusion behind his visor.

"I took you for a lot of things, but not a coward," Harald growled. "Your mother was right to throw you from that bridge, you worthless piece of-"

"Sleep," Zahra sighed as Amani planted her at his side. She dragged back her windswept hair and looked down at Lucia. "You have a lot of explaining to do."

"What is there to explain?" Lucia sighed, exhaling her anger as she watched Harald's head slump back. "We killed all the bad guys. We won."

"You slaughtered hundreds of people!"

"People who would have done the same to us! To the College!" Lucia growled. "Maybe your perfect life in that stupid desert of yours is all sunshine and rainbows, but let me tell you - death is the only solution in this hellhole of a kingdom."

Zahra shook her head as she backed away. "Maybe what they say about you is right," she said, staring up at the crumbling ruins of Revani Tower. "Maybe you are a monster."

Lucia looked again at her reflection in Harald's gut. Her skin was dark and worn, her eyebrows half-vaporised and her hair scorched completely black, with but a remnant of blonde remaining at the tip of her ponytail.

"Monsters don't feel," she grinned darkly, swelling with conviction. "And right now, I feel *really* good."

Her sickening words made Zahra ill. Cupping her mouth, she turned her back on Lucia and looked gravely upon the blazing remains of Revani Tower. It was true that the men Lucia killed would have done the same and that they would surely have been executed had they survived. Still, it was harrowing to think that Lucia felt not a shred of remorse, even after all she had been through. Truly, that girl had a twisted sense of justice.

"Is everyone alive?" Lucia asked as she scrambled to her feet.

Zahra took a deep breath. "Brooke's injured, but yes," she sighed. "We did it."

Lucia sighed with satisfaction as they watched Bruno trudge into the courtyard, a dust caked Emilia following in tow. Isadora appeared atop a crumbling building and slipped elegantly to the ground, slinging her bow over her back and wandering merrily to meet them.

"We get all of it?" Lucia called.

"Yep, reduced to ash," Isadora chirped as she skipped to Lucia's side. "All in a good day's work, I'd say!"

Emilia tried to hide her laughter while Lucia received Isadora's high five. "You two have become pretty chummy, huh?" The dark glare that she received was enough to turn her away.

Zahra stepped into the open and flung out her arm, smiling as Amani swooped down and wrapped her feet around her wrist. The drake's mouth was smeared with blood and her golden scales were battered by flame and ash.

"Deb Amani besan?" she whispered, carefully stroking the drake's snout. "Emilia, Bruno! You okay?"

"A few aches here and there, but I can't complain," Bruno boomed. "Turned out, these chaps didn't have many weapons outside of those stockpiles, mostly had to deal with a bunch of idiots waving rocks at me."

"Yeah, fun time!" Emilia chirped. "I only lost two fingers!"

"What?!"

Emilia stuck up her hand and waved it about nonchalantly. The pinky and ring fingers on her right hand were reduced to stumps, spilling a torrent of blood down her arm.

"I am in a great deal of pain," Emilia smiled.

Zahra span around, taking cover behind her hand as she tried to scrub the image from her mind. "I- what- you... how did that even happen?"

"The mage guy froze me and when he chucked me through a wall, they kinda just... snapped off," Emilia said, her voice becoming more and more strained.

"You're a biomancer! Can't you just heal it?"

"Yeah, I was just waiting until I'd spent the shock value," Emilia smirked. She grasped her stumps in her left hand and in a quick flash of pink light, regenerated the flesh and sealed the wounds. "Done!"

"Great..."

"Um, guys?" Isadora asked. "I know Nearchos is helping the captives home, but... where are James and Brooke?"

"I... don't know," Zahra mused, folding her arms and glancing up at Amani. "They're definitely alive, I saw them."

"Maybe, they went home?" Bruno suggested. "Ah, what does it matter? Let's just get this mess cleaned up and get back to campus."

"Speaking of - What do we do with him?" Zahra asked. "I assume treason is a death penalty here too?"

"Please, loitering can be death if you're in the wrong person's garden," Lucia muttered. "I'll straighten things out with the battlemages, make sure he ends up in House Severin's custody. House Tarantis can do whatever they want with the rest."

"Won't they be a little pissed about all the destruction?" Isadora smirked.

"What're they going to do, arrest me?" Lucia sneered. "I'm a full half of a great house, I'm practically untouchable. You idiots scram and I'll take care of the cover up."

"Are you sure?" Zahra asked.

"Of course, I'm bloody sure!" Lucia snapped. "Get the hell outta here!"

Zahra shrank away and waved the others along. Bruno and Emilia marched off, while Isadora lingered at Lucia's side.

"Proud of you," she smiled.

"Fuck off."

Chuckling to herself, Isadora span around and skipped after the others. Lucia took a deep breath as she started her march towards the front gate, her head held high with pride. For the first time in forever, she felt a glimmer of hope, small but with plenty of room to grow. Maybe, in time, she would overcome her anger after all.

An explosion shook the ground, displacing rubble and throwing dust into the air. Lucia watched as the compound's gate skidded by, a cloud of fading smoke in its wake. From the veil emerged five soldiers, four men and one woman, all cloaked in turquoise robes and clad in silvered armour. The battlemages marched into the courtyard, their hands aglow with spells and clenched around blades. One of their number moved ahead to confront Lucia, staring at her narrowly through his golden eyes.

"Apologies for the racket, gentlemen," Lucia smiled. "No need to worry, this is official House Severin business."

"Wh- Lady Severin?" the battlemage scoffed. "What are you doing here?"

"Just tying up some loose ends. Lord Mortan betrayed his oath and fled to Abenfurt, thought he was untouchable in his little compound," Lucia muttered. "I have thusly proved otherwise. I have personally seen to the traitor and my men have dealt with his."

"And... where are your men?"

"Oh, I sent them home. Figured it was best left to House Tarantis to deal with what happens next, being their city and all."

"So, you led an attack on a property within Abenfurt *without* notifying the local guard?" the battlemage growled. "With all due respect, Lady Severin, this was an illegal raid. In the eyes of the law, you are currently a criminal."

Lucia stepped closer, leaning in and glaring into his eyes. "Are you threatening me, soldier?"

"Well, I... no, ma'am."

Lucia planted her hand firmly on his shoulder and gave him a sweet smile. "Great. Now, I suggest you obey my orders before *I* start threatening *you*."

"O-of course, my lady."

"That's the spirit," Lucia smiled darkly. "You and your men can have your way with this place. All I require is that House Severin receives Harald Mortan in chains. Can you do that?"

The battlemage nodded intently, stiff with fear. Lucia slapped him heartily on the shoulder and moved on, grinning at the other mages and laughing as they shrank away.

"You can discuss the logistics with my brother," she called as she stepped out of the gate. "I expect that man in Jordenholm by the break of dawn, so chop chop!"

Flicking her charred hair, she strode triumphantly into the street, watching over her shoulder as the guards looked on baffled. Never had she felt so confident, so full of purpose. Never had she felt so alive.

James watched as Brooke slumped onto the ledge, cradling her arm as she sank onto the rooftop at her back. From four stories up, they could see for miles around, from the smouldering ruins of the compound to the rolling canopies of the Abenwood and to the distant ocean in the west. It was beautiful, a collage of blues, greens and flickering lights.

"Do you think we did the right thing?" Brooke sighed as James sat down beside her. "He seemed like he meant well..."

"Maybe, but he was going to destroy the College," James muttered. "It's like Nearchos said - that would've set the world back centuries."

"And I guess it would have sucked for us too…" Brooke smirked. "I don't know what I'd do if it were gone."

James nodded his head and suddenly, they were silent. Aside from the pained breaths that Brooke exhaled, not a sound was exchanged between them as they simply sat there, twiddling their thumbs. James looked back and forth between her and the horizon, afraid to stare for too long.

"You know, um… you were amazing back there," James mumbled. "As usual, I guess."

Brooke looked up at him, scarlet swamping her cheeks. "You-you think I'm… no, no, I'm not that good, I just… If anything, *you* were amazing! I mean, you only have the sword and the shield, but you still fought him a- and we won!"

"Yeah, because you kept saving me!" James laughed. "That fight was all you."

"Well, I… I guess I kind of did do a lot," Brooke muttered. "B-but you were still really cool! You know, with the sword and the shield and the… and the… the thing! Th-that thing that you do."

"The thing?" James smirked.

"Yes…" Brooke smiled. Her quivering smile suddenly dropped and she buried her head in her good hand. "I'm sorry, I'm sorry! You're my friend and I don't know anything about you, I'm so sorry! Stupid, stupid…"

"Brooke, it's okay," James urged.

"I'm a terrible friend, this is why nobody likes me!" Brooke moaned. "I try to be nice and I just ruin everything and I-"

James grabbed her arm and pressed his lips against hers. For that long few seconds, she sat frozen, staring wide eyed into space as her head swelled with heat. She pushed him back, her heavy breaths becoming quickly panicked. Her body trembled, her eyes welled up and her mouth quaked as it tried to produce anything beyond crazed mumbling.

"I-I'm sorry, I… I shouldn't have done that," James stammered, reaching out slowly to calm her down. "It's just… it's just I really like you an-and I thought… I thought you-"

She grabbed his shoulder, dragged him close and kissed him as hard as she could. Brooke pulled herself away and gazed into his eyes, tears streaming down her cheeks as the two of them broke down into giddy laughter. She flung her arm around him and buried her face in his shoulder, spilling tears down his neck as she wept.

"Why are you crying?" James asked through uncontrollable laughter.

"I don't- I don't know!" Brooke giggled. "After everything that's happened, I guess I can't believe it's real. I mean, we just saved the College and now…"

"Now what?" James asked, toying with her hair as he rested his head on hers.

"I don't know," Brooke smiled. "Why do anything?"

"Because your arm is broken?"

"Ah, it can wait," Brooke sighed, her voice barely strained by the agony. "Let's just stay a while, enjoy the company."

"Just don't fall asleep on me, alright?" James chuckled. "I kinda need you to get down."

Brooke heaved a drawn out yawn as she cozied up to him. "No promises... at least you'll have a nice view."

"Yeah... guess I will."

"I meant the scenery."

"I know."

The two of them giggled childishly as James sank into her greasy hair - it smelled horrible after a night of sweating, but he didn't care. He was on top of the world and there wasn't a thing that could bring him down. All that was left now was to win the Triarcanum.

Chapter Eleven - Finale

The dull clang of a distant bell jolted James from his sleep. The air was cool and fresh, a gentle morning breeze caressing his skin. Birds sang, wind whistled and the sun had begun to slip from the horizon, bathing the city's spires in golden light. He glanced down with a smile at Brooke, who lay snoring quietly on his lap. As he ran his hand through her hair, another clang struck, one that saw his eyes shoot wide. He tilted his head to the culprit, a clock tower that bore grave news indeed.

"Brooke!" James hissed, grabbing the girl's shoulder and shaking her erratically. "Brooke, wake up!"

"Huh, wha?" Brooke mumbled, rolling over and looking up at him through groggy eyes. "Hey… it wasn't a dream."

"Brooke, you have to get up right now," James urged. "The final is in two hours!"

"What?!" Brooke gasped, whipping upright and whimpering at the pain of her arm. "Oh my God, oh my God! Th-th-this is my fault, I shouldn't have- I was so stupid, I-"

"Calm down!" James snapped. "Look, we've got plenty of time - I'm already suited up and I can live with dirty clothes. You've just gotta get me to my team."

"Okay, okay, I can do that… I can do that."

Brooke stuck out her foot and summoned her disc, stepping off the rooftop and extending her hand to James. She pulled him on and smiled as he wrapped his arms tight around her.

"Alrighty, where are we going?" she asked.

"If they're not still waiting outside the red dorms, they'll be on their way to Gladewatch. Just follow the road."

"Aye aye!" Brooke concurred, thrusting out her arm and propelling them forth.

James still could not help but laugh as the wind surged by - it was a feeling he expected would never get old. They soared over the skyline and traversing such a small city, arrived at the College in minutes. Brooke drew them to a halt, hovering outside the red dorm tower, and peered down at the ground.

"Nope, they're gone," she said, moving them gently along. "But it looks like they were here recently - I can still see Nearchos' footprints."

James glanced down with an eyebrow raised at a trail of water droplets leading down the path. "Huh, I never noticed that."

"Yeah, he uses a thin layer to keep himself cool in the sun," Brooke said. "I'm, uh… kind of a loser. I stare at boys a lot."

"Eh, guys stare at girls all the time," James said. "But not Lucia. Never Lucia."

"Yeah, poor Harmodius..." Brooke smirked. "Hey, there they are!"

They looked down upon Zahra and Nearchos, who were wandering away from the main path and towards the biomancy building.

"Alright, put me down around the corner," James said. "I'll pretend I ran here from my dorm."

"They won't believe that!" Brooke giggled.

"Won't know until I try," James smiled confidently. Brooke hovered him to the ground outside the library and he hopped off the disc. "Guess I'll talk to you back at the dorms."

"Guess so," Brooke sighed. "Might want to wait til tomorrow though - it'd be kind of awkward if Ava answered the door."

"You live with Ava?" James scoffed.

"My parents paid her entry fee, got a discount by having us share a room."

"Huh... cool. See you later!"

"Hey, wait up!" Brooke called, hurrying after him. "I need to go get my arm checked out, so I... I won't be there to support you."

"Ah, it's fine. You don't have to-"

Brooke's hands smothered his cheeks as she dragged him into a kiss. She was a terrible kisser, bunching up her lips as if she'd eaten a lemon whole, but it was the thought that counted.

"Kick Lucia's ass for me, will you?" she grinned, shoving him back and leaping back onto her disc. "And don't get killed!"

Watching as she soared into away, James breathed a sigh of satisfaction and wandered to meet his friends. Their eyes lit up as he rounded the corner, waving awkwardly as he approached.

"James?" Zahra gasped. "Goddess, you had us so worried!"

"Yeah... sorry about that," James mumbled, a plastic innocence on his face.

"Where did you go?" Zahra snapped. "Did you have to sleep that bad?"

"Yeah, something like that," James smirked. "What did I miss?"

"Not much. Lucia caught up with us, said she sorted things out with the battlemages. The official story is that a group of Severin knights raided the compound and demolished it with magical charges."

"Will House Tarantis buy that?"

"Maybe not, but I'm sure they would rather keep this under wraps as well," Nearchos said. "The idea of a bunch of students taking the law into their own hands wouldn't exactly reflect well on their battlemages."

"So, we're in the clear?" James laughed.

247

"We won't be if you talk so loud!" Zahra hissed. "Look, let's just agree not to make a habit of it, okay? And maybe never talk about it again."

"Agreed," Nearchos sighed. "I think Emilia has learned a valuable lesson about keeping her mouth shut."

"You guys are boring," James chuckled. "I had a pretty good night."

"Then I'm sure you'll make a great battlemage," Zahra muttered. Her eyes darted suddenly to a second floor window as they approached the biomancy building. "Was that Emilia?"

"Huh?" James looked up at the window, where a smeared drool mark remained on the glass. "Is she not meant to be here?"

"We're not here for her, we were coming to visit Laurent," Nearchos explained. "I guess Emilia had the same idea."

"Huh. The more the merrier, I guess."

They wandered through the silent halls of the biomancy building, destined for the medical ward. It was a drab room painted in a number of different greys, lined with several improvised beds - stretchers planted on tables and draped with blankets. Emilia was drifting around the room on a wheelchair, pushing herself along with a broom. Laurent, who mostly looked as good as new, greeted his friends with a wide smile from his bed.

"And so arrive the all-conquering heroes!" he yelled, raising his arms in the air. "I understand you lot have been quite busy."

"You could say that," Zahra smirked. "You look good."

"I feel it! Well, not in the legs - I still can't feel those."

"You don't seem that down about it," James observed.

"Because I'm not," Laurent smiled, watching as Emilia span around in circles. "Going after Emilia was my choice and it is one I would happily make again. My career as a knight might have come to an early end, but I fulfilled my duties all the same."

"You're okay with this?" James asked.

"It's not ideal… but there is no greater honour for a knight than to give his body for the sake of his charge. I was made for this."

"So, what happens now?" Nearchos asked. "For you, I mean."

"Well, there's always a career out there for even the most broken of mages," Laurent sighed. "Perhaps I'll take up enchanting full time. Certainly seems like the way to go."

"Mm, most enchanters tend to go down the route of battle enchantment," Nearchos mused. "You'd have no problem finding a career with the battlemage guard."

"I could get behind that," Laurent smiled. "A life of law enforcement is a noble one indeed. Anyhow, I don't want to keep you too long. After all, you've a tournament to win!"

"Hell yeah, we do!" Emilia growled, springing from her wheelchair and pumping her hands into the air. "Let's go!"

"You gonna be alright on your own, Laurent?" James asked.

"Ah, I'll keep myself preoccupied," Laurent sighed. "My only regret in all of this is that I won't be there to cheer you on."

"I'm sure Emilia can fill you in once we're done," Zahra smiled. "We'll bring you back a good story."

"I'm counting on it," Laurent grinned.

With a nod and a wave, Zahra marched out of the door, Nearchos in tow. Emilia strolled to James' side as they stepped out into the hallway, chuckling quietly to herself.

"So... you and Brooklyn were noticeably absent last night," she whispered, her face creased by a smug grin. "The rest of our rag-tag gang might've been dull as dishwater, but I'm no fool."

"No idea what you're talking about," James smirked. His cheeks were awash with a rosy glow and his eyes avoided contact at all costs.

"I see how it is," Emilia grinned. "Well, I for one am proud of you - didn't think you had it in you. I guess our little James is all grown up!"

"Did you just call me James?"

"No idea what you're talking about," Emilia muttered. "You're not gonna tell anyone?"

"Not yet," James sighed. "There's a time and a place."

"Well, your secret's safe with me," Emilia smiled. "Now, why don't we go crush this stupid tournament?"

The atmosphere at Gladewatch was one of sheer insanity. The crowds roared with feverous chatter, magical fireworks boomed in the sky and myriad bands drowned the venue in music. To merely wander behind its walls was to lose all cohesion in thought, for the sounds and songs of the Triarcanum final were deafening.

James took a deep breath as he stepped up to the arena's edge and surveyed the audience. It was good to finally see everyone alive and well - Bruno, Isadora, even the jerks that they'd had the privilege of saving. His eyes drifted to Team Severin's end, where Lucia was barking like a drill sergeant at her team. *Her* eyes however, were glued to him and his friends, a combination of excitement, amusement and bloodlust in her dark smile.

"Gods, how is she so scary?" Nearchos sighed.

"She's like a demon, only angrier," James mumbled. "Don't get me wrong, I'm happy for her now that her disorder is... under control? But that doesn't make her any less crazy."

"Just more powerful," Nearchos whispered.

"Can you babies cry already? Your whining is *killing me*," Emilia groaned. "She's just one girl. One very angry and stupidly powerful girl, but still!"

"Just stick to the plan and she'll be no problem," Zahra said. "Come on, let's do this."

They marched together onto the field. The crowd fell quiet as Gerard cleared his throat, yet a low static of anxious chatter remained to fill the void.

"Welcome, ladies and gentlemen, to the grand finale of this magnificent tournament!" Gerard boomed, ceasing that static as the crowd thundered with applause. Today, you will witness a titanic clash of the best that this College has to offer! My friends, lend your applause to our glorious finalists - Team Severin and Team al-Masir!"

The mere mention of her name filled Zahra with dread - a name that would represent this kingdom's first real impression of her people. She had to prove herself to them.

"Sadly, both teams appear to be down a fighter, so we have a four versus four battle on our hands! With all the stand-out talent in these teams, I hardly need to remind you who will be taking to the field, so let's waste no time!"

The horns began to count down as the teams took their positions. Lucia's glare was fixed upon James, who screwed up his fists and returned a snarl of his own.

"You look ridiculous," she yelled through cupped hands.

"Not as ridiculous as you're about to look!"

Lucia grinned darkly and rubbed her hands together, igniting them with flame. Matheas and Josef edged away from her and into the middle, while Isadora took up a position on a distant flank. Team al-Masir split into pairs - James and Zahra on the left, Nearchos and Emilia on the right.

"Emilia, I want you to promise me you'll stick to the plan," Nearchos warned.

"Of course! What do you take me for?" Emilia sneered. "Just don't get jealous when I single handedly crush their team."

"And here I thought you'd gotten over that ego," Nearchos groaned.

"Just because my essence isn't pink, doesn't mean I'm anything short of flawless," Emilia said smugly, giggling as he rolled his eyes. "I'm kidding… I know I'm not invincible. Just outrageously resistant and in some capacities, impervious to physical harm."

"You have done nothing to reassure me."

"I wasn't trying to," Emilia smiled, patting him on the back. "Just try not to get killed, okay?"

Nearchos took a deep breath and nodded as the final few horns blared. Zahra looked her team up and down, receiving glowing smiles from the lot of them.

"Everybody ready?" she asked.

"I need the toilet," Emilia moaned.

The final horn rang across the arena and the eight combatants sprang into action. Zahra thrust out her hand and immediately halted an incoming blast of flame. Lucia's arms sagged slowly to her sides, her face frozen in horror and her eyes fixed to the ground.

"Lucy?" Isadora yelled, firing an ice arrow into Nearchos' water jet. "Josef, keep Nearchos suppressed! Matheas, protect Lucia!"

"Perfect…" Emilia grinned, rising from cover beside Nearchos. "Water Boy, send me in."

Nearchos ducked into cover as a lightning bolt ripped overhead. Emilia leapt into his arms, light as a feather, and hardened her skin with an eager squeal. Nearchos aimed Emilia towards Matheas' shield, sidestepping a lightning bolt and detonating a massive blast of water against Emilia's back. She soared through the air like a comet, shattering Matheas' barrier in an instant and knocking both him and Lucia flat.

"No!" Zahra gasped as Lucia collapsed into cover. "I need line of sight! Get her where I can-"

Three arrows struck the ground ahead of her, flaring with blue light an unleashing an avalanche of smoke before her. James moved in front of Zahra while she took control of Amani, but both of them knew what was coming.

Emilia punched a hole through Matheas' seventh barrier and grabbed him by the collar, hurling him out of the arena with a flick of her wrist. She glanced to Josef with a wide grin, watching as Amani ran circles around him, spraying fire at his feet. As a jet of water sent him flying, she turned back upon Lucia.

"You bastards have a lot of nerve!" Lucia growled, rising to her feet and cloaking herself head to toe in flame. "You should know better than to piss me *off*!"

Her blazing fist slammed into Emilia's forehead, detonating an explosion against her face. As the smoke cleared, Lucia withdrew her stinging knuckle and groaned as Emilia smiled back at her.

"And you should know better than to mess with me!" Emilia laughed, discarding her crumpled glasses and charging her opponent.

Lucia dodged a meteoric punch and blasted herself away, skidding to a halt metres back and opening fire. Bolt after bolt of crackling fire exploded against Emilia's face to little avail, barely slowing the girl's steady advance.

While Lucia and Emilia beat each other senseless, the rest of Team al-Masir found themselves cut off by a rolling cloud of smoke. James and Nearchos stared anxiously into the veil, their eyes darting about as footsteps pattered in its midst. A single arrow broke from the smoke and shot high into the air.

"What was that supposed to be?" James asked as they watched it soar into the air.

"A distraction!" Isadora yelled.

Another arrow slammed into the ground before James, exploding with jagged ice and cutting him off from Nearchos. As Nearchos fired a jet into the veil, Isadora leapt into the open and fired an electric arrow into the water. She charged him as he ceased his attack, smashing him over the head with her bow and drawing another arrow.

The distraction arrow struck the ground behind her as she swivelled around him and blasted him off his feet with a wind arrow. Watching as he sailed over the first arrow, she clenched her fist and detonated a blast of wind that propelled him high into the air.

"Oh, Lucy!" Isadora called, dispelling the smoke with a wave of her hand. "I've got something for you…"

Lucia whipped around and fired a beam of light over her shoulder, blasting Nearchos out of the sky. Amani swooped to his aid as he went spinning into the distance, barely catching him as he soared over the arena's border. Depositing him by the bench, Amani swept around and dived upon Isadora.

"Really, Zahra?" Isadora laughed, reaching for another arrow as the drake swooped overhead. "I've killed beast five times the-"

Her face dropped as her hand clasped nothing but air. She span around and watched with sagging shoulders as Amani flew out of bound with several arrows between her claws. Turning back upon Zahra, she sidestepped a blow from James' sword and jabbed him immediately in the gut.

"Bad idea," Isadora grinned. She thrust her bow into the air and ignited it with electricity.

"Aw, crap…"

Wielding her bow like a quarterstaff, Isadora leapt at James. Kicking his shield aside, she ducked beneath his sword and caught it with her bow. In one graceful motion, she disarmed him of his weapon and smashed him simultaneously in the chin. Dazed by the jolt of energy that shot through his skull, James staggered back and threw out his shield. Isadora slammed the tip of her bow into the shield and discharged her weapon's electrical charge into its centre, punching a whole through it and watching as it collapsed in on itself. She grabbed James' sword and kicked him to the ground, stepping over him and raising his blade.

"I like this thing," she smiled, marvelling at its discordant form. "Might get one myself."

She cleaved the sword down upon him. Isadora's hands sailed past and slammed into her groin as the blade disappeared from her hands. Materialising in James' grasp, he struck her across the face and sent her reeling back. He scrambled to his feet as Isadora laughed giddily and reignited her bow.

"Turn around," James said.

Isadora held her stare for a few seconds before caving into his persistence. She swivelled around and readied her bow, only to receive a face full of Emilia. Amani released the girl and bowled Isadora off her feet. She and Emilia tumbled several metres before they rolled gradually to a halt. Emilia sprang up, kicked Isadora in the gut and wandered to James' side.

"Fear not, your hero has arrived!" she declared, placing her hands on her hips. Her face dropped as Lucia emerged from the fading smoke, her flame cloak burning brighter than ever.

"Get back here, you tiny freak!" Lucia growled.

She blasted herself off the ground, falling like a meteor upon Emilia while James ran for cover. A colossal explosion bathed the battlefield in smoke once again, from which echoed blast after blast of flame. The grim smog lit up with yellow, dwarfing the occasional flicker of pink. James and Zahra watched as Emilia tumbled out of the cloud, her skin sagging and the pink in her eyes fading.

"You know… i-in a stalemate such as this, I think it's important to consider new options," Emilia stammered, panting for breath as she staggered away. "If you're willing, I'm totally open to talking this-"

A bolt of flame slammed into her shoulder and cast her effortlessly out of bounds. Lucia stepped into the open, the flames around all but her arms flickering away. Her eyes were worn red, her nose dripping blood. Her fiery pupils waned, dancing between a dull yellow and their natural blue.

"That girl can take a beating," she groaned.

As Zahra threw out her hand, Lucia blasted her position with a burst of flame. James' shoulders slumped as Zahra went up in flame, before turning back upon Lucia and summoning his shield.

Lucia gritted her teeth and buried her face in her hand, the flames on her arms growing weaker. "It's just me and you now, Serith," she sneered, withdrawing her hand and returning confidence to her flickering eyes. "This is your last chance to walk away."

"I'm not going anywhere," James growled.

"Hm. Suit yourself."

Lucia threw out her arm and fired a gout of flame from her palm. She was utterly blank as little more than a handful spewed out and dispersed into the wind. A grin spread across James' face as he drew his sword to his shield and charged.

"Well, aren't you clever..." Lucia smirked, snuffing what little flames remained on her arms. "Alright, Serith, let's see if you're tough enough to beat up an unarmed teenage girl."

She barely had to move her head as his thrust went straight over her shoulder. Grabbing the blade of his sword, she slammed her boot into his groin.

"Not a great start," she chuckled as he stumbled away.

He fell back upon her and swung his blade down, cleaving past her and jamming into the ground. Lucia cackled as he tried to pry it free, her foot deflecting barely off his shield as it swung for his face. As she drew back her fist, he released his grip, summoned his baton and jabbed her throat as she opened her guard.

Lucia's tone quickly changed. Her smugness was wiped away, replaced once again by raw aggression. She grabbed the end of the baton and shattered it over her knee, kicking him in the head as he yanked the sword from the ground. He took a clumsy swing as he back away, one that was easily dodged and countered with a left hook. Sidestepping another blow, she punched the edge of his shield and propelled it into the side of his head, slamming him against the rocks.

"A word of advice, James," Lucia smiled. "Maybe learn how to *use* a sword before bringing one to a tournament."

"Maybe *you* should learn to be more aware of your surroundings."

James ran at Lucia and hurled his sword over her head, where it fell into Zahra's hand. Lucia span around and took a blow to the jaw, spilling blood from her mouth as she bit down on her tongue. She ducked below Zahra's second strike and caught James' baton in her hand. A punch to the nose was all it took to wrest the baton from his grip. She span back upon Zahra, deflected her strike and smashed her across the face with the baton.

"Damn it, James!" Zahra hissed, clutching her cheek as she reeled back.
"Sorry!"

He thrust out his hand and recalled the baton. As he charged back towards her, Lucia grabbed Zahra by the wrist and thrust up the sword in front of James' strike. Deflecting the blow, she punched Zahra in the gut, turned to James and caught his incoming shield. She pulled him close and head-butted him, sending him spinning in a daze.

"You're embarrassing yourselves," she laughed, stepping aside as Zahra swung down upon her. "Here, I'll show you how its done."

She punched Zahra in the jaw, took hold of her arm and smashed it into her knee. Her opponent's grip loosened, Lucia yanked the sword out of Zahra's hand and struck her across the face with it. James' attack was parried with little effort. She whipped his leg with the tip of the blade, dropping him to one knee. Her hand clenched the edge of his shield and with a smug grin on her face, she rammed the sword through its centre and shattered it apart.

"You've got spirit, James, but you're terrible at what you do," Lucia sneered.

"Actually, a free hand is exactly what I needed!" James hissed.

The sword vanished from her grip and materialised in his left hand. With a defiant roar, he charged her with his weapons in either hand, falling upon her like whirlwind. His strikes were clumsy and uncalculated, but they were fierce. He battered down Lucia's arms and struck her across the face with the baton. She stumbled further and further back as he jabbed and slashed at her body, painting her skin with glowing, red marks.

Her hand caught his sword mid-swing and ignited with flame. He stared with horror into her eyes as the flared with fiery yellow light. A firebolt slammed into his gut and sent him flying back. Cackling maniacally, Lucia whipped around and caught Zahra's hand mere inches from her face.

"Time's up," she grinned, flames surging down her arm. "Maybe this time you'll *stay down!*"

Her right arm burst suddenly into flame and swung at Zahra, sending her flying with a compressed explosion. James watched without breath as his friend disappeared into a cloud of black smoke. With barely an ounce of essence left in him, he truly was out of time.

"Ballsy move, trying to wear me down like that!" Lucia laughed, grinning darkly as her body set ablaze once again. "You almost had me."

She raised her hand, the flames around her body surging down her arm. James dug in his feet and raised his arm, his mind burning as he forced his shield back into reality.

"But, let's face it - you were never going to beat me," Lucia sneered, her hand glowing a blinding white. "Don't get me wrong, I'm impressed you got this far, but… all good things must come to an end."

A flick of her wrist painted his vision white. Robbed of his senses, James felt only a wave of heat, a sharp backlash and the rush of the wind around him. He let slip a feeble wheeze as the light faded, watching as the arena's boundary emerged before him. His body sagged as he felt the arena's invisible barrier ripple against his back his ears ringing as he sank into the grass.

Lucia withdrew her smoking hand, her face bright with pride. While tears trickled from James' tired eyes, she laughed with delight and span elegantly around.

"Sleep!" Zahra cried.

The silence was deafening. Lucia's blank face peeled away from Zahra's palm and she collapsed flat on the ground. Zahra glanced up at James, a look of sheer disbelief on her face as the horns began to sound.

"Ladies and gentlemen, in a most outrageous turn of events, victory goes to Team al-Masir!" Gerard roared, spreading his arms as the crowd exploded with ovation. "Give it up for this year's Triarcanum champions!"

Zahra could barely stand up straight as her legs wobbled and swayed. She broke into hysterical laughter, throwing open her arms as James ran to meet her.

"Zahraaaa!"

Emilia leapt from a nearby trench and clung to her like a rabid monkey, toppling her face first onto the grass. As she tried to pull herself from Emilia's grasp, she was tackled by James and flattened into the dirt.

"*You did it!*" Emilia growled, shaking Zahra violently by the shoulders.

"And I'll do it to you too if you don't get off me!" Zahra laughed. She shoved the girl to the ground and rolled onto her back, watching with the widest smile as Nearchos jogged to meet them.

"I thought it was over…" James gasped, shuffling onto his knees. "How the hell did you sneak up on her like that?!"

"I used an illusion to make myself appear invisible to her," Zahra said. "I preferred to keep an extra trick up my sleeve."

"You are the best person in the world," James laughed, squeezing her tight in his arms. "I couldn't think of a better person to represent Novekhir."

Zahra's smiled beamed with warmth, herself swelling with pride. "Maybe because you've never been there," she chuckled.

"Well, *maybe* we ought to change that someday," James smiled. His face dropped as he glanced over her shoulder "Uh oh."

The rest of the group turned around, watching in terror as Lucia clawed her way off the ground. She glanced around the arena in a daze, laying her eyes upon her glum team and receiving an awkward thumbs up from Isadora. The emotion in her face was indiscernible as she stalked towards Team al-Masir, her hands behind her back.

"Lucia…" Zahra stammered. "I, um… I can- I don't-"

She flinched as Lucia thrust out her arm in front of her. "Well played," Lucia smiled. Zahra's face was left empty, her mouth searching for words that would not come. "What, you really thought I'd freak out over losing fair and square?"

Zahra stared blankly at Lucia's hand. "Hand… shake," she mumbled.

Hesitantly, she wrapped her hand around Lucia's fingers and shook it violently. Suddenly, her hand began to sting and Lucia leant in close with darkness in her eyes.

"You are *so* dead," she whispered. As Zahra's face drained of colour and her eyes shot wide with terror, Lucia could barely contain her laughter. "I'm joking!" she giggled, smacking Zahra hard on the shoulder. "You need to work on that handshake."

"And you need to work on your jokes," Zahra muttered.

"Yeah, I'm kind of new to it," Lucia smirked. "Enjoy the praise, morons."

Watching Lucia march back to her team, Team al-Masir exchanged several glances, both exhausted and relieved.

"That was surprisingly tame," Nearchos whispered. "I think she might like us."

"I'd rather go with 'she no longer hates us'," James said. "Anyway… how about we finally get those drinks?"

"Calm down, Polymedes," Nearchos laughed, receiving empty stares from his audience. "Seriously? Not one of you?"

"I literally speak a different language," Zahra said.

"I am wasted on you people," Nearchos sighed. "Still, maybe we ought to wait until *after* the ceremony?"

"Where's the fun in that, Water Boy?" Emilia sneered. "Let's get wasted!"

"There is no way they'll let you have a drink," James chuckled. "You look like a ten year old."

"*Maybe I'll drink your blood instead!*" Emilia hissed.

Zahra backed far away from Emilia. "Good to see some things don't change…" she muttered. "Nearchos is right, you can all get drunk later. Except for Emilia."

Emilia narrowed her eyes and wandered slowly away. "You'll rue the day you crossed me."

Later that day, as the sun began to fall in the sky, an excited crowd swelled at the centre of Gladewatch, packed into an overgrown courtyard and placed before a vast podium. While the faculty fell into place and Gerard hastily scribbled some cue cards, Team al-Masir lined up beside the podium.

"God, I didn't think it would be this scary," James mumbled, hopping up and down in an attempt to shake off his anxiety.

"You're telling me, I have to give a speech!" Zahra hissed. "Come on, Zahra, you've trained all your life for this… you can do it."

"Are you sure?" Emilia asked. "You sound less confident than a fly in a web."

"Thank you *so much* for the support," Zahra snapped. "Okay... Okay, here we go. I can do this."

They stood in silence as Lady Amelie stepped up to the podium, a beaming smile on her face.

"My friends, on behalf of House Tarantis and the College of Arcana, I thank you dearly for making the three hundred and eleventh Triarcanum one of, if not the best yet! It truly has been a pleasure, not only to enjoy your company, but also to behold the incredible talent we have seen this week. This year, we have witnessed possibly the most promising batch of students that the kingdom has ever seen - I can say without a doubt that they will go on to do incredible things!"

The crowd roared with applause as Amelie stepped back from the podium's edge, waving as she went. Zahra tensed as Gerard took position once again and cleared his throat.

"Thank you all once again," Amelie smiled. "And I look forward to seeing you all next year."

"Thank you, mother," Gerard sighed, trying to subtly shuffle his cue cards. "And now, let us move swiftly onto crowning this year's champions! Please, welcome to the stage - Zahra al-Masir, James Serith, Nearchos Phokinas and Emilia Arrenni!"

The four of them stepped onto the podium and marched in single file to the centre. Zahra and James were stiff with terror, Nearchos was fairly unfazed and Emilia was oozing a toxic amount of smugness. As for the crowd before them, as many were elated as were furious - where much of their class hailed them with praise, the other classes were largely unimpressed. Franz avoided looking upon Zahra as best he could, while Meridian glared at Emilia with seething contempt.

"Despite a lacklustre performance from much of their team in the monster stage, Team al-Masir returned like a phoenix from the ashes! Though their combat stage was not the smoothest, stellar performances from each of their number won them a place in the final and through sheer will and determination, they did what we all thought impossible!"

"Um, excuse me, sir?" Zahra whispered. "Laurent..."

"Ah, of course," Gerard murmured. "Sadly, due to injuries sustained in training, Laurent Bouchard could not be here today, but he will receive his award nonetheless. Now, Miss al-Masir, I trust you have a few words for our audience."

Zahra turned to the waiting crowd, her heart pounding as they awaited her words in deathly silence. "Yes... Being a part of this has been possibly the most amazing experience of my life. Despite its ups and downs, the

Triarcanum has been wonderful - I've made new friends, done things that I never imagined I could do and discovered a few things about myself along the way."

She paused as the audience pattered with a light applause. Her cheeks blushing, she continued through a timid grin.

"I would, of course, like to thank my team, who told me that I had what it takes and supported me even when I'd lost hope. Maybe I wasn't the best leader - maybe for most of the tournament, I was barely a leader at all… but I did have my team. To use a popular expression here in Athaea - from the bottom of my heart, thank you. It has been truly wonderful."

"Well said, Miss al-Masir," Gerard smiled, patting her on the shoulder with his meaty hand. "I'm sure I speak for everyone when I say it's been a pleasure having you. Now, onto the-"

Amelie tapped him delicately on the shoulder and peered around him. His eyes widened as she whispered to him and he turned back to the ground with an apologetic smile.

"Ah… we're forgetting the trophy!" he laughed, glancing back at Caesia. "One moment, she doesn't do crowds."

"Why did you rope me into this?" Caesia spat as she trudged to her mother's side. Like Lady Amelie, her voice wasn't amplified. She turned to Zahra with a sigh and forked over the trophy. "Congratulations."

Zahra took the trophy in hand - it was a small, crystalline statuette of five men holding up the six-pointed star of House Tarantis. She looked up at Caesia with a smile, but the girl had already scampered away.

"Isn't she pleasant?" Amelie smiled, extending her hand to Zahra. "Well done. You've represented your country well."

"Thank you, my lady," Zahra said, taking her hand and shaking it about.

"Hm… I think you ought to work on that handshake," Amelie smirked. "You'll need it once we open negotiations."

She patted Zahra on the side and retreated back to Gerard's side. As Team al-Masir took their position at the back of the stage, he continued to shuffle through his notes.

"That wasn't so bad," James sighed. "I liked your speech."

"You did?" Zahra smiled.

"And now… for the bonus awards!" Gerard declared. The silence of the crowd was enough to convey their astonishment - there had been no mention of such awards. "After a great deal of deliberation, we have decided to introduce two secondary prizes that will award our most promising students with a chance to expand their horizons."

"I would have preferred them to disclose this information…" Nearchos muttered.

"Oh, chill out," James sighed. "What's the worst that could happen?"

"First of all, we have the award for best team leader, as decided by observing faculty members," Gerard said. "In recognition of their charismatic leadership and the resultant high morale of their team, this award goes without a doubt to Ava Trausch!"

Half of Ava's melted face lit up with shock as Brooke shoved her out of her seat. Her cheeks glowed red as she edged her way to the podium, shaking Lady Amelie's hand with a frozen smile.

"I, um... thank you!" Ava gasped, her voice utterly incoherent. "Thi-this means a lot, but... I'm not really interested in the internship."

The thunder of the audience died suddenly away and many confused glances were exchanged as she turned to Gerard and took a deep breath.

"If you would allow it, sir, I'd like to give my prize to my teammate, Brooklyn," Ava smiled. "I couldn't have done it without her and... well, she was as much the leader as I was."

Brooke cupped her mouth in her one good hand as hundreds of eyes fell upon her, every inch of her skin painted immediately red. Gerard leant into Amelie, who whispered to him through a smug grin.

"Well, what a noble act!" Gerard laughed. "I suppose the award for best team leader goes to Brooklyn De'Claire!"

Ava hurried down from the podium and was intercepted by her quivering friend.

"Wh-what... what are you doing?!" Brooke hissed. "I-I-I'm not the leader, you- I don't-"

Her arms fell to her sides as Ava wandered past without a word, only a sweet smile on her lips. Brooke turned back to the podium and drifted like a ghost up to Lady Amelie, who shook her trembling hand and mumbled something inaudible to her.

"I... I... oh God," Brooke gasped, wiping down her sweat-drenched face as she looked over the crowd. "I-I guess I should say... thank you! And, um... I'd like to thank Ava. For the award, which I think, really, she deserves more, but... that's all."

She span around and walked stiffly to James' side, smiling awkwardly as the patter of reluctant applause echoed behind her.

James placed his hand on her shoulder and leant in. "That was-"

"Terrible, don't try and tell me otherwise," Brooke mumbled. "But, I... appreciate the support."

"Finally, in recognition of the sheer potential of the mightiest amongst you - the elimination award!" Gerard declared. Lucia bolted upright as the eyes of the entire crowd fell upon her. "I... I don't need to announce this, do I? Get up here Miss Severin!"

Emilia laughed as the faces of her friends collectively dropped, watching as a smug grin shot across Lucia's face.

"You've got to be kidding me!" Zahra spat. "She scarred three students for the rest of their lives and they're rewarding her for it?!"

"At this point, are you really surprised?" Nearchos asked.

Lucia flicked back her fringe as she strode to the podium, an Emilia-level of swagger in her step. She took her trophy with a sweet smile and heartily returned Lady Amelie's handshake.

"Thank you, thank you so much," she smiled as the crowd died down. "There was a... dark time when I thought my powers were a curse. All I ever wanted was to get rid of them, I would have done anything... but thanks to my friends, I understand now that this... this is a gift. A gift that will bring law and justice to this glorious kingdom!"

"That doesn't bode well..." Zahra mumbled as the crowd applauded the girl's words.

"But all that aside, I'd like to thank my friends - Isadora and... and Hasso. They were there for me when nobody else was and I just wanted them to know that I'm thankful. I wouldn't be here today if it weren't for you."

James' eyes fluttered in disbelief as she strode to Brooke's side, the thunder of applause at her back.

"You idiots look like you've seen a ghost," she smirked as she fell in line. "Guess you didn't know I was capable of displaying affection, huh?"

"I guess not..." James muttered.

"And there you have it, my friends," Gerard smiled. "Seven students, each extraordinary in their own right. This week, we have seen some truly historical talent! I think it's clear to see that the future of our world is brighter than ever and that those who inherit what we leave behind... their legacies will put ours to shame. Give it up, one last time, for this your Triarcanum champions!"

As the crowd roared with applause and sang the praise of their champions, Gerard paced over to the students with a wide grin on his chubby cheeks.

"Congratulations," he smiled, reaching out and shaking Zahra's hand. "Hm, you need to work on that handshake, my girl... Anyhow, the guard will be in touch."

Zahra stared at him blankly, her eyes shrinking. "The... guard?"

"About the internship?" Gerard smirked. "She does speak common, right?"

"Of course, of course!" Zahra laughed through gritted. "Th-thank you, sir."

Exhaling heavily through her nose, she hurried off, followed in tow by the rest of her team.

"So, anyone got any plans?" Brooke chirped, skipping after them.

"We were going to head down to the Cauldron for some drinks," James said. "You want to-"

"Yes!" Brooke gasped. "I mean, if that's okay with everyone else. I don't want to assume, it would be kind of rude for me to intrude, considering I'm not part of you team…"

"It's fine," Zahra smiled. "The more the merrier!"

Well, since you're offering," Lucia hissed, slipping to their sides. "Surely, you weren't thinking of getting drinks without me…"

"Um, I don't know…" Zahra mumbled. "It was kind of going to be a-"

"Perhaps you need convincing," Lucia smiled. "What if I told you I could buy out the whole tavern…?"

"The whole thing?" James scoffed.

"The whole thing," Lucia grinned. "On one condition - Isadora comes too."

"Whatever," Zahra sighed. "Guess there's no harm in it."

"Oh, can Ava come?" Brooke gasped.

"We should invite Bruno as well," James suggested. "We kind of owe him one."

"Yeah, yeah, just bring the whole class, why don't you?" Zahra groaned. "That was a joke, by the way."

"And it sucked," Lucia muttered.

Zahra buried her face in her hands. "Ala'mir… Let's just go."

Epilogue

That night, the victors and their closest friends gathered at the Cauldron. Lucia was there an hour early, having barged in with Isadora and thrown a sack of money at the owner. They were already drunk when the rest arrived. Some time after the others, Emilia barged Laurent through the door in a wheelchair and did not take well to being refused alcohol. So did she find herself sitting on a broken chair that evening.

"You might as well give up now!" Bruno roared, nearly collapsing onto a table as he swigged another mouthful of beer. "I am invincible!"

"Oh, please, you're barely standing!" Isadora laughed. "I once drank three priestesses of Euphraea under the table *at the same time*."

"I don't know what a Euphraea is, but you are screwed," Lucia chuckled, snorting with laughter as she laid down her head on the table. "Does anyone else have a really bad headache?"

"Yeah, my ears are still ringing from your rendition of Arrows of Fire," James sneered, drawing laughter from much of their company.

"Hey, can you go back to being a spineless loser?" Lucia groaned, burying her face in the table. "I liked you better that way."

"You *are* pretty cute when you're scared," Brooke whispered.

"Says you," James laughed, playfully shoving her shoulder. "You've apologised more in the past week than I have my whole life!"

"I'm just scared I'll offend someone…" Brooke mumbled.

"Kind of looks like you have," Ava smirked. "Zahra's been giving you the eyes for at least ten minutes."

"Huh?" Brooke glanced to the end of the table, where Zahra was sitting silently, swirling her tankard of water and staring into the wood. "You liar, don't scare me like that!"

"I'm telling you, it's hysterical," Emilia said through a mouthful of chicken. "He thinks that I think he's overweight, but I've called him fat so much now that he's beginning to question it himself!"

"Truly?" Laurent scoffed. "But this is Bruno we're talking about! He's all muscle!"

"Or is it flab?" Emilia grinned. "Who can say for certain?"

She glanced across the table to Bruno, who was face down in a pool of beer beside a rather smug Isadora. As Emilia surveyed the length of the table, her brow dipped at the glum sight of Zahra.

"I'll be right back," she said, sliding along the bench and cozying up to Zahra. "Why the long face?"

Zahra stared at her for a moment, pain in her eyes. "I messed up," she sighed, glancing across at James. "I tried to play the long game and now he's dancing on another girl's strings."

"I thought you had an arranged marriage…" Emilia smirked, raising an eyebrow as Zahra shook her head. "Well, that's what he told me."

"Wait, he- *Ala'mir*!" Zahra moaned, sinking into her seat. "Ugh, I made that up so Vivienne would stop harassing me about marrying her brother."

"Oof. So, he thought all this time that you were taken, when…"

"I'm such an idiot," Zahra groaned, planting her face on the table. "Whatever. This is a happy day, I should be celebrating, not moping… and as your people say, there's plenty more fish in the ocean."

"Yeah… something like that," Emilia chuckled. "Well, I suppose there's never been a better time to try a drink!"

Zahra glanced across the table at a cluster of murky bottles. "You know, I think you're right," she sighed, scooping one up and toying with it in her hands. "In fact…"

She sprang to her feet, wiping down her face and raising her drink at her side. The room fell gradually silent, though Lucia was totally vacant and Bruno was unconscious.

"Ladies and gentlemen, if I might say a few words," Zahra announced. "When my mother told me I was being transferred to some foreign institution, an ocean away from home… I cried. I was terrified because… because the impressions I made, the people I met, I was told they would mould the future of Novekhir."

She looked to James and Nearchos with a warm smile and stared down upon an infatuated Emilia, who patted her gently on the back.

"And thanks to my friends, not only can the future of our nations be bright, but I can also stay in this place that I've come to love. For all its imperfections, Verdenheld is a wonderful place. So, I guess what I'm saying is… thank you all for making me feel so welcome."

James led a round of applause, added to vigorously by Emilia and even reluctantly by Lucia.

"Ahem… well, I think a toast is in order," Zahra smiled. "Not only to our victory, but to us. To new friends and… acquaintances."

"Up yours," Lucia groaned.

"And to those who made great sacrifices so that we might stand here today. I think we can all agree that, for better or for worse, this week has changed our lives. Thank you all for being a part of this… *crazy* adventure."

She raised her drink high in the air, taking a deep breath as others rose around her.

"Here's to us," Zahra said. "And to the future, where I'm sure many an adventure lies ahead. I look forward to being a part of them."

Everybody burst into laughter as she knocked back her beer and choked on its bitter taste, spilling an avalanche of the stuff down her chest. At that, they raised their drinks in concert and cheered for their fearless leader.

Books by Jack Wright

ELARIA

Ashes of Verdenheld

Winds of Change

OTHER BOOKS

Battlemages

Printed in Great Britain
by Amazon